Murder

AT

HEATHERSTONE HALL

KATHRYN REISS

Time Portal Press

email: timeportalpress@gmail.com

www.kathrynreiss.net

Cataloging-in-Publication, Library of Congress
Reiss, Kathryn.
Murder at Heatherstone Hall/Kathryn Reiss

Summary: An ancient manor house turned-hotel-and-spa is the scene of murder, and sixteen-year-old American-born Juliana attempts to solve the crime—and save herself—while unraveling a mystery from the past. [Adoption—Fiction. 2. Hotels—Fiction 3. Family life—Fiction. 4. England—Fiction. 5. Mystery and detective stories.] 1. Title. 2015

ISBN 978-0-9862602-1-6 pb

Text set in Minion Pro and Gill Sans with calligraphic flourishes
Designed by Daniel Strychacz and Bonnie Britt
Front cover by Kelly Eismann

Printed in the United States of America

Praise for Novels by Kathryn Reiss

Blackthorn Winter—"New York Public Library Book for the Teen Age."

Dreadful Sorry—"Suspenseful and difficult to put down."—Voice of Youth Advocates

➤ "…wondrously effective…another fine spellbinder from the author of *Time Windows*."—Kirkus Reviews

➤ "…spooky and satisfying…fabulous…"—Bulletin of the Center for Children's Books

➤ "With its skillful plot twists, the book will have readers anxious to solve the mystery."—School Library Journal starred review

PaperQuake: A Puzzle—Nominated for the **Edgar Allan Poe Award** by the Mystery Writers of America for Best Young Adult Mystery.

➤ "Reiss weaves in well-timed twists and eerie coincidences that set the plot thrumming with tension."—Kirkus Reviews

For my son
Nicholas Strychacz,
a hot-tub trickster
whose underwater antics sparked this story.

"Truth will come to sight; murder cannot be hid long."
—William Shakespeare,
"The Merchant of Venice,"
Act II, Scene 2.

I know he is meant to be mine. Only mine.

Knew it from the first time I saw him.

Sat with my darling today, took his poor hand in mine. His hot brow under my fingers... oh how I wish I could heal him with my touch. Talked of his time in France. Talked of childhood, the village, his family...He seemed cheered by the talk of times gone by.

I've known forever that we're destined to be together, but I didn't speak of that. Know in my heart he feels the same way.

Left him when he fell asleep, looking again like the boy I remember. We will be together—forevermore.

1

"Wasn't that the turn?" Dad interrupted. "The directions said to take the first turn on the left."

"I never heard it say that," Mom snapped. "And the first road on the left was miles ago so we should have turned then. You must still be jet-lagged!"

"I'm fine—except that now we're lost. If you'd watch the road, we might get to meet Juliana's grandfather—*today*."

I dug my fingers into my forehead, trying to press away the headache I could feel starting up. I'd been crammed into the backseat with my brother and sister for hours, driving into the heart of East Anglia to visit my grandfather. He wasn't anybody else's grandfather, just mine—a quirky state of affairs that could exist only in a family like my own.

"Oh, so now I'm not driving fast enough, is that it? First I'm driving too fast, and now not fast enough, and you're just sitting there brooding because you don't want Juliana to have a boyfriend. She's sixteen, and Duncan's a lovely chap."

"I never said he's not a nice kid. But when you're setting up a show, you're gone for hours and hours. I just don't want them gallivanting around London unsupervised, and it really would be better if she came back to California with me."

"*Gallivanting*—there's a good word!" Mom looked over her shoulder at me. "Do you *gallivant*, Juliana? Is that what you and

Duncan do together?"

I refused to be drawn in to their stupid fight.

"Stop here," Dad ordered, consulting the map. "Turn around. Back to that last village."

My parents *were* lost—in more ways than one.

"All right, everybody," said Mom grimly as the turned the car around. She craned her neck to glance at the three of us in back. "We'll be meeting Mr. Ellis for the first time, and I want you all on your best behavior. That means you, especially, Edmund, do you hear me? We want him to see what a wonderful family Juliana has."

Edmund and Ivy, bopping along to their music, headphones hooked into their ears, nodded as if they'd heard her.

I leaned my cheek against the window and wished I could be making this first visit on my own. My parents and siblings were coming for moral support and—face it—to satisfy their own curiosity. But I could have just taken the train by myself, no problem. It would have been so much easier.

"Mr. Ellis will have to take us as we are," Dad declared. "I refuse to put on a special show for him."

"Who said anything about a show?" asked Mom. "I just want civilized behavior."

"It will be a fine visit," Dad said. "And it's important for Juliana."

"I don't feel ready for this," grumbled Mom.

"Well, Hedda, guess what? This isn't about *you*."

"That's what's really upsetting you, isn't it?" Mom turned to glare at him so long she nearly ran us off the road into the hedge. She swerved back, shoulders hunched. "You're angry that I needed to move here—angry about my art…"

I closed my eyes and wished for those days when everything seemed so simple, back before Mom and Dad separated, back before Mom moved us to England while Dad stayed in California. Dad was a big-deal architect, and Mom was a painter. I think Dad was proud of Mom's new show in London, but they both seemed content to be living far apart. We kids were not at all content with the arrangement, but whenever Dad came to visit, they bickered the whole time. I hated it.

Dad was visiting now, during our summer holidays. He'd been in England a week, and was going to take my ten-year-old brother and sister—known as the Goops because of their perpetually grimy hands and faces—back with him to California in a few days. My sister and brother would be staying with our grandparents for a month—and our little cousins would be visiting them at the same time. Ivy and Edmund were ecstatic about having a whole month with the eight and nine year olds. I had been less thrilled at the invitation—suspecting I'd end up the babysitter—and so I'd begged off. I wanted to stay at home in Blackthorn so I could hang out with Duncan, who was my dearest friend and possibly—fingers crossed—becoming something more. His mum was dead and his dad had run off to Brazil years ago, and he lived with his grandparents. Duncan was sixteen, like me, but extremely tall and lanky, with a cute mop of red hair. I'd met him the same day we'd moved to England last winter—and never looked back. Now we were just trying to figure out where this thing was heading. Were we friends—or more than friends? Even if the romance we kept dancing around didn't go anywhere, I just loved being around him.

But Mom said no way was I staying alone in Blackthorn. If I wouldn't go with Dad and the Goops to California, I was coming to London with her, where she'd be spending the month setting up a big art exhibition. I could help her with that, she said, and then I could explore the city. Duncan might be able to come to London on weekends to hang out with me, if his grandparents didn't mind.

I wasn't thrilled with this version of my summer, but at least I'd see Duncan *sometimes*. So that's how things were until fate, in the form of a letter dropped into our postbox about a week ago, changed everything.

The envelope was large, square, and dove-gray. It was addressed to Miss Juliana Martin-Drake in formal, sort of old-fashioned writing, and the return address on the back was embossed.

It said *Heatherstone Hall and Spa,* and under that *Heatherstone, nr. Norwich, East Anglia.* At first I thought it was some advertisement. But then I saw the handwritten name penned above the hotel's address, and my stomach did a little flip: Lloyd Ellis.

Lloyd Ellis was a name we'd all recently heard of, a name that had surfaced after a neighbor in Blackthorn discovered that my birth mother had been an old schoolmate of hers, and had come from a village near Norwich. I think all adopted children want to know, sooner or later, something about their biological family, and I sure was no exception.

Inside the envelope was a glossy brochure featuring pictures of an incredible manor house—the hotel and spa, apparently—and a short, handwritten note from Lloyd Ellis, introducing himself as my grandfather. He said he would like to make my acquaintance, and my family's, and would we please contact him as soon as possible.

I had written back that same day, telling him a little about myself, and my mom had included a short note saying that maybe we could meet him during the summer holidays. And next thing we knew, he had telephoned and arranged that we should come to visit him at the hotel he owned, which was also where he lived. He offered to let us stay as his guests as long as we wanted. I was eager to go, but Mom and Dad balked; if we had to go meet the guy, and they supposed we should, we would go just for the day. Even though it meant a whole lot of driving. But we were not going to stay overnight, we didn't know him, it would be too awkward. I offered to go alone by train and save everyone the trouble, since they obviously didn't care about meeting him.

"Of course we care," said my dad.

"Yes, we do," my mom said, and since it was one of the rare moments when they agreed on anything these days, I didn't argue.

I could tell Mom and Dad felt vaguely threatened, as if this new relative of mine might somehow try to sweep me out of our family and into his. But I was happy about meeting this birth relative, and I'd go by train or car—no matter how long it took—and so here we were. Or, at least, *almost.*

Mom finally turned off the main road and onto a narrow, winding lane lined with hedgerows that eventually brought us into Heatherstone, a small village of shops and stone houses. She was driving so fast that the whole village was mostly just a blur out my side window. After another mile she drove past a pair of huge stone gates. "There it is!" my brother yelled, and she slammed on the brakes. "You went too fast this time, Mom. You missed it."

Mom backed up the car, grinding the gears, probably grinding her teeth, as well. I craned my neck to see beyond the tunnel of trees to the grandeur of the house. *"Whoa,"* I said.

It was like something out of those "Glories of Britain" shows Mom liked to watch. Ancient stone gleamed gold in the late-afternoon sun. "Look how *ancient* it is!" my sister Ivy exclaimed, pulling her headphones out of her ears. "The date on that arch says 1654!" She adored old things, old places.

"I've got butterflies in my stomach," Mom muttered.

"I do, too," said Dad. "I wish you'd slow down and—"

"I wish *you'd* go back to California," Mom snapped.

"I'm here for the kids," Dad said tersely to Mom.

"I betcha the old man will be a hunchback!" Edmund's strident voice rang out. I knew Mom and Dad were upsetting him. All three of us kids hated the constant tension when they were together. Much as we hated to admit it, their separation was a good thing.

"He won't be a hunchback." Ivy frowned at Edmund. "He'll be handsome and nice. You're just jealous because Juliana gets to meet a birth relative—and you don't."

Edmund crossed his eyes at her. She laughed.

The two Goops never stayed mad at each other for long.

My parents had adopted Edmund from an orphanage in Russia

when he was a baby, just after Ivy's birth. The Goops liked to tell everyone they were twins, because they had the same birthdate. They did look a lot alike, with their pale blond hair. Mine was blond, too, but darker.

"*Not* jealous," countered Edmund. "I'm just *saying*. Anyway, here he comes!"

An elderly man with a shock of white hair was making his way down the wide stone steps of the immense house. Mom parked in the shade of trees by the side of the gravel drive. She turned off the ignition and just sat there, staring at her hands.

"It'll be fine," Dad said. "Let's do this."

"Company manners, kids," Mom said grimly, and opened the car door.

We walked to meet him, passing an ornamental stone lion at the base of the wide stone steps of the manor house. Ivy stopped to pat its head.

"Hello, hello there!" called the old man.

"David Martin-Drake," Dad announced in a hearty voice, pumping his hand. "Delighted to meet you!"

The old man leaned hard on his cane and smiled at us. I sucked in my breath as he released Dad's hand and reached for mine. Up close I could see his eyes were wide and gray. So were mine.

My family's chatter seemed to disappear as if someone had pushed a "mute" button. All I could hear was the beating of my own heart. I was struck by the random thought that this absolute stranger and I shared DNA and chromosomes, and without him I could never have been born. How weird was that?

"Hello, hello, and welcome to Heatherstone Hall." His voice was raspy. "Juliana? Let me look at you!" His fingers around mine felt cool and dry. "Yes, I'd know you anywhere, lass," he said hoarsely, "You look like my Barbara-Elizabeth. Just exactly the way she looked when she ran off to California, never to be seen again. Oh, she was a wild one, that girl of mine." He clutched my hand more tightly, frowning.

"Are you a wild one, too?"

"Juliana isn't the *least* bit wild," Mom said repressively, putting her arm around my shoulder.

She made me feel like some tame, boring farm animal. But I know Mom was just nervous about making a good impression.

The old man winked at me, then released my hand to shake hers. "I'm very pleased you've come." He shook Ivy's hand, and Edmund's. "I'll be 'Grandfather Ellis' to all you young ones, how's that? We're all family here, eh?"

Then, as if his words had summoned them, three people stepped out of the open front door and lined up on the top step: a man, a woman, and a girl my age. The man was tall and dark-haired, but both the girl and the woman were fair and small, with wild, curly manes. They were dressed in the most fashionable jeans and tops, and I felt wrong in the stupid skirt Mom had made me wear.

"Ah," cried Grandfather Ellis. "Ross, Josie—and Pippa! Come and meet my new granddaughter. My only blood kin left in the world, I do believe!"

The woman reached past Mom and Dad to shake my hand. "Hello, Juliana, darling." She pronounced it *dahling*. "I can see the family resemblance. Long blonde plait and big eyes—I've seen the photos of Barbara, you know. How lovely to meet you at last. It was so exciting when we learned of you. Imagine—a granddaughter popping up out of nowhere! Lloyd was *that* thrilled."

"California is hardly *nowhere*," said the laconic voice of the dark-haired man behind her. He pumped Mom's hand, then Dad's. "Nice to meet you. I'm Ross Foxworth, manager of this hotel. My wife, Josie, does the bookkeeping."

"And I'll be running the new spa," she added brightly.

"Nice to meet you," Mom and Dad both said.

"And our daughter, Pippa. She's helping out as well, during her summer hols."

"Slavery," said the girl. "Drudgery."

"Good pocket money, though, and you know it," said Grandfather Ellis in his raspy voice, then broke off to cough alarmingly. Looking abashed, the girl named Pippa patted him on the back until he recovered. "You're just about Juliana's age, eh, Pippa?"

"I'm fifteen," she said.

"I've just turned sixteen," I said.

"There, now, you see?" Grandfather Ellis cleared his throat roughly. "Cousins. You'll get on smashingly, I daresay."

I smiled at this cousin, feeling suddenly shy. She looked past me to the Goops. "More cousins?"

They surged forward in their usual, noisy way, clamoring for attention, making charming nuisances of themselves. I edged closer to Grandfather Ellis.

"Ross has all sorts of credentials in hotel management," Grandfather Ellis was saying proudly, clapping Pippa's father on the shoulder. "Hopes to take over this place from me one day. Keep it in the family."

Mom looked puzzled. "So...Ross is your son?"

"Ross is my wayward stepson."

"And Lloyd is my evil step-father." Ross and Grandfather Ellis grinned at each other. "That makes me an uncle to you, Juliana," Ross explained. "Or a step-uncle, or something like that."

"Something like that," Grandfather Ellis echoed with a shrug.

"You men," said Josie, rolling her eyes at my mom. "It's perfectly clear." She smiled at me. "Ross is your uncle, Juliana. Plain and simple. He was Barbara-Elizabeth's half-brother."

"Ah," said my mom, nodding.

Josie clarified things further. She explained that Ross's mum, Jane, had been married before, and his dad died when he was about five. Cancer, it was. Then his mum married Lloyd Ellis when Ross was ten. And then Lloyd and Jane had Barbara-Elizabeth, who became my birthmother. Josie raised her eyebrows at me. "All clear now?"

I thought I got it, but it still seemed complicated. Mom was nodding; she was always good at that sort of thing, instantly understanding intricate family relationships like halves and quarters, steps and twice-removeds. "So Ross is your half uncle," Mom clarified for me now. "And that makes Josie your half-aunt-in-law. And their children are your half-cousins."

"Oh, let's do away with the halves and the steps," said Josie lightly, "and just be *family*."

"Sounds good to me," I said, relieved. I saw Mom turn away, her forehead furrowed in a frown, and I knew she wasn't happy to count all these strangers as family. But while *she* felt anxious, *I* was delighted.

I couldn't see, right then, past the gleaming stone of the grand old manor and the welcoming smiles of the family, to the shadows.

2

Ivy, a major fan of all things historic, changed Mom's frown back into a polite smile with her chatter. "Your house is so awesome," she said excitedly, pushing in between Mom and Dad to stand close to Grandfather Ellis. "That's what's so cool about England. I can feel the past all around me."

Grandfather Ellis looked down at her in surprise. "You can feel the past, can you, lass?"

"Yup."

"How interesting," Grandfather Ellis said. "My daughter used to sense the *future*,"

With a start I realized he was talking about my birthmother.

Ross snorted. "Barb was just having you on," he told the old man, winking at me. "She could always pull the wool over her dad's eyes about anything."

"About some things," Grandfather Ellis conceded. "But my mum said *her* old granny claimed to see flashes of the future, and I rather think our Barbara-Elizabeth had that gift as well."

"If so," said Ross grumpily, "she didn't use it very wisely, did she? Running off and getting herself killed?"

"I think it would be *brilliant* to be able to see the future," Pippa interjected.

"I think it would be scary," Ivy said solemnly. "At least the past is over and done with. Except for the leftover vibes."

"Ivy's always feeling vibes." Edmund was proud of Ivy's weird talent. "She's always *sensing* stuff."

Ivy had been the first one to sense that all was not well with our parents. She was the first to guess they were splitting up. Edmund and

I hadn't wanted to believe it. Maybe divorce is harder on adopted kids because it's yet another loss.

"Ah, and are these vibrations from the past like *ghosts?*" asked Grandfather Ellis with interest. "I've never seen anything around here myself, mind you. But we've had guests who have."

"Cool!" said Edmund.

"Tourists like ghost stories," he chuckled, turning to my parents. "A ghost or two is good for business." His chuckle turned into a rough cough that shook his entire body.

Ross patted the old man on the back. "All right?" he asked in concern.

"Fine, fine," Mr. Ellis wheezed.

"Sometimes guests say they see people—you know, ghostly people, walking in the maze," said Pippa, turning to me.

"Don't be silly," said her mother.

Pippa shrugged. "They've also seen them down by the lake. Having romantic…you know. *Trysts.* I wouldn't mind a tryst or two myself. Do you have a boyfriend, Juliana?"

"What are trysts?" interrupted Ivy before I could answer, but no one told her because Edmund was jumping up and down in excitement.

"Did you hear that, Ivy?" he crowed. "There's a *maze!*" He grinned up at Grandfather Ellis. "Can we go in it? Please?"

"*May* we go in it," Mom corrected him under her breath.

"You certainly can *and* may," Grandfather Ellis said genially. "It's a lovely old boxwood maze. Very popular with our guests. After lunch you must all explore it."

Then Grandfather Ellis raised his arm to beckon to a smiling, heavy-set woman about his own age who was hurrying toward us down the wide front steps.

"Now Lloyd," said the woman. "What are you on about?"

"Just telling them about the maze."

"And about the ghosts," added Edmund.

"That's pure nonsense, Lloyd, and you know it." She smiled at us, her eyes warm. "Hello, everyone."

"This is Edith Grey, an old friend *and* our housekeeper." Grandfather Ellis patted her round shoulder affectionately. "Not to mention the hotel's chief cook and resident nurse."

Mom and Dad shook hands with her.

"This place couldn't run without Mrs. Grey, that's for certain," Grandfather Ellis continued. "She's been here forever and loves every stone." Then he urged us inside for a tour of the manor. Mrs. Grey excused herself to get our lunch ready. Ross said he needed to get back to work but would join us at lunch. Pippa and her mother came along for the tour.

Edmund kept trying to race ahead and had to be restrained by Dad. Ivy was entranced. She listened intently to everything the old man said, drinking in the age and atmosphere. I just stared around me, trying to imagine what it would be like to live in such a place— not as a hotel guest, but back when it was a manor house owned by a wealthy family. In his letter to me, Grandfather Ellis had written that he had bought Heatherstone Hall, it had not been his family home. *Too bad,* I thought. It would have been very cool to be descended from people who had lived here hundreds of years ago.

As we climbed the broad, curving staircase, Ivy clutched my arm. "Do you feel it, Jule?" she whispered. "The vibes of all the people who have lived here?"

"I was just wishing they'd been my relatives," I told her with a laugh.

"Me too. But…don't you feel the vibes? I can."

"Nope. I don't believe in ghosts."

"I'm not talking about ghosts," my sister said. "*Vibes.*"

Dad, Mom, Edmund and Grandfather Ellis moved down a long hall. Josie and Pippa followed. I could hear their voices receding. But Ivy and I still stood on the stairs. She had her head cocked to one side and stood stiffly, as if listening. "Come *on,*" I said. She was so weird.

"Ssshhh!" She held up one finger; she seemed to be listening to the house. "They're *mostly* good vibes," she said slowly. "But...there's some bad mixed in, too. A touch of evil."

"You're giving me the creeps," I said, then hurried to catch up with the others. We saw a few bedrooms that were unoccupied (the house had twelve double bedrooms and four suites for guests, Grandfather Ellis told us). We passed several young women who wore black aprons tied over their jeans and black T-shirts. The aprons had an outline of the manor house in white on the large pocket. They were all carrying piles of towels. Grandfather stopped and introduced them to us as Bee, Maggie, and Harriet, three of the hotel's maids.

"Bee and Maggie are part-time help," he said. "Bee's parents are my landscape designer and my doctor. And Harriet is Edith's granddaughter, and is working for us full-time."

"Everybody else calls me Hat," the tall, pretty girl with the cloud of dark hair told us. "But Mr. Ellis never will."

"I've got half a dozen hats hanging on the stand in the hall," he told us with a chuckle, "but there's only one Harriet."

"He's sweet," she said to us. "I was excited to get a job here at the place Granny and I love so much. She's worked here most of her life, one way or another, and I lived with her off and on when I was still in school because my dad's on the road most of the time. He was gone a lot—over to France and Germany—but I never minded if I could stay at Heatherstone. But—no offense, Mr. Ellis—I have to say I'd rather live here as lady of the manor than as hired help!"

"Hat's saving up her pay to do a catering course in London, she is," said the plump girl called Bee. "She's ever such a good cook already, and she wants to have her own restaurant."

"Someday!" said Hat with a wide smile.

"Well, you've had the best teacher in your gran," said Grandfather Ellis. "She's a marvelous cook—as you'll soon see," he added to my family.

"The sooner the better!" said Edmund, who was always starving. Mom shushed him.

"Pippa's working as a part-time maid this summer," Josie told us. "Earning some pocket money."

"It's hard work," Pippa said. "I could never manage a full day like Bee and Maggie and Hat and Doreen!"

"And where is Doreen?" asked Grandfather Ellis, looking around. "Isn't she here today?"

The three maids glanced at each other uncomfortably. "She went down to the village on her lunch break, Mr. Ellis," said the young woman named Maggie. "And she hasn't come back yet. Trying to keep away from Lewis, I'm sorry to say. He keeps trying to…er…talk to her—you know. He really gets on her nerves."

"On mine, too," said the girl called Bee with a roll of her eyes. "He's a right *pest,* and I'm trying to be polite."

"Yes, yes, quite," interrupted Grandfather Ellis quickly. He started coughing hard, and Pippa darted over to pat his back. The maids glanced at each other again, and I wondered what was going on between the maid named Doreen and the guy named Lewis. "Well, well," said Grandfather Ellis when he recovered his breath. "You lasses get back to your work, eh? It must be nearly time for our lunch."

"*Yes!*" chirped Edmund.

Mom shushed him again.

We said good-bye to the maids and descended by another staircase to the billiards room. We walked through the library—a room I would have loved to linger in, with acres of books behind ornate iron grills. Then Grandfather Ellis led us into a grand glass-walled room filled with plants and small tables covered with white cloths, set with silver cutlery and pretty china plates. "I suspect Mr. Mustard in the conservatory with the lead pipe," whispered Edmund loudly.

This time *I* shushed him.

"How charming!" Mom said. She had grown less defensive as we wandered through the house and met the maids, and she was almost friendly now.

"Definitely the lap of luxury," Dad agreed. "And solidly built. Excellent examples of domestic architecture from several periods."

Our host beamed at their reactions, then motioned for us to be seated. Ross rejoined us, and sat next to his wife. Mrs. Grey and the maid called Hat brought tea, plates of little sandwiches cut into triangles, and a basket of scones with cream and jam. Then they left us. I think everyone was glad for the food to keep us occupied so we didn't have to talk much. Josie told us about their son—Pippa's older brother, Hugh. He was a university student in Norwich, living with a group of friends in a flat. "You'll meet him next time you visit," Josie said. "He and Pippa are thrilled to have a California cousin…"

"Mum," said Pippa, "control yourself." She turned to me. "Mum's the one who's absolutely chuffed that you're from California. She's counting on you to invite us there and show us round Disneyland and introduce us to all your Hollywood friends someday."

"We lived in northern California—nowhere near Hollywood," I told her. "And besides, we live in England now. But of course you can visit me when—*if*—I go back."

"See, Mum? All your hopes dashed to dust." Pippa smirked.

"Don't be silly," Josie said with a little trilling laugh.

After the Goops had stuffed themselves, they begged to be allowed to explore the maze. I pushed back my chair; I wanted to go with them.

"Go on, all of you, if you like," Grandfather said jovially. "Pippa will show you the way. Perhaps you'll run into our cousin, Lewis."

"Lewis Paine," muttered Pippa. "Oh, joy."

Grandfather frowned at her.

"And who is Lewis Paine?" asked my dad.

Ross Foxworth cleared his throat loudly. Josie sighed.

"Lew is a cousin of my late wife," Grandfather replied, frowning at Ross and Josie. "He works here as our assistant gardener and landscape designer. The maze draws people in like a magnet, but it requires a lot of upkeep." He smiled at us. "Anyway, Pippa, you let them try to find their own way—see if they can get to the middle and out again. In under an hour!"

"How will we know we're in the middle?" queried Edmund. "Is there a sign?"

"There's a stone bench dead center," Ross said. "You'll know when you get there."

"*If* we get there!" added Ivy with an eager giggle. She linked her arm through Pippa's.

"Have fun, kids," Dad said, and I think he wanted to go, too. But maybe Mom was stepping on his toe under the table because he stayed in his seat.

"Don't be too long," Mom said, and I could hear in her voice that she felt strange sitting with Grandfather Ellis and Ross and Josie without us kids. That is, without *me*—to connect them.

"We'll be as fast as we can," I said, and I headed off with the Goops and Pippa, out of the conservatory, under the shade of a stone portico topped with a row of big stone pots in the shape of Grecian urns. The urns were planted with dark green ivy that hung over the portico in leafy tendrils. We ran down the slope of manicured lawn toward the lake. The entrance to the maze was there on the left, before we reached the water.

The hedges were dark green walls rising more than seven feet high. A rose covered trellis marked the entrance. We walked under the roses together, then needed to proceed single file. "Cool!" breathed Edmund.

Almost immediately the path branched in four directions. Ivy stopped in front of me and I nearly ran into her. "Now what?" she asked. "Which way?"

Smiling, Pippa shrugged. "What do you think?" she asked. "Take a guess."

The Goops fell to discussing the merits of each possibility. But I was silent, peering as far as I could see down each of the paths. I could hear voices talking in the maze, a man and a woman. A shriek—then a man's laugh.

"Get away, you great ox," hissed a young woman's voice quite near me—through the hedge. I couldn't see anything, but I heard the deep laugh again.

"It's no use pretending," the man's voice said. "Come here, my charmer."

I could hear swishing sounds as bodies brushed against the hedges; I could hear the pad of footsteps when people passed us unseen on the other side of the hedge walls. It must be some of the hotel guests running around in there.

But Pippa snorted. "Grandfather wanted you to meet our cousin Lew—well, now you've met him, and you're welcome to him. Such a bloody nuisance."

I was about to ask if the girl's voice belonged to that other maid—the one who had gone to the village to try to escape Lewis Paine, but Ivy clutched Pippa's hand. "We've decided," she announced. "*This* way—but let's stick together."

"This one on the right," shouted Edmund, starting off.

"No, wait," called Ivy. "I said this second path on the left looks better. See how the sun sort of falls right into it? It's like a sign to us, pointing the way."

"Whatever," said Edmund, and he veered obligingly to the left. "They all look pretty much the same to me!"

Pippa set off after them. Ivy looked back at me. "Come on, Jule!"

I followed slowly, then stopped. When I stared down those sun-dappled paths, I felt uneasy. Each path would lead us farther into the maze, twisting and turning us around, moving us toward the voices and footsteps of the unseen people who were in here with us.

I wasn't like Ivy, I reminded myself, feeling vibes from the past…it was more that the *present* in this maze didn't appeal. And so, instead of moving forward with my brother, sister, and new cousin, I found myself inching back to the rose arbor.

"You know what, guys?" I said conversationally. "I think I'll go back to the house." The Goops stopped and looked at me in surprise.

"Why? Is something wrong?" demanded Pippa.

"Nope," I said. "It's just—well, I really should stay and talk to Grandfather and the others. Your parents. That's why we came here, after all. "

Edmund shrugged. "Whatever. Just send out a search party for us if we're not back when it's time to leave!"

"You're sure, Jule?" Ivy peered at me as if trying to see into my head.

"Totally sure. See you later." I waved and stepped back onto the lawn. Ivy gave me a long look before taking Pippa's hand and following Edmund down the second path on the left.

Everyone looked surprised when I returned to the conservatory. I pulled out my chair and sat back down at the table. "The explorers have set off," I reported.

"You didn't feel like exploring, too?" asked Dad.

"I'd rather stay here with you."

"I could go with you," he offered.

I shook my head.

"Your grandfather was just telling us how he came to buy this manor house," Mom said brightly. "How he and his wife had a dream of running a really grand hotel somewhere, but the opportunity never came while Jane was alive—that was your grandmother, sweetheart."

"And then poor Lloyd was busy trying to raise Ross and Barbara on his own," Josie continued. "Ross was soon off to school, and doing well—but that sister of his! I never knew her," Josie added, "but I've heard the stories." She winked at Mom. "Of course, I know from raising Pippa that teenage girls aren't the easiest beasts on the planet to tame. I imagine you know what I mean!"

Mom gazed back at her impassively. "Juliana has never needed taming."

I winced at Mom's tone, but Ross let out a nice deep chuckle. I wondered if my birthmother had had a laugh like his. "Well, I guess you adopted her in time, then," he said. "If she'd been raised by Barb—*look out!*"

Grandfather coughed into his napkin. Then he told us how he'd always hoped his daughter would go into the hotel business with him, but she ran off and was not heard from again. He was glad when the local manor house, then falling into ruin, went on the market at a bargain price, and he was able to buy it. He was delighted when his stepson, Ross, offered to move in and help run the place. They had dreams of fixing Heatherstone Hall up into a really fine hotel.

He beamed at me. "And now we have. With Edith Grey to keep things running in the house, and John Bainbridge, a local landscape gardener, to keep things running on the grounds. Lewis Paine has been his right-hand man. He's got a landscape degree, he does, and a creative vision. And now we're opening a luxury spa—that's Josie's special project. Swimming facilities, massage therapy—did I mention that our Josie's a certified, licensed massage therapist?—and steam saunas and a hot tub. Ahh, it's all going to be most excellent. All the staff will be helping and even Pippa has signed on for duty in the spa before school starts again in September. Earn some more pocket money, eh?"

"This spa has been my dream for ages," explained Josie, eyes glowing. "I trained as a massage therapist, and I'm going to be offering all sorts of services. Lloyd, have you shown them?"

"I was leaving that to you, Josie."

"Oh, you must see the spa! It's absolutely *fabulous.*"

So Josie took us off to see the new wing added on to the back of the manor, and it *was* fabulous. The spacious glass atrium contained a large, kidney-shaped pool with a small island in the middle. The island was landscaped with ferns and flowers and had just enough room for a few reclining deck chairs. There were two steam saunas and a bubbling hot tub, also surrounded with lush plantings. Behind a bamboo screen were two massage tables draped with white cotton sheets. There were treatment rooms for salt rubs and seaweed wraps, a laundry room with piles and piles of thick white towels stacked and ready to be used, and a snack bar. "We open next week," Grandfather Ellis told us. "And Josie has the massage appointments already fully booked!"

"I signed all the family and staff up for massages last week," Josie said, beaming. "Gave them the full treatment. First a swim, then a massage, then a relaxing dip in the hot tub. Everybody loved it—well, Mrs. Grey, of course, only had the massage and the hot tub. She doesn't swim. Doesn't much like the water."

"It all certainly sounds tempting," Mom said, her eyes lighting.

"We may have to book a weekend here ourselves sometime," Dad agreed heartily.

I liked the idea of my whole family coming here. I wished we were staying now.

"As I've said, you are most welcome to stay tonight," the old man said. "You've got a long drive home."

I smiled. "I'd love to—Grandfather." It was the first time I'd called him that.

"And we can offer you a very special discount rate," Ross added quickly. "A special rate for long-lost relatives."

"Oh no, Ross!" Grandfather looked scandalized. "They would be our *guests*. Our *honored* guests. Juliana is my own granddaughter, after all. My only blood kin."

I saw Ross's face darken, and I remembered he was Grandfather's *step*-son, and his children were Grandfather's *step*-grandchildren. I saw Mom and Dad exchange a glance. Talk of blood kin seemed to make everyone uncomfortable.

"No, no," said Mom. "We really do need to be getting home tonight."

They thanked him for the tour and the lunch, and promised to stay in touch. The Goops were retrieved from where they were playing frisbee on the lush green lawn with Pippa (having successfully negotiated the maze and, as Edmund reported, disappointed, seen no ghosts *or* guests at all). I glanced over at the high hedges of the maze, the cheerful rose-covered entrance hiding the dark twists and turns of the paths.

Grandfather Ellis took my hand. "Dear girl," he said softly to me, "you are the image of my Barbara-Elizabeth, but you have your own special spark. I should very much like to know you better."

I squeezed his hand. "I'd like that, too, Grandfather."

He cleared his throat as if to say something more, but started to wheeze. Ross strode over and pounded him so heartily on the back, I was afraid he'd knock the old guy right over.

Then Grandfather, Ross, Josie, Pippa, and Mrs. Grey all stood on the gravel drive to say good-bye. The maid called Hat leaned out an upstairs window and waved. A couple of guests were walking up from the lake, and the man lifted a walking stick or cane and waved to us, too.

Mom and Dad never looked back, but Ivy, Edmund, and I waved out the car windows as we drove down through the green tunnel of trees. The sun glinting off the old glass in the manor house windows made them seem to wink like eyes, as if they knew secrets we weren't in on.

Well, this is something I didn't expect—and it's hard not to hate her. In fact, I do hate her.

Oh, she's friendly as can be, and efficient, and useful...but it's so clear she wants him, and thinks he wants her as well.

A situation impossible to ignore.

Or forgive.

Dreams come, fantasies of how to fix everything once and for all so that we may go on as before...

And, finally, from my dreams a plan emerges.

Such a simple plan!

So that we will be together as we are meant to be.

Forevermore.

3

Just a few days later, we kids were all sitting with Mom in the garden behind our cottage, a fresh pot of tea on the wrought iron table, when Dad came walking into our garden. He was staying at the Old Ship Inn in Blackthorn, where he always stayed when he was visiting, though he came to us for meals. Mom seemed all right with this arrangement, on the whole, but the Goops still held hopes that he'd move in properly. I'd given up hoping for that, but I did notice times when they seemed to forget they were mad at each other, and stood together with their shoulders touching, or their fingers reaching out for each other's hands. It almost seemed, sometimes, as if their bodies still remembered how nice they could be together, even if their heads were telling them it was all over.

Today Dad had collected our letters from the postbox just outside our stone wall and, as he came walking in through the door in the wall, he sailed an envelope over to me like a Frisbee. "Heads up, Jule!

I reached out and caught it—something I rarely manage with Frisbees. The envelope was large, square and pale gray, embossed with a return address on the back flap: *Heatherstone Hall Hotel and Spa*.

It was addressed to me.

I withdrew a single folded sheet of paper. A little tickle of excitement pounced across my shoulders. I unfolded the letter, looked at the signature—Lloyd Ellis—written with an old-fashioned flourish. Reading the letter, I left the table and walked into our cottage.

Grandfather Ellis wrote that it had been lovely to meet me and my family. And he wanted to see me again soon. Very soon—in fact, as soon as possible. Would I like a summer job? Starting right now? One of the maids had left suddenly, and now they were short-staffed at the hotel. I would help for the month of August, part-time like Pippa, working a bit in the kitchen, serving meals, assisting Josie in the newly opened spa. And Grandfather had a special favor to ask me: turned out that the Landscape Designer in charge of the grounds, a man named John Bainbridge, needed a new assistant because cousin Lewis Paine, whom we had not met but had heard about, would soon be traveling to Canada. Perhaps I knew a strapping lad who would also like to work at Heatherstone Hall this summer, filling in while Lewis was gone? We would both be paid as regular employees, but as Lloyd Ellis's only blood granddaughter in the world I would, of course, be a pampered guest as well. *Please come,* he wrote. *I long to get to know you better. My only true blood kin left in the whole wide world!*

The thought of spending the final month of the summer washing dishes and scrubbing out saunas and disinfecting hot tubs didn't thrill me, but the invitation did. I walked back out into the garden, where Mom and Dad still sat at the table over their tea cups. The Goops were now chasing a ball across the lawn. I handed the letter to Mom.

"I want to go," I said. "Please."

She read it swiftly, then looked up at me and laughed. "I can't picture you as a maid."

We both knew I was none too tidy around the house, but so what? "I *want* to go," I repeated softly. "It's important to me."

Mom passed the letter to Dad, who read it with a furrowed brow. "Did you know he was going to send this, Juliana?" he asked. "Did your grandfather talk to you about it secretly while we were there?"

"Not at all. This is a surprise—and I want to go."

"What about London?" Mom said. "We're going to have a lovely time together, you and I, setting up my new exhibit." She pressed her lips together.

"Look, I need to get to know him," I told my parents. "All of them. Everybody. They're related to me. They're my *family.*"

"We're your family!" Dad's voice rumbled like thunder.

"They're my *other* family." I could feel tears pressing behind my eyes. "You know they are. We're *connected.*"

Mom took a sip of her tea and I could see she was trying to stay calm. She had this way of tightening her mouth and squaring her shoulders as if she were mentally counting to ten. The Goops ran over to see what we were talking about, nosy little things. "Connected, are you?" Mom said softly. "Well, my grandmother always said people are *all* connected. All links in the same chain. But, Jule, we've already made plans. It's too late to change everything."

"But *why?* You don't need me in London. And I know Duncan would like working at Heatherstone…"

"A strapping lad…" giggled Ivy, who was reading the letter now.

"Like a lumberjack," chortled Edmund, reading over her shoulder. "Juliana's big and burly *hunk…*"

I shot them a look. Mom sat back in her chair and crossed her arms. Her legs were crossed, too. Now she didn't look angry. She looked vulnerable.

"Mom," I said gently. "Whether or not Duncan can go, I want to. It's only for a month. And it—it's not like I'm…switching sides. I know which family I belong to most—and it isn't to Lloyd Ellis's."

Mom caught her breath. She leaned forward and put her hand on my arm. "I don't think you're in danger of forgetting us, honey," she said, laughing a little. "Not really."

"You're our girl forever," said Dad. He looked out over the garden. "But I guess you can be their girl, too."

"I don't like it," said Ivy, hands on hips. "I don't want you to go away."

"Me neither," said Edmund. He kicked the table leg.

"You guys will be in California, living it up with the cousins," I reminded them. "We'll all be back here together in Blackthorn at the end of August, right?"

Dad looked at Mom. "I'm thinking it could be good for her to stretch. See what new things she can handle."

"You find out what you can handle when you're wrestling in the dirt."

"As your granny used to say," said Dad. "But the woman was a pessimist."

"A realist. It means things can get messy."

"But then you find out if you can handle them," Dad pointed out.

I waited, not saying anything, just holding my breath. Links in a chain, wrestling in the dirt, *whatever*. I wanted to go.

Mom cradled her tea cup. Dad shredded a paper napkin.

"We don't know those people, not really," Mom said after a long moment.

"Mr. Ellis is an old man," Dad pointed out quietly. "Juliana may not have many chances to get to know him."

"Hey, what if he does die?" asked Edmund. "Will Juliana inherit that manor house? That would be so cool, wouldn't it, Ivy? We could all live there and hang out in the maze and—"

My parents looked at each other consideringly, then at me. Then back at each other. Their old parent-code was still working, despite their separation and the troubles between them. They were sending each other a message with their eyes. I could tell—the Goops and I could always tell—but I couldn't read its meaning. Then, as if they'd rehearsed it, they said in one voice, "Oh, all right."

"All right—what?"

"We can go live there when the old man dies?" cried Edmund. "Cool!"

"No, kiddos. We mean that Juliana may take the job and get to know her grandfather," Dad said. "All right, Hedda?"

"Just for the month."

"Thanks!" I hugged each of them, Mom first, then Dad. We all laughed a little, slightly awkward together.

Before I phoned my grandfather to say I was coming, I called Duncan and told him about Grandfather's invitation, and the house, and the spa, and the maze, and the lake, and the gardens. "It's an amazing place, Dunk. So what do you think? Can you take the gardening job and come with me? Pretty please?"

"Oh man. A whole month with you?" I could hear the smile in his voice. "That sounds *brilliant*. I've hated the idea of your being away in London till school starts. But, I'll have to see—" his voice trailed off.

"Your grandparents?"

"Right. I'll have to check if I can get away." Duncan lived with his grandparents and took care of them just as much as they took care of him.

"Let me know as soon as you can," I urged him. "Then I'll phone my grandfather and tell him I can vouch that you're the strapping lad he's looking for."

"Fingers crossed."

We hung up and I collapsed on my bed and stared at the ceiling, waiting, waiting, waiting. I pictured him telling his grandparents, describing the work, asking if they could get along without him for a month. How long before they phoned my parents to ask for further details about my grandfather and his household?

The phone rang downstairs and my mother answered. I smiled, listening to her end of the conversation. "Hello, Mrs. Hooper. Oh, yes! Yes, it does sound like a good job. Yes, they seem like very nice people. I can give you the phone number so you can discuss it with Mr. Ellis yourself..."

She sounded like she'd never had a single reservation about my going to Heatherstone Hall at all.

*   *

Three days later Duncan and I were on our way. Grandfather Ellis was delighted we could both come. And so Mom and Dad and the Goops, as well as Duncan's grandparents, all saw us off on the train to Norwich. We stowed our backpacks and suitcases on the overhead racks and found seats together. Two elderly women boarded in Oxford, and sat across from us, chatting quietly, their knitting needles clicking companionably. I gazed out at the wet green fields as the train rolled east, my head resting against Duncan's solid shoulder, my hand in his. Sure, it would be fun to get to know Grandfather Ellis and the other relatives. But hanging out with blood kin was only the half of it. *Adventure and romance, here we come,* I thought contentedly as the wheels of the train clicked against the track, and the drizzly English afternoon flashed past.

Grandfather met us at the station. I introduced Duncan, and knew things were off to a good start by the way Grandfather and Duncan shook hands. "Strong grip," Grandfather said approvingly. "You'll do very well."

As we drove out of the city in Grandfather's posh car, the countryside opened around us, soft and green. Duncan sat in the back seat and was mostly quiet. I sat up front next to Grandfather and felt a little shy, too, at first. Grandfather, in true English tradition, talked about the weather. It had been cool, he said. Wetter than usual. Hadn't hurt business much, at least not yet, he thought, but it seemed there wasn't a day this week when a drizzle hadn't passed over. Good for the gardens, of course, but not for the honeymooning couples who wanted to fish on his lake or lie out with a picnic in the fields. Mrs. Grey had had to serve Afternoon Tea on the verandah every day this week because of the mist off the fens.

We nodded and said all the polite things like we didn't mind the weather, and it was a treat to be able to come to Heatherstone. I still hadn't got used to how chilly the summer had been so far. Very different from the bone-dry summers in California. Then, as we left the city limits, my grandfather—that staid old gentleman with his cane—turned into a speed demon.

He gripped the leather-wrapped steering wheel, concentrating on the road as we careened along narrow country lanes. Occasionally the hedgerows parted to allow us blurred glimpses of fields yellow with mustard flowers.

I opened my window and sniffed. In Blackthorn the salty scent of the sea was ever-present, but in East Anglia the fields and marshland made the air smell wet and green. As we sped along, Grandfather told me again how glad he was that I'd agreed to come. The maid named Doreen had left ("in something of a huff, Harriet tells me," he confided) and I was doing them a big favor. Duncan was a Godsend, too, with cousin Lew off to Canada soon.
Another gardener was desperately needed to finish up projects before the winter. "We're fencing in the entire property, so there are a lot of post holes to dig, I'm afraid, lad," Grandfather called to Duncan in the backseat. He whizzed to the left, onto an even narrower lane.

"Looking forward to it," replied Duncan, hanging on. I turned around to grin at him.

"Here's Hethel," wheezed Grandfather, hardly slowing at all as we passed a cluster of houses and an old stone church. "Lived here as a boy, I did. Expect to be buried here someday as well. Blink and you'll miss it!"

The car raced on. "Heatherstone is next." Grandfather did slow down slightly as we passed through the small village. Heatherstone had a main street, with a row of stone houses and shops, a post office, a pub on the corner. "There's the Pike and Drum," Grandfather said, pointing. "Old folks like me seem to prefer downing our pints here; most of the young folk get together at the other end of the village…" he pointed ahead, and in about two seconds we were there—"at the Dirty Duck."

The wooden sign hanging from chains above the door was shaped like a swan. I craned my neck to read the back of the sign as Grandfather veered left around a corner. "The White Swan" was painted on the other side.

Duncan, in the back seat, laughed. "That's classic," he said. "There must be a couple dozen pubs in Britain with that same name."

"You'll be back here soon enough, I'll wager," Grandfather said cheerfully. He gunned the motor and raced along like a madman. "Hat and Pippa and Hugh will bring you."

I hoped I lived long enough.

Finally Grandfather slowed to point out the cobbled lane leading into a grove of trees. "Mill Lane," he said. "That's where Bee lives—you remember her? She's working as a maid until her time comes. Her dad is John Bainbridge—he's the man who will be your boss, Duncan, after me, that is. And her mum is my doctor. Mina Fuller. Lovely lady, our Dr. Fuller. You'll meet them all, soon enough."

He braked suddenly and I clutched the door handle. Before I could ask what "time" would be coming for Bee Bainbridge, Grandfather had rolled down his window to call to a man who was leaving that same lane on foot, sprinting across the main road.

"Lew! Hullo there, Lew!" called Grandfather, but the man did not stop. He disappeared around the corner, heading back into the village.

"That was Lewis Paine, our cousin," said Grandfather, speeding up again. "Off to the pub, I suppose—though I had hoped he would be at the house to welcome you. Ah well, the others will all be there."

Then the car turned into the big stone gates and started up the gravel drive. Heatherstone Hall loomed ahead of us, and even though I'd seen it just a short time before, the sheer grandeur of it came as a fresh shock. *So big—and so old,* I thought, feeling almost reverent. I remembered Ivy's talk of vibes, of hints of evil—but that was just Goop nonsense, of course.

"Now that's what I call *massive.*" Duncan sounded impressed.

Grandfather Ellis parked on the gravel drive in front of the house. "Come along, you two. Do you need help with your luggage?"

"Oh, no, we can manage just fine, "I told him, getting out of the car and shouldering my backpack. The drizzle had stopped, and the air was cool and damp. I let Duncan pull my suitcase from the trunk—

the *boot,* as they called it here in England. Here was his chance to show Grandfather what a fine, strapping lad he was. The late afternoon sun slanted gold on the facade of the house as we started up the wide stone steps. The old glass in the windows glinted. I turned to smile back at Duncan, who was wrestling with our suitcases. He grinned at me.

Behind him the lawn glowed emerald green, the winding paths tumbled down to the lake, and the late afternoon sun gleamed on the water. I saw a young couple walking there, arm in arm, the woman steadying the guy who leaned on a walking stick. *Hotel guests out for a stroll,* I thought. Soon it would be Duncan and me, just the two of us, just like that. Well, without the cane.

Then the light shifted and another fine mist of raindrops came down. When I blinked, the couple had vanished.

4

I glanced back over my shoulder as Grandfather led us up the steps of the manor house. The couple had probably just moved behind a clump of bushes, that was all. Probably were already making out, hot and heavy. Newlyweds probably didn't even notice the rain.

Even in this drizzle, I wouldn't mind a walk around the lake with Duncan, but we followed Grandfather through the marble entrance-way into a grand, long-windowed, high-ceilinged room. It was elegant but comfortable, furnished with richly upholstered leather couches and chintz-covered armchairs and small tables with reading lamps. We had seen this room on our family tour, but no one had been in it, then. Now several people were clustered in each seating area.

"The hotel guests socialize in the library," Grandfather said, taking my elbow and ushering me across the room. "But this parlor is reserved for family and special friends." He raised his voice: "Here she is, everybody! My miracle granddaughter, Juliana Martin-Drake."

Mrs. Grey bustled over, smiling. "It's lovely you've come back to us," she said. "And is this your young man?"

Grandfather looked surprised, as if he had already forgotten about Duncan. I reached for Duncan's hand. "This is Duncan McBennet," I said.

"He's going to work with John Bainbridge," Grandfather explained. "Filling in when Lew leaves for Canada." He turned to Duncan. "You did say you like to garden, eh, lad?"

"I help my grandparents with their garden quite a bit," Duncan said. "Pruning and weeding, and tending the vegetables."

"Good lad," said Grandfather.

Josie and Ross greeted us both warmly, and Josie linked her arm through mine. Pippa loped across the parlor like a graceful gazelle. She curtsied dramatically in front of me. "Hail the returning princess!"

"Um…whatever that means," I said.

"It means you're the prodigal granddaughter! The main topic of conversation around here all week. No, really, I'm glad you've come back," she said. "We'll have fun." Then her eyes slid past me. "Well, *hullo there!* Who are you? Please don't say you're another cousin!"

Duncan stuck out his hand and shook hers. I loved that he had such perfect, old-fashioned manners. "Duncan McBennet. No relation to anybody here, as far as I know."

"That's good," she said, dimpling at him.

I slid my arm through Duncan's. *He's with me,* I wanted to say as Pippa clung to his hand. "He's my friend from Blackthorn."

How I wanted to be able to call him my boyfriend, but somehow we weren't that far along yet. We weren't officially a couple, but I felt we were close.

Pippa's eyes shifted to me and back to linger on Duncan's face. "Soon to be my friend, too, I hope."

"So you live here?" he asked her, extricating his hand from hers.

"In the old stable block. We're not *royalty* around here like Juliana. She gets a big room upstairs. But if you're a lowly gardener, you'll be living right by me. Most of the stable block has been converted into cottages. We can hang out when you're off duty." Her eyes shifted to me. "You, too, Juliana. Of course."

"Come, Juliana, darling, you and Duncan must meet Hugh." Josie turned me firmly. My fingers were gripped in the warm, strong hand of an exceptionally gorgeous guy. "Hugh, darling, this is your California cousin, Juliana, and her friend, Duncan." Josie turned back to me. "Hugh is a graduate student at the University of East Anglia.

We're very proud of him!"

"Hullo," Hugh said, grinning at us.

He had the same cork-screw curls as Pippa, but his were dark, like his dad's. Gorgeous brown eyes. Straight, white teeth and a very cute smile. I had to grin back.

Duncan seemed to be waiting for me to take the lead; after all, these were my relatives, though I had a hard time holding on to that fact. "Um—hi," I said. "So, what kind of grad student are you?"

"Creative Writing," he said. "And what Mum says about their being so proud isn't quite true. Mum may be, but my dad thinks writing is a total waste of time."

Ross strolled over and clapped his son on the shoulder. "Write a best-seller and I'll revise my opinion then. I don't have anything against writing. But you've got to be able to earn your way in the world."

"Dad wants me following in his footsteps, helping to run the hotel. So I'm stuck working here for the summer."

"Hotel management is an excellent area of study, and running this hotel someday would be a fine future for you. You're nearly twenty-five years old, and I want—"

Hugh turned away. He looked back at me intently. "Anyway, it's great to meet the mysterious long-lost cousin everybody's been talking about," he said, talking right over his father, who was still muttering on about hotel management.

"Well, not really long-lost. In fact, I haven't been lost at all."

"Of course you haven't," Hugh agreed. "Just unknown to us."

"But how nice that now she *is* known to us," said Mrs. Grey comfortably, joining our group. "And back in the bosom of her family."

Good thing Mom wasn't here to hear that.

Pippa linked arms with Duncan. "Let's go sit down. I want to know everything about you." She dimpled up at him flirtatiously. "Come tell me about your...*hobbies.*"

Grrrrr, I thought. But before I could do anything, Grandfather took my arm.

"Look, Juliana, speaking of family—our cousin Lewis has joined us after all." Grandfather pointed across the room where the thin man we had seen crossing the road in the village earlier was standing with another couple—a woman about my mom's age, though with dark hair in a smooth pageboy, and a large man built like a football player (an American football player, that is). His hair was gray, but his face was youthful. He had huge shoulders and hands like hams.

Hands in fists—that's what I noticed as Grandfather towed me over to meet these people. The large man had his hands in fists and was looking like a steam valve about to blow. The three people were locked in such furious conversation, they didn't even notice us until we were next to them.

"What are you suggesting, man?" the broad-shouldered guy was saying in a deep growl. "Dammit, spit it out."

Lewis Paine cocked an eyebrow. "I only commented on how your wife sparkles tonight. Plenty of gold and glitter." His expression seemed to hold a challenge.

She spoke up quickly. "John, it's nothing at all. We'll talk about it at home, dear—"

"Lew!" Grandfather clapped the thin man on the arm. "You must meet my granddaughter!"

The heavier man backed up and took a deep breath. The woman raised her hands and smoothed her dark hair nervously. Then she turned to me with a quick smile.

"Hello there!" she said warmly. It was obvious she was glad of our interruption. "You're Juliana. I'm delighted to meet you."

I shook her hand. "Hello."

"I'm Mina Fuller, local doctor," she continued before I could say more. "And my husband, John Bainbridge."

The big bear of a guy clasped my hand, and Duncan's. "Greetings," he said gruffly.

"Mina and John are Bee's parents," Grandfather explained. "You'll be working with Bee while you're here."

Lewis Paine snorted. "Working, hah! The maids just stand about chatting all day, far as I can tell. Especially that Doreen. Didn't do a lick of work."

"As far as I can tell, all the girls work very hard indeed," Mina said, narrowing her eyes. "Bee certainly does. And as for Doreen—well, perhaps she found it hard to work under certain trying conditions."

Her husband looked from Mina to Lewis and back again. "What's all this then?"

Lewis Paine raised his eyebrows sardonically, but before he could speak, Grandfather began wheezing. Mina hastened to pound him on the back. Lewis rolled his eyes at me and shrugged.

After a moment Grandfather caught his breath. "Ah, thank you, Mina! There—you see, Juliana, lass? What I'd do without Mina and her family is anyone's guess. John is the landscape gardener I mentioned, the one who has designed all of the new gardens you will see, and restored the old ones…with Lew's help, of course. And Mina, ah Mina. Mrs. Grey is a wonderful nurse, don't get me wrong, and we're very lucky to have her here if the guests should need anything, but it is Dr. Mina Fuller who keeps me on my feet. And she's the only doctor for miles around who still pays house calls—"

Grandfather broke off, coughing hard, and Mina pounded his back. Lewis just stood there, lanky arms crossed. "Yes, Mina is incredible," Lewis said with a sardonic smile. "And very fashionable, too. Gorgeous earrings she's got on tonight. Don't you think so, John?"

John Bainbridge scowled at him, then glanced at his wife. Her face was red. Her ears sparkled with fiery blue stones set in gleaming gold.

"They *are* gorgeous," I told her as Grandfather caught his breath.

"See? Another lady ready to snatch up quality when she sees it,"

Lewis said. He was gazing at Mina Fuller with an unpleasant knowing sort of expression.

But what is it he knows? I wondered. *Or thinks he knows?*

There was a strained silence. Then Lewis Paine encased my hand in a killer grip. "I'm delighted to meet such a pretty new cousin," he told me.

He was younger than Ross, younger than John Bainbridge…maybe in his thirties. He had lank sandy hair falling limply into his eyes. He was very thin, almost gaunt, but muscular. My fingers were aching as he explained that he was, to be precise, Grandfather's wife's second cousin on her maternal side, which made him my second cousin twice removed…

Whatever. "Nice to meet you, too," I said, extracting my hand from his and looking around at the others. "All of you."

"I'm sure we'll be seeing you often," said Mina. "But—come on, John. We need to go."

"Right-oh."

"Why don't you two stay to dinner?" Grandfather invited them.

"Not tonight. I—er…I still have a patient to see in the village. Maggie has agreed to drive Bee home when they're through cleaning up after dinner." She towed John quickly toward the door, saying good-bye to people as they passed.

When they'd gone, Grandfather turned to the thin man. "Glad you made it back from the village so fast."

Speedy driving must run in the family, I thought to myself. Maybe I'd be speedy myself—not that I'd get a chance to find out anytime soon. It was a sore point for me that teenagers in England had to be eighteen before they could get a driver's license. If we were still in California, I'd be on the road by now.

"Now you must meet Juliana and her friend *properly,*" Grandfather said to Lew. Taking us each by an elbow, he towed us back to where Pippa was still flirting with Duncan.

"Hello *properly* to my beautiful cousin and hello to her friend," Lew said, smiling first at me, then at Duncan. Finally he turned to Pippa. "And hello again to my other little cousin. Isn't this one adorable, folks?" He flicked his fingers through Pippa's curls.

Pippa backed away. "What kind of cousins are we, Lew? Second or third step-cousins once or twice removed? Something distant, anyway. Very very distant."

"Lew's family emigrated to Canada years ago," Grandfather told us, "but Lew stayed on in England. But he's going off on an extended holiday in two weeks' time, so it's very lucky that your Duncan was able to step in to fill his shoes."

My Duncan. I liked the sound of that. Then I looked for my Duncan and saw Pippa pulling him across the room to meet an old man in a wheelchair.

Lewis Paine reached for my hand again. "Those will be big shoes for your friend to fill. I'll have you know I'm no run-of-the-mill gardener! I've got a degree in Landscape Design." His boastful voice sounded aggrieved, and his whole manner was aggressive. "Won't be working as anybody's assistant much longer, I can assure you. I've got plans to open my own business someday very soon. In fact, I could take over the grounds-keeping of this place, no sweat, right now. I've got the skills to manage the entire place."

"That's nice," I said, trying to extricate my hand just as, behind me, Ross let out a derisive snort. There were undercurrents between these men, just as there had been undercurrents between Lewis Paine and the other couple, but I couldn't tell what any of them meant.

"It is nice," he said, gazing deep into my eyes. "And so are you. And I am bowled over! Absolutely charmed to meet such a lovely, *sexy* young very distant cousin." His teeth when he smiled were long, with a yellow cast. "So very like your mum, you are. A real charmer. If you know what I mean." He gave me a wink.

Whatever!

Behind me, another snort from Ross. Then Josie snatched my hand from Lewis Paine's. I felt like thanking her, but Lewis was still talking.

"It really is astonishing to have you turn up after all these years," he said. "All the way from California, eh? Land of golden sunshine?"

I nodded. "Well, I live here in England now, in a little village called Blackthorn. But my dad still lives near San Francisco. Have you been there?"

Lewis Paine pursed his lips. "I've never been to the States—nor anywhere foreign. Never saw the need, actually."

"But you're going to Canada," I said, "aren't you?"

"Well, my parents are both gone now, but I've still got an aunt and uncle over there who've been after me for ages to come for a visit. I hear they've got a large property near Toronto. Think it's time I go take a look."

"Because maybe they'll leave it to you in their will, eh, Lew?" Pippa's voice behind me sounded snide.

"I wouldn't turn it down if they did, Pip-squeak," he said with a wink at me. Then he shrugged. "But I won't be gone long. Don't like to travel much, and I'm quite happy right here." His thin lips lifted in a smile. "There's just something about England."

"That's what my mother says," I told him, returning the smile. "She's English, you know, even though she lived in America for years. She says something always draws her back here."

"Your mother?" Lewis Paine darted a look over at Grandfather.

"Not my *birthmother,* not Barbara-Elizabeth," I clarified. "My *mom.*"

"Ah, that's right. Lloyd said you'd been adopted. So you're happy with those people, are you? It's all working out then?"

I sighed inwardly. This guy seemed to think my adoption into the Martin-Drake family was just some sort of arrangement we'd decided to try out. Some people just didn't get it, didn't understand that adoption is forever. "My family is great," I said simply.

"So there, Lew," said Pippa. "Juliana's *got* a family. She doesn't need us."

"Doesn't need is not the same as *doesn't want,"* said a heavily accented voice, and I turned to see that the portly old man in the wheelchair had rolled up behind us. "One can always use more family!" He folded his newspaper in his lap and reached out to shake my hand.

"Hello," I said, happy to be diverted from conversation with Lewis Paine.

"Pleased to meet you. I'm Otto Stifelmeyer, from Germany." His voice was deep and rich.

"Guten Tag," I said.

He brightened. *"Ach, Sie sprechen Deutsch!"*

"Sorry, I don't really speak German well. I've had just two years at school."

"Well, it is a start," the old man said with a smile. "The more languages we can speak, the more we enjoy other cultures. Other countries. In fact, I couldn't help overhearing, and I must say that I understand how your mother feels about England. I know what she means about this country drawing one back." His shiny head, completely bald, gleamed in the shaft of sunlight through the panes of glass. "I have just returned to England myself for the first time after almost sixty years, but I have often thought with great affection about this land."

"High time you made the trip, Otto," Grandfather said heartily. "Highest time!" Then he put his arm around my shoulder. "Mr. Otto Stifelmeyer, that is—*Herr* Otto Stifelmeyer—is from Bonn, Germany. We met many many years ago—back when his English was very rusty indeed!"

"Back when it was practically non-existent, I'd say," laughed the German. "But I learned fast. I needed to."

"And you have remained fluent all these years," said Grandfather.

Otto Stifelmeyer looked pleased. "I am delighted to meet Lloyd's granddaughter," he said heartily. "I myself have three granddaughters, about your age. My son's children."

"That's nice," I murmured.

"And next time you come, you must bring them all with you," said Grandfather. "Bring the whole family! They'll be our honored guests! We'll show them a good time, won't we?"

Everybody agreed that of course they would.

"When word of this elegant new spa gets out," said Mr. Stifelmeyer gallantly, "I think you'll be too busy here to pay special attention to any particular guests. Have you seen the new spa, young Juliana? You will be most impressed!"

"I saw it last week," I said. "But Duncan hasn't."

"Well, he must do so! Its opening has created quite a stir. It was written up in the—how do you say it?—the travel supplement? Yes, in the newspaper in Bonn. And when I saw the name of the place, I knew immediately I had to come back here as soon as I could. I arrived only yesterday."

"Back here?" I repeated. "So when were you here at the hotel before?"

Mr. Stifelmeyer and Grandfather exchanged a smile. "Many long years ago," Mr. Stifelmeyer said. "A lifetime ago. But it wasn't a hotel back then."

"Surely we can tell them the story?" said Grandfather. "No reason it has to be our little secret, eh, Otto?"

"Of course we can tell them. It's quite a story, really!" The old gentleman ran a hand over his bald head and smiled at us all. "You see, I was here during the war."

Mrs. Grey looked at him in surprise. Ross leaned forward with interest. Josie stopped chattering to Hugh and peered at him.

"World War Two?" asked Hugh.

"World War Two, it was," the old man clarified. "A dreadful time. I was drafted into Hitler's army, just a young pilot, and sent to fly bombers over the city of Norwich. I did not want to do this, you must understand. And so I was secretly glad when my bombs failed to deploy. But nothing else was working properly on my plane, either—and there was engine trouble. I was forced to eject from my plane before it crashed, and I parachuted into a field in Hethel, where I was promptly taken as a prisoner of war."

"Oh heavens!" cried Josie. "You poor thing."

"Well, he *was* flying a bomber," said Ross drily. "What would you expect?"

"I was brought here to Heatherstone Hall," the old man continued softly, "which was in use as a military hospital. Two badly broken legs, and many broken ribs, and lucky I was that it wasn't worse. I was brought here to mend. To—*ach*, what is the English word?"

Mrs. Grey cleared her throat. "Recuperate?" she suggested.

"Ja, that is it! To recuperate. And the nurses, they were so very helpful and kind."

"Especially one of them, eh, Otto?" said Grandfather, his voice droll. He winked at Mrs. Grey.

Mrs. Grey clasped her hands together as if she were praying. "Now Lloyd—"

"Ach!" exclaimed the old German. "Am I correct in thinking you were a nurse here at that time, Mrs. Grey?"

Mrs. Grey nodded, her face coloring. "I was indeed."

"A happy coincidence, then, that we should meet again. I don't recall your face, but the years have taken—how do you say it?—taken their toll on my memory, and it isn't what it used to be, I'm afraid. And of course for much of my time here I was under sedation. Mercifully. The memories are quite vague..." He shook his head. "Perhaps I will remember in time."

"I'm afraid I don't recall you either," Mrs. Grey said sharply.

Mr. Stifelmeyer laughed heartily. "I had quite a bit more hair in my youth—bright red it was, too! Like this young man here." He nodded toward Duncan, then patted his corpulent belly. "I've fattened up since the war."

"Red hair, you say?" Mrs. Grey was frowning at him, as if still trying to remember.

"Perhaps you would call it orange, really. My dear mother used to call me—*ach*, how would you say it?—Little Carrot Top! *Ja, ja,* there were so many young nurses here, and all so kind, even to an enemy soldier."

I smiled at the thought of this old gentleman as a young pilot with bright orange hair like Duncan's. It was hard to think that he had once been the enemy.

"So many injured lads…" said Grandfather reminiscently. "Remember, Otto? British lads and German prisoners of war, together. Our nurses certainly had their hands full. Oftentimes they never did learn our names, did they?"

"They just knew us as 'shattered hip in Ward 1,' or 'shrapnel wound in Ward 2,'" said Herr Stifelmeyer with a smile.

"Or handsome heir to Heatherstone in Ward 3! Eh, Edith? Remember how the nurses flocked to watch Dorian sleeping?"

"Nonsense," said Mrs. Grey. "We nurses were much too busy to watch patients sleep. We'd fall asleep ourselves at the first lull; it was that busy around here."

"The heir to Heatherstone was a patient here, too?" I asked, confused.

"Well," said Grandfather. "Well, yes, I'm afraid he was."

He went on to explain that Dorian Heatherstone's family had owned Heatherstone Hall since it was first built. Dorian grew up to be a handsome young man. Village girls would swoon when he drove past in his motorcar. (Here Grandfather winked at Mrs. Grey.) During World War Two he enlisted as an army officer. Apparently he was popular with the young men under his command, and he had unusually egalitarian ideas for a young man so highborn. When he was injured in the war and shipped home, he insisted on being treated like one of his soldiers—wanted to lie on a ward rather than upstairs in his private room. His father was quite annoyed. But that was nothing new; the way Grandfather heard it, Lord Heatherstone was always threatening to disinherit young Master Dorian for some reason or other and turn the whole estate over to his twin sister, Lady Diana. "She's the one who inherited it in the end," Grandfather told us. "And the one who, many years later, sold it to me."

"So Dorian was disinherited after all?" asked Duncan. "That's harsh."

Herr Stifelmeyer and Grandfather exchanged a look. Grandfather cleared his throat. "No, he wasn't disinherited. The truth of the matter is that poor Dorian never fully recovered. That is to say, he died." He shook his head. "It was a sad time."

"It was dreadful," agreed Mrs. Grey. "So many young men didn't make it."

"Granny?" The girl named Hat had stepped inside the room during Grandfather's account of Dorian Heatherstone's history and stood along the wall with Hugh, listening. Now she took Mrs. Grey's arm. "The guests are gathering in the dining room."

"Goodness, look at the time!" exclaimed Mrs. Grey. "It simply won't do to have the sideboard bare." She smiled at everyone. "Please excuse me. We're a bit short-handed just now, with Doreen gone." She bustled out of the room. Hat followed, tossing a brilliant smile over her shoulder at Hugh as she left.

I wondered if I should go along to help, but Grandfather kept hold of my arm. "You'll start work soon enough. No need to rush off on your first night with us."

"You go, Pippa," ordered Josie.

Pippa tossed her curls and looked ready to refuse, but then rolled her eyes at Duncan. "Slavery," she murmured. "Drudgery. I'm glad you're here to help me forget my misery."

"Misery," said Herr Stifelmeyer ruminatively after she left. "These young people know nothing about misery. When I think back to the war…"

"Yes, those were dreadful times," Grandfather agreed. "But now most of Europe has been at peace for a generation, and is finally unified. I am glad I've lived to see it." He laughed. "I'm glad to be alive, period!"

Herr Stifelmeyer nodded. *"Ja, ja.* Here we are, the two of us old men now, but alive. Look at me in this wheelchair! My doctor says I must get up at least three times a day and walk. And he insists I must climb up and down the stairs for exercise as well!"

Grandfather's expression was rueful. "I'm not so good on the stairs myself these days. My knees, you know. So perhaps, Josie, you will show Juliana to her room?"

"Certainly," said Josie. She took my arm. "Come along, darling, you'll want to unpack. Lewis, will you take Duncan out to your flat?" She turned to Duncan. "You won't mind sharing with Lew, will you? His flat has two bedrooms."

"No, that will be fine, as long as Lew doesn't mind."

Lewis Paine gave Duncan the thumbs up signal. "Glad of the company."

Duncan looked over at me and smiled, and I could tell he was sorry, as I was, that he wouldn't be sleeping in a room near mine. But we'd make time to see each other anyway.

I felt eyes on my back as we left the room. "So that's your girl, eh, Duncan?" I heard Lewis Paine say in his deep, rumbly voice. "She's a charmer."

"Juliana is a lovely girl," Grandfather's voice affirmed. "Does my old heart good to have her here." He came out into the hallway and smiled at me. Then he set off down the corridor to the kitchen.

The old man was sweet. I craned my ears, eager to hear what Duncan might say about me, but Josie beckoned impatiently. As I started up the stairs behind her, there came a short bark of a laugh from behind the door of the parlor. "Better hope this charming princess doesn't become heir to the kingdom," I heard Lewis say.

Someone snorted. Ross? "Right. Must be on guard against gold diggers, eh, Lew?"

Heir to the kingdom? Princess? Gold diggers? I glanced up at Josie, but she showed no sign of having heard. Duncan and Lewis Paine came out into the hallway then. I looked at Duncan and raised my eyebrows, but he just shrugged.

Oh, the frustration! Why on earth does she always hang about? Of course he is polite; it is his nature to be polite—chatting and smiling through his pain. It doesn't mean anything.

Doesn't she realize he is only humouring her?

It is still quite clear that he wants one thing only: me, me, me. I know he wants what I want.

That we shall soon be together. Must be together.

I want to carve it in stone. Or across her pretty forehead.

Must.

Be.

Together.

5

Josie led me up the curving staircase to the next floor, where hallways stretched left, right, and straight ahead.

"You're down here on the right, Juliana, pet," said Josie. "In number eight. The blue room. There's a lovely view of the lake." She opened the door, then handed me the key.

I gazed at the expanse of soft blue carpet and the four-poster bed with a blue lace canopy. "Oh, how pretty!"

"Your suitcase ought already to have been brought up—yes, here it is," Josie said. "Oh—and you have an *en-suite* bath. This room is one of the nicest. Your grandfather wanted you to be comfortable. Only the best for his new granddaughter! Of course, our rooms don't automatically come with telly and phones, the way hotels do in America. Some rooms have those extras, some don't. Will this suit you?"

"It's perfect," I said, though I wasn't quite sure what an *'en-suite'* bath was. "I have a cell phone—a mobile, I mean. And I don't watch much TV."

"Well, if you want to watch, your Grandfather has one in his room, and of course there's one in the parlor for the guests. And I'm sure Pippa will invite you round to our place to watch a film, if you like."

"Thank you. This is great."

She left the room, closing the door softly. I figured out *en-suite* meant a private bath, because there it was, tiled in bright, clean white, with a large, old-fashioned, claw-footed tub and gleaming chrome fixtures. I walked over to the long windows and looked out at the sun-dappled garden. The rain had stopped. People strolled up from the lake, heading toward the house for dinner. I opened my suitcase and stowed my clothes in the large dresser, then pulled my laptop out of its case.

I sat on my bed and texted my parents to say we'd arrived safely. Then I lay on my back, staring up at the canopy. I felt like a princess in this fancy room. And, fittingly, Pippa had even called me 'Princess.'

Heir to the kingdom? Had Lewis and Ross meant that someday Grandfather might leave me this whole huge manor house in his will—as Edmund was hoping? Would he, really?

I grinned, loving the idea of it. *Princess!* Me!

I lay there entertaining myself with fairy-tale fantasies of how Duncan and I would become the new lord and lady of Heatherstone Hall until it hit me that such a scenario could come about only if Grandfather Ellis *died.* And I'd practically just met the man!

I didn't want to lose him any time soon.

* *

We couldn't eat our meal until the guests had finished theirs, Mrs. Grey explained when I came down to the kitchen. The maids I'd already met were introduced to Duncan: Maggie, Bee, and Mrs. Grey's granddaughter, Hat. Maggie and Bee lived in the village with their families, but came to the house each day to clean and to help prepare and serve the meals. Hat was living here at the Hall with her granny.

"It's lovely having her back," Mrs. Grey told us. "She was here quite a lot while she was growing up because her dad's work took him away to foreign parts. As a girl she liked to sleep with me, and even now she's sharing my suite. Just as well, with the hotel crowded as it's been. I quite like having a roommate."

Hat smiled at her grandmother and swept back her cloud of dark hair. "Granny tosses and turns like a ship in a storm," she said. "It's a good thing I'm nearby to pick her up off the floor and tuck her back in."

"Oh, I'm not that restless, I should hope!" laughed Mrs. Grey. "Though Hat does tell me I talk in my sleep. Poor dear girl says it's as bad as living with somebody who snores!"

"Worse," said Hat. "Because I have to hear all your stories of the olden days."

I laughed.

Mrs. Grey and Maggie sat me down to explain my duties. Starting tomorrow, Mrs. Grey said, I would wear the same sort of uniform as the other maids: blue jeans, black T-shirt, and an apron with a silhouette of the manor house emblazoned on the pocket

Josie would show me my duties in the morning. Mrs. Grey herself prepared the breakfast every day, a light lunch for the staff and guests who ordered lunch ahead of time. The number of guests who chose to dine at the hotel was up considerably since the spa had opened. Not only the hotel guests, but also people from the nearby villages and as far away as Norwich, liked to come for a massage or a swim and then stay for a meal. Business, Maggie informed me tiredly, was booming. My help was very welcome.

I would primarily be working at the spa, but at dinner I might make myself helpful, Mrs. Grey told me, by walking through the dining room and stopping at each table to enquire whether the guests liked their food.

This was easy enough, and I ended up chatting with a family of Americans—a mom, dad, and two little boys named Ryan and Dylan—from North Carolina. Their familiar American accents made me a little homesick. Right now Dad and the Goops were on an airplane, flying to California.

"Sit down, boys, and stop wiggling!" ordered their harried mother. "They're always up to something," she told me with a sigh.

"Real mischief makers," agreed the dad. The two boys beamed at me, then started tossing breadsticks back and forth.

I retreated hastily to the next table, where Herr Stifelmeyer sat alone. He was reading a German newspaper while eating his stew. He put the newspaper down and started chatting, telling me how he wished his wife were here with him, how she'd always enjoyed traveling, how sad he still was about her death over two years ago. He told me about his son, who was a lawyer, and about his three beloved granddaughters, all at university. He said if I ever wanted to practice my German, I should come to him. He seemed too chatty a person to enjoy eating alone, and he had an air of loneliness about him, somehow. Maybe it felt strange to him, being back where once he'd been a wounded prisoner. Maybe he'd like to eat with Grandfather who had been, after all, a friend.

Besides the American family and the German, I met three honeymooning couples, three Japanese businessmen, and two elderly sisters—one of whom sat watching all the other diners with narrowed, considering eyes while the other giggled through each course of her meal like a school girl Ivy's age.

The watchful one reached out a surprisingly strong hand as I passed and grabbed my wrist. "Now you're a new girl here, aren't you? What's your name, dearie, and how did you come to be here? Tell me everything."

I pulled out of her grip and rubbed my wrist. "I'm Juliana Martin-Drake," I began politely, but before another word was out of my mouth, she broke in.

"American, eh? Coming here to sightsee, I imagine. England does have the most beautiful countryside on God's green earth."

"My family lives here now," I said. "I'm not a tourist."

"Come to take jobs away from hardworking British people, eh?" the old woman persisted querulously.

"Now, Aggie," chided her birdlike companion.

"It's true, Sue-Sue. Foreigners come in search of a better life, and then they stay. Now I ask you—"

This time *I* broke in. "My mother is English," I said squelchingly. "And Mr. Ellis is my grandfather and he wants me here, so I'm hardly taking a job away from some British person—"

"What's that you say?" yelped the woman. "Your grandfather? So—you're the one!"

"Something you didn't know, eh, Aggie?" asked the one named Sue-Sue slyly. "How astonishing. Just like you didn't recognize the German! You're slipping, sister. Slipping badly."

"Of course I recognized him. It just took me a minute. But then I recalled that carrot-orange mop. Oh yes, I remember him! A dastardly pilot he was. Shot down! No less than he deserved."

"And I'll bet you were sweet on him, Aggie," said Sue-Sue, slanting me a look.

"He was the *enemy,*" the one named Aggie said repressively.

Sue-Sue turned hastily back to her meal, giggling like a lunatic.

Her sister frowned. "So," she said, turning to me with a sniff. "You're the long lost granddaughter everyone was talking about. The only blood kin! Lovely to meet you—lovely, I'm sure. I am Miss Agatha Moggs."

I nodded. "Hello. I'm Juliana." I turned back to my duties, but she kept talking.

"My sister and I were intrigued when we heard about the new spa opening here at Heatherstone Hall because I used to be in service here, decades and decades ago. I was but a scrap of a girl when I first came. Sue-Sue was too sickly to work, so our mum kept her at home, but me—me they sent out to earn my keep. I was a serving girl—right here in this very dining room!"

"Does it feel strange to be back?" I asked, mainly just to be polite.

"Worked to the bone, I was," continued Miss Agatha Moggs by way of a reply. Her sparse eyebrows drew together fiercely. "Worked from long before dawn till long after dusk, I tell you. Weren't any unions to monitor the servants' hours or working conditions, no indeed not. I was on my own, with my bruised knees and my bleeding, chapped hands—bruised and bleeding from kneeling on the hard flagstones and scrubbing with hot water! And all the while we maids were to keep silent, to be invisible. We were to glide about without getting in anybody's way—like *ghosts,* we were supposed to be!"

"Hush, Aggie. Mind your tongue," tittered Sue-Sue.

"Bloody ghosts," repeated Agatha Moggs with relish. "Quiet as the grave! And I was good at it." She fixed her eye on me. "Got quite good at creeping about so people didn't notice me. Oh, I could tell you a few things as went on here that would shock your socks off."

"Ooh, Aggie," breathed Sue-Sue. "Do tell!"

"Secrets," said Agatha Moggs, shaking her gray head at me. "You have it soft here, girl. We were tough back then—forced to be. But I intend to make up for it now with some serious pampering. Scurry off to the kitchen now, young Juliana, if you please, and bring me another helping of this lovely sticky toffee pudding."

"All right," I said obligingly. I'd rather stay, though, and hear those secrets.

"*Yes, Madam* was the correct response in my day," said the old woman tartly.

I hurried to get her dessert. Josie was waiting for me in the kitchen doorway. "You mustn't pester the guests, Juliana."

"I wasn't pestering," I protested. "She wanted to tell me all sorts of stuff."

"Yes, I'm sure she did, and I daresay you meant well, chatting with her for so long. But the guests need to be left in peace." She smiled to take the sting out of her words, but I was pissed off. I hadn't been bothering anybody.

"Well, the guests seem mostly very friendly," I said, keeping my tone mild. "They seem to want to talk. The ones at that table by the window—they were telling me about their wedding. And the family in the corner—they're American. And Herr Stifelmeyer was telling me—"

"About the war?" Hat interrupted sharply. "About how he suffered here as a prisoner? All his old dreadful memories?"

"Not at all." I glanced at her, surprised by her tone. "He just talked about his family. I think he's lonely here."

"Perhaps," said Josie. "But that's none of our business. You're not to bother him or any of them. Remember—you're hotel staff."

Hat nodded in agreement.

"Sorry," I said, irritated. *Hotel staff* didn't sound nearly as good as *Heir to the Kingdom*. I took Miss Agatha Moggs another serving of Mrs. Grey's sticky toffee pudding.

"Here you are, Madam," I said, setting it on the table with a flourish.

The old woman looked at me appraisingly, then nodded to her sister. "She'll do."

Lewis and Duncan returned from their stable flat, and then it was the staff's turn to eat dinner. We sat in the kitchen on benches at the long scrubbed pine table, with Mrs. Grey presiding at one end and Grandfather at the other—almost as if they were hosts of a banquet, or parents of a large, unruly brood. I was seated between Duncan and Pippa, with Maggie, Hat, and Bee across from us. Lewis Paine and Josie sat farther down. Ross and Hugh were nowhere to be seen.

Immediately the table was buzzing with conversation. Maggie talked about her husband, who worked at one of the pubs in the village. They'd been married three years, were blissfully happy, and had a toddler son that Maggie's mum looked after while Maggie and her husband were working. Maggie often left the hotel before the meal in order to have time with her baby before he went to bed. But she'd been staying later ever since the other maid, Doreen, had left. Now that I'd come, she'd get home earlier again. That would be a relief. She missed her little boy while she was working.

"You might well be wondering why poor Doreen left us," Maggie added, passing around a wallet-sized photo of her smiling curly-haired toddler. "Since that's how you've come to have this job." And though I hadn't especially been wondering about Doreen, I nodded.

Maggie sent a sidelong glance down the table, and then lowered her voice. "She was *that* fed up, I'm telling you."

"With Lewis?" I whispered. The other maids and Pippa exchanged a dark look.

"Dead right," Pippa whispered back. "The evil Lewis."

"He was always pestering her," Hat said. "He's been after all of us, one after the other, but with Doreen it was the worst. Always cornering her in the garden or in the maze, or downstairs in the laundry. 'Come on, just a kiss,' he'd say. You've got to watch out for blokes like him."

I remembered the voices I'd heard in the maze, and the protest: *Get away, you great ox!* and the deep rumble: *Come here, my charmer…*

Yuck. That was harassment.

"It's just how he acted with you, Bee, before Doreen," Hat said to her.

"That man is a bloody nuisance," agreed Bee. "And now he's even after my mum!"

I wanted to ask what had happened with Bee, but Lewis Paine was staring at us from his place at the other end of the table. I wasn't sure whether he could hear us or not.

So Hat started talking about the catering course she was hoping to do in London—but how hard it would be to live away from Heatherstone Hall even for a year. "I grew up here, and the place is in my blood."

Her grandmother, carrying a basket of bread to the table, smiled fondly. "It's in both our blood, I think, child. We both came here as girls and fell in love with the place. I was a scullery girl here in this very kitchen when I was only thirteen years old!" She looked around. "We didn't have all these mod cons back then."

"Modern conveniences," Duncan translated with a grin. "Microwave. Dishwashers."

"I know what she meant!" I said.

"Hat came to live with her gran when she was about six," Pippa said. "Right Hat?"

"When my mum ran off and my dad was always working," Hat said cheerfully. "I'm lucky my granny was here."

"I'm the lucky one, Hat, dear," said Mrs. Grey, beaming.

Then Hat told us how she was hoping to become a fine chef and own a top restaurant someday. "A really trendy one," she vowed. "Maybe one right here at Heatherstone. Granny, you'd work in it, too!" Then Hat started asking me about the San Francisco and Napa Valley restaurant scenes—not that I knew a thing about them—but even as she talked she kept craning her neck, looking beyond me.

"Hugh is in the study, looking over the bookkeeping with our dad, Hat, so stick your eye stalks back in," Pippa said.

"Sod off, pipsqueak," returned Hat across the table, but without venom. They grinned at each other.

Pippa leaned toward me. "What Hat really wants is to marry my brother, which would be bloody horrible for her, but she won't listen. She'd better make a lot of money at her restaurant, that's all I can say, because he's never going to make any money writing stories."

"Hugh's going to be a famous novelist *and* be running this hotel someday, you wait and see," Hat said airily. "And I'll run the restaurant here—and turn it into a 5-star world-class event! You and Maggie and Bee will be on my staff. Juliana, too, if she likes."

"I won't be working here then," said Bee. "I'll be raising my babies. But Henry and I will come to eat at your restaurant, Hat. Don't worry." Bee pushed back a bit from the table and rubbed her belly. With a start, I saw there was a pronounced bulge.

"Yes she's preggers," Pippa said to me. "Did you just think she was fat?"

I could feel my cheeks heat up. But the other girls were all laughing at me, so I shrugged. "You must not be very far along," I said. "When is your baby due?" I was remembering how Grandfather had said Bee would be working "till her time comes." I didn't ask all the other questions I wanted to ask: Who was the baby's dad? What about school? Wasn't she worried about becoming such a young mom?

Bee smiled tremulously. "Just five months along," she said. Then she told us how her parents were furious, but what's done was done. Her boyfriend was in the army, but when he was home on leave last Christmas, they'd taken the train up to Scotland and gotten married. "I hope he's all right," she said, her brow furrowing. "I've written twice this month, but haven't heard a thing."

"Maybe he doesn't want to write," suggested Lewis Paine coolly from further down the long table. I realized he could hear our conversation perfectly well. "Maybe the lad doesn't think it's his baby."

Bee flushed. "Shut up, creep," she snapped. "It *is* his baby! And we're legally married."

"My goodness," said Mrs. Grey from her end of the table. "I'm surprised at you, Lew."

"He's just having a joke, aren't you, lad?" said Grandfather from the other end.

Lewis gave him a thumbs up. "Of course I am. I wish the happy couple all the best. In fact, I'm thinking of writing Mr. Henry Harrison and offering him my heartiest congratulations on his impending daddy-hood." He grinned around the table at us all. "Nothing like a new blood relative, eh?"

No one grinned back. Bee was glaring at him, her cheeks bright pink. I glared at him, too, wanting to say something—but what? Duncan pressed my foot gently under the table. Then Mrs. Grey stood up and started serving the dessert, and the awkward moment passed. Mrs. Grey's beef and potatoes had been delicious, the salad crisp and tangy, and now her sticky-toffee pudding proved to be luscious.

We all made complimentary remarks, and then Bee told me she had left school when she was sixteen to do a hairdressing course, but in the end decided she didn't really like being a hairstylist. Her parents were always after her to finish school, to go on to university, but she just didn't want to. She knew she was a huge disappointment to them, but she didn't want to become a boring old landscape designer like her dad and *Lewis*, God forbid, or, God forbid even more, a stressed-out doctor like her mum. She'd met Henry through a friend of a friend when he was in Norwich visiting his cousin, and they'd just clicked. You'd think her parents could understand that, seeing how madly in love *they* still were—even after being married a million years. You'd think they'd be happy for her and Henry! He was brilliant, he was from Scotland, he was *so* handsome, and they'd fallen in love. It was fate! And it was horrible, just horrible, when he was sent to Iraq. But then at Christmas he'd come back, and they married, even though her parents were dead set against it. But too bad! She was almost eighteen, and people could marry in Scotland at *sixteen*, and it was *her* life and *their* marriage and *their* baby.

I nodded through all this information. "Sure, wow, uh-huh, of course…"

Bee said she was glad to work at the hotel now; it was good of Mr. Ellis to offer the job when he heard she was looking. "He's ever so kind, Mr. Ellis is," Bee told me, "You're lucky to have him as your grandad." She twinkled at him.

Grandfather waved his fork at her and smiled.

"And as soon as Henry is back, we'll be together. Maybe we'll live on one of the bases. It should be interesting, being an army wife."

Lewis Paine snorted and muttered under his breath. I frowned down the table at him. "What is your *problem?*"

"Don't even go there, Juliana," Maggie said in a low voice. "I assure you, you don't want to tangle with your cousin."

Second cousin twice removed, I reminded myself, grateful for the distance.

He smiled. "I was only having a joke."

"Well, you're the joke," Pippa said. "I'm sorry Grandfather hired you, and I'm sorrier that you're related to any of us at all."

"Now Pippa," remonstrated Mrs. Grey. "Be kind."

"You and your family don't want *any* blood relations at Heatherstone Hall, eh, Pip? Might make it just that little bit harder for your daddy to inherit the place someday, am I right?" He winked at me. "Watch your step, Juliana, my girl."

"Oh, shut up, Lew," Pippa retorted hotly. "You're babbling."

She and Lewis both glanced over to see whether Grandfather had overheard this exchange. He was talking to Josie. Lewis winked at me, then stood up and carried his plate over to the sink. He made a great show of washing up.

"My dad can't stand him," Bee confided to me in a low voice so Lewis wouldn't hear. "But he said Lew knows his shrubberies and has a way with roses. Plus, Mr. Ellis said to hire him because he's a relative. On his wife's side, you know. Not blood kin to Mr. Ellis, but still a cousin." Her dad, she told me, was Lewis's boss, after Grandfather. "He'll be your boss, as well, Duncan—at least for the month. And I bet you Dad gets on with you much better than he does with Lew."

"You know the reason why your dad can't stand Lew," Hat whispered.

"Well, it's a dirty lie," retorted Bee. "As if I ever would!"

"Lew says you did."

"Well, he's a dirty liar!" flared Bee, and I sat there trying to figure out what they were talking about.

Maggie leaned toward me. "Lew claims that *he's* the father of Bee's baby," she explained. "And Bee's dad—he believes it. Makes him furious because he can't stand Lew."

"They're bloody awful," hissed Bee. "Both of them. But I think my parents will like the baby, when it comes. They'll want to babysit all the time! See if I'm not right."

I didn't know what to say to any of this. I just sat there, listening, nodding. Maggie spoke soothingly. "I'm sure they'll be brilliant babysitters, Bee." Then she turned to me. "Did you know your mum was my babysitter when I was little?"

"You mean Barbara-Elizabeth?" I looked at her with interest. "I didn't know you knew my birthmother."

"Well, I was very young," Maggie said. "Our mums were friends."

"*Your* mum doing all right, Bee?" Lew called from the sink, where he was filling the electric kettle.

"Why wouldn't she be?" Bee shot back.

"Oh, I saw her in the village today and she was acting a bit daft. Slinking out of the shops, skulking in the shadows along the street like a spy…"

"Shut up, Lew. You are truly bizarre." She turned back to us and lowered her voice. "Anyway, my mum is crazy about babies, even though she never likes *any* bloke I bring home. She's so critical. Hates them all."

"That's not true," interrupted Maggie. "She likes Hugh, for instance. She just wants you to choose higher-class lads."

"Too late," Hat said abruptly. "Hugh is taken."

Pippa rolled her eyes. "Don't be so sure, Hat," she murmured. "My big brother's not ready to settle down. It's just our *mum* who wants him settled."

I spooned up the last of my dessert, just listening to all this, and dabbed at my mouth with my napkin. Ross and Hugh Foxworth finally came in, still arguing about the merits of getting a degree in Creative Writing versus running a hotel. Mrs. Grey hurried to warm up plates of food she'd set aside for them. Grandfather leaned his elbows on the table and smiled indulgently at me. "Have you had enough to eat, lass?"

"Yes," I told him. "Mrs. Grey is a super cook."

Mrs. Grey looked pleased.

"And your rooms are satisfactory?" inquired Grandfather, including Duncan in his smile.

"Mine's great," Duncan said. "I've got a good view of the maze, too. I'd love to explore it tomorrow."

"And so you must," said Grandfather. "How do you like your

room, Juliana, lass? I gave you one of the best rooms, one usually reserved for paying guests. I wanted you near me."

"My room is beautiful," I told Grandfather. "Is yours on the same hall?"

"Yes, just at the end. Corner room. Number 12. Come and see me any time. Any time at all. We must get to know each other better while you're here. My dear granddaughter! My own child's child!"

Lewis Paine dropped the spoon he was holding. It clattered onto the floor, launching two sugar cubes under the table. He bent to pick them up, exchanging a look with Ross Foxworth. I couldn't read it, but I knew the look was about me, somehow. I hated the feeling of being the subject of conversation I couldn't hear.

"Lew, just leave the sugar for the girls to sweep up," Josie said. "Next thing we know, you'll be dropping the good china." Then she turned to me. "You get this first night off from kitchen work, Juliana. But I'll give you a tour of the spa and explain what your duties will be, starting tomorrow."

"Ah, Josie, let the tour wait till tomorrow morning, too," said Grandfather. "I rather fancy having a nice chat with my granddaughter in the parlor on her first evening here."

Josie frowned. I smiled brightly and pushed back my chair. "I'd love to chat, Grandfather," I said. *Ten points for me!*

Maggie and Pippa started clearing our dishes and carrying them to the sink. Hat started loading the dishwashers while Maggie and Pippa filled the sink with soapy water for the pots. Bee wandered over to the window and stood there, staring out at the courtyard, rubbing her round belly.

I watched Lewis Paine gazing at Bee. And there was an odd, somehow wolfish expression on his face that made me think of a crafty, hungry predator. "It's time for you to be getting home now Bee, don't you think?" he said suddenly. "I'll give you a lift."

"Maggie is going to drive me."

"But Maggie's busy helping with the washing up, and you're looking tired. Ladies in your delicate condition need their rest."

"Leave her alone, Lew." Maggie whirled around from the sink. "I'm taking her as soon as I finish here."

"I'm only trying to help." Lewis Paine looked offended. "Never mind! Well, all right, then, I'm off. Want to come with me, Duncan? I've got some good films."

"No—Duncan's coming with me!" Pippa linked her arm through his, though her hands were dripping soapsuds. "Come to my house," she said, and her voice was low and sultry—how come I couldn't sound like that? "We'll find *something* to do until Juliana joins us…" She stood on tiptoe to whisper in his ear. I saw his cheeks turn pink, and my own started burning.

Get your mitts off him! I wanted to shout, but of course did not.

"Righty-oh. Let's leave them to work it out, shall we, lass?" Grandfather struggled to his feet and reached for his cane. I moved to take his elbow, afraid he might fall.

I said good-night to the others, wishing I could wait to see whose film Duncan would choose to watch. "See you in the morning." Then, as we walked out of the kitchen, I remembered a question I needed to ask Grandfather. "I'm wondering about Herr Stifelmeyer."

"And what is that, lass?"

Josie followed us out of the kitchen, frowning. I ignored her. "I think your old friend seems lonely," I said. "Do you think maybe he could eat in the kitchen with us instead of by himself?"

"Now, Lloyd, I already told her the guests eat separately," Josie interjected before Grandfather could reply.

And Mrs. Grey wheeled around, dessert platter in hand. "That's absolutely correct," she said firmly. "The man is a guest, and he belongs in the dining room. Next thing, you'll be wanting to bring all the honeymooners and businessmen in here, too—and that awful Agatha Moggs."

"But—" I tried to explain.

"No!" The housekeeper cut me off abruptly. "Let's not hear

another word about it."

I was surprised. Grandfather seemed surprised, too. He raised his eyebrows and shrugged. "We'll see, lass." Then he looked over at Mrs. Grey. "So it is the same Agatha Moggs, is it? You're quite certain?"

Mrs. Grey nodded. "Yes, with her sister Sue-Sue, the most down-trodden birdlike creature I've ever met. Not surprising, with an over-bearing sister like Agatha."

Mrs. Grey rolled her eyes and turned away, but Grandfather chuckled. "Have you met our Miss Moggs?" he asked me.

I told him I had.

"Well, brace yourself, lass. Because she informed me today that she and her sister plan to stay another week or two—at least."

Mrs. Grey winced. "Agatha Moggs worked for the Heatherstone family many years ago, and she was also here as a nurse's aide during the war."

"Yes, that's when I met her," Grandfather said, nodding. "She was a bit difficult."

"Difficult?" Mrs. Grey laughed wryly. "Lloyd, you are a tactful gentleman. Agatha Moggs was a nosy old busybody when she was young, and from what I've seen of her this past week, she has not improved with age. No one was sorry when she left Heatherstone after the war, and I for one will not be sorry when she leaves the hotel, either! She's come back because she saw the advert for the opening of the spa. She's proud of herself, she is, because she and her sister came into some money and opened a shop in London and have done quite well for themselves. She's been snapping her fingers at me and demanding service ever since she arrived, and she's terribly chuffed about returning as a fine lady to the place where she once was in service."

Josie folded her dishtowel. "That explains it," she said. "Miss Moggs has been acting very queenly. I hadn't realized she'd once worked here." She turned to me. "We'll have to do our best to cater to the old dear. She's made her fortune, and if she wants to spend it at our spa, I'm not going to discourage her! So I'll be waking you up early, Juliana. Get a good night's sleep." She looked over at Grandfather. "Don't keep her up too late, Lloyd, please. We don't want her tired on her first day of work."

She left the kitchen, her low-heeled shoes tapping smartly on the tiles, blonde curls bobbing.

Then Grandfather headed for the parlor, and as I followed him through the swinging door, I glanced back over my shoulder. Pippa was back at the sink now, up to her elbows in bubbles, giggling at something Duncan was saying to her as he dried the pots. Maggie wiped the countertops, Hat scoured the stove, and Bee rather haphazardly swept the floor. Ross was lecturing his son, gesturing with his knife as he ate, while Hugh slumped in his chair, arms crossed. Mrs. Grey now stood at the windows, gazing out at the courtyard. And Lewis Paine was sitting at the table, staring straight at me with his head cocked to one side, his long nose like a beak in his thin face, watching me watch all of them.

He reminded me of some predatory creature, but now I wasn't thinking of a wolf; now he was reminding me of some sort of graceless bird. An eagle—but no, an eagle was graceful, majestic. Still, some bird of prey. *More like a buzzard,* I thought.

Flashing that long-toothed, yellow grin, he blew me a kiss.

6

"Come have a chat with an old man, lass," Grandfather said, ushering me ahead of him into the parlor. "The rest of the staff will be going home now, or off to watch the telly. And the guests will be in their rooms or in the parlor. Some go down to the village for a pint. We'll have ourselves a nice pot of tea together, what do you say?"

"I say that'll be perfect."

He motioned me toward a leather armchair by the fireplace. There was no fire in the grate (this was August, after all, despite the cool weather), but I could imagine how cozy it would be in here on a rainy winter night. Grandfather pulled an old leather-bound photo album from a glass-fronted bookcase. He handed it to me. Then he sat himself down in the chair next to mine and watched as I turned the pages slowly, offering his commentary as we looked at all the pictures of my birth family. We spent a long time looking.

There was a younger Grandfather with a dumpling of a wife, and a schoolboy I could see was Ross. Then there were the photos of a fat, smiley baby—Barbara-Elizabeth. I studied her chubby cheeks as if in memorizing them I would find something of myself. There she was as a fair-haired toddler, just learning to walk, reaching one hand out to the camera. Grandfather smoothed his hand over the faded photo.

Here she was in a garden, holding a bird's nest. Here was her first bicycle! Ross had been the one to teach her to balance, Grandfather murmured, turning the page. That one there—oh, that was just after her mother died. Cancer it was. Very sad. But look here—here she is on her first day at school, wearing her smart new uniform, her perky braids tied with blue ribbons.

"And here she is with her new Border Collie puppy, Butch," said Grandad, running his finger over the next photo. "Poor dog."

"What happened to Butch?" I asked.

"Killed a year later," he said. "Flattened by a lorry. Poor lass was that upset. She'd feared it would happen, you see. When she first held her new pup she looked up at us and said we'd have to be very, very careful to keep him away from the road, especially from the round-about at the end of our street where all the lorries passed by."

A *lorry*, I knew, was what the British called a truck. I gazed down at the photo and felt sorry for the puppy and the little girl, both dead too soon.

I leaned closer as Grandfather Ellis turned the pages, fascinated to see this child who looked so much like me growing up, turning into a teenager. As Barbara-Elizabeth grew older, the pictures were fewer, and in them the girl's expressions turned sour.

"Turned into a rebel, she did," murmured Grandfather. "Started running with the wrong crowd. Drank too much, I'm afraid. Maybe got into drugs…And I was running the hotel, trying to make it pay. Not this one, mind you. I bought this place years later, after she was gone. But I was always working hard. Had no patience with her rudeness and her drama. Sometimes I think…ah, maybe if I'd taken more time with her…"

I didn't know what to say to comfort him, this man whose daughter had run away from home and ended up dead in California—especially since maybe she'd run off to get away from *him*. It was so strange to think that I had grown inside her body, been born to her, ended up being put up for adoption after she'd died. I barely remembered her—and my birth father even *less* than barely. Still, such a shame, two people dying so young.

"Rough living and bad choices," Grandfather murmured now, as if he could read my mind. With a sigh he closed the albums and folded his gnarled hands on top of them. He coughed, cleared his throat, coughed again.

The coughing didn't stop, but grew more intense, and Grandfather's face turned an alarming plum color. I jumped up and patted him the way I'd seen others do, but it didn't seem to help. "Let me get someone," I said anxiously, and started for the door, but then it opened and Mrs. Grey bustled in, followed by her granddaughter, Hat.

"Oh, good," I said. "I don't know how to make him stop—"

Hat hurried to his side and took his arms. She lifted them above his head. "Sometimes this can help," she said. "Mina showed us how to do it."

Sure enough, the coughing subsided and Grandfather regained his breath. "Thank you," he gasped. "Thank you, Harriet, dear. I'm fine now."

Mrs. Grey looked at him critically. "I don't know about fine," she said. "But you might live long enough to look at another photo album before you go off to bed."

"I don't look at these often," Grandfather said, still wheezing a bit. "And they take a lot out of me. So many memories! They're all I have left of Barbara…well, these and the boxes of her things I've packed away. And it's your history too, lass." He brightened and looked at me. "Perhaps you'd like to have something of Barb's to keep for your own? Something from her childhood?"

I said I would like that very much.

"Then you'll have to have a look up in the attic, in her boxes. I stored them up there when I first came to Heatherstone, years back. Up with all the other old trunks." His expression grew pensive. "People die, lass, but their stuff lasts forever."

"Nothing ever gets thrown away around here," Mrs. Grey agreed. "I keep meaning to go through it all again sometime. There's the stuff your grandfather brought with him when he moved here, and there's my own stuff. Years and years of it all boxed away up there…"

"It's just junk," said Hat. "I've been up there. There's nothing worth bothering about."

"What about things from the Heatherstone family?" I asked.

"Oh, Lady Diana got rid of most of that," Mrs. Grey said. "Whatever was valuable she sold, then she tossed the rest. I don't know that there's a whole lot left up there anymore. Mostly it's just my own castoffs, and your grandfather's."

"But you're welcome to look through Barbara's things," Grandfather said gently. "Keep whatever of hers you like."

"I daresay the girl would like to have something that belonged to her mum," conceded Mrs. Grey. "Just don't look too closely at all the dust."

"It's a mess up there," said Hat. "I wouldn't bother." She followed her grandmother from the room.

Grandfather rubbed a hand over his wrinkled face, then reached down and pulled another album out of the bookcase. "Here—have a look at these. Here's a photo of Heatherstone Hall when I first bought it."

I leaned closer to him in order to see. He lifted one veined hand and tapped the album page. "See how dilapidated it was becoming? Gardens all overgrown, old stones crumbling. Lady Diana inherited the house when her parents were gone, but there wasn't much money to keep it going, you see. She had to let the staff go, all the servants and groundskeepers. Sold off acres and acres of land to developers. Turned parts of it into flats. It's the same story with so many of England's grand old homes and palaces, I'm afraid. In the end, she was ill and old, and the house was a burden to her. She tried to get the National Trust to buy the house, but they said it didn't have enough historic merit or some such nonsense. Been too much altered and modernized over the years." He shook his head. "Can you imagine?"

"It's hard to see how a place that's over four hundred years old doesn't have enough historic merit," I agreed. "We hardly have any buildings at all in America that are this old!"

"Well, lass, the world is a strange place, and don't you forget it. Anyway, then word got around that Lady Diana was ill, and she hated the idea of going into a nursing home. And the hall was for sale...well, I was interested. I was running a smaller hotel in Norwich at the time, and it was doing well enough, but I didn't mind selling it if I could buy Heatherstone Hall. I knew I still wouldn't have enough to buy it outright, so I came up with a special offer: I wrote to Lady Diana that if she sold me Heatherstone for a price I could afford, and let me run it as a hotel, she could remain in her home as long as she wanted, at no charge. She would be treated as a pampered hotel guest! She agreed to my offer, and Edith Grey, who was here as her housekeeper, agreed to stay on as her nurse. She lived only another year, but she was happy during that time, I believe. And she was glad to see the repairs being made to Heatherstone Hall. She always talked about how it was to have been her brother's inheritance, you see, and Dorian would have lived here with his bride, and he never would have let it fall into disrepair. Ah, well."

"Who was going to be his bride?" I asked.

Grandfather was silent so long I thought he wasn't going to answer. But then he sighed. "There was a young army nurse that Dorian loved. They met while they were both serving in France. She was sent here to work, and then he ended up here as well, when he was wounded."

"That's so romantic," I said. "But—wow. It must have seemed strange for the nurse, working in the place she'd one day be mistress of...well, in the place she *would* have been mistress of, if Dorian hadn't died. She must have been totally *devastated*."

"She was inconsolable," Grandfather said, and his eyes stared past me, as if looking at something far away. "Couldn't bear to live without him." Abruptly he shut the photo album. "I'm tired now, dear girl. Shall we say good-night?"

I helped him out of the chair, and we walked together up the stairs. After we'd said good-night, I went into my room and texted

Duncan, just saying hi, waited a minute and texted again—*sleep tight!*—but he didn't answer. Probably still watching the film with Pippa and Hugh and Hat.

The canopy bed was comfortable, but I couldn't sleep. I lay there listening to the silence of the vast house, feeling its hugeness all around me. So many things must have happened in these walls over four hundred years. The old walls were basically the same as they'd always been, except for the hidden wires and pipes affording modern electricity and plumbing, telephones and internet access. There must be so many stories, so many people's lives lived out within these walls. And now these walls still were full—with hotels guests from all around the world, with the staff, with my family members. So many new faces—

Their names and faces swirled in my mind, and I suddenly missed my family. I thought of my dad and the Goops, on the plane to California. I thought of my mom, settling in with her friends in London.

I thought about Barbara-Elizabeth who had run away when she was not much older than I was now. She'd had a baby very young, and turned to drugs—that much I knew—and had not been able to take proper care of me. *But she loved me!* I thought fiercely. Somehow I knew it was true. I *remembered* it was true.

These thoughts led me to the brink of sleep, but then I heard the pad of someone out in the hallway. I sat up again, hoping for Duncan and a midnight cuddle.

But there was only silence. Probably just a guest passing by in the hallway. I punched my pillow and settled back down in the bed—then jumped when I heard voices. Tense, listening, I sat up again.

Men's voices, hushed and angry, rose out in the hallway. After a long moment I wriggled out of bed and stood in the center of the room, straining to hear.

"...only the *stepson,* and don't you forget it..."

"...sick of all your meddling..."

"...leave it all to the girl—just you wait!"

Moonlight flickered through the cloud cover outside the windows. Gusts of wind rattled the panes of old glass. I crept to the bedroom door and slowly turned the knob, opening it just a crack. I couldn't see anyone, but the rumble of voices was coming just around the corner, at the top of the stairs. It was hard to make out everything, but I could hear the angry voices.

Someone hissing: "I've seen you with Doreen...No wonder she left...Don't you try anything...Juliana...Pippa—just a girl...I'll kill you, you bastard—"

I felt chilled. Whose voice was it?

And then laughter in response: "...course not...a misunderstanding...What do you think I am—?"

Was that Lewis Paine?

A deep rumble: "You don't want to know what I think you are—"

The voices faded. I opened the door farther and peered out.

The corridor stretched away in two directions. To the left it angled out of sight. That was the way to the main staircase. To the right it stretched off into the distance, all the way down to Grandfather's room, dimly lit by the moonlight through the long window at the far end of the hall and by the low-wattage nightlights set into the walls at intervals.

No one in sight.

Who had such deep voices? Grandfather was the only man—besides the various hotel guests—who slept in the house itself. But I didn't recognize it as Grandfather's voice. Hugh and Ross should be out in the Foxworth's cottage; Lewis and Duncan slept out over the stable block. I knew it hadn't been Duncan—at least I was sure about that.

But...whoever it was had spoken my name. They had been talking about *me*.

If I didn't get some sleep, I told myself, I would be useless on my first day of work. But as I climbed back into bed and pulled up the covers, snippets of memory formed in the darkness and ran before my wide open eyes like frames of a film: Grandfather running his hand over the photo album; a red-faced Ross arguing with Hugh; Pippa laughing flirtatiously, linking her arm through Duncan's, Lewis Paine baiting Bee at dinner. I remembered the sparkle of Mina Fuller's earrings, Josie's shrill laugher, Miss Agatha Moggs ranting about how she'd been worked to the bone, and the old German in the wheelchair telling war stories with Grandfather. I remembered snuggling against Duncan in the train, remembered the voices in the maze, remembered my little sister standing on the wide stone staircase—feeling her vibes.

As I drifted, at last, into sleep, I wished I'd asked what Ivy meant by "a little bit of evil."

7

I dreamed I was home in California, biking with my friends, Jazzy and Rosy, along busy city streets, then out of the city—the road like a long, shining ribbon curving up hills and down—to the ocean. The sun beamed down on us, hot and bright, and the hills grew steeper and steeper until finally I knew my legs couldn't pump any harder. I was dripping with sweat and gasping for breath, and I just had to stop. When I did stop, I looked around me and saw no sign of my friends or of anyone else. The road stretched out on either side of me, sunbaked, empty, and I was all alone.

As I tried to catch my breath, I awoke to a gray morning light filtering through the lacy curtains of my bedroom at Heatherstone Hall, in England, and I heard the patter of rain outside the window.

Summer in England, I thought. *Not California.* And I wasn't all alone; there was a whole hotel full of people waiting for me to serve them.

But despite the strange dream, I'd had a peaceful sleep after all. My nervousness in the night struck me now as completely stupid, and I stretched under my duvet and reached for my watch from the bedside table. Nine-thirty! I was surprised no one had wakened me earlier. Didn't maids start working at the crack of dawn?

There came a tap on my bedroom door, and I realized it had been an earlier knock that woke me. Pippa poked her curly head inside. "Rise and shine, Princess. Mum's got her knickers in a twist."

That particular British expression always made me smile. But I didn't want Josie to start the day mad at me. "I didn't mean to sleep so late," I said to Pippa. "I was dreaming about some friends…" I suddenly missed Rosy and Jazzy sharply. You'd think with email and all the social media it would be easy to stay in touch with far-flung friends, but somehow we weren't very good at it.

"Grandfather said to let you sleep late this morning," Pippa told me. "But Mum's been pacing around like a panther. Now that the spa has opened, all the guests are signing up for massages and herbal wraps, and steam saunas…and people are coming in from miles around. Mum's desperate for everything to run smoothly." Pippa slanted me a smile. "I owe you. Usually she has me working by eight during the summer hols, but Grandfather said I could wait till your training starts. Bless his old heart!"

I pushed back the duvet and swung my legs over the side of the high bed. "My training?"

"Care and maintenance of the spa, and pampering of rich guests. It's not too bad. Better than chopping vegetables in the kitchen and washing the bed linens down in the laundry, which is what I did for the first half of the summer. Anyway, you're up now. I'll wait for you in the kitchen."

Hat stepped into the room as Pippa turned to leave. "Oh, good, you're up. Here—catch!" She lobbed a balled-up wad of cloth at me. "Your uniform. We have to look the part. This black T shirt with your own clean jeans. And this apron." Another balled-up wad flew through the air.

I caught and unfolded these new clothes. The black T-shirt was the same as Pippa and Hat were wearing, and the apron was also black, with a white silhouette of the house on the pocket and a sash to tie around my waist.

I headed for my bathroom. "I'll be ready in two minutes," I said.

"If you hurry, there will still be some breakfast for you." Hat left the room behind Pippa.

I showered, marveling that here, at last, was a decent shower.

That there was any shower at all was a marvel in itself. Our cottage in Blackthorn had only a bath, and a very small water heater, so there was never enough hot water. My friends in Blackthorn all made do quite happily, it seemed, with tepid baths. They didn't seem to care about this deprivation—or even notice it.

They didn't know what they were missing.

This shower was modern and powerful, and I stood under the blast, enjoying the heat and the water pressure for longer than it really took to get clean. Then I twisted my hair into a single, long braid, pulled on the black T-shirt and my nicest jeans, tied the apron around my waist, and left my bedroom. I hurried along the hall, slowing down when I saw Miss Agatha Moggs walking ahead of me. I waited until she had gone into her room, and then nearly bumped into the German guest, who was slowly heading for the stairs, leaning on two canes.

"Oh! I'm sorry!" I cried, reaching out my arms to steady him. I was surprised to see Herr Stifelmeyer out of his wheelchair.

"Kein Problem—nothing to worry about," he said in his accented English. "I am sorry to be so slow. How was your first night at Heatherstone Hall?"

"I slept very well, thanks." I smiled at him. "Can I help you down the stairs?"

"Thank you, but no. I can manage, but it takes me a while. I am very slow in the mornings—like a garden snail. But my doctor insists walking is good for the old bones, and so I must walk. And my doctor says climbing stairs is also good—so I climb. Down, and up again."

He did seem to be managing fine, so I smiled and told him I'd see him later, and I moved ahead of him. But when I reached the landing I stumbled, careening down three steps to the landing. In a panic I clutched at the handrail and jerked to a halt. My heart thudded hard.

"Lieber Gott!" cried Herr Stifelmeyer above me. "My dear girl, you must take care! You could have fallen and been badly hurt."

Panting, I steadied myself, looking back up at him. "I-I'm all right—just clumsy." I looked down the curving expanse of ancient stone steps and knew it had been a close call. My arms ached from the jolt of catching my fall.

Bustling along the hallway came Mrs. Grey, with Hat at her side. "Now what is going on here?" called the housekeeper. "Herr Stifelmeyer, be very careful near the stairs!" She hurried over to him. "Hat, you help this gentleman to his room."

"I'm fine," protested Herr Stifelmeyer. "It's Juliana who nearly had an accident."

Mrs. Grey peered down at me on the landing. "An accident? You'd better hustle down to the kitchen, Juliana. Bee has a plate of breakfast keeping warm for you, and Josie is waiting with a list of duties as long as your arm. I'll be down in just a minute myself." Then she frowned. "Do I see wet hair, young lady? You'll catch a chill and it will be the death of you."

"I'll be fine," I said, though my knees were still shaky at the close call. I looked up at the German. "I *am* fine."

In the kitchen Bee was sitting at the table buttering a slice of toast. She got up and removed a plate of food from the oven. "For you," she said, setting the plate on the table. "Nice and hot."

I blinked at the feast. At home I usually just managed a sip of orange juice.

Bee laughed at my expression. "Mrs. Grey always insists we start the day with mountains of food. I haven't been able to look at food in the morning ever since I fell pregnant. But every morning when I get here, there's always *this* sort of thing waiting. You can dump it in the rubbish when she's not looking. It's what I do."

"Well—" I began, but then Mrs. Grey appeared and started fussing.

"It's important for young people to eat a hearty meal to start the day," she said, pouring me a glass of orange juice. "Now you sit down and eat properly, and Mrs. Foxworth will have a better worker in her spa for the wait." As I sat down, I felt her hand close over my braid. "Tsk, tsk," she muttered. "I knew it! You do have wet hair. Here—let's get it a bit dryer…" She started dabbing at my head with a dish towel.

I laughed and tried to dodge away. "Where's Duncan?" I asked, and was disappointed to learn that he and Lewis had eaten earlier and were already working in the gardens. Pippa had wanted to wait for me, but Josie had just dragged her off to the spa.

"I'd better get in there, too," I said, but Mrs. Grey picked up my fork and handed it to me.

So I tried to do justice to the fried eggs and sausages and toast and fried tomatoes. I washed the meal down with the juice and a cup of tea, then wiped my mouth, feeling ten pounds heavier than I had when I'd sat down. *If I dove into the pool right now, I'd sink like a stone*, I thought, pushing my chair back. "That was delicious, thanks."

The elderly housekeeper beamed at me. "I like to see young girls eat. Now get along to the spa. And, Bee, luv? You're to start on the guest rooms, and you need to take extra care with the Moggs sisters' rooms. Agatha is very particular, and I daresay her sister is as well. They've been complaining about wrinkles in their bedsheets and a cobweb in the corner."

"She can stuff that cobweb up her bottom," said Bee.

"Now Bee," remonstrated Mrs. Grey, but I heard the smile under her stern tone. "It's a treat for her to be waited on when she was a maid here herself, once."

"And she doesn't miss a chance to crow about it," Bee muttered.

"Well, you be sure to pop back in here for a snack before lunch," said Mrs. Grey. "You're eating for two, don't forget."

Bee and I walked out to the front hall together, then parted ways. She started up the stairs, and I headed out to the new spa wing. As soon as I stepped through the double glass doors at the end of the long corridor, I was enveloped in warm lavender-scented air.

I inhaled deeply. "Ahh!"

"It's lovely, isn't it?" Josie bustled up to me with her arms full of fluffy white towels. "Makes you feel pampered just to walk through the doors, doesn't it?" She handed me the armload. "Here, Juliana. These are clean. Just out of the tumble dryer. You can fold them while I out-line your duties. Come over here. Oh, Pip, please fetch the next load. It should be ready now." Josie shook her head. "It's so much nicer to dry towels out on the line, I always think. But we can't be waiting around for sunshine when we've got a hotel of guests to cater for."

Pippa was already folding stacks of thick white towels. I went to help her, and the two of us folded towels while Josie outlined our work schedule. Then she took me on a tour of the spa, stopping to greet various guests as they entered. We said good morning to Hat, who was busy applying thick green cream to the face of a heavy-set woman in a reclining chair.

"We offer beauty procedures as well as invigorating health-enhancing treatments like the steam bath and hot tub," Josie trilled. "We want the entire spa experience to be one that our guests will remember forever. They come here to be pampered, and they're paying top price, so they deserve every bit of it!"

Josie led us into the massage room—a calm and elegant space designed with low lighting and a state-of-the-art massage table to give hotel guests a relaxed and soothing break. She swooped down on the elderly woman lying on the massage table with her hair wrapped in a turban. "Are you ready for your salt rub, Miss Moggs? It's the best thing to improve circulation, you'll see. And you'll enjoy popping right into the hot tub for a nice soak after. I'll be right with you after I set these girls to work."

"Yes, yes, do set them to work," croaked the old woman, sitting up and eyeing us intently. "Set them to work and work them hard. To the bone! That's the way I was worked when I was in service here. On my hands and knees from dawn till dark, I was. Still have the scars…look here!" She flicked back her white fluffy towel to reveal boney knees. "See those scars? Came from kneeling on the flagstones in the scullery, scrubbing them day after day."

Pippa and I peered at her knees, but I didn't see any scars. Still, I made a small gasp of astonishment, as if I were looking at a terrible sight. Pippa just turned away.

"Your poor knees," murmured Josie soothingly. "We'll add extra lotion to give them a treat, shall we?"

Pippa rolled her eyes at me, maybe embarrassed by her mother's fawning manner. I sure would be. We left the turban-wrapped guest and went over to the weight training area on the far side of the atrium. Already, even so early in the day, there were a few men and women working out. They were all shapes and sizes, using all sorts of exercise equipment. I felt weak and out of shape, just seeing them. My huge breakfast sat like a lump of lead in my stomach. "Do we get to use the weight training stuff and the stair stepper?" I asked Pippa as Josie breezed past, waving cheerfully at her hard-working patrons. "And have a soak in the hot tub?"

"Only during the lunch hour, or when the atrium is closed for cleaning."

"Who does the cleaning?" I asked.

"We do."

My heart sank.

We folded towels for hours, it seemed. There were zillions of them. While we worked, Pippa quizzed me about Duncan. How had I met him? What was his family like? What did he like to do for fun? How long had we been friends. And…what kind of friends were we? Were we, like, *dating*?

I told her the truth, that I'd known him only since we'd moved to England last winter. That we were friends—and only just getting to be more than that. And that nobody really dated in Blackthorn, the little village where my mom had decided we would live while she resurrected her career as a painter. Duncan and I just hung out a lot, watched movies, went on walks up Castle Hill, had lunch at the Angel Cafe…

Pippa's eyes sparkled. "So he's not *officially* your steady, then? Because I think he's brilliant. Veeerrrry adorable."

"Now hold on just a second," I objected, because Duncan and I were *attached*, even though we weren't engaged to be married or anything. We'd come here for a month together and I was planning we'd *stay* together, and this new cousin of mine was going to have to rethink her romantic scheme…But Pippa was off in dreamland, telling me how she'd always lusted after lads with ginger hair like Duncan's, and how the boys at her school were all so daft, it was a relief to meet someone like him who was smart and sweet and *super* sexy…And she continued jabbering right over me when I tried to get a word in edgewise. She said her brother Hugh was a very nice sort of chap, even if he was her brother, and he didn't have a girlfriend, even though Hat was after him here and there were loads of girls always after him at university. He had told Pippa only last night that he thought I was gorgeous. "*Gorgeous*, that's what he said, Juliana. Don't you think you could fall for our Hugh? He's pretty gorgeous himself, don't you think?"

"He's my *cousin*, Pippa," I said dampeningly. "Same as you are."

"Cousins can marry, you know," she told me, wide-eyed. "Even first cousins! Mum was telling me about that. It's perfectly legal, and happens all the time."

"Not in California," I said, although I wasn't really sure about this. "There's something about people who are closely related having deformed babies or something. Anyway, I just met Hugh, and I have no interest in marrying him. And Duncan and I—"

She cut me right off and kept on chattering, a mile a minute. "Well, really, we're just your step-cousins, anyway, isn't that right? So there's no reason in the world that you couldn't marry Hugh, if you wanted to! Then we'd be sisters *and* cousins!"

This was certainly a girl with her eye to the future. Now it was my turn to roll my eyes. And then Mrs. Grey came into the spa. She waved to us and headed over to the alcove off the main atrium, where there was a snack bar. "You'll need a break soon, girls. It's nearly time for elevenses!" *Elevenses*, I knew, was the mid-morning tea break in England. And even though I wasn't the least bit hungry, I finished the towel I was folding and followed Mrs. Grey. I'd heard more than enough from Pippa.

Slipping behind the counter, Mrs. Grey started slicing the home-made cake. Herr Stifelmeyer sat there in his wheelchair, chatting with the other Miss Moggs, Sue-Sue. She was frail and birdlike, but had no problem at all tucking into coffee and pastries. When Herr Stifelmeyer saw me he raised his hand in greeting.

"I would like a word with you, Juliana," he said.

The family I remembered from last night's dinner ambled through the atrium, heading straight for the pool. Their kids shrieked with excitement.

Josie stepped into the alcove. "Americans," she said. "Such loud people!" But, far from looking disapproving, Josie was beaming. "I just love the hustle and bustle. Isn't it lovely? This wet, cool weather really brings in the crowds from town, too. And isn't this just the perfect place for hotel guests to gather on a rainy day?"

She turned to me. "Doing all right, are you? Have you finished the towels? Right! Then Pip will work in the exercise room until your break, and I'd like you over by the hot tub and steam rooms. You'll need to keep picking up the used towels and taking them to the laundry room. Bring out fresh ones and pile them here. Wipe up wet spots on the floors—heaven knows we don't want anyone slipping and getting hurt. Help people in and out of the tub if they need assistance. Any questions?"

When will I have time to simmer in the hot tub with Duncan? In fact, when will I get even a second alone with Duncan around here? "Um—no questions," I said. At least I'd get a little time off from Pippa. "I'll talk to you during my break," I told Herr Stifelmeyer.

He regarded me from beneath his fierce eyebrows for a long moment. "I shall wait for you," he said. Then he turned back to his companion.

The work wasn't hard, but it was constant. Mopping up splashed water from the pool and the hot tub was the least of it; I ran around gathering up wet towels and laying out stacks of fresh ones, monitored the chlorine levels on the pool and hot tub, scrubbed down the wooden seats in the steam sauna, ran back and forth to the little refrigerator in the snack bar for more cucumber slices (eye treatments!) and plain yogurt (skin masks) so that Josie, with her degree in cosmetology, could pamper the guests who paid extra for such treatments. Outside the atrium, rain drummed on the glass.

I emptied the trash bins and swept around the snack bar and took over the cash box for Mrs. Grey for awhile when she went off to the kitchen to make fresh coffee. Pippa called to me across the atrium. "Sit with me at break?" She waved her mop.

"I've already promised to sit with Herr Stifelmeyer. Anyway, when *is* our break?"

"Whenever you remember to take it. Mum will never remind you, so you've got to look out for yourself." She started mopping up spilled Coke by the pool.

Hat and Mrs. Grey came into the spa pushing a cart laden with jugs of fresh coffee and pots of tea. Hat and I poured ourselves cups of tea, and I perched on a stool at the counter with her, sipping it. My legs felt tired from standing so long. Hat said her arms were aching from scrubbing the guests' bathrooms.

The snack bar was filling up now as hotel guests came dripping from the pool area to warm themselves with hot chocolate or a pot of tea, and others left the hot tub in search of a cold drink. Besides the American family, there were the two Moggs sisters, a couple who looked as if they might be on their honeymoon from the way they kept gazing into each other's eyes, and a single middle-aged guy who had the look of a businessman about him, even though he was wearing a bathing suit.

Herr Stifelmeyer and Josie came out of the massage room. I was surprised to see him walking with just one cane—no wheelchair in sight. He seemed to be standing straighter as he walked over to a table and carefully lowered himself into a chair. Josie followed, fluttering her hands. "Now take it easy for a while. The effects of a good massage should last you all day."

"Ach," he said, smiling broadly, "that felt so good. Heavenly, Mrs. Foxworth! Simply wonderful." He nodded over at Mrs. Grey and me. "I tell you, this woman has hands of steel. I do believe she has done more to help my poor aching back than all the doctors have."

Josie looked pleased. "Thank you, Herr Stifelmeyer. That's very kind of you. I believe you'd get even more benefits from massage if you would let yourself relax more, close your eyes—let yourself drift…"

He winked at me. "Mrs. Foxworth means that the old man talks too much!"

"Nonsense," Josie objected, laughing brightly. "It was very interesting, hearing about your time here during the war. I'm amazed that your memory of so many decades ago is still so clear. It's fascinating."

"What do you remember?" Hat asked him. "Every detail? Do tell."

"Oh, only certain memories are still sharp, I'm afraid. So much of my time here was spent in sleep…To dull the pain, you see, the nurses needed to give us medication."

Mrs. Grey, pouring out tea for the Americans, paused and looked at Herr Stifelmeyer consideringly, as if still trying to remember the young man who had been a wounded prisoner of war so long ago, right in this same house.

Herr Stifelmeyer skirted around the table where the Moggs sisters sat. Agatha waved to him. "There's room for you here, dear Otto!" she caroled. "I'll talk about the past with you any day at all. So much more interesting than the present, don't you agree?"

Dear Otto didn't seem to hear her, and went to sit at a small table in the corner. I figured Agatha must remember him from wartime, when both were here and the manor house was a hospital. I wondered about that *dear*. Did Agatha Moggs once have a thing for a young red-headed enemy soldier?

Before I could go chat with Herr Stifelmeyer, Lewis Paine, wearing damp overalls and muddy boots, ambled across the atrium and into the snack area. Just as Mrs. Grey took Herr Stifelmeyer's order, Lewis plonked onto the counter an insulated travel mug of shiny black plastic with the Heatherstone Hall logo on it. "I'll have a coffee, right in this cup, Juliana my love. Fill it full and make it hot. And give me a slice of that cake, to go. Make that two slices. Thick ones. Thick—and luscious." His voice was low and intimate. "*Dripping*—with frosting."

I looked at the door, hoping to see Duncan behind Lewis, but he'd come alone.

"Oh, Lew, look at the mess," Josie chided. "You've tracked half the garden in here."

"Take off your boots, man," Hat said. "You're a walking disaster."

Lew lifted one muck-encrusted work boot and laughed. "Want to lick the mud off for me, Hat, luv?"

"A total disaster," Hat snapped, turning away in disgust.

"Where's Duncan?" I asked, partly to change the subject, but mostly because I hadn't seen him yet. "Isn't it time for his tea break, too?"

"He's digging holes, and he'll get his break when he's finished. Now where's my cake?"

"I'll get it for you when I have time, Lew. Juliana has other things to do." Mrs. Grey handed me a cup of coffee. "You'll see your young man at lunch, dear, I daresay. Now take this to Herr Stifelmeyer," she directed. "And I'm going back to the kitchen to get lunch ready, dear. You'll have yours in about forty-five minutes. It's just sarnies, but they're good ones, if I do say so myself."

"Sarnies?" This was an English word I hadn't heard yet. I imagined some kind of fish, maybe a sardine, and thought I'd rather just have a slice of bread and some cheese.

"Sandwiches," Lew translated. "Don't they speak English over in

California?"

Mrs. Grey frowned at him. "Yes," she said to me. "It's just sandwiches, my luv. I usually make a few platters and leave them on the table for the staff and family to take when they get a free moment. Chopped egg and watercress, tuna and onion, bacon and brie. Help yourself to an apple as well, and you'll be ready to get back to work."

"Sounds yummy," I said, then sighed at the idea of a whole afternoon of folding towels. I headed for Herr Stifelmeyer's table, glad to get away from Lewis. But before I reached him, Agatha Moggs called to me.

"Your first day going all right, dear?" she asked me. "You look tired. I recall how very tired I was when I was in service here. Worked to the bone I was."

"I'm fine," I replied, but I glanced longingly over at the bubbling hot tub where two guests were soaking, their cheerful chatter muted by the surging jets. I didn't feel exactly worked to the bone, but I wished Duncan and I could steal a nice long hour in that hot tub.

As if Mrs. Grey had read my mind, she said, "No reason you young people shouldn't have a dip in the pool on your lunch break— or before dinner tonight." She left the snack bar and headed for the double glass doors. "One of the first things I learned as a young nurse was not to let my own self get run down. Then I'd be no use to anybody else."

"Hummmph," said Agatha Moggs bitterly to her sister. "It's all very well for her to say. She wasn't worked to the bone as I was! Made herself *quite* a favorite with the family, she did! Put on airs *quite* above her station."

I carried the coffee to Herr Stifelmeyer's table. I'd see Duncan at lunch, and maybe we *would* have a swim. Or a soak in the hot tub. "*Vielen Dank*," he said. "Many thanks." And then in a grave voice he added, "Will you join me for a moment?"

"Sure," I said. "Of course." This was the second time he'd asked. I wondered what he could possibly need to say to me so urgently.

Apparently Agatha Moggs was wondering that, too. She hitched her chair closer to our table, the better to eavesdrop. But Lewis Paine was even bolder. He strode over, pulled out a chair, and plonked himself down. "Mind if I join you?"

Herr Stifelmeyer looked pained, but shook his head. "Not at all," the old German replied courteously. He reached out to pat my hand. "We'll speak later, then. After dinner."

"Ah," Lewis Paine said expansively, stretching his legs. "Good to take a load off. My back is killing me. I'm going to need Josie's magic massage fingers—or more likely the services of our good Dr. Fuller before the day is over. It's all the digging that's making things so bad. I've been digging post holes for new fencing all morning, along the drive, and it's done me in, I tell you. I think I fancy a dip in that hot tub."

"Yes, I plan to go into the bath myself. But Mrs. Ellis offers a delightful massage," Herr Stiefelmeyer told him. "Perhaps you will feel the same relief I just had."

"Yeah, how about it, Josie, luv?" Lew called over to where she was still standing with Hat and Pippa at the snack bar. "I'd like a *delightful massage*—right now."

Hands on hips, Josie strode over to our table and stood over him. "Back to work, Lew."

Lewis looked around at the guests seated at other tables and raised his wiry arms in mock supplication. "I tell the woman my back is aching and she sends me away, do you all hear that? It's lovely and warm in here, and outside it's appalling—and I'm sent out to work myself into an early grave! Feels like knives stabbing me with every step, and she sends me back into the deluge! Rain dumping down like cow piss—"

"Lew!" exclaimed Josie furiously. The American kids laughed, but I could see that Josie felt Lewis Paine was lowering the tone of her fancy spa and she wanted him out. I did, too. Wherever he went, I was learning, he caused some sort of scene.

"At least it's not as bad as cow *turds* plopping down!" called one of the American boys.

"Ryan, watch your manners," remonstrated his mom.

"Cheeky lad," muttered Agatha Moggs. But Lewis laughed hard, showing all his teeth.

"Right you are, my boy. Mud on the boots is one thing, but cow poop on the head would be worse." He reached out, picked up Herr Stifelmeyer's still untouched cup of black coffee, and took a loud slurp. Making a comical face at the women, he drawled, "Ahhh, now that's what I call *Java*. A bitter brew, but really puts hair on your chest." He winked at Herr Stifelmeyer and poured the rest of the cup into his travel mug. "A man's brew, eh? Keep me going till lunchtime, I daresay."

You are one rude jerk, I daresay, I thought, standing up to get Herr Stifelmeyer a fresh cup of coffee.

Lewis shoved back his chair and sauntered out of the spa, while Miss Agatha Moggs regarded him with watchful, narrowed eyes.

8

Finally, about half an hour later, Josie poked her head into the laundry room where Pippa and I were folding more towels, and said it was time for lunch. "Take just an hour, please," she said. "Mrs. Grey is waiting in the kitchen."

Sarnies, I remembered.

Pippa licked her lips. "The woman can cook."

The atrium had been bustling all morning but was now completely quiet. All the guests were gone, the snack bar was closed. The hot tub was still. Pool water lapped softly against blue tile. Outside the windows I could see Lewis Paine heading toward the garden shed. He was walking slowly, a little unsteadily. I wondered if he had a drinking problem, if maybe he didn't sip something stronger than just plain coffee in that travel mug while he worked.

"Here, Juliana, put these complimentary drinks on the serving cart by the hot tub so they'll be ready for the guests," Josie was saying. She handed me four large thermoses labeled COFFEE, TEA, SPRING WATER, BLACKCURRANT JUICE. "Always be sure to lock the glass doors when you're leaving on a break," Josie instructed. "We don't want anyone using the pool when it's unattended. The spa opens again at 2:00. Now you, Juliana, should be back at 1:30 to check the chlorine levels. Pippa can help me with some things at home."

"What things?" demanded Pippa.

"Just some family business, darling. All right, Juliana? You'll be able to work on your own till we get back?"

"Yes, I'll be fine." I arranged all the thermoses and the paper cups and napkins on the cart, then followed Josie and Pippa down the hallway to the main house and the kitchen.

I peeked into the dining room and saw that Maggie had arrived for her afternoon shift. She was arranging trays of sandwiches on the sideboard. At my greeting, she smiled. "It's going to be a crowd today," she said. "On account of the rain. On fine days they all stay out playing golf or sight-seeing."

Today Mrs. Grey had made piles of the famous *sarnies*, as well as a vat of barley soup. The guests filed into the dining room and helped themselves, while Bee and Hat zipped around the room, bringing drinks to the tables. Still no sign of Duncan.

Ross and Hugh were seated at the kitchen table, devouring large baguettes filled with bacon and brie. I was famished, and pulled out a chair, eager to get started on my own. But first I had to smile and chat with Bee's parents. John Bainbridge, in charge of the hotel grounds, had been working with Duncan all morning, showing him around, explaining his duties. His skin was ruddy, his eyes bright blue. His graying hair was short and curly from all the rain. His hands were stained but clean, and he, unlike Lewis Paine, had remembered to take off his muddy boots before coming inside. Dr. Mina Fuller turned to me with a quick smile, and smoothed her dark hair. Again she wore gorgeous earrings—this time a single teardrop stone, deep red, maybe a ruby, hung from a silver thread through each ear. She reminded me of some sort of fairy-tale pixie. I remembered that Bee had said her mum would come over to the hotel this morning to check on Grand-father.

"Is my grandfather very sick?" I asked her.

"Quite ill, I'm afraid," she informed me. "With emphysema, no doubt due to his years of smoking pipes. I've weaned him off those, but the damage is done. So far the proper medication has kept everything under control."

"I hope he'll be okay," I said fervently. I had only just discovered this birth-grandfather, and didn't want to lose him. "And I think it's really cool that you make house calls. I don't think there's a doctor left in America who does."

She smiled, looking even more like a pixie. "I believe one must always do what one can."

"I agree," said Mrs. Grey. "We should always look around and see what needs to be done. Neglecting to take action—it's just plain wrong."

"We'd better spring back into action then," said Ross jovially, pushing back his chair.

"Oh, hooray, more bookkeeping," intoned Hugh, and with a dazzling show of reluctance followed his dad. I had to giggle.

Lewis Paine didn't show up for lunch and nobody missed him. But I did miss Duncan. Pippa was keeping her eye on the door, too— no doubt waiting for him, too. One by one, the rest of the hotel staff left the kitchen and went back to their duties. Josie and Pippa went off to their cottage, John Bainbridge said he hoped Lewis and Duncan had finished the post holes so they could set the posts into concrete this afternoon, now that the rain was stopping. He left to look for them. I thought I should stop in to say hello to Grandfather before I started working in the spa again, but Mina Fuller said he was having his lunch with Herr Stifelmeyer in the parlor. "I've told him he can have another fifteen minutes, and then he simply must rest for an hour. His wheezing gets worse the longer he's up socializing. You'll see him at teatime, I'm sure. Now I'm needed at the clinic, so I'll say good-bye."

She left the room, too, and I sat there with Mrs. Grey, just taking in the silence. After so much hustle and bustle all morning, I was glad of a little quiet. I thought about my family, wondered what Dad and the jet-lagged Goops were doing in California right at this very moment. Wondered about Mom in London. Hated that Mom and Dad were so far away from each other again—eight *thousand* miles away. And where was Duncan? As much as I was getting to see him around here, he might as well be eight thousand miles away, too.

"More tea, dear?" asked Mrs. Grey. "Or are you miles away?"

Startled, I laughed. "In a way, I was," I said. "I was just thinking about my family. My dad and brother and sister just flew back to California…"

"And you're wishing you had gone with them?"

"Oh, no, not really. I'm happy to be here. And it's nice that Duncan is here, too!"

"He's your special lad, I can tell," she said, nodding cheerfully. "Just like Hugh is Hat's special lad. Ah," she said, pouring out another cup of tea for herself. "How lovely it will be if Hat really does marry him someday. I know it's what she longs for, and I feel certain it will happen. She has always loved this place—we both do. Gives me something to live for—daydreaming about how my own granddaughter might one day be mistress of Heatherstone Hall. Or at least run the hotel, which is almost the same thing!"

"That's about as much of a manor house as anyone can have these days," I said.

"Hat even heard me talking in my sleep about how I want her to marry Hugh," Mrs. Grey confided. "Didn't you, luv?"

Hat had just stepped through the door with a tray full of dirty plates and glasses. "Oh, yes, Granny. You chat on and on about all sorts of things in your sleep. In fact, you'd be surprised at how much you tell me."

Mrs. Grey looked disconcerted. "Oh dear. I hope I haven't given away all my little secrets," she said lightly.

"Every one of them," Hat replied sharply. Then she winked at me. "But don't worry—I won't tell." She dropped a kiss on her grandmother's gray head as she left the kitchen.

"Why, I hope I haven't said anything embarrassing," said Mrs. Grey, her cheeks pink.

"My brother Edmund talks in his sleep, too," I told her. "Rambles on in a kind of gibberish, sometimes, and then other times speaks perfectly clearly. Sometimes he even shouts things out. Once he yelled, 'I'm hungry! Give me the green umbrella!' Who knows what he really meant? We don't even have a green umbrella! But we'll tease him about it forever. Whenever he asks what Mom's making for dinner, she says, 'Green Umbrella stew!'"

Mrs. Grey laughed. "The things you say in your sleep don't really mean anything," she said decisively. "Everyone knows that." She carried her teacup to the sink, then left the room.

Time for me to get back to work. I stood up and rinsed my lunch plate. Then I heard a sound behind me and turned, grinning at the sight of Duncan in mud-spattered overalls, holding out his hands. "Can a bloke get a wash around here?" he asked.

"About time!" I moved aside so he could plunge his hands into hot, soapy water.

Duncan glowered at me from under mud-flecked eyebrows. "It's tough work, and I've been at it mostly alone, since that third cousin of yours, or whatever he is, likes to play foreman. *Slave-driver* is more like it. He stands there rabbiting on and on about his aches and pains—hey, that's a good one, get it? *Pain*? Lewis *Paine*?" His voice was weary. "He doesn't do a thing, but points out where I should do all the digging. Claims his poor back won't let him do his share. Oh well, maybe it's true."

"He came in for the tea break. You should have, too."

Duncan splashed water on his face, then dried his hands and face on a tea towel. He sank onto a chair and helped himself to the last sandwich on the platter. "I would have if I'd known. He just told me to keep at it, and wandered off. So I did, till John Bainbridge stopped by to see how things were coming along. He said it was time for lunch. Told me a lot of other things, too, like how he'd like to throttle Lewis Paine with his own bare hands for getting his daughter pregnant. He's furious."

"But Bee says the baby's dad is in the army—"

"John Bainbridge doesn't believe that. Nor does Bee's mum. They think she got pregnant by Lewis, but then decided she didn't like him much after all. So she married the bloke in the army as her cover." He shrugged. "The way I see it, now Bee's eighteen, and old enough to do what she wants. It's her business, really. Not her parents'."

"So that's what you told Bee's dad?" I ladled out a bowl of the barley soup.

"No way!" He smiled his thanks as he took the bowl and started eating. "I want to keep my job. We only just got here—and your grandfather pays well."

"If you eat really fast, we'll have time for a soak in the hot tub."

He slanted me a glance with those piercing dark eyes. "Do we have to wear suits?"

I snapped him with the dish towel. "This is a high class, luxury establishment, good sir!"

"Puritan American," he teased.

I raced up to my room to get my swimsuit, wishing we dared go skinny-dipping.

The hot tub was bubbling and steaming invitingly when I unlocked the double glass doors and entered the atrium with Duncan. We didn't have much time till our lunch hour was over. *Check chlorine levels,* I told myself. *Fold towels.* Outside, the rain had stopped and wavering yellow sunlight showed through the clouds. Through the glass walls I could see the lush green lawn stretching down to the lake. The two figures were walking there again—it must be the newlywed couple, I decided, though it was hard to see in the mist that had come up off the lake. "Look there," I said, poking Duncan. "Do you see those people? I keep seeing them, but then—" I blinked and peered closer through the glass. "Like that! I keep thinking I see them, but then they're gone."

"I don't see anyone." But Duncan was hardly sparing a glance outside. He was taking in the spa, which he had not seen yet. "Whoa, this place is great! Look at all the steam. That is one serious hot tub." He undid the straps of his work overalls, dropping them and stepping out. Underneath them he was wearing jeans and a t-shirt, which he also stripped off—down to his dark blue boxer shorts. I stared at his long, lanky body, noting how the muscles rippled along his arms and chest. He strode into the men's changing room, then returned with a towel. Dropping it at the edge of the hot tub, he lowered himself into the hot water with a groan of pleasure. "Ohhhh. Perfect."

Chlorine levels, I reminded myself firmly, and went to check them. Finding everything in order, I folded the last of the laundered towels, changed into my bright blue bikini in the privacy of the massage room, then grabbed one of the fluffy white towels I had just folded. I stopped at the table near the hot tub to pour out two cups of cold spring water.

Duncan was chest deep in the bubbling water, leaning back, eyes closed, a great grin on his face. "This is heaven."

I set our waters at the edge of the hot tub. Duncan reached out and closed his fingers around my ankle.

I stepped down onto the bench next to him, and the bubbling water closed deliciously around my legs. "Ahhh," I sighed rapturously, easing down to sit next to him. I leaned back and closed my eyes. Foam tickled under my chin. My long braid floated out like a rope. Duncan's hand found mine as jets of water pounded the small of my back.

We sipped our cold water. The sound of bubbling water filled our charged silence.

After a while I stretched out my arms under water and pushed myself off our fiberboard seat and floated. The pulsing froth of water buoyed me up as if I were a bottle in the ocean. *A bottle with a message inside*, I thought dreamily. *A message saying, kiss me, Duncan…I want you, I want you…*

He pulled me onto his lap. His kiss tasted sweet—and a little like barley soup. Eyes still closed, I floated back onto the bench, adjusting myself so the jets pounded my shoulder blades. Duncan stroked my arm with his fingers. *Yes*, I thought. Lying here in the hot, surging water I wanted something more than that. I wanted to feel his body against mine—

Yes, like that, I thought, as his leg pressed against mine under the water. *Like that and more than that...*

His leg bumped me again, and then his hands—fingers brushing my knees.

My eyes flew open. I sat bolt upright with a gasp. *Wait a minute, wait a minute*—Duncan's arms were around me. His fingers were caressing my arms. Then he turned me to him, entwining his fingers in my hair. His lips touched mine in the sweetest of kisses.

We were alone, just the two of us. So—what had bumped against me under the water?

His hands were in my hair. So—whose fingers were still fluttering on my knee beneath the surging foam?

I jerked away as hot panic flooded me. "Duncan—"

"What is it?"

I longed to leap out of the hot tub, but I made myself reach down, down, down to grab—whatever was there.

Whoever was there.

My hands touched flesh. My fingers felt hair.

9

My scream echoed through the vast atrium as I thrashed my way out of the water, gasping for breath. Duncan's bellow was loud enough to wake the dead—but the someone down there, down under that water, did not wake.

I hit the switch that shut off the pump and lowered myself back into the hot tub, where Duncan, face ashen, was grappling with the body. As the foam cleared, I could see white swimming trunks. I grabbed the hair and yanked hard to lift the head free of the water.

Water cascaded over the face of Lewis Paine.

"What happened? What's wrong?" called a voice, and there were Ross and Hugh at the glass door. "We heard screams " Ross said

"Are you all right?" asked Hugh.

"Hurry," I called. "It's Lewis!"

"What the—?" Ross ran to us.

"Help me lift him out," ordered Duncan. "Who knows CPR?"

"Is he still alive?" I cried. "Oh, no…"

The two men and Duncan pulled Lewis Paine out of the hot tub and laid him face down on the tile. Hugh immediately bent over Lewis and tried pumping his back while Ross pulled out his cell phone to call the emergency paramedics. When no more water gushed from Lewis's mouth, Hugh turned him face up and listened for a heartbeat, felt for a pulse. "Nothing," he muttered. He tilted Lewis's chin up, grasped the nose firmly, and began CPR.

I watched, horrified. Then I couldn't watch anymore. I stumbled away, sickened. Duncan followed me and we clung together.

Lewis had been in there all the time. In there with us. He'd been submerged while we lounged around, kissing. I retched into a large potted palm. In memory I felt again that bump against my leg, those limp, floating fingers at my knee. I knew it was no use. I knew that Lewis was dead. It was all very well to try to revive him—it was the right thing to do—but it couldn't work. He had been under the water too long.

Josie burst in then, took in the scene by the spa, and sort of squeaked in horror. Pippa sidled into the atrium behind her mum. I was surprised to see the two of them because I thought they'd gone back to their cottage. Josie ran over to me and wrapped me in a towel. I needed some mothering right then.

"Poor girl, you're shivering. And Duncan? Were you...? Did you...?"

"Did *you* find the body, Juliana?" whispered Pippa. "You and Duncan?"

When we nodded, Pippa gasped, then started wailing.

"Be quiet!" snapped Ross. "Get a hold of yourself. Josie, where's Mina? Is she still here? We need a doctor—fast!"

Josie pulled Pippa into her arms. "Mina left for the clinic, right after lunch. Call her on her mobile—maybe you can get her back here. Oh, this is terrible, just terrible!' She took a deep breath, then made a visible effort to calm herself. "All right. All right, we have to deal with this. Ross, have you called the ambulance? Of course you have. Then, quick, Juliana? Duncan? You come with me. You're in shock." She moved toward the glass doors. "Pippa, you, too. Hugh, you be sure to lock the doors behind us. The last thing we need is to have the guests come walking in on this."

"But...Lewis?" My voice sounded tinny and far away, even to my own ears.

She was bundling me out of the atrium as she spoke to me in a soothing voice. "Ross and Hugh can handle things, I'm sure."

Just outside the glass doors, Herr Stifelmeyer was approaching in his wheelchair. "Ahh, good timing!" he greeted us, obviously not having heard the news yet. "Please hold the door." His voice trailed off as Josie barred his way.

"You can't go in there," she said.

He looked surprised. "No? But I was planning a little dip in the— how do you call it? The hot bath? That is so lovely on a rainy day—"

"I'm sorry. There's been an accident."

"Oh?" His voice sharpened. "What has happened?"

Even as Josie explained, the paramedics were arriving. Grandfather, looking pale and leaning heavily on his cane, led them into the atrium. "This way, this way," he barked. "Hurry! He may still be alive!"

I felt very sure Lewis was not alive. But I was relieved to be leaving the spa, glad I didn't have to watch any attempts to jolt Lewis back to life. Murmuring agitatedly, Herr Stifelmeyer allowed Duncan to push his wheelchair back to the library where some of the guests were hanging out to escape the rain. Duncan settled the old man at one of the tables, and left him there to tell the others what had happened.

Soon the rest of us settled at the kitchen table, wearing dry clothes, sipping mugs of hot tea. I finally stopped shivering—until I let myself remember the feeling of that leg bumping against mine underwater. I reached over to clutch Duncan's hand. His fingers were cold, uncomforting.

Mina Fuller raced into the kitchen, panting. "I had a message on my mobile!" she cried. "To hurry back to Heatherstone. Is it Lloyd? But I just left him—he was fine! "

"No, it's not Grandfather—" I began.

"Bee?" Mina asked. "Is it Bee? Losing the baby?"

"I'm right here, Mum," Bee said, drying her hands on a dishtowel and giving her mother a hug. "It's nothing to do with me. It's *Lewis*, Mum. Lewis Paine is *dead*."

Mina's face paled. "What happened?" She looked shocked, but there was something else in her expression that caught my attention and held it.

She looked…*relieved.*

Quickly the others filled her in on what had happened. I sat there, staring after her as she hurried down the hall to the spa wing, to Grandfather and the paramedics—and Lewis Paine.

Mrs. Grey served hot cinnamon buns with trembling hands. I couldn't eat a thing. Nor could Pippa. But Duncan gobbled his and both of ours as well. Josie hovered, worriedly flitting about the kitchen, then leaving to check on the guests in the library, then returning to the kitchen. There was no sign of Maggie and Hat, who must be working elsewhere in the hotel, but Bee stood at the sink, chopping vegetables for the evening meal. From time to time she stopped to rub her pregnant belly. Round and round. She had a little smile on her face.

Grandfather entered the kitchen slowly, accompanied by Mina Fuller, Ross and Hugh. They all sank into chairs at the table.

"Lloyd," whispered Mrs. Grey. "Tell us. Tell us what's happening…"

"The paramedics couldn't do anything," Grandfather said heavily. "He was already gone. Now they've taken his body." He sat silent for a moment, then sighed.

"Cardiac arrest," Mina said crisply. "I expect we'll find it was a heart attack."

"Lewis's mother died of a wonky heart, now that I recall." Grandfather reached over to pat my hand. "A young man doesn't just drop dead unless he's got something wrong inside. There must have been a genetic problem."

"So that's it, then," Bee said over the running water as she rinsed the sliced potatoes.

"Don't sound too sorry about it!" commented Mrs. Grey sharply.

Mina looked up, frowning. "Of course she's sorry. We're all sorry. It's very sad." She ran her hands over her smooth pageboy. I noticed she wasn't wearing the sparkly earrings anymore.

"We will get a full report," said Grandfather heavily. "It grieves me terribly. He was family. My wife's blood kin." He squeezed my hand. "Like you're *my* blood kin, Juliana!"

"Poor, poor Lewis." Mrs. Grey sounded near tears.

"He was an awful person," Bee said. "I for one won't miss him one jot."

"You keep a civil tongue in your head, Beatrice Bainbridge!" Mrs. Grey snapped. "It's a *tragedy*, that's what it is!"

Mina opened her mouth as if to object to Mrs. Grey's yelling at her daughter, but then she saw the housekeeper had dissolved in a flood of tears. "Come now, Mrs. Grey. It's just one of those sad things."

"I know, I know, but it's tragic." Mrs. Grey mopped at her face with a dish towel.

A tragic accident. I hadn't liked what I knew of this third cousin of mine, but now he was gone, and it was such a shame. He must have been basking in the hot tub just as Duncan and I had, then suffered a sudden heart attack. I hated to think he might still have been alive when Duncan and I first slid into the spa. If we had found him sooner, could we have saved him? I touched Duncan's foot under the table. Our eyes met and held. I knew he was wondering the same thing.

"I feel awful," Duncan said in a low voice. "I saw his work clothes and boots in a pile on the changing room floor when I went in for a towel. I'm afraid I didn't give them a thought. Maybe if I had..."

"He was probably in there the whole time we were eating lunch," I said. I couldn't bear for Duncan to feel guilty about Lewis.

"You mustn't blame yourself," said Grandfather.

Maggie and Hat appeared at the kitchen door with wide eyes. "Mr. Ellis—there are two police officers at the door," Maggie announced. "They said they need to speak with you."

Grandfather's face was grave. "Ah, yes."

"The police?" Bee's voice came out a shriek.

"But what are they doing here?" asked Hat, her voice rising. "What do they want?"

"It's just a formality." Grandfather coughed hard into his hand-kerchief. "I'm sorry, Harriet and Maggie. Haven't you heard the sad news? Lewis is dead. Heart attack, we think."

Maggie pressed her hand to her mouth. "Dead? Oh—no." She leaned against the doorframe, as if needing extra support.

"But why are the police here?" demanded Hat again.

"The paramedics rang them. Standard practice when it's unclear how an accident occurred. No doubt they'll want to speak to Juliana and Duncan since they're the ones who found Lew. Please show them in, Harriet, lass."

Leaning heavily on his canes, and wheezing with every breath, Grandfather left the kitchen after Hat.

Maggie sank into a chair at the table. "Poor Lewis…"

Bee turned to Mina. "It *was* a heart attack, right, Mum?"

Mina was looking after Grandfather, her face etched with concern. "Heart attack…yes. At least that's what I thought when I first heard. But there was so much water in his lungs, Ross told me, that now I'm thinking it may not have been a heart attack that actually killed him. He may simply have drowned. We'd have to see the autopsy results to know for sure."

Pippa put her head down. "Please don't talk about autopsies. I feel sick."

Josie pushed back her chair. "I'm going to see what the police are doing."

Hugh, his face pale, followed her. And Mina Fuller said, "I'll come with you. I'm worried about Lloyd. His wheezing is worse than ever."

"It's the shock," diagnosed Mrs. Grey. "It's going to be the death of him."

"Let's not have any more deaths around here," objected Mina, leaving the room after Josie and Hugh. "One is enough."

Mrs. Grey followed. The rest of us sat silent for a long moment. Duncan reached over and squeezed my hand.

Then Bee shrugged. She untied her apron and hung it on the hooks by the back door. "It's terrible how he died, I'll give you that much. But let's face it. Nobody is going to miss him! At least nobody here. He was always so full of himself, and so insulting to everybody, and always coming on to girls…He was awful."

"Yeah," agreed Pippa. "Look what happened with Doreen! But if we complained, Grandfather just said he was family, and that with family you'll get all kinds. He doted on Lew because he was some relation."

Bee snorted. "Family counts a lot with Mr. Ellis." She slanted a look over at me. "Just like *you* count a lot with him, Juliana. Blood kin, and all that."

"Well, I'm glad to have a chance to get to know him."

"He is so thrilled to have a *real* granddaughter!" Bee slanted a glance at Pippa. "I bet you'll inherit this whole place someday."

"You're joking," I said, trying to act as if the idea had not occurred to me before.

"Not at all. My dad said that Ross and Josie are worrying themselves sick over that possibility. They didn't like it when Mr. Ellis hired Lew—and not only because Lew was such a wally. They didn't want some other relative getting close to the old man because then he might leave Heatherstone to *him* when he dies, rather than to Ross."

"But Ross is his son," Duncan pointed out.

"Ross is his *step*-son," Bee said pointedly.

"Shut up, Bee," Pippa flared. "It's none of your dad's business. Or *yours*. And a step-son is still a closer relative than a wife's cousin, or whatever."

"Well, pardon *me*." Bee rolled her eyes, then headed for the back door. "Tell Mrs. Grey I'm walking around the lake. It's hardly raining at all now, and Mum says walking is good for pregnant ladies." She patted her bump. "Walking helps with back pain. And my back's been killing me." She put her hand to her mouth. "Oops. Pardon the choice of words."

Then she was gone. Duncan, Pippa, Maggie and I remained at the table, slumped in our chairs. I knew all of us were thinking about Lewis—poor Lewis whom none of us had liked, but who would never pester anyone again. How terribly sad that was, after all.

It surprised me that I was feeling so bad because, really, why should I care about Lewis? But I thought suddenly of a poem we'd studied in my lit class at school—a sermon, really, by an old British poet, John Donne. There's a line that says 'For any man's death diminishes me because I am part of mankind...' And I saw now that it was true. Lewis Paine was no one's favorite, but we were all altered, even diminished, by his death. There was one fewer of us—and it mattered.

Because he was a link in our collective chain, my mom probably would have said.

Then Pippa spoke up—but not about Lewis. "It's true," she said softly. "What Bee said about relatives. It's all my parents seem to talk about. You should hear them going on."

"Going on about what?" asked Duncan.

"About how my dad is only Grandad's stepson. About how maybe he'd leave Heatherstone to Lew. Or to Juliana now that he's found her—because she's Barbara's daughter. His real, *blood* grand-daughter. They have such hopes and dreams for this hotel, and they're worried Grandfather has other plans he's not letting them in on."

"I'm sure you're wrong," I told her. Maybe it's because I was adopted that I bristled when people acted like the blood connection had to be so important. I wasn't related by blood to my own parents, but I knew that didn't affect how much they loved me. "Anyway," I continued to Pippa, "Grandfather hardly knows me and, anyway, I wouldn't know the first thing about running a hotel. Besides, your parents have worked really hard here. *They're* the ones who deserve to inherit it someday. But I hope that day won't come anytime soon—it would be terrible if Grandfather died..." My voice trailed off as Josie appeared in the kitchen doorway, eyes wide. Mrs. Grey was behind her.

"Lew didn't have a heart attack," Josie announced.

Pippa raised her brows.

"They know that already?" asked Maggie.

Josie glanced over her shoulder, out into the hallway, then looked back at us. "They're pretty certain. They've found a *residue* of some sort in that coffee mug he always had with him. They think it might be—well, some sort of *drug*. So they've taken the coffee mug for testing. And the thermoses of drinks."

"Of course they must test everything," said Mrs. Grey. "But I prepared those flasks myself and gave them to you to take to the spa." Her tone was righteous. "They were full of perfectly good mineral water and Ribena."

"I gave them to *you*, Juliana," Josie said slowly, turning to me.

"Yes, and I set them out on the cart just as you asked me to." My voice rose. "Are you saying you think I drugged them?"

"Of course she's not," said Mrs. Grey, patting my shoulder. "The very idea!"

But Josie was frowning at me with suspicious eyes. I frowned right back.

She was a fine one to try to cast the blame on *me*. What had *she* been doing when Lewis Paine stepped into that hot tub? She had a key to the atrium, after all. At lunch she'd told us that she and Pippa had things to talk about at their cottage—but had they really gone home? Or had they crept into the spa to drug Lewis and then hold him under the water till he was dead?

I couldn't really picture either of them as cold-hearted murderers, but they had certainly despised Lewis. Then again, so had Bee. And so had her parents...

I rubbed my eyes. No, no, no. It was crazy to think anyone had killed Lewis, and Josie was looking accusingly at me because she was stressed out, and probably also worrying that a death in her precious new spa would be bad for business. We were *both* being crazy.

Maggie reached across the table and squeezed my hand. She frowned at Josie but her voice was gentle. "Lewis's death was an accident, pure and simple."

"Amen to that," added Mrs. Grey.

It is a perfect plan. And afterward, freedom. Hand in hand we can leave the house, no need to skulk, no need to wait for dark.

We will show everyone.

We will not have to hide.

We will not have to slip into the quiet of the boathouse, nor will we seek privacy in the heart of the maze. We will stand right out in full sunlight, ready to start the rest of our lives together.

It is time now.

Ready...steady...

Go.

10

All of us at the table looked up, startled, as Grandfather stepped into the room with two police officers following. "These are Detective Inspector Richards and Constable Henderson," Grandfather said. "Officers, these are my granddaughters, Juliana and Pippa. He introduced Maggie, then faltered as he tried to recall Duncan's name. His brow furrowed. "And this fine lad is on our staff, helping out in the gardens."

"Duncan McBennet," supplied Duncan.

I gave Pippa a look, hoping she had noticed how Grandfather had called us *both* his granddaughters. But she was staring at the officers with worried eyes.

They didn't look particularly intimidating, I thought. Detective Inspector Richards was a middle aged woman about my mom's height, with sleek short brown hair. Constable Henderson was a man about the same age, taller and darker, with a friendly face. Grandfather introduced Mrs. Grey, Maggie, Hat and Bee.

Constable Henderson pulled out a notebook and pen, and waited for the detective to speak. Detective Inspector Richards smiled at us. "So Juliana and Duncan, I understand you're the ones who found the body. So I'll be wanting to talk to you first, then. Separately. Juliana, please come with us to the library. The rest of you please wait here. We shouldn't be long."

I wished that Duncan could come with me, but Grandfather touched my shoulder and I stood up, alone. Maggie gave me an encouraging smile. Josie was still frowning as I left the kitchen with the police officers.

"Have a seat," Detective Inspector Richards offered, pointing to the loveseat by the library fireplace. She sat across from me on the piano stool while Constable Henderson perched on the window seat. "Lewis Paine was your cousin, as I understand," Detective Inspector Richards began. "We're very sorry about his death, of course, and also very sorry that you had the shock of finding him. Your grandfather says you didn't know him well?"

"No, I just met him." I explained to her how Grandfather had asked me to work at the hotel. How I'd just arrived yesterday. It seemed much longer ago than that.

"Ah, yes." Detective Inspector Richards nodded. "But in the short time you knew Mr. Paine, were you able to form an opinion of his character? Did he have friends here? Was he a happy man? Did he seem troubled?"

"Well…" The silence stretched out between us. Lewis Paine's sly smile flashed before my eyes. "He wasn't very nice. I don't think a lot of people liked him."

"And why was that, in your opinion?" Her gaze sharpened.

"Well, he was always saying snide things." Lewis Paine's smirking face rose in my mind like a ghost. I pressed my hands against my eyes, as if by doing so I could push away the vision. "He was always sort of smirking. And coming on to girls. And just sort of being in your face."

"In your face?" repeated the officer.

Was that some sort of American slang? "He was always a pest," I rephrased it for her.

"I see. And do you know if he was ill or in pain? Did he talk to you about his health?"

I nodded. "Well, he complained a lot about his back hurting badly."

Constable Henderson wrote on his pad. Detective Inspector Richards asked me to describe how I'd discovered Lewis in the hot tub, and I steeled myself to go over it all again. She listened, nodding. Constable Henderson was scribbling the whole time. "Thank you," Detective Inspector Richards said finally. "That will be all for now."

She stood up and, hastily, I did as well. "Um, I have a question," I said. "Josie—that's Mrs. Foxworth, who runs the spa—she said you think Lew might have been drugged, and that the drugs might have been in the thermoses. Well, she's the one who gave them to me, and I just put them on the cart! I didn't even open them—!" My voice was shaking.

Constable Henderson scribbled furiously. Detective Inspector Richards raised her eyebrows. "We're looking into every possibility. No one is accusing anyone of anything at this time. Your cousin's death might very well have been an accident—or, well, suicide."

Then she opened the door and there was Agatha Moggs, standing so close to the door of the library I felt sure she'd been trying to eavesdrop. Her face brightened as Constable Henderson showed me out.

"Hello, Sir," she said. "Are you the copper? Well, you'll be wanting to speak with me, I expect. I used to be in service here, many years ago. And now I've returned as a guest. Isn't that lovely? It was hard here, back in the old days, I don't mind telling you. Oh the things that went on then. Scandalous, really. And we were worked to the bone, I tell you. Worked to the bone. And I've learned a thing or two about human nature, I have. I can tell you, the man who died always had a kind word for me. We walked in the garden together yesterday, and he was a lovely gentleman. Have you seen the gardens? There's a very intriguing boxwood maze you might enjoy exploring, young man. What is your name?"

The officer looked at her blankly for a moment. "I'm Constable Henderson, madam. Detective Inspector Richards will be wanting your statement very soon. But please wait in the lounge with the other guests until we call you."

Muttering under her breath, Agatha Moggs made her way down the hall.

Constable Henderson escorted me back to the kitchen. Josie jumped up from her place at the table. "I'm next," she said.

"No, next we'll speak with the lad," Constable Henderson said, glancing at his notes. "Duncan McBennet." He peered down at Josie. "Please wait patiently. We will call your names one by one."

"Oh, certainly, Officer. I just thought you wanted to see me—and my daughter, Pippa."

"We'll want to speak to everyone eventually."

"Just sit *down*, Mum!" Pippa's expression was pained. "They'll get to you!"

As Duncan left the room with the police officers, I sank into his seat at the table. Josie leaned toward me. "What did they ask you, Juliana? What did you tell them?"

"Just what happened. How I found Lewis." A headache was starting to bloom at my temples.

Grandfather and John Bainbridge were in the parlor with the guests, but everyone else was gathered in the kitchen. Josie kept firing questions at me, Pippa sat silent with her arms crossed. Maggie sat at the table with her head in her hands. Mina Fuller and Hugh spoke together in low voices. Mrs. Grey sailed across the kitchen carrying the large brown teapot, with Bee right behind her with a plate of scones.

"Poor dear," the housekeeper said to me. "Questioned by the police! Let's let the girl rest her nerves with a nice cuppa." She poured out a cup of tea and set it in front of me. "I'm sure your parents will be aghast to learn what's happened since you came here. I wouldn't be surprised if they wanted you to leave immediately."

"*Aghast*," Maggie repeated in a low voice. "That's a good word for what we all are."

"That's right," said Josie quickly. "You may have to leave immediately, Juliana. You and Duncan both." Then she frowned. "No surprise if the guests start leaving now, as well."

"I feel like leaving myself," murmured Maggie.

"You?" Pippa laughed shortly. "You're not the one who found

him. Why should you leave just because Lewis committed suicide?"

Mina Fuller's teacup clattered against the saucer, spilling tea across the pine table top.

"I'll take care of it," said Hat, swooping down with a cloth.

"There's no reason for anybody to leave, Mum," Hugh said, quirking an eyebrow at Josie. "It's sad about Lew, of course, and a terrible shock for Juliana and Duncan, finding him like that. But there's no reason to leave. And the guests won't leave, either—you'll see. There's a certain romance to death. It lends an air of tragedy to a place. Guests like that. They'll be arriving in coachloads."

"You're a ghoul," said Pippa.

*   *

After the police had talked to everyone and gone away again, no one seemed to be able to buckle down to work, not even Josie. John Bainbridge and Duncan wandered out to the gardens, then came in again. Ross and Hugh went to the study to work on the hotel accounts, only to emerge a short time later, saying they couldn't concentrate. John told Ross that the fence construction was taking longer than he'd thought it would, and he'd like to hire day laborers to help. Ross didn't look pleased by this news, and muttered that the point of hiring Duncan was to avoid having to hire day laborers. Ross pointed out that Duncan had discovered a dead body today and might need a day or two to recover from the experience. And Lewis Paine would no longer be designing gardens *or* building fences. Mrs. Grey bustled in and out, trying to spread calm among us all. I could just imagine her as a nurse back during World War II, wandering among the wards of wounded soldiers, calming them with kind words and endless cups of tea.

Bee complained of feeling dizzy and Mina took her home. Pippa and Maggie chopped vegetables for dinner while Hat deftly stirred up batches of Yorkshire puddings. I peeled potatoes. Josie wandered into the kitchen and back out again, getting on my nerves. Grandfather's cough sounded awful—deep and wrenching—but he refused my suggestion that he lie down and rest. Instead, he dragged Josie and Ross off to mingle with the guests over cocktails before dinner. "Just don't talk to them about Lewis, do you hear me, Josie?" Grandfather said fiercely. "We'll talk about the weather instead!"

"Tell that to that dreadful Agatha Moggs," Josie said wearily. "She and her sister are all atwitter with the excitement of it." She shuddered. "Vultures, they are. Feasting on the carcass."

"*Mum!*" objected Pippa.

* *

As soon as dinner had been served to the guests, Maggie headed down to the village. "I'm going home," she said. "Can't stay another minute—I'm that sick over the poor man. No one liked him, but it's a shame. I just want to hold my baby."

Now the rest of us had finished our own meal, and Pippa, Hat, and I were clearing the dishes. Hugh pulled out a deck of cards and started showing Duncan a card trick. "Pick a card, any card," Hugh directed.

Everyone gathered closer to watch. Hat left the sink to hover behind Hugh so she could see, too. Then the telephone rang.

Ross jumped to answer it. The room grew quiet for a moment. "It's the police," he told us. "And they want to talk to you, Lloyd."

Grandfather took the phone into the study and closed the door.

"What? What is it? Oh, Ross, what in the world is it?" cried Josie, bobbing around her husband like a little bird.

"It's good news," Ross said. "Babe, will you calm down? It's good news, I'm telling you!" But he wouldn't say another word until Grandfather returned to the kitchen. Josie looked ready to burst.

Grandfather finally came back to his seat. "With poor Lewis dead, I'd hardly say this can be called a day for good news of any kind. But

Detective Inspector Richards rang with the toxicology reports. She says there were no drugs in any of the four thermoses—not that we thought there would be. But in Lew's coffee mug they found quite a lot. Very strong painkillers. Too much."

"The plot thickens," intoned Hugh. His father shot him a dark look. "Sorry. I'm just trying to lighten the mood around here. I never liked Paine, and that he turns out to be a junkie doesn't surprise me."

"I don't think he was a junkie, Hugh my boy," Grandfather corrected him mildly. "The residue in the coffee mug was from Lew's prescription pain pills—the ones Mina prescribed for his bad back. He had dissolved them in his coffee—more than enough to knock himself out."

"Did he leave a suicide note?" demanded Ross. "Did they find a note?"

"The police checked his room above the garage. They didn't find any sign of a note."

"Perhaps it was a sudden decision, while his back pain was especially bad," Grandfather conjectured. "The police are figuring Lewis came in from the garden while everyone else was at lunch—he had keys, of course—and changed out of his work clothes and climbed into the hot tub to ease the back pain. He usually had a soak in the hot tub after work, didn't he?"

In a flash I remembered how I'd seen Lewis Paine lurching across the grass before lunch. I'd wondered at the time if he were drunk, but maybe he was just in terrible pain. Or maybe he had already taken his pain pill overdose…

"That's right," said Mrs. Grey, wiping her eyes with her apron. "It was his habit to soak while everyone else would be having their tea and scones. Who would have thought he'd change his habits today! It's just horrid! Awful!"

"He must have been in a lot more pain today, so he came to the hot tub earlier than usual. And he may have taken more pills than he should have, trying to manage the pain. "

Mrs. Grey nodded. "It's hard to judge properly when you're in pain."

Hat looked up from her Yorkshire puddings. "So that means he fell asleep in the hot tub while the rest of us were eating lunch?"

"Oh, the very thought," whispered Mrs. Grey. "The poor man."

"Couldn't rouse himself even when the water was closing over his head," Hugh said grimly. Pippa squealed—which might have been why Hugh said it. "Puts me right off my food," he added.

Grandfather shrugged his thin shoulders and bent double, coughing hard. "In any case," he wheezed, when he'd recovered enough to speak, "the police are thinking it was an accidental over-dose, not deliberate suicide." He shook his head. "Such a rotten thing to happen. And he was such a young chap, too."

We finished cleaning up in silence. Slump-shouldered, Grand-father left the room, telling us he must phone people with news of Lewis Paine's death. My parents and Duncan's grandparents would need to know what had happened here today, and most importantly Lewis's relatives in Canada would need to learn the sad news.

He left a message on my mom's phone. I was relieved that she was busy, that she hadn't answered. I didn't want her telling him that I must leave Heatherstone Hall at once.

When Grandfather called Duncan's grandparents, Duncan spoke to them, too, reassuring them that although he and I had found the body, we were not too badly traumatized.

But maybe that wasn't quite true. Because when Ross and Josie invited Duncan to sleep at their cottage rather than in the flat he'd shared with Lew, and Pippa squealed with excitement and took Duncan's arm possessively, I didn't even feel my usual flare of irritation. When Duncan asked if I'd like to sit out under the portico for a while before bed, I shook my head. So off he went with Pippa and Hugh, and I said good-night to the others. I went straight to my room and sent an email to my parents.

to: **artmama@blackthorn.uk**; drake@homedesign.com
from: californiadreamin@blackthorn.uk
subject: don't worry

Mom, I know Grandfather phoned, but you didn't answer. And, Dad, I started to phone you, but then I realized it's still nighttime in California. So I thought I'd just write to you both to tell you I'm okay. It's totally sad about Lewis, and strange. He was some sort of cousin to me, second or third, or whatever. I'd only just met him, and it's a shame he's dead. Finding the body was a big shock for me and Duncan, but everybody is being really sweet and looking after us. Turns out there's not going to be a funeral because the relatives in Canada want his body shipped home to be buried there.

I hate the idea of coffins flying in the hold of airplanes, but I guess it happens all the time and the passengers just never know about it. Ugh.

Anyway, I hope you and the Goops and the London art show are all fine...Please don't worry about me because I'm fine too. And please don't overdose on anything because I love you!

I felt exhausted. This day had lasted forever. But outside my bedroom windows the long summer evening was ending, with the setting sun casting a pink glow on the lake. Even places this far north were ready, at last, for sleep.

I stretched out on the bed, my head resting on the soft pillow. I wished for Duncan's arms around me. Why had I just let him go off with Pippa? I wanted to be the one to comfort him. I wanted *him* to comfort *me*.

11

One thing about running a hotel: you've got to keep it going even when something sad happens. The guests are still there, even if there's been a death in the family. So the next morning after Lewis Paine's drowning, I was back in the spa, mopping up water from the pool and folding towels almost as if nothing had happened. The hot tub had been emptied and cleaned out and refilled, but no one felt like going in it. No one was talking much about Lewis Paine, but his unexpected death hung over us. Mrs. Grey kept wiping away tears. Grandfather tried to comfort her, and he kept checking in with me: How was I feeling? Was I all right? He didn't want his sweet next-of-kin to be distressed.

I kept telling him I was fine, and it was mostly true, though the shock of discovering Lewis's body would return from time to time, and I'd suddenly remember the feel of that underwater nudge against my leg, or the light flutter of fingers. But mostly I could keep the images away by staying busy.

The American family was out sightseeing that morning despite the low-lying fog, but planned to be back later for Mrs. Grey's buttery scones at Afternoon Tea. The honeymooning couples luxuriated in the spa or walked the grounds, glad that the rain had stopped. It was nothing to any of them, really, that a staff member had died of an overdose of his medication. Of course it was sad, but accidents happened. Life—and luxury holidays—went on.

The Moggs sisters played cards on the terrace. Herr Stifelmeyer

sat in his wheelchair in the parlor all morning. He seemed preoccu-
pied. I kept meaning to have a chat with him, but Josie kept me busy
serving at the snack bar and dusting the guests' bedrooms. At break
time she took Pippa to the dentist in the village. John Bainbridge and
Duncan continued working on the fencing project they'd begun with
Lewis Paine. No guests left early. But no buses full of tourists arrived,
either.

"Want to pop into the village with me on our break, Juliana?"
Maggie invited me mid-morning. "I often give my James a quick
cuddle before Mum puts him down for his sleep. Would you like to
meet my sweet boy?"

"Love to," I replied. "That is, if General Josie won't shoot me for
deserting my post."

"She's off to the dentist, remember? And besides, Mr. Ellis won't
let anybody give you the sack." Maggie smiled. "We won't be long, and
it might do you good to get away for half an hour or so."

So I left with Maggie, her little car scattering the wisps of fog
along the driveway. And I didn't think it was my imagination that
made the whole day seem brighter once we exited the big stone gates
and turned onto the road toward the village. Even the sun came out. I
let out a giggle of relief as Maggie rolled down her window and
accelerated. I hadn't realized how much tension I'd been holding in
back at the house.

Maggie glanced over at me. "You look so much like your mum,"
she said. "And you even *sound* like her when you laugh."

"Really?" I laughed again, experimentally. "You said my birthmother was your babysitter. Did she laugh a lot?"

"Yes, she was, and yes, she did," Maggie told me, veering off the
main road onto a narrow lane that led to a row of vine-covered stone
cottages. "She was a jolly sort. Lots of fun. Just a big kid herself, really.
About your age, too, I think—sixteen or seventeen—when I knew
her. And I was—oh, quite small. Around four. But I remember her
well." Maggie parked the car outside the cottage at the end of the row

and waved as an older woman stepped out the front door, a toddler balanced on her hip.

"There's my mum." Maggie opened the car door. "With James. Come meet my lovely little lad! She minds him every day while my husband and I are working. We have a little flat on the high street, but there's no proper garden for the baby to play in. Hullo, Jamsie! How's Mummy's sweet boy?"

Maggie's mother set the little boy down, and he pelted straight into Maggie's arms. She swooped him into a hug, then turned to me and made introductions.

"Mum, this is Juliana—Mr. Ellis's granddaughter from America. Juliana, my mum—Amy Beaton."

"Hello," I said. I shook her hand.

"My word," she said, raising her hands to neaten the bun she wore at the back of her neck. "Barbara-Elizabeth's daughter! And don't you have a look of your mum about you!"

"Thanks," I said. It was new to me, this being told how *like* someone I looked. Adoptees often long for the family resemblances that the rest of the world takes for granted.

Hearing that I looked like Barbara-Elizabeth gave me mixed feelings: happy to look like my birthmother, sad that I could never know her.

"Dreadful business up at the hall, Maggie was telling me. That poor man."

"I know," I said. "It's really horrible."

"Of course, nobody liked him much, really," the woman said cheerfully. "From what I've heard."

"Mum!" chided Maggie. "Here, Juliana, you must meet Jamie. James Christopher, he's called. After my dad." She handed me the little boy.

"Hello, James," I said, wincing as he clutched my braid. He was heavier than he looked.

"D'you have time for a cuppa?" asked Mrs. Beaton. "I'll just put the kettle on."

"Sorry, no, Mum. We've got to get right back."

"Then I'll get the lad's bottle warmed up," she said, and returned to the cottage.

James yanked my braid even harder and kicked his plump legs, wanting to get down. Maggie came to my rescue. "Here," she said, taking him into her arms. "He can run around on the grass for a minute."

She set him down and he toddled away. "Stay out of the lane, Jamsie!" Maggie called. She turned back to me, her face grave. "It's a dangerous lane, with that blind curve just ahead." She pointed. "In fact, your mum saved my life there—I don't expect you knew that."

"No—how?" I asked, intrigued.

"It was right there, just past the bluebell woods. Barbara-Elizabeth came to babysit while my mum and dad went out dancing at the church hall on a Saturday afternoon. We knew Barb because my dad worked for Mr. Ellis at his hotel in Norwich. We went skating that afternoon, along the lane right here, she holding me up by the hand, sort of towing me along. Both of us laughing like mad. And then, all of a sudden, she just picked me up and *threw* me with all her might— really threw me!—sending me sailing right through the air into the brambliest hedgerow at the side of the lane over there. And then she threw herself right on top me, knocking the wind right out of both of us, just as a gigantic lorry barreled along at top speed, swerving right around that blind corner. It clipped the hedgerow just where we'd been skating. It missed us by inches, Juliana. Inches! When we could breathe again, we were both screaming—it had been such a close call."

"Whoa," I said. No wonder Maggie remembered my birthmother, even though she'd been so young. "How had she known the truck was coming?"

"She said later she didn't really know, but sort of felt vibrations in the road." Maggie watched her little boy bend down to pick a flower. "She sensed it, somehow. Thank God!"

She scooped James into her arms and rubbed her cheek against his silky, tousled hair. "And do you realize, Juliana? By saving us that day, she made James's life possible. And yours, too. And any children you both will have some day. Grandchildren, even! Isn't that an odd thought?"

It was.

By sensing those vibrations and shoving Maggie out of the path of that truck, my birthmother had done more than save just herself and one little girl. She'd sent a whole lot of other things in motion. Maggie's whole life—growing up, falling in love, having James, working at the hotel…And me, too, growing up in California, coming to England…A whole chain of events.

"Links in a chain," I told her.

"Exactly." Maggie grinned, and the solemn moment passed as the little boy let out a shriek and struggled out of her arms to chase a cat across the garden.

"That little chap needs a sleep," Mrs. Beaton called from the cottage doorway.

"Indeed he does," Maggie replied fondly. "And we must be getting back to work."

I said good-bye to Mrs. Beaton and James, and Maggie showered them both with kisses. Then we drove back to Heatherstone Hall, zooming right past the bluebell woods and around the blind curve.

After lunch Duncan asked me to come up to his flat. He wanted to get some things to take over to Pippa's house. They had a nice little guest room for him, he said. It was cozy there.

"I could ask Grandfather to let you sleep in the house with me," I said. "I mean in a room on the same hall."

"But they're all full of guests, aren't they?"

That was true. "Well, maybe someone will leave soon."

I walked Duncan to his flat. I climbed the narrow stone stairs at the side of the building with Duncan right behind me, and stood aside on the narrow landing while he unlocked the door at the top. We stepped into a small living room—the *lounge*, as they called it in England. "Whoa!" I said, awed. "The police really ransacked this place!"

Duncan laughed shortly. "Nope," he said. "The mess was all your cousin's. Good thing his death has been ruled an accident, because even if he'd left a suicide note, nobody would be able to find it. The chap lived like a pig."

"That's unfair to pigs," I said, looking around at the incredible mess. Dirty cups and plates were stacked on the table. The couch was draped in newspapers and clothing. Piles of magazines lurked in the corners, and crumpled wrappers from chocolate bars and potato chips—*crisps*, they were called here—littered the carpet. Empty beer bottles stood randomly on every other surface, except for the space at the end of the room by the windows, where nine of them lay on their sides.

Duncan waded through the chaos to pick up a tennis ball by the television. "This is what Lew and I did that one night we stayed together here," he said, tossing the ball from hand to hand. "Lined up those bottles and bowled them down. Lew was really quite proud of his aim. Knocked 'em all down every time."

"So you had time to talk with him?" I sat gingerly on the edge of an armchair piled with laundry, dirty from the look—not to mention the *smell*—of the socks.

"I wouldn't say we actually had a conversation," Duncan said. "He talked, I listened. Same thing while we were working together— he talked. After a while I stopped listening because it was all the same."

"Same what?"

Duncan laughed, but it wasn't a cheerful sound. "Same rubbish about how irresistible he was to women. And all about his plans to find the perfect lady, take over this place someday and make it into a major resort holiday destination. He mentioned Hat a few times— seems he had a thing for her, but I doubt it was returned. Anyway, whoever she turned out to be, he and his bride were going to be incredibly wealthy, he said. He would enlarge the gardens, and then turn the fields into a theme park of some sort, you know. Charge admission for rides and for the maze. Rent out paddle boats on the lake."

"Wow. Sounds like he'd turn this place into a sort of Disneyland." I wondered if Grandfather had known about Lew's plans. "It would be really tacky..."

I walked over to peek into the small kitchen. Down a short hall were a bathroom and two tiny bedrooms, each with a single bed, a chest of drawers, and a wardrobe. I peeked into Duncan's room, where the bed was neatly made, with his laptop open on the pillow. His backpack and duffle bag lay next to the dresser. Then Duncan and I crossed the hall to Lew's bedroom. It was a tumble of bedclothes, muddy overalls, more crumpled crisp packets and chocolate wrappers, and beer bottles. A tablet of lined paper lay on his bedside table. I picked it up and read the neatly penciled lines on the top page:

Glitter and gold...
I saw you!—so bold!

That was puzzling. Was my cousin trying his hand at writing poetry?

A few sketches in pencil, torn from the same lined notebook, were tacked to the wall. I leaned over the messy bed to inspect them. They seemed to be neatly drawn plans for the expanded gardens he hoped one day to create here. Formal flower beds and meandering paths, fountains, reflecting pools, even a waterfall were all detailed and labeled in the same precise hand:

The Waterfall with Coloured Lights.
The Magical Maze.
Fountain of Bubbles.

"Pretty cool," I murmured.

I hadn't liked my cousin, and his scheme to turn Heatherstone into a garden amusement park would have probably come to nothing. But the sight of those sketches on his wall brought a lump into my throat. He'd been a man with talents, a man with a plan. Now his plans had all come to nothing, for Lewis Paine was dead. He'd been no one special to me—yet I continued to feel unsettled.

I told this to Duncan, and he nodded. "Of course you're unsettled, Jule. We both are. Why do you think I asked you to come with me to this flat? I want my stuff—and I don't want to be here alone, because it was *his* flat. We found his body, and I'll never forget how it was there, floating under the water, bumping against our legs. Just thinking about it freaks me out, so it's no wonder you're not in top form yourself."

He was right, I knew that.

But still…my unsettled feelings stayed with me after I returned to the spa and worked under Josie's eagle eye. My unease wasn't only over our having been the ones to discover the body in the hot tub. What haunted me now was the memory of those careful sketches tacked up on the wall by Lewis's bed. And not only the drawings, the snatch of poetry: *Glitter and gold…* The little couplet ran through my head.

Saw who? I wondered. *Doing what?*

*   *

Finally it was time for Afternoon Tea and the popular scones. Mrs. Grey asked me to go to her little kitchen garden and pick some mint to make a pot of mint-leaf tea. The herb garden was like a miniature maze but held no mystery because even the tallest plants were no more than a foot or two high. I wandered along, reading the neatly handwritten labels staked among the plants: *Lemon Sage, Rosemary, Basil, Thyme.* Idly I picked a leaf or two to rub between thumb and forefinger, then to sniff. Duncan and I should be ambling through these fragrant paths together. We should make some romance for ourselves. We should go out in rowboats on the lake, like the other romantic couples.

I peered across the lawn to the water. The sun wasn't warm today, either, and the water in the distance looked gray and choppy. Only a few rowboats were out on the water. Summer in England was proving to be as chilly as winter in Northern California. I shivered and wrapped my arms around myself.

Aha. There was the plant I'd been searching for, properly labeled *Mint.* I picked a dozen leaves, then turned to go back to the house.

"Juliana, dear girl, you look like somebody who is fed up with English summer weather and are about to chuck your job for a new one in the south of Spain." The friendly voice startled me, and I was surprised to see Mina Fuller come around the corner of the potting shed. "I always enjoy walking these garden paths, almost as much as walking in the maze." She untied her sweater from around her trim waist and handed it to me. "Here, put my cardigan around your shoulders. And if you're headed back to the house with those mint leaves, I won't mind coming with you and begging a nice hot cup from the kitchen."

"Thanks," I said, accepting her fleecy white sweater. I slipped it on. "This takes the chill off." I checked my watch. "But I can't really have that hot cup of tea just now. I need to get back to work."

"I'll walk up to the house with you," Mina said. Then she peered furtively over her shoulder. "I don't mind telling you, there's a spy in this garden and I'd like to give her the slip."

"Who?" I asked, looking around.

"It's that dreadful Agatha Moggs. See? Over there behind the lavender! Such a busybody—I've never seen the like. Always creeping about, hovering outside doors. I don't mind telling you, I've seen her peeking in the windows of houses when she walks down in the village. And I caught her in the act when I finished examining your grandfather this morning and opened his bedroom door. There was the woman, ear pressed against the door. And cool as you please, she just smiled at me and said that when she'd been in service, she'd had to sleep up in the attic, and how lovely it was now to be in a nice, big bedroom."

"She is odd," I said. "And nosy." Then I hesitated a moment. "So, how is my grandfather? Is he all right?"

"He'll do. But some days are harder than others."

"The shock about Lewis doesn't help."

"True. Your grandfather doted on the man." Then, under her breath, she muttered. "Can't see why."

"He wasn't very nice," I said. "Lewis I mean."

Mina Fuller had the grace to look embarrassed. "I shouldn't have said that. He was your cousin, too. But he wasn't always a very nice person. In fact, he could be quite…dreadful."

"I know," I said.

"If your grandfather didn't have such a special interest in his blood kin connections, I don't think he'd have given a chap like Lewis the time of day."

We had reached the house. "I'll pop into the kitchen and see how Bee is getting on," Mina said brightly. "And then I must get to my appointments at the clinic. But I do worry about my girl."

"Will her husband be able to come home before the baby is born?" I asked, partly, I admit, to see what sort of reaction my mention of the soldier boy would provoke.

Mina wrinkled her nose. "Husband—such a funny word for that young man. They're both babies, really. Babies having babies! It's absurd. Of course we have to hope they'll be happy together and somehow make a go of it, but really we just want to wring their necks." Then she smiled at me. "I sound terrible, don't I?" she asked ruefully. "It just takes some getting used to—having your only child go down a path you'd never pick for her. John and I gave Bee every advantage: an excellent school, lessons in music, riding, art, dance…We traveled as a family and did all the right things parents are supposed to do to bring up bright, clever children. But Bee is mule-headed. Stubborn girl. It's infuriating! But I'm getting over it—slowly."

We went our separate ways. Josie sent me up to put fresh towels in all the guests' bathrooms. I ran into Bee in the hallway.

"Oh, hi. I was just talking to your mum. She went looking for you in the kitchen."

"Has she got her knickers in a twist again?"

"She just wanted to see how you are before she goes to the clinic. She told me she worries about you."

"Well," said Bee. "I worry about her. She's the one who has been acting so daft. She's really taken it hard, my getting married. Hasn't been the same since Christmas when I came back from Scotland with Henry."

"How has she changed?" I asked as I knocked briskly on a bedroom door, waited, then used the key Josie had given me to open the door. Bee followed me in to the bathroom, where I laid out the clean towels.

"Oh, she was just furious at me all the time. It's like she couldn't stand being in the same house with me. She stayed late at the clinic or went out shopping. She never used to like shops. She used to laugh at the sort of women who shopped all the time, but then became one of them herself and bought all sorts of expensive junk. She'd come home with tons of new clothes, and dripping with jewels!"

Glitter and gold…

I stared at Bee, wanting to ask—what?

"Hello, may I help you with something?" asked a man's voice, and I whirled around to find a honeymooning couple, whose bathroom we were standing in, peering at us.

"Oh, sorry, we're just bringing you new towels," I said, smiling at both of them. The woman smiled back, but the man checked his watch.

"Almost done in here?" he said. "Because we need to change and wash up, and they're serving scones downstairs and they're to die for."

His wife elbowed him in the side and he looked abashed. "Oh, sorry. Sorry! Poor choice of words. I just mean we don't want to miss After-noon Tea."

"But we can wait," said his wife, "if you need more time."

"No," I said. "We're finished here. Come on, Bee."

Bee smiled at the couple. "We'll save you some scones, don't worry."

"Now that's service!" the woman said. "And we appreciate it, don't we, Ralph. How the hotel staff is still being so friendly and help-ful, when we know how much you must be grieving."

Bee snorted rudely and I kicked her ankle. "Yes," I said. "Thank you. My cousin's death was a shock."

The woman leaned toward me, lowering her voice to a tone that invited confidences. "So sad. And I hear that one of the maids found the body in the hot tub!"

"Uh-huh," I said, stepping away from her.

"How gruesome is that?" the woman said. "That poor maid! Do you know her?"

"Intimately," I said, and the guest's eyes widened. Bee snickered.

Bee and I hurried downstairs to help serve the guests. "People really are horrible," I said. "They love the details."

"The nastier the better," Bee agreed.

Afternoon Tea was served in the conservatory and outside under the portico. It was a daily ritual the guests loved, and most of them arranged to be back at the hotel from whatever sightseeing they were doing in the area in time to gorge themselves on Mrs. Grey's delicate little sandwiches and plump currant-studded scones.

"There you are!" Josie said when we appeared. "Pippa and Maggie could use some help, please. Hat and Mrs. Grey are baking a third batch of scones—they disappear so fast! They're stuck in the kitchen." Josie handed Bee a platter stacked with tiny sandwiches cut into triangles, then sent me outside to see if Herr Stifelmeyer, in his wheel-chair down by the lake, needed help coming back across the lawn.

He was sitting there with a deep frown creasing his face, but he looked up and smiled as I walked toward him across the lawn. "*Hallo,* Juliana. The very girl I am wanting to see."

"*Guten Tag,*" I greeted him. "I'm sorry I've been so busy."

He motioned for me to come closer. I knelt at his side in the grass and he leaned toward me. "I am very sorry about your cousin's death. And I need to tell you something. The pills he was taking for the pain in his back—they are very strong. They work very well to relax the muscles. I know this because I use them myself for the pains in my knee, and they always make me drowsy." His lined face creased into a frown. "But yesterday, the day your cousin died, my pills were gone."

"Would you like me to ask Mina Fuller to prescribe a refill?" I asked helpfully. "Or you can email your own doctor in Germany and pick up the medicine in the village—"

"No! Dear child, you must listen to me. I keep the plastic bottle for my pills on the table next to my bed. And yesterday morning—the day Mr. Paine died—my bottle was empty. Just sitting on the shelf by my sink as I'd left it, but empty."

"Are you thinking Lewis took them?" I asked. "Maybe he came to your room to ask you if you had any painkillers, and you were out. Maybe he saw the pill bottle, realized they were the same kind, and just took them."

"I am thinking—*ach*, child, I don't know what I am thinking. That Lewis took many, many pills—too many—this we know for sure. Did he really think if one worked well, two would work even better? And three better still? Six, seven—twenty? That does not seem to be the thinking of an intelligent man like Lewis. Would he take my pills because he had used up all of his own, and he was in a lot of pain with his back? Why would he not just ask his doctor for a stronger prescription? And how did he know I had the pills? That is what I am wondering."

"Hmm," I said. "I guess you could tell the police. But since Lewis is dead, they could hardly arrest him for stealing your pills. And they don't think he intended to commit suicide."

"No, not suicide. He did not seem the type, although I have learned we can never know what goes on inside another person's head. And I am not worried about theft, not exactly—" Herr Stifelmeyer broke off as Duncan came around the side of the house from the stables.

"Need some help?" he called, crossing the lawn to us.

I released the brake so I could push the wheelchair over the grass. "Shall we have some scones, Herr Stifelmeyer?"

He was silent. I grinned at Duncan, who came striding toward us. "What about you, Duncan?" I said. "Ready to stop building fences and sink your teeth into some scones?"

"Absolutely!" He smiled down at Herr Stifelmeyer. "Shall I give you a hand with this chair? It's hard to push on grass…"

With Duncan pushing, we moved swiftly up the hill toward the house. "I've been working over by the maze," he said as we reached the gravel drive. "Had to sneak a peek, but I didn't go far because I thought I'd get lost and then John Bainbridge would fire me. But I can't believe we've been here *two days* already and haven't gone in."

"Well, there's been a lot going on," I replied quickly. "And it's not like we get much time to ourselves."

Duncan sounded frustrated. "I'm dying to explore." He looked embarrassed, just like the honeymooning guest, at his inadvertent choice of words. "That is—I'm *longing* to explore."

"*Ja*, the enchanting maze," murmured Herr Stifelmeyer. "I remember there was a time when the maze was full of wounded boys, limping along on crutches. Back during the war. It was a great diversion. I remember one lad whose eyes were bandaged, finding his way to the center and back by touch alone."

"You mean he got himself in and out again just by feeling along the hedges?" Duncan looked impressed.

"*Ja*, that is what he did. I had a difficult time finding my way with my eyes wide open and two guards at my side!"

"Guards?" I asked. We had reached the portico at the side of the house. Deep green ivy cascaded down the columns from two immense stone urns at the top.

"I was a prisoner of war, you must remember," Herr Stifelmeyer said quietly. "Though I was treated kindly enough, I was not allowed to forget that I was in enemy hands. Two guards were stationed on my ward to keep watch that I did not try to escape. As if I could, with two shattered legs! But I healed slowly, and finally I was allowed to walk on the grounds if one of the guards walked with me. They were nice lads. My favorite one was your grandfather, Juliana."

"It's hard to believe England and Germany were at war," I said. I shaded my eyes from the sun and looked toward the maze. Its hedge-rows were dark against the lighter green of the manicured lawn, and the rose trellis framed the entrance. It looked romantic and inviting, but I remembered that sense of unease I'd felt on my first visit here, and I was not as eager as Duncan was to discover its secrets. Still, with him at my side, I would be brave. "The whole idea of wartime soldiers and prisoners doesn't seem to fit this setting, somehow," I said resolutely, pushing the thoughts of the maze out of my mind. "Do you know what I mean?"

"*Ach, ja,* but those were dark times," said the old German. "Times have changed, and for the better, that is certain. But old memories do not die."

His words chilled me and I pushed my hands deep into the pockets of the sweater I wore—Mina Fuller's cardigan. The fingers of my right hand closed on something—a crumpled scrap of paper. I pulled it out, smoothing it open, then turned away to read it.

I read it once, twice, and my breath caught in my throat.

12

I shoved the paper back into the pocket, unable at first to think what to do.

Duncan pushed Herr Stifelmeyer's wheelchair over to one of the small wrought iron tables set out on the grass just outside the conservatory "It's turned sunny again," he said. "Let's sit here. Or would you rather go indoors?"

"No, this is very good. Let's stay out in the sun. We must make the most of what summer sunshine we can catch."

Maggie came out and set down three plates for us. Bee brought over a tray laden with scones, clotted cream and jam. Duncan sat down and patted the chair next to him, indicating I should sit there, but I needed to talk to him privately, desperately.

"Excuse us, please," I said to Herr Stifelmeyer, snatching Duncan's hand and yanking him away from the table, back down the lawn.

"Bloody hell!" protested Duncan, stumbling after me. "What in the world is wrong?"

Old memories do not die, the old man had said—and neither did recent memories. I pulled the crumpled slip out of my pocket and thrust it at Duncan. "Listen, this is terrible. Remember what we found in your flat? Lewis's poem?"

"What about it?"

"Read this."

He glanced at it. "Another poem? Why are you panicking? I don't see—" He broke off then because, suddenly, he did see.

"This isn't a poem," he said slowly, handing it back to me and then wiping his hands on his jeans as if the scrap of paper had dirtied them.

"No, I don't think so either," I replied.

"It sounds like a—like a blackmail note."

"That's what I thought, too." I stared down at the scrap of paper. The words were printed neatly—in Lewis Paine's handwriting.

> **Glitter and Gold—**
> **I saw you! So bold...**
> **the good village doc,**
> **wife, mummy—what crock!**
> **'Oh, what <u>will</u> people say?'**
> **Not a word...if you pay.**

Duncan's face darkened. "Where did you find this?"

"In this sweater. Mina gave it to me to wear, and I just found the note in the pocket. Oh, Duncan, it's awful."

"Yes it is. But why does Mina have it? Who is blackmailing her?"

"*Was*," I said. "I think Lewis was blackmailing her."

"How do you figure that?" demanded Duncan.

"Well, the note is in his handwriting, and it was in her pocket!" My mind was racing with what I'd heard, what I'd seen since I'd come here to Heatherstone Hall. "But there's more than that. I heard Lewis talking to her, saying strange, sort of insinuating things. About her jewelry—remember? And in the note it says 'glitter and gold.' But what could he mean?"

"Hmm." Duncan reached for the slip of paper and read the poem again. "Blackmailers have power only if they catch someone doing something the person doesn't want other people to know about. Like committing a crime, or having an affair, or something."

"Was Mina having an affair with...someone?" I whispered. "And he gave her gifts of jewelry? And...and Lewis knew and was threatening to tell her husband if she didn't pay him to keep quiet?"

"Could be," murmured Duncan.

"Oh, Duncan, I bet that's it. You remember the things Lew was saying that night we first arrived, complimenting Mina on her jewelry, drawing John's attention to it…all our attention. How nervous she seemed…"

"The swine," Duncan said. "Even if it's true, blackmail is a really slimy crime."

"Who is it, I wonder? Oh, Duncan, you don't think Mina was sleeping with *Lewis*?"

Duncan laughed shortly. "I rather doubt it, don't you? Though I have no doubt he had his eye on *her*."

"Well then, it must be someone else. Maybe from the clinic," I conjectured. "But it's strange for Mina to be having an affair. Bee told me her parents are crazy about each other."

Duncan raised an eyebrow. "I'm not sure their daughter is the best person to know whether their marriage is working," he said. "I was just about the last to learn my parents were getting a divorce…"

"True," I conceded. It wasn't as if I completely understood my own parents' marital troubles, either, though it seemed to me my parents were in love with their careers these days rather than with other people. "But if Mina isn't having an affair, what other reason for blackmail is there?"

Duncan considered this. "Well, if she had committed a crime…" he suggested. "Like, if she'd stolen those jewels, and Lewis saw her, he might have threatened to tell John. Or she might have been terrified he'd alert the police."

"But it doesn't really make sense," I said. "I mean, she's a *doctor*; she obviously makes a good salary. Why would she steal things she could just buy for herself…?"

My voice trailed off as I remembered something that had happened at school in California, when one of the most popular girls in my class was caught stealing things from a teacher's desk. When the principal confronted her, the girl cried that she hadn't meant to, really—but she was just feeling so stressed about things happening at home, the theft was her way of feeling some sort of relief. I remember how surprised I was to discover she didn't have a perfect life after all.

Could a successful doctor like Mina also feel stressed out? Maybe because she was upset about her daughter's pregnancy?

"She could be mentally ill," Duncan said. "I remember hearing a news report about some famous actress who got caught shoplifting things she could perfectly well afford to buy. Her defense was that shoplifting was some sort of mental disorder, and she didn't mean to do it. Kleptomania, it's called. People aren't responsible for their crimes if they suffer from Kleptomania."

"I think shoplifting is a crime no matter what," I countered. "But so is blackmail. Mina should have called the police and reported Lewis—oh! Except then the police would know what she had done."

"Exactly. Which is why blackmail works," Duncan said. "Bloody nasty business."

"Murder is even nastier," I murmured. "This note explains every-thing."

"What? What does it explain?" he asked me. "I'm not following."

My legs felt shaky suddenly. Weak, trembly. "It explains why Mina killed him."

"Killed—?"

"Shhh!" I sank down onto the grass and wrapped my arms around myself. Duncan bent down and looked at me in concern. Then he sat next to me. Herr Stifelmeyer, still all alone where we'd left him under the portico, was watching us.

Duncan waved to him and smiled as if all was well. Then he turned back to me. "Now let me get this straight. You think Mina Fuller killed Lew. Because he was blackmailing her."

"I don't *want* to think this," I said. "But she had a motive—and she had a method, too. Herr Stifelmeyer was just telling me that his own pills had been stolen—the same drug that Lew was taking. Mina could have done that, drugged Lew. And left him to drown."

"She wouldn't need to steal Herr Stifelmeyer's pills. She's a doctor! She could just get them from the clinic."

"Yes, but she wouldn't want to be caught. Taking someone else's drugs makes someone else look guilty."

"True," agreed Duncan. "So—what should we do now? Tell your grandfather what we suspect? Tell the police? Or ask Mina about the note? Hope that we're completely wrong?"

"If she killed him because he was blackmailing her, then she's dangerous," I replied. "Oh, Duncan, it makes me feel sick." I stripped off the cardigan. I had chills running up and down my back, but wearing Mina Fuller's sweater was not going to warm me.

Duncan took my hands. "Let's sleep on it and decide what to do tomorrow. Since the blackmailer is dead, Mina isn't likely to hurt anyone else." He picked up the sweater and shook it out, folded it neatly, and handed it back to me. "We're safe enough, I think, as long as she doesn't know anyone knows…"

He pulled me to my feet, and together we started back to the house.

Tea was still being served. Guests were milling around in the conservatory and on the lawn. With gracious smiles, Bee and Maggie and Pippa were serving second helpings of sandwiches and scones.

We rejoined Herr Stifelmeyer at the wrought iron table. "The sun's gone behind the clouds," I said cheerfully. "Would you like to move indoors now?"

"That would be lovely, child, if it's not too much trouble—" He broke off as we heard a cracking sound from above our heads.

Duncan started maneuvering the wheelchair toward the portico, but I craned my neck to see what was making the noise.

"Juliana!" shouted Duncan, and I whirled around, just as one of the massive stone urns filled with ivy fell from overhead—leaves grazing my cheek—and crashed directly at my feet.

13

The ground reverberated with the thud. Stone shards and potting soil settled around us. I stood completely frozen, stunned.

Duncan wrapped his arms around me. He was shaking. "That was close. Are you hurt?"

"Another inch—" I expelled my breath in a shaky laugh. "Just one inch, and I'd be dust." I didn't know why I was laughing. I felt like throwing up. I had to turn away and kneel on the gravel, holding my stomach. The stones gouged my knees, but somehow that pain felt good because—because it meant I *could* feel. That I was still alive to feel. *I was alive.*

Duncan's arms went around me again. "It's okay, Jule. It's okay." His voice was shaky, too. "It missed you by an inch. A huge, long, full inch."

I stood slowly, hanging on Duncan's arm, and stared at the wreckage. *A blessed inch.* Herr Stifelmeyer struggled out of his wheel-chair, hands gripping the arms, his knuckles white with strain. Duncan reached out his other arm to steady the old man.

The French doors opened under the portico and Josie stepped out, followed by Pippa. "What is going on out here?" Josie cried shrilly. "What was that terrible crash?"

"What *happened*?" Pippa echoed. "We could hear it all the way in the kitchen!"

Duncan pointed to the shattered urn. "A very close call."

"By a hair." My voice came out as wobbly as my legs.

Herr Stifelmeyer was still staring at the wreckage, muttering under his breath in German. Josie and Pippa fixed their gazes on me. "How?" Pippa gasped. "How did it happen?"

I stood there, shaking my head. The realization of just how close a call it had been suddenly made speech utterly impossible.

"How indeed?" whispered Herr Stifelmeyer raggedly, this time switching back to English. He raised his voice commandingly. "How *did* it happen? We must know this! What made it fall?" He stood taller, craning his neck to look up at the portico where the other giant urns stood as they had for hundreds of years, immoveable through all seasons. "Did someone push it?"

Josie fixed him with a stern eye. "What a suggestion, Mr. Stifelmeyer!" Then she shouted for Hugh and Ross, with an edge of hysteria. "Ross! Hugh! Come out here!"

They arrived, with Mrs. Grey just behind them, wiping her hands on her apron. "What in heaven's name?"

"Juliana was nearly killed just now," pronounced Herr Stifelmeyer slowly. "It would have been a second death in just as many days."

"What a dreadful thing!" exclaimed Mrs. Grey. Her face was ashen. She reached out grandmotherly arms and embraced me.

Then Grandfather appeared, leaning on a cane. He stared at the shattered stone, the spilled dirt, the uprooted ivy. "What has happened here?" He reached out his free hand to me. "Lass, did you bring one of your California earthquakes to Norfolk?"

Hugh laughed, but Ross frowned, and I still couldn't seem to find my voice.

"Nobody felt an earthquake," Ross said grimly. "So I'd like to know how that pot fell."

Curious guests started filtering out onto the lawn from the conservatory. "Is something happening out here? What was that crash we heard? Has someone been hurt?"

Grandfather nudged me toward the house. "Don't stand out here, lass. Let's get you indoors." He turned to the guests, trying to reassure them, to make light of the incident. "No problem here at all, but we were lucky. These ancient stones do tend to crumble over the centuries…But it was only an old stone pot and no one is injured in the least. Not to worry!"

Mrs. Grey took charge of me. "Come, dear. You, too, Duncan. Here, Mr. Stifelmeyer, you sit back down in your chair and Hugh will wheel you indoors. Come, come, my ducks. You all need a hot cup of tea and a plate of scones. That'll put you to rights. Plenty of jam and cream."

"We must discover what happened!" Herr Stifelmeyer demanded insistently. "What caused it to fall? The girl was nearly killed—right in front of our eyes!"

"It *was* a narrow escape," agreed Ross, his voice terse. "But Juliana's safe. So let's not dwell on it."

Herr Stifelmeyer pressed his lips together. "Then let us go inside where we can talk. Juliana, you must come."

Wide-eyed, I followed as Hugh pushed the wheelchair all the way to the kitchen. Ross and Josie, Pippa and Hugh, Mrs. Grey and Hat all followed. Pippa, Hugh, Josie, and Grandfather sat at the table; Ross strode to the sink and stood glaring out the windows. Hat jumped up to sit on the counter until her grandmother's scowl pulled her off again. She shrugged and grinned. Mrs. Grey hovered over the wheelchair, twisting her fingers together. Duncan and I stood together near the door. Duncan squeezed my hand.

Bee and Maggie came into the kitchen carrying their cleaning supplies, and stopped in surprise at the sight of all of us. "Oh, are we having a staff meeting?" inquired Maggie.

"But then what's Mr. Stifelmeyer doing here?" wondered Bee.

Grandfather told them to get busy elsewhere, but Herr Stifelmeyer interrupted. "No, no, it is good that you join us. You must hear this as well, what I have to say."

We all stood there, waiting. *What in the world?* I wondered.

"When Juliana almost fell down the stairs yesterday morning," the old man began gruffly, "I thought of course that it was just bad luck, just an accident." He shifted in his wheelchair and met my eyes. "You went down to breakfast, and I went to my room, but I kept seeing in my mind how you had staggered, how you had—how do you say it?—you had *pitched forward* as if you'd tripped over something. What had tripped you, I was wondering. So I left my room and returned to the stairs to check."

"But nothing was there," Mrs. Grey said earnestly. "I know because of course I checked before we helped you back to your room, Herr Stifelmeyer." She looked worried. "It is my job to be sure no one has left a suitcase on the stairs, or any personal belongings. We must keep the passageways and staircases clear and safe for our guests."

Herr Stifelmeyer thumped his fist on the table top. "I went back to look at the stairs. And nothing was there—"

"You see?" Mrs. Grey interrupted with satisfaction. "I'll not have anyone saying I don't keep a clean and tidy house! Even a house as big as Heatherstone Hall!"

"Nothing was there," continued the old German, frowning at us all, "but I saw that *something had been there.*"

I glanced at Duncan, who just shrugged. A shiver tingled at the back of my neck.

"What are you on about, man?" demanded Ross, turning from the windows.

"How could you see something that wasn't there anymore?" asked Josie reasonably.

"Is he talking about ghosts?" Bee asked Maggie, looking confused.

"Shh," said Maggie.

We waited. Herr Stifelmeyer drummed his fingers on the table top. Grandfather's cough filled the kitchen. "Just say it, old chap," he said impatiently, and then wheezed heavily. "Just spit it out. Tell them all what you told me earlier! Tell them what you're imagining!"

"I imagine nothing. The holes are there." Herr Stifelmeyer pointed his finger at me. "There are holes. Small holes in each of the wooden railings at the top of the stairs."

"I still don't understand—" I began, but he cut me off.

"Those holes could be nail holes. Stretching a rope across the stairs. To trip someone."

"What—on purpose?" I couldn't think where he was going with this, but the intensity in his voice betrayed how upset he was. "But...I would certainly have seen a rope."

"Not a rope, he means a *wire*," wheezed Grandfather. "Or a *string*. Some sort of trip-line."

"Loony," muttered Hat. "He's gone daft on us, he has."

"He took me aside yesterday to tell me about it," Grandfather told us, "and I had planned to discuss it with you, but then we found Lewis...and it did not seem important. I dismissed it as his imagination. Still do. This is an old house, after all. A very old house. The wooden railings are very old. There could be any number of reasons for small holes in the railing bases."

"Cracks in the carvings. Signs of woodworm," Ross itemized them on his fingers.

"And I would have seen a trip-line," I said. *This* is what Herr Stifelmeyer had been worrying about? I shook my head.

"I was there, too," Hat spoke up. "I saw nothing on the stairs."

"Nor did I," said Mrs. Grey. She pressed her fingertips to her forehead.

"And why would anyone want to trip me, anyway?" I murmured.

"Why would anyone want to drop a stone flowerpot on your head?" Herr Stifelmeyer countered. "Or drown you in the hot tub?"

"Otto!" Now Grandfather sounded not merely impatient but angry with his old friend. "Surely you're not suggesting—"

"I am suggesting only that Juliana be very, very careful," he said sternly. "She was at the top of the stairs with me. She was in the hot tub. She was very nearly under that falling urn." Then he folded his wrinkled hands in his lap, and would not look up at any of us.

After an uncomfortable silence, Hugh laughed, but it wasn't a merry sound. "Right. So that's it, then. Let me take you back to the parlor…" He stood up and took hold of the wheelchair handles. Before the German could utter another word, Hugh had wheeled him abruptly out of the kitchen. The rest of us looked at each other.

"You see?" Josie spoke up acidly. "That's why we don't eat with guests in the kitchen."

"*Germans*," said Hat sourly. "So melodramatic."

Mrs. Grey started pouring tea—clearly her cure for everything—into our cups. "Now, now, he's a good man, I don't doubt. But very strange. Why would anyone want to hurt Juliana? That is the most bizarre thing I've ever heard."

"Of course it is," Ross said harshly. "The very idea." He patted my shoulder as he strode out of the room after Hugh.

"Crazy as a loon," said Pippa. "Isn't that the expression?" Then she looked puzzled. "What's a loon, anyway?"

"Some sort of bird," Duncan replied tersely.

Mrs. Grey sank into her chair at the table. "My goodness. What a lot of bother."

I sat silently, fortifying myself with tea and two delicious scones topped with jam and clotted cream. Duncan, too, had little to say as he ate. Josie sent Pippa off with Maggie and Bee to change sheets in the guest bedrooms, but when she turned to assign some new chore to me, Grandfather cleared his throat.

"I'd say Juliana needs the rest of the day off, Josie, dear. Don't you think?"

"Oh—no. There is still quite a lot to be done," Josie objected predictably.

"She's had a shock," Grandfather said. "She'll think Heatherstone Hall is nothing but trouble if we don't give her a nice, peaceful afternoon." He turned to me and put his hand on my arm. "You go on, lass. You're off duty until you report for breakfast tomorrow, eh? And take your lad with you—that is, if you want him."

"You mean Duncan?"

"You have another lad here that I don't know about?" Grandfather laughed, but then his laugh turned into a coughing fit. I had to jump up to pound him on the back.

"Thank you, thank you," he wheezed. "There now—much better. Eh, Duncan? Do you fancy a walk round the lake? Or a stroll through the maze?"

"I'm dead keen to see the maze." Duncan's voice was eager.

"Then off you go."

"The center of the maze is lovely," Mrs. Grey said from the sink where she was loading the dishwasher. "Many a time I've sat there when I need a spot of peace."

"But—" sputtered Josie. "But they have *work*!"

"The work will get done sooner or later," Grandfather said amiably. "Harriet can help."

"Trusty old Harriet," groused Hat. But then she winked at me. "Go on, then."

Duncan and I left the room. "So," Duncan said, reaching for my hand in the quiet of the hallway, "what do you think?"

I knew what he was asking. "I didn't see a trip-line," I murmured. "But I did feel a sort of grab to my ankle. Listen, I want to get a look at those nail holes. Come on."

We passed the parlor and saw Herr Stifelmeyer sitting by the window. His newspaper lay still folded and unread on his lap. "Take care," he called to me.

Duncan and I exchanged a glance. "I'll be careful," I promised.

And Duncan added, "I'll watch out for her, sir."

The *sir* was a nice touch, I thought, slanting a smile at my classy boyfriend. Still, I could feel Herr Stifelmeyer's troubled gaze as we passed. It was sweet of him to be worried about me.

When we reached the wide staircase, I squeezed Duncan's arm and started up the steps. When I reached the top, I turned. The late afternoon sun glinted through the windows onto Duncan's russet hair. "Okay," I said. "This is where I was standing that first morning. I was talking to Herr Stifelmeyer—he was right there, standing with his canes." I put one hand on the banister. "I started down—like this—and then felt a catch at my ankle, and I tripped—" I stepped forward. "He dropped his sticks and grabbed for me, and we both sort of crashed against the railing—here." I knelt down. "So the nail holes ought to be about...here." I stared at the dark brown wood. The railing was thick and carved richly with spirals and flowers. *How old is this?* I wondered, amazed at the sort of attention to detail people had paid in the past even to utilitarian things, decorating railings as if they were fine works of art.

There were nicks and cracks in the wood, as Grandfather had said. But—yes, there they were: two small holes, one on each side of the staircase, about six inches from the base.

I tried to remember the sequence of my movements that morning. I had talked with Herr Stifelmeyer. Then I'd tripped—and he'd saved me. Then Mrs. Grey and Hat had come to us, and I'd hurried straight down to breakfast. Herr Stifelmeyer was helped to his room. *If* a string had still been stretched there, surely one of us would have noticed. But if I had broken it with my ankle, it could have fallen over the side of the stairs and hung there from the nail, unnoticed, until someone had removed it, cleaned it away.

Someone? Mina? Had that been her first attempt to kill him?

But, Lewis hadn't slept upstairs. Mina couldn't have expected to trip him.

The American family came trooping into the center hall then and surged up the stairs, laughing and chattering about their day of sight-seeing in the fog. "Ryan! Dylan!" the mother called. "Don't run! Mind your manners!" They passed us with nods and greetings.

It would be stupid to try to kill Lewis Paine with a trip-line on these stairs. You'd be more likely to kill one of the guests. I shook my head. "Probably those holes are just ancient woodworm holes, like

Ross said," I murmured to Duncan. "And Lewis was already dead when that urn fell. So what happened today can't be anything to do with him or Mina. Mina isn't even here. She left for the clinic ages ago."

Duncan put his arm around my shoulders. We started walking back down the stairs, but then I stopped. "Wait," I said. "I want to check something else." And I led the way back up to the hallway.

Instead of walking toward my room, I walked the other way. Down the corridor, around the corner, into another passageway that must be, I figured, near the conservatory. Yes. The long windows looked out over the jutting roofline of the glass conservatory. The flat roof of the stone portico jutted out along one side. From this hallway, three long windows looked out over the roof of the portico—the portico with its long line of stone urns forming a sort of balustrade at the edge.

I stood looking out of the first window. I unlocked it and tugged at the handles, but it did not open.

"What now?" asked Duncan. "You don't want to go out there—"

"No, but I want to see if someone else could have gone out there," I said tersely. "Because either Herr Stifelmeyer is totally paranoid and bizarre, or he's not. And if he's not—then maybe someone *did* go out there and push the urn." I moved to the next window, which was also stuck fast, or painted shut. Then I tried the third.

The third window slid up easily.

Duncan and I stared at each other. Then he stepped cautiously over the sill and stood up on the flat surface of the roof. "Careful," I whispered, climbing out after him.

We edged over to the urns. There had been twelve of them; now there were eleven. The sight of the empty space where the fallen urn had stood made me shiver. The entire edge of the portico was full of cracks, and the stone was worn and, in some places, crumbly. Grandfather was right: the stone was very old. The mortar had crumbled in places. The urn could have become loose over the centuries. But what had made it fall? Had someone stood up here only a short time ago, looking down at all of us on the lawn with our tea and scones, watching…waiting…taking aim?

I looked closely at the empty space. Were those scratches made by a person chiseling the urn loose in the dead of night? Or had they been made by the original stone masons, hundreds of years ago? There seemed no way to be sure.

Duncan took my hand and together we climbed back through the window. We walked silently down the stairs. We left the hall and crossed the gravel drive to the lawn. When we reached the rose trellis marking the entrance to the maze, he stopped and put his arms around me. "Listen, I don't know what's going on—or even *if* anything is going on. I think people are probably just upset because of Lewis. That's all. But if I'm wrong—if something *is* going on—then you do need to be careful. Promise me you will be."

"Are you saying that you *do* think I'm in danger?"

"I don't know what to think."

"Well I know what *I* think. I think Mina killed Lewis because she was being blackmailed. It all fits. I found that note. She would have access to the drugs." I took his hand again. "And so that means the urn fell by chance. By coincidence. Lewis is already dead, and Mina wasn't even there when the urn fell. She'd already left for the clinic. So what we have to decide is whether to tell Grandfather about Mina first or just call the police."

"I don't think we have enough evidence for the police."

"Oh, they'll be interested in that blackmail note," I said. "It may not be proof against Mina, but it proves there was something going on. At least maybe they'll reconsider their accidental overdose verdict."

We had reached the entrance to the maze. The lake sparkled in the late afternoon sun, and the breeze whipped up little choppy waves that lapped the shore. One of the honeymooning couples was launching a rowboat into the water. We stepped under the rose arbor and the maze seemed to close around us, cutting off the light of the summer afternoon. Immediately, the paths branched before us. Which of the four paths would lead to the path that might lead to the path that would lead to the center?

As I had when I'd stood in this spot with the Goops and Pippa, I stared down each path as far as I could see. The two center paths went straight for about ten or twelve feet, then twisted, one to the left, one to the right. The other two paths veered immediately left and right. I turned around and looked back out through the rose trellis. As before, I felt the urge to leave the maze before I'd even started.

Then, from the path on the left we heard a rustling sound.

Was there an animal in the maze?

We heard a cough.

"Hello?" Duncan called out.

More rustling, then footsteps. I tensed.

"Oh!" exclaimed a voice in surprise, and Bee's mum, Mina Fuller, came around the corner, smooth dark hair swinging against her cheeks. Little diamonds glinted in her ears. But swiftly she put her hand to slip the earrings out. She tucked them into her pocket.

"Well, hullo there," she said softly.

14

"Hi," I said, thinking: *don't panic.* "I thought you'd gone to the clinic." My voice came out sounding falsely hearty. Fake.

"Well, I decided to take the afternoon off instead," Mina said lightly.

"Ah—but you missed Afternoon Tea," Duncan said. "What a shame."

"Well, I do enjoy Mrs. Grey's scones and sandwiches," Mina allowed, "but today I just felt like a walk in the maze. I love it, don't you? Clears the head." She smiled at us and her eyes were as sparkly as the diamonds in her ears had been. "Mazes are wonderful places for meditation."

"That's what Mrs. Grey said, too," I told her, edging closer to Duncan.

"Yes, I've often found Mrs. Grey sitting on the bench in the center. It's her special spot."

"We haven't gone through the maze yet," Duncan said. "We were just picking a path."

"Oh, you can start anywhere," Mina advised. "Don't worry. Just choose any path and start walking. You'll find the center sooner or later. And the searching itself can be soothing."

"Soothing?" I murmured. "It seems stressful to me."

She put her hand on my arm and I had to steel myself to keep from flinching. "Yes, soothing." She peered closely at me. "You know the old saying about the journey being the point, rather than the destination? That's how it is in a maze. And do you know the difference between a maze and a labyrinth?"

We shook our heads.

She seemed eager to tell us. I was eager to get away from her.

"Well, a labyrinth is one single circuitous path, you see," she said. "It loops round and round, turning this way and that, but there's no way to get lost. You're always on the right path. It's just one road leading to the center and out again. People find that walking a labyrinth is soothing, meditative. Some even say it's a spiritual experience, which is why many churches have labyrinths of tile or stone laid out on their grounds. But a maze is different. A maze has wrong turns and dead ends. It's possible to get frustrated, to get lost. A maze is like a puzzle, designed to confuse you. Which," she added with a quick smile, "is why I find it so enticing. I deliberately take a different route each time."

As Mina's words washed over me, my mind was racing along a completely different track. *She was not at the clinic, she was here in the maze…She was here while we were having tea and scones. She was here at Heatherstone Hall when the urn nearly crushed me…* A dawning horror was spreading through me as I realized she might suspect I knew she'd killed Lewis. And if she knew, she might have tried to kill me, too, so I would not be able to tell. What if—what if she had not been walking the maze while we stood with Herr Stifelmeyer on the patio? What if she'd been climbing out the hallway window to the roof of the portico to push that urn right down?

Maybe Herr Stifelmeyer isn't so crazy after all, I thought wretchedly. My body was so tense, it was all I could do not to race away from Mina and her mini-lecture about labyrinths, just race away down any one of these paths. Whatever weirdness I felt about the maze was nothing compared to my unease standing here next to a killer.

But instead of running, I untied the cardigan from around my waist and thrust it at her. "Here," I said abruptly, interrupting. "Thanks for this. I don't need it now."

"Oh, anytime, dear." Mina said, her eyes meeting mine. There was a long, awkward silence. "Well," she said brightly after a moment. "I'm off to take Bee home now. I'll see if John has finished up for the day, too. It's nice when we can all get home around the same time and have our meal together. Bee tires easily these days, and goes to bed early." Her expression darkened. "Pregnancy is hard on a young girl. John wishes she'd thought about *that* when she and Lewis were wandering this maze together! Oh, I know, I know. She has a husband now, and she says he's the father of her baby, but we have our doubts." She looked at Duncan, and her gaze sharpened. "You look like a nice young man, but you're far too young to become a father. So see that you don't."

Duncan's face flushed as red as his hair. "I will! I mean, I won't. Come on, Jule. Let's get going."

"Wait, Mina, I just wanted to ask you something." I decided to be bold. "Was Lewis your patient? I mean, did you give him a prescription for his pain pills?"

She turned back. "What—you mean the ones found in his coffee? Yes, yes, I wrote him the prescription because he was limping so badly with the back spasms. I recommended chiropractic treatment, but he wasn't interested."

She didn't seem particularly defensive, I noticed. Just answered my questions easily.

"But you didn't like him," I said softly. "You thought he'd seduced Bee."

Duncan stepped on my foot. *What are you doing?* I knew he was asking.

"No, I didn't like him at all. But I'm a doctor, Juliana. The man came to my clinic and wanted something for his pain. I don't let personal feelings get in the way of my job. The pills I prescribed for him offered him very strong relief. But of course he was only to have taken the recommended dosage. He was a fool, and a very unpleasant character, but the personalities of my patients do not concern me when it comes to their medical care. I can't get involved personally. He came to see me quite a few times at the clinic soon after he moved to Heatherstone Hall…" She pressed her lips together as if to keep herself from saying more.

Then she smiled brilliantly. "I must be off!"

We watched as she strode up the lawn toward the hall. "Whoa," Duncan said.

"She took off her earrings when she saw us," I said.

Duncan nodded. "I saw that, too. Whipped them right into her pocket."

"Yeah. She definitely felt guilty about something."

"Do we believe she doesn't get involved personally?"

"Not one bit." I was remembering the couple of times I'd seen Lew and Mina Fuller together. How he'd seemed to watch her in amusement, as if he knew something, as if he had some sort of power. I remembered what he said to John Bainbridge the night I'd met them: *"…your lovely wife seems to sparkle tonight."* And later: *"Gorgeous earrings you've got on tonight, Dr. Fuller…Another lady ready to snatch up quality when she sees it…"*

I remembered the look in Mina's eyes that night. I remembered her eyes on me, just now. Had she pushed that urn over to keep me from telling what I suspected about Lewis Paine's death?

"You okay?" Duncan asked me.

"Not really." I told him. "I'm wondering if Mina knows that I know. That we know. I mean—could Herr Stifelmeyer be right—that I'm in danger?"

He gave my fingers a squeeze. "Let's hope not…"

A quarter of an hour later we were still twisting, turning, and backing out of dead-ends. We tried leaving little markers to show where we'd already been, for each path looked like every other path; we broke off small twigs and laid them at cross roads, pointing the way we were going. We scratched lines in the dirt path to indicate which route led to nowhere so we wouldn't inadvertently head that way again. My unease had disappeared almost entirely as the two of us applied ourselves to the challenge of finding our way. We didn't speak very much; the maze seemed to cast a spell of silence. Despite my misgivings, I was finding this wandering relaxing. Finally, *finally*, we rounded a corner and our efforts were rewarded, for there in a little circle of a low stone wall was the welcome sight of a wrought iron bench. We had found the center.

"All right!" Duncan crowed in triumph and leaped up onto the bench. He punched his fists in the air and did a crazy victory dance. I joined him, and we laughed and hugged each other, and congratulated ourselves on our cleverness. Finally we sank down to sit on the bench and luxuriate in our success. I leaned against him and my uneasy feelings about Mina Fuller, the trip-line, the fallen urn all dissolved. The air smelled of boxwood, warm and fragrant.

Duncan slid his arm around my shoulders. I traced my fingers on his leg, marveling that I had come to England and found this boy. We'd liked each other from the start, right from the day we'd met, soon feeling as right together as if my mom's whole decision to move to England had, in the end, not been about her career as a painter but about my need to meet Duncan.

His thoughts right then must have paralleled mine, because he clasped my fingers in his and murmured, "I didn't know it back when you first moved to Blackthorn, of course, but I think somehow I'd been waiting for you."

Romantic words from a usually straightforward lad—and definitely words to wipe all thoughts of murder from my mind. I lifted my head for a kiss, but then we both froze as the hedge rustled. I jerked, and would have fallen off the bench if Duncan's arms hadn't been around me. Had Mina Fuller doubled back, come back into the maze? Was she following us?

Just to my left, just beyond the stone wall, the branches moved.

We pulled away and waited…but there was no further interruption. Finally we laughed a little. No doubt it was just a squirrel or bird, or some other common hedgerow dweller like a badger or a hedgehog. But then just as we settled back into each other's arms, another sound caught our ears: a little cough.

Badgers and hedgehogs didn't cough.

Duncan released me and stepped over the stone wall. "Hello?" he called. "Mina?"

No answer, but I could sense someone nearby, listening, waiting. I jumped onto the stone wall. "Hey, Mina! We know you're there!"

Again, there was no reply, just the soft sound of footsteps padding along a path. The back of my neck prickled, which I tried to tell myself was stupid because, of course, there could be any number of hotel guests wandering the maze. Maybe those American boys, Ryan and Dylan. Probably they'd simply been trying to peer through the hedges to see if they were anywhere near the center.

After a moment, we sat back down on the bench. We clasped hands, but the magic had been spoiled. I was feeling edgy. "Look, let's go," I said softly. "It might take forever to find our way out of here."

"We'll follow our markers. It will be dead easy." He stood up.

We headed out of the circle. At the first intersection I tripped over a branch in the path. And clutched Duncan for support. "This branch wasn't here before," Duncan said with a frown.

"How do you know we've been this way before?"

"We have—look, there's the line you drew in the dirt. This branch is someone else's marker."

Someone else?

We pressed on. I couldn't shake the feeling that we were still being tracked from behind the hedges.

15

I froze, tense and ready to run. But which way? I felt trapped. A thread of ice ran though my veins. I wanted to hide. But where? There was no place to hide.

"What? What is it?" Duncan was staring at me.

Stop it, I told myself. *Don't panic.* Now I was even worse than Ivy, with her vibes. I must be reacting, somehow, to my near-miss with the falling urn.

"Someone's in here with us," I gasped, clutching his arm. "Someone's watching. Get me *out* of here!"

Instead of grabbing my hand and running at top speed, Duncan reached for me, folded me into his arms. Pressed against his chest, I could hear his heartbeat. I felt some of the tension in my body soften, vanish. "It's okay," he murmured into my hair. "We're okay. It's no wonder you're upset. You've had a really rough day."

Then he took my hand and we set off again, with me still holding onto his arm. We walked in silence, rounded a bend and there, blessedly, was the rose arbor entrance. I exited the maze in relief, and started laughing. "Sorry," I said. "I don't know what that was all about."

"As I said, it's been a rough day. And probably someone was in the maze. One of the hotel guests, maybe the kids pretending to be spies..."

Someone was stalking us. But I made myself smile. "You're probably right," I said.

We crossed the lawn to the house and saw that the broken urn had been cleaned away. No broken pieces lying on the patio, no dirt, no tangles of ivy. I looked up at the row of urns atop the portico and saw no one loitering there.

I kissed Duncan under the portico before we went inside. "Thank you, valiant sir," I said, trying for lightness, though my head was aching and I felt like an idiot. "Thank you for protecting me from the seen and unseen."

"The known and unknown!" he bantered back, but I could see concern in his expression.

There was still half an hour until dinner would be served, but when Duncan suggested a game of snooker in the billiards room with the guests, I begged off. I just wanted to get up to my room, close the door, and collapse on the bed. I needed to be alone to sort out the tangles of this afternoon. Grandfather said they could do without my help tonight, and I must have a rest. Maggie would bring me my dinner on a tray, if I liked.

Gratefully I climbed the stairs to my bedroom. I locked the door behind me and went into the bathroom. Splashing water on my face, I stared into the mirror. My eyes were wide, troubled.

When Maggie brought my food, I unlocked the door and accepted the tray, only to end up picking at the food—though Mrs. Grey had outdone herself once again with crispy baked fish and delicious fries—called *chips* in England—as well as grilled vegetables and chocolate pudding. My stomach was too tense to accept much food.

I sat on my bed and read the emails from my parents. Both were concerned, both sorry to hear about Lewis's death. Both wondering if I wouldn't rather leave here and get the next flight to California, or join my mom in London, or go back to Blackthorn to stay with my friend, Kate.

I stared out at the evening beyond my window. It didn't get dark here in summer until after ten p.m., so I wasn't very good about judging time. It looked as bright as noon, though downstairs everyone was eating dinner. The smooth lawns glowed emerald green. The lake beyond shimmered like a mirror. Such a beautiful place, such a lovely old house. Did I want to leave here already?

I knew my mom would be delighted to have me join her in London. I knew my dad would book me a flight to California as soon as I asked. I knew Kate would love having me stay with her in Blackthorn.

I rubbed my eyes and lay back on my bed. If I really thought someone was out to get me, I shouldn't stay another night in this house. But Mina Fuller had gone home to her house in the village. She wasn't here anymore. We were all safe.

And there was no proof of anything. What if I were only imagining the blackmail—imagining that Mina Fuller had drugged Lewis and killed him? If I really thought Lewis Paine had been murdered, I had to take action, tell Grandfather, go to the police, not just run home to my parents.

Someone had been stalking me in the maze.

Or maybe not.

I had to be reasonable, rational. What did I *really* think? What was I going to *do*?

I started typing a list of what I knew. Or what I thought I knew. Maybe seeing it all written down would help me.

I opened a blank document and wrote:

one dead cousin in the hot tub—

one blackmailer—

one killer doctor (maybe)

one tripwire (maybe)—

one falling stone urn—

footsteps in the maze—

And a partridge in a pear tree, I thought, shaking my head as I read over my list. These were the things that might make me leave Heatherstone early. Should I go or stay?

A tapping on my door startled me and I leaped off my bed to answer. Hat stood there, her long hair fluffed prettily around her face. Usually she wore it pulled back in a tight ponytail, but now she wasn't wearing her work apron and jeans, either. She had on a pretty, short dress and high heels. "We're going to the pub," she said. "Hugh and I, Pippa and Duncan. He—er—we *all* wondered if you're feeling up to coming with us."

I grabbed my purse off the chair. "Yes," I said. "I am totally coming with you." No way was I leaving Duncan to have a double date while I stayed locked in my bedroom, tearing my hair out. I had been wondering whether to leave Heatherstone Hall, and now here was an invitation. It was what I desperately needed: a nice, normal night out. I would figure everything else out—later.

Downstairs, I checked with Grandfather, who said that a night out and about would be good for me. He pressed a twenty pound note into my hand. "Live it up, lass."

Miss Agatha Moggs jumped back from the door as I left the room. She and her sister Sue-Sue followed me to the front hallway, where Pippa, Duncan, Hat, and Hugh were waiting. "Off to the pub, eh?" Agatha Moggs inquired, obviously feeling no shame at having eavesdropped.

"Gallivanting about," added Sue-Sue.

"In my day," Agatha continued, "maids stayed here and did their work. We knew how to put in a day's labor, we did. And at night we rested up for the next day's work! None of this taking time off to wander in the maze or run around town with suitors, no ma'am." She frowned at us. "All this socializing can only bring disaster," she muttered. "I've seen it all before."

"Hard work builds character," stated Sue-Sue.

We ignored them both and headed out the door. Hugh's car was parked by the door—an old Mini with only four seats. I walked to the door and waited, wondering how we'd all fit. Hugh cocked an eyebrow at me. "Are you going to drive, Juliana?"

I had to laugh; I was always forgetting, here in England, that the driver sat on the *right* side.

"*I* shall sit up front with Hugh," Hat told me. "The rest of you are the sardines."

I walked around to the other side, where Duncan and Pippa were climbing into the back. Somehow I managed to wedge myself between them, half on Duncan's lap, which was not a problem for me in the least. Hugh folded his long frame into the driver's seat, and Hat slid in to the passenger seat next to him. "All right?" inquired Hugh, craning his neck to look back at his passengers. "Everybody in?"

"To the pub, James," ordered Pippa in a posh, nasal voice. "And don't spare the horses."

"At your service, Madam," Hugh replied, and roared down the drive, scattering gravel in his wake.

I had not been back to the village of Heatherstone since the day I'd careened through it on my way to the hotel, with Grandfather at the wheel. However much Grandfather went on about *blood kin*, Hugh was definitely a chip off the old block, or off Grandfather's block, anyway, the way he took the curves like a racecar driver. I clutched Duncan and shut my eyes as we swerved left, then right along the narrow lanes. *And I thought I was in danger back at the hotel?* I asked myself shakily when—*finally*—we screeched to a stop in the pub's parking lot.

The Dirty Duck was small, and crowded with villagers and a few hotel guests. One of the Japanese businessmen recognized us and waved from his place at the bar. "Let's sit in the garden," Hugh suggested. "That all right with you lot?"

We said it was. Duncan took my hand and we walked to the bar to order, then followed the others outside in search of a table. Picnic tables dotted the manicured lawn, and there was a wooden play structure built like a pirate ship—complete with a skull-and-crossbones flag—at the back of the garden. I knew Ivy and Edmund would have taken over the ship for the rest of the night, if they'd been with us. For a moment I missed them.

Hat and Hugh had their heads together, talking in low voices and sometimes smooching. Pippa pulled out her phone, tapped a number. She walked over to the pirate ship, away from us, while she spoke. I was still recovering from the wild ride in the Mini, still holding tightly to Duncan's hand, when the waitress brought our drinks—beers for Hat and Hugh, sodas for the rest of us. I sipped mine gratefully. Pippa returned to the table, and Hat and Hugh came up for air, and we had the garden to ourselves for the first half hour. It was fun sitting there, listening to Hugh and Hat and Pippa talk about life at the hotel. Then the other tables started filling up with couples—I recognized one pair of honeymooners from the hotel—and a few groups. Old people, teenagers, everyone seemed to like this place.

"Hullo, there!" called a familiar voice, and Bee Bainbridge came walking across the grass from the lane. "Thanks for ringing me," she said to Pippa. "I really could use a night out, but I had to wait till my mum started watching the telly. She's always going on about how pregnant ladies need their sleep. She'd have me tucked into bed at eight o'clock if I didn't put my foot down."

We were all glad to see her, but I had to keep pushing thoughts of Bee's mother out of my mind. I was glad Mina Fuller had not decided to join us at the pub.

The waitresses were kept busy bringing drinks and snacks, and some people at other tables even ordered late meals. Bee ordered a lemonade, which I had already learned during our time in England was, disappointingly, not at all like American lemonade, but more like a lemony soda. I asked for a bag potato chips with the unlikely flavor of 'Roast Ox' just because they sounded so weird. Duncan obligingly ordered the other weird flavor, 'Prawn Cocktail,' so I could try those, too.

"What, you don't have crisps in California?" asked Hat.

"Of course we do, but the most exotic flavor you'll find is salsa," I said. "Or maybe sour cream and chives."

"How dull for you," said Hat. "And here I thought California was cutting-edge."

"California," murmured Bee dreamily. "Movie stars and surfer boys and—"

"Earthquakes," supplied Duncan.

"Someday I'll travel there," Bee said. "It's on my list."

"After 'Get Married, Have Baby, Clean House'?" teased Hat. She rolled her eyes.

"It won't all be drudgery, Hat," said Bee. "But I'm not opposed to keeping house. I want to be a good mum who stays home with my kids, if we can afford it. At least while they're young! I'll be content to raise a family and be a wife. I'm not like you—wanting riches and greatness and my own business."

"We're going to have all that," Hat said, "aren't we, Hugh? When we're married and you're a famous writer and I'm running the hotel."

"You're going to run the hotel?" asked Duncan.

"Well, when Mr. Ellis dies and Ross inherits. That's the plan, see?" She glanced at me. "Sorry, Juliana. Don't look like that! It's not like I'm hoping he dies any time soon—it's just that I'm a realist. He's an old man now. And with those breathing problems? He can't last long."

I shrugged, but I didn't like how cold-blooded she sounded.

"Anyway," she continued, "Ross is desperate for Hugh to join the family business, but Hugh really doesn't want to…and Hugh won't have to because his lovely and talented wife—that would be *me*—will be perfectly delighted to handle everything. That way Hugh can write his novels, and I'll run the hotel. It'll be a five star luxury palace, you'll see! And eventually—"

"Now don't go killing off my parents, Hat," laughed Hugh.

"Of course not. But *eventually* they'll retire to the south of Spain or somewhere, and we'll be running it completely on our own. I've always wanted to be lady of the manor!"

Everyone laughed.

"You've really got everything planned, don't you, Hat?" said Pippa. "But I wonder if it's really going to work out that way."

"You mean you think Hugh won't marry me?" Hat reached over and tickled him, and they wrestled a bit, with Hat shrieking delightedly. "Oh—yes he will! He'd better!"

Pippa raised her voice so she could be heard. "What I meant is that maybe my dad isn't going to inherit Heatherstone Hall. He isn't *blood kin*, after all."

Hat and Hugh stopped wrestling and stared at her. Then both sets of eyes turned to me. "Don't look at me," I said, raising my hands as if to ward them off. "I have no plans to run a hotel. Or to inherit anything!"

"Bee is the one who will need some sort of inheritance," Hugh said, turning to her. "Right, Bee? How else are you and your soldier boy going to have enough money for a holiday in California—or anywhere?"

"We'll save up," Bee said. "Or maybe Henry will be posted to a base in America. California has army bases, doesn't it, Juliana? I bet there are all sorts of exchange programs."

"I don't know," I said. "But if you *do* go, I'll come too and show you around. Not that I know any movie stars."

"But—surfer boys?"

"Oh, absolutely," I assured her.

"And you a married woman!" Hat shook her head at Bee. "Brazen hussy."

Hugh and Duncan laughed. Hugh ordered more drinks. I relaxed. The troubles at the hotel seemed to recede as everyone sat talking and joking.

Then a voice broke through our evening. My hand shook and my soda sloshed onto the table. "Bee! Beatrice Bainbridge—there you are!"

It was Mina Fuller, moving full steam ahead across the garden to our table. "What in the world are you doing here?" she demanded. "I thought you had gone to bed ages ago!"

"Well, I didn't," said Bee resentfully. "I went out. As you see."

"Isn't it enough that you spend all day with these people?" Mina asked. "Why do you sneak out to see them at night, as well?" Her eyes raked across the rest of us. "I hope you weren't drinking beer, Beatrice. Alcohol is damaging to unborn babies."

"Thank you, Doctor Fuller, but I was drinking lemonade. Not that it is any of your damn business! You don't care about this baby at all! And you don't care about me!"

"Oh, Bee..." Mina lowered her voice. "I was just going up to the hotel to pick up your father, who has been working late, and I stopped in your room to make sure you were all right...and you weren't there. I was so worried."

"So worried about what, Mum? Hasn't the worst already happened? Your only daughter, teenaged and pregnant, and not going to university."

Mina sighed. "Come on now. I'll drop you off at home on my way to collect Dad."

Hugh stood up. "The rest of us ought to be getting home now, too, Bee. We'll see you tomorrow."

"I'm sorry, Dr. Fuller," said Pippa politely. "I rang Bee to ask if she wanted to sit with us. I didn't mean to get her in trouble."

"You did not get Bee in trouble, Pippa," said Mina wearily. "She got herself in trouble. As it were."

We all got up and left the beer garden. In the parking lot, Hat slid into the front passenger seat while Hugh waited for the rest of us to pile in to the back of the mini again. Pippa climbed in first, then Duncan, and just as I was about to launch myself across Duncan's lap, Mina Fuller called to me.

"Juliana! Come here, dear. No need for you to wedge yourself in there when I'm headed in the same direction. It's not safe without a proper seatbelt. You come ride with me."

"Oh," I said. "Um—thanks, but I can fit just fine…"

"Don't be daft," Hugh said in a low voice, moving me gently out of the way and pushing the seat back into place. "Go with them. She won't yell at Bee as much if someone else is there."

He slid into the driver's seat, and I had no choice but to join Bee and her mother. I saw Pippa wrapping her arms around Duncan in the back seat of the mini. I saw Duncan give me the thumbs up sign as Hugh screeched out of the parking lot. *Right*, I thought. *I don't mind riding with murderers at all. And leaving Duncan all snuggled up with Pippa? No problem.*

The Bainbridge-Fuller House (that's what it said on the metal plaque by the door) was substantial and square, and built of the same warm stone as Heatherstone Hall. It was only a minute's drive along one of the narrow lanes off the main road, and so in seconds we were parked in front. "See you in the morning, Juliana," Bee said as she got out of the car. And then she added meekly, "Sorry, Mum." She went into her house and closed the door, and then I was alone in the car with Mina Fuller.

"So," said Mina. "Here we are."

"Yes," I said softly from the backseat.

"Just the two of us."

16

As Mina turned the car around and drove down the lane toward the main road, I edged closer to the door, and closed my fingers around the handle. I could jump out if I had to, I told myself. I would leap away from the moving car and roll into the ditch, and before she could run after me, I'd be tearing through the fields. I was fast. I could outrun a middle-aged doctor…

The automatic door locks clicked into the locked position.

In the silence that followed, I felt those Roast Ox flavored crisps lurch in my stomach. If I threw up, Mina would have to open the door, wouldn't she?

Mina drove much more slowly than Grandfather and Hugh. Much, *much* more slowly. *Clearly not in the family*, I thought, and I could feel a sort of hysterical giggle welling in my throat. *Not in the family at all.* I pushed back the urge to laugh.

She wasn't going the same route that Grandfather had; she didn't make the left turn at the edge of the village—she drove straight on down the road. I opened my mouth to tell her of this error, but then closed it, a sick feeling washing over me. Of course she knew the way to Heatherstone Hall. She went there every day. Her husband and daughter both worked there.

Why would she miss the turn?

Because she wasn't going to Heatherstone Hall at all. Because she was taking me—wherever killers took their victims before they killed them. Wherever they would leave the bodies so no one could find them.

How would she explain my disappearance to Grandfather? "Oh, I was just driving her home and suddenly she leaped out and ran away through the fields…" Would Grandfather believe that? Certainly Duncan wouldn't.

But it would be too late by then. Too late for me.

Oh, *why* hadn't I said something to Grandfather earlier? Why had Duncan and I decided to 'sleep on it' and call the police in the morning? *Mom*! I called out mentally. *Dad*! I wished fervently that I had never heard of Heatherstone Hall, never begged to take the summer job, never come to this place…

"Juliana." Mina's voice was low.

I couldn't find my voice. It was all I could do to raise my head and look at her. She was watching me in the rear-view mirror.

"Juliana, I want to talk to you."

"What?" I croaked.

"You returned my cardigan this afternoon." She hesitated. "Do you have anything else to give me?"

I stared at her. Was I imagining it, or was *her* voice shaky?

"Like what?"

"Like—what you found in the pocket?"

No doubt about it, her voice was trembling. She was scared—of me. Wonderingly, I poked my fingers deep into my jeans' pocket and pulled out the blackmail note. I handed it over the seat to her.

Her hand closed around it tightly. "You read this."

It was a statement, not a question.

"Yes."

There was a long pause. Miles sped by as we drove along the dark road. "What are you thinking?" Mina asked me.

I was thinking I wanted my mommy. But I took a deep breath. "That Lewis liked to write poetry?"

Mina let out a laugh that sounded more like a sob. "Come on, Juliana. You're a clever girl."

She wasn't going to get me to say anything she could attack me for. I sat silently.

"Don't you recognize a blackmail note when you see it?" she cried suddenly. "Surely you read it and understood what it meant!"

I thought of lying, of saying, no, no, I don't know what you mean, but there was desperation in her voice. Suddenly she didn't seem quite so dangerous. "Lewis was blackmailing you," I said cautiously.

"Yes. Yes…he was, Juliana."

"That's…terrible. Blackmail is terrible…" My voice trailed off.

"Lewis was terrible," she said. "But I—I did a terrible thing, Juliana. I'm so ashamed."

She was going to admit to murder. And what could I do? Could people really make a citizen's arrest? Did it work the same way in England as it did on American TV shows? And what did you do if the person you were arresting wouldn't allow herself to be taken off to jail?

"He was blackmailing you," I said, stalling for time. "That must have been so scary."

"He knew," she murmured. Then I saw we were at the entrance to Heatherstone Hall, after all, right near the big stone gates. We'd simply taken another route. The car started slowly up the drive. "I'd like to tell you. Will you sit with me for a moment?"

I hesitated. "All right," I said. Then, as she circled around behind the house to the stable block, I took a deep breath. "Will you—will you please unlock my door?"

"Of course!" She clicked a button and my lock sprang up. "But why? What were you thinking? Oh—? Oh, no."

I sat silently, waiting, not sure what she was talking about, but ready to leap from the car if I had to. *If* I could get out before she locked the door again.

She took a deep breath and turned in her seat so she was nearly facing me. "Lewis was blackmailing me, Juliana, and I didn't know what to do. So I had to stop him. I had to…" She lowered her head.

"To stop him," I whispered when she couldn't continue. "And

you did."

"Yes."

I opened the door and jumped out.

"Juliana! Wait—come here!"

I backed away.

John Bainbridge came loping around the stable block. "Hello there! Perfect timing," he said. He was washed and scrubbed and no longer wearing his gardening coverall.

"John!" cried Mina. "She thinks I killed Lew!"

"What?" he thundered. He strode toward me and I backed away even faster. Of course he would support his wife. Likely they were in on the murder together, to silence the blackmailer before he could expose Mina's affair or whatever she'd done. Now they would need to silence me.

As I turned to run, John Bainbridge lunged and caught me. Before I could do more than yelp, he'd bundled me back into the car and thrown himself in next to me in the rear seat.

I opened my mouth to scream, and he clapped his hand over it. "John!" objected his wife. "Do stop. You'll give her a fright!"

"I want her to listen." Then he turned to me, his hand still hard on my mouth. "Juliana, Mina did not kill Lewis Paine. I promise you that. She did not kill anybody. Now, will you please sit quietly for a moment? No one is going to hurt you."

I nodded and he released me. I took a shuddering breath.

"Now open your door," he said to me. "Go ahead. Leave it open so you can run if you think you need to run. But I want you to listen. Mina has been through hell. We both have." He looked at his wife. "Go on, then. You tell her."

With the door open and the cool night air blowing into the car, I calmed down. With Bee's parents sitting back in their seats and not acting so scary, I listened.

And it was not about an affair, as Duncan and I had first suspected, but about a crime. We had partially guessed the truth. Mina had been depressed and disappointed over Bee's pregnancy. She'd started buying things to cheer herself up—jewelry and clothing from a little shop in the village. Then when Bee ran off and married, Mina sank to a new low. She had been spending wildly, but now she started shoplifting.

"Jewelry," I whispered. "Glitter and gold."

Mina put her hands over her face for a long moment. Then she looked at me. "I'm dreadfully ashamed, Juliana. I just felt the compulsion—as if somehow I'd feel better if I just took that one thing, or that, or that. Of course I felt worse and worse—especially because the shop is right here in the village, and belongs to an old school friend of mine, a very nice man."

With my door open, the interior car light was on, and so I could see the tears streaking Mina's face. "It went on for a few months," she continued, "and I felt so terrible. I kept trying to stop myself. I knew it was very wrong. I'd tell myself I was not going to take even one more thing, and I was going to return everything I'd taken…but I didn't. It got worse. I took even more! I was so ashamed, and also very afraid I would be caught. What would my family think? And what about my career?"

"Then someone did catch you," John said grimly.

"Yes. Lewis was in the shop one day. He saw what I took. He started following me. He started sending me little notes, little horrid poems he'd written, demanding money. Or kisses."

John Bainbridge punched his fist into the seat of the car. "That swine."

"It was horrible," Mina said faintly. "But I felt so wretched. I felt I deserved to be blackmailed that way, as punishment. So I paid him what he asked. But then he didn't want money anymore—he just liked having power. He started asking for other things. Like, he wanted me to talk to Lloyd—to your grandfather. He wanted me to convince Lloyd to make Lewis his heir so that he could turn Heatherstone Hotel into some sort of theme park. I did try to talk to Lloyd, but he just laughed. I was glad! Then Lewis threatened to tell the police what I'd done, to expose me to my clinic colleagues and patients, to ruin me professionally if I didn't get Lloyd to change his will to favor Lewis. He threatened to hurt Bee..."

She was silent a long moment, wiping tears away. Then she took a deep breath and continued. "Finally I realized I could not live this way. I had to tell John what was going on. I realized I needed help. It was the night I met you, Juliana—that night Lewis was being so insulting and insinuating, remember? I knew John was wondering what was going on. So when we arrived home that night—once Bee was in bed—I told him everything. How messed up I was. What I'd been doing. And...and he forgave me." She took another deep breath as John reached over the seat and squeezed her shoulder. "And then we went together, early the next morning, and I talked to my old school friend, the shop owner. I told him everything, and returned everything I'd taken—plus I insisted on paying for it. He didn't want me to—he was very forgiving, but I felt I had to pay. He gave me one pair of earrings to keep—said I'd earned them by coming clean..." Now she started crying harder and reached for her husband. He was in the back seat with me, but stretched his arms out so he could hold her. I felt strange, watching. But my heart felt lighter, and I was no longer afraid.

"Those were the earrings you took off in the maze," I said. "Today, when we saw you."

"Yes. I'm afraid it was a guilty reaction, even though those earrings are mine to keep, bought and paid for. It's just that I've been feeling guilty for so long."

I believed Mina's story so far. Her account had the ring of truth.

"The very next day after I told John," she continued, "I made an appointment with a psychologist, someone I can talk to about all this. It's a sickness, really. And as a doctor myself, I know that most sicknesses have some sort of treatment or cure. So I was feeling hopeful for the first time in a long time. Then I arrived at the hotel to check on your grandfather, and I learned that Lewis was dead."

John ran his hand over her sleek, dark hair. "It was a shock," he said.

"Oh—a terrible shock, yes," she concurred, "but also—I admit it—a relief." She looked me full in the eyes. "But I did not kill him, Juliana. I swear to you. I am a doctor. Killing someone—even someone as twisted as Lewis Paine—is against everything I stand for."

I leaned against the back seat and relaxed. I even smiled at her. "I—I think I believe you," I said, and it was very nearly true.

"That means a lot to me tonight," she said softly. "But now that you've suspected me of murder because of the blackmail, I'm having second thoughts about the cause of his death. I thought at first it was a heart attack, then agreed with the police verdict that it was an accidental overdose—because he certainly never seemed suicidal. But now I'm thinking that if he was blackmailing me, he might also have been blackmailing others. I can well believe he would have other enemies."

John reached out and stroked his wife's cheek. "I still think it was an accidental death, luv," he said. "I mean, look around you at the other suspects. Which of us at Heatherstone Hall is a murderer? The staff? The guests? Lloyd Ellis himself?" He slanted a smile at me. "Or—what about the new granddaughter and her gardening friend? Come on, now." Then his expression grew serious. "Juliana, I'm sorry. I had no right to grab you like that. To cover your face. I—I was just afraid you would scream and bring people running, and then we'd have to tell everyone about Mina's…crimes. I hope you'll forgive me."

Mollified, I nodded slowly. I was feeling better now, and I let John walk me to the house, while Mina waited in the car. "No one else knows about the blackmail," John said to me in a low voice as we reached the house. "I'd appreciate your discretion—though of course it is up to you. We'd hate for Bee to know—or any of Mina's patients. She's so very ashamed of what she did."

I murmured something and stepped inside the house with John right behind me. We surprised Hat and Hugh in the front hall, where they were half hidden behind one of the vast marble pillars, kissing like maniacs. They came up for air pretty fast when they saw us.

"Oh, there you are, Juliana!" Hat exclaimed, as if I were the very person she'd hoped to see just then.

And Hugh added: "We were wondering if Mina had taken a wrong turn somewhere!"

John Bainbridge squeezed my shoulder gently. "Seems she did take a wrong turn," he said. "But she found the right road again soon enough." Then he nodded good-night and left.

Hat stared after him. "That's odd," she said with a sharp bark of laughter. "I was only joking. Dr. Fuller has driven here a zillion times. She could drive here in her sleep."

I shrugged, and left the two of them to get on with it. Duncan was waiting for me in the kitchen. I took him up to my room and told him everything—the scary ride home, being jumped by Duncan's own boss and forced into the car, Mina's confession.

"Do we believe her?" he asked when I'd finally finished my story.

"I think we do," I said. "And it really could be just as the police think—that Lewis died of an accidental overdose. That's what John Bainbridge believes. But I keep thinking what Mina said that Lewis could have been blackmailing someone else. And if he was, then *that* person might have drugged and drowned him...And that person is still out there."

"Dropping urns on you?" he asked. "I don't see the connection."

"I don't either. So the thing with the urn must have been an accident, too." Maybe if I said it a zillion times, I'd actually believe it.

"We'll keep our eyes open and ears to the ground," Duncan said, twirling an imaginary moustache. "We'll learn every secret. Uncover every plot. All will be revealed."

He was trying to be light-hearted, trying to cheer me up, but it wasn't really working. It wasn't working because, in my heart, I didn't believe in accidental overdoses and accidental crashing urns, but I did believe that someone here at Heatherstone Hall had murdered Lewis Paine in cold blood—and hot water.

Why on earth is she always hanging about? Is she really so thick that she cannot see he is only humouring her?

Of course he is polite! It is his nature to be gentlemanly. He was brought up to chat and smile through his pain. It doesn't mean anything.

Still…maybe a new plan is in order, for it is ever so clear now that our destinies are entwined.

We must be together.

Must be together.

Must be.

Together.

17

I dreamed that night of California sunshine, and kayaking at the beach with Jazzy and Rosy, and then awoke to find that the new day in England was also, finally, sunny and bright. The unaccustomed sunshine made me want to forget my dark suspicions, and put my worries and fears out of my mind. As I got dressed, I even tried telling myself I was here to work, and to get to know my grandfather, and so that's what I'd do. And I wouldn't let myself feel the least bit uneasy about anything...

But it didn't work. All the sunny days in the world couldn't change the fact that I now suspected just about everyone of murder.

Down in the kitchen the rest of the family and the staff looked as if they hadn't noticed the sunny morning. They all looked as if the stresses of recent events weighed heavily on them. Pippa slumped in her seat, her expression glum. Josie greeted me with her usual disapproving frown. Ross would not meet my eyes, but spoke in a low voice to Hugh, who glanced up at me, waved briefly, then looked away. Mrs. Grey seemed to have a secretive air about her as she bent over the sink. And Hat just leaned against the counter with a dish towel in her hand, looking bored. Bee looked sullen, and her father, John Bainbridge looked irritated. Even Maggie, just in from the village, seemed out of sorts. And Grandfather kept wheezing as if he were a steam engine. What were they all thinking? Who among them was putting on an act?

One of them had killed Lewis Paine.

There was no sign of Mina Fuller because, Grandfather told me, she had morning hours at the clinic. But I'd heard *that* story before, when she was very much at Heatherstone Hall.

Then Duncan walked in the back door. He smiled at me and said good morning in a fairly cheerful, normal way. But I hated the way Pippa perked up at the sight of him. He sat next to her at the table, and she kept touching his hand and hugging his arm and otherwise monopolizing him. I sat down on the other side of Duncan and ate my breakfast in silence, and nobody realized I was considering each of them in turn, asking myself which one most wanted Lewis dead.

Then Josie kept me busy from dawn till dusk, and I began to feel a kinship with Miss Agatha Moggs. Worked to the bone, I was, and sour of disposition, and suspicious of everyone except Duncan. I folded towels and more towels in the spa, checked chlorine levels, served food at the snack bar, cleaned up after each massage and readied the cubicles for the next client.

John Bainbridge kept Duncan outside—busy with fence building, mowing, pruning, watering—but we met in the back hallway for a few seconds after lunch, and he wrapped his arms around me. I leaned into him, and his kiss was sweet.

I kept the memory of the kiss with me all through the afternoon, and it—along with the bright sunshine that continued without even a hint of rain—lifted my spirits. It was hard to remain troubled and uneasy in good weather.

Ross kept Hugh holed up in the study, no doubt learning the ins and outs of hotel management. Grandfather and Herr Stifelmeyer played a few games of snooker. The Japanese businessmen left for a three-day tour of the Lake District, but assured us they would be back to conclude their conference in Norwich at the end of the week. I did not see Mina Fuller all day, but her tearful confession played over and over in my head. She had *not* killed Lewis. If he *had* died by accidental overdose, then all the other things that had happened were also most likely just unfortunate accidents. The tripping on the stairs, the falling urn—nothing to worry about.

The air was warm and balmy as I headed in golden light to the patio for Afternoon Tea. It would be fun to go out on the lake with Duncan this evening, I thought, as I shared a few scones with Grandfather and Herr Stifelmeyer. I kept looking around, hoping Duncan would join us, but he did not appear. Nor did Pippa. I retreated to my room for a break before serving dinner, and as I collapsed on my bed, a text popped up from Duncan.

> *I hope you saved me a scone with clotted cream.*
> **Nope—you had to be there.**
> *no rest for the wicked, as my granny always says, but you'll be glad to know that all the fencing is in place.*
> **I dreamed about kayaking last night. When will we ever have time for a romantic boat ride?**
> *do they have kayaks here?*
> **rowboats...**
> *i have to finish mowing now. but after dinner, what about watching a film with me and pippa?*
> **you and PIPPA???**
> *Probably Hugh and Hat, too. Maybe even Bee. Don't get your knickers in a twist.*

Despite my annoyance that my evening plans with Duncan would have to include Pippa, the bizarre British expression made me laugh. The Goops used it whenever possible because *knickers*, in England, meant *underpants*. It always made them crack up—or, as they said in England, *fall about laughing*.

I pressed my lips together and typed:

> **Depends what you're watching.**

Then I wrote quick messages to both my parents, telling them that it was very sad about Lewis Paine's accidental overdose, but I didn't need to leave my new job earlier than planned. I loved them and missed them, but everything was, as they said here in England, *brilliant*, and the sun was even shining.

I lay on my bed reading a magazine called *SCULPT* that I'd

picked up in the spa. I'd thought it would be an artsy magazine, like the kind my mom had lying around our house. But it turned out to be about body-building and exercise. When I'd had my fill of buff bods, none of them nicer than Duncan's, I brushed and braided my hair, tied on my black apron, locked my bedroom door behind me, and stowed the key in my jeans pocket. Out in the hallway, I stopped and looked down the curving staircase to the marble tiles of the hallway below. I did not crouch to examine the nail holes in the base of the carved railings, but resolutely continued down, holding the smooth wooden bannister.

As I rounded the corridor into the kitchen, I ran into John Bainbridge. He was wearing his gardening overalls, and was covered with grass clippings. There was a sheen of sweat on his face. "Hello, Juliana," he said. "Your lad is a hard worker. He's under the shower just now, but should be along in time for his meal. I'm taking Bee home with me early. We want to have a quiet, family evening tonight." He leaned toward me, lowering his voice. "Mina and I want to thank you—for being so understanding. She is sorry you were frightened last night. It was a misunderstanding."

"I know," I said. "I'm fine. But I didn't see her here today. Is she all right?"

"It was a busy day at the clinic, but she'll be round tomorrow to check on your grandfather."

Then he left, and I went on to the kitchen, where I could hear Pippa's trilling voice and Hat's bark of laughter even before I entered the room. I worked through the dinner service with Maggie, Pippa, and Hat, smiling and cheerful, chatting with the guests—but not chatting *too* much because Josie's eagle eye was on me. Herr Stifelmeyer was not at his table, and Maggie told me he'd asked for a tray to be brought to his room.

I took orders and waited on the tables, poured drinks and cleared up spilled milk, courtesy of the American boy, Dylan. Or was it Ryan? Then the staff gathered to eat, but Hugh wasn't there. Ross said he'd had a few errands to do in the village but would be back in time to watch the film with us. Josie and Ross went back to their cottage, and Grandfather shared a glass of brandy with Herr Stifelmeyer up in his room while I stayed in the kitchen with Pippa and Hat and Mrs. Grey, washing up, polishing the countertops till they shone. Maggie left after dinner to go home to her husband and little James.

Nobody mentioned Lewis Paine at all. Nobody mentioned my near-miss with the falling urn, either.

After dinner I walked with Pippa, Hat, and Duncan over to the Foxworth's cottage, a converted section of the old stables. Pippa slithered, eel-like, to walk between Duncan and me. She linked her arms through mine and Duncan's, and giggled up at him as she told him what big muscles he had. She stroked his bicep and hung on his arm, begging him to try to lift her, to carry her. To his credit he eventually shook her off, but not as fast as I'd have liked. And he didn't kick her, either, which was a shame.

This was the first time I'd been to Pippa's house. A bright blue door in the old stone building was a cheerful welcome. And as much as I hadn't really wanted to come, but was determined to thwart her attempt to seduce Duncan, I looked around the cottage with interest.

Pippa's dad was lounging on the couch, playing a riff on an acoustic guitar. Ross looked different here in his own home, more casual. At the hotel he was always wearing a jacket and tie, looking every inch the hotel manager/accountant. I'd have liked to hear him play more, but he set the instrument down when he finally noticed us.

"Hullo there," Ross greeted us. "Welcome to Foxworth Lodge, Juliana. It's your first time here, eh? The Princess comes to the Stables! Well, *former* stables! I'd give you the grand tour, but you can basically see everything from here. Lounge, dining area, kitchen…and the loo. Upstairs there are three bedrooms about as big as the beds themselves. It's no palace, for sure."

"But someday we'll be living in Heatherstone Hall proper, and we'll have room to stretch out," said Josie, coming in from the little kitchen. She, too, looked different in her own home. For one thing, she'd scooped her usually elegant hair back into a simple ponytail. She looked younger, more like Pippa's older sister than her mother.

"It's very cozy," I ventured, looking around the small room crowded with two chintz-covered couches—called *settees* here in England—and a large TV—the *telly*.

Ross let out a short bark of laughter. "Well, yes, we're ever so cozy. Like sardines in a tin."

"Hugh should be along any minute," said Josie. "Had to nip out to the shops before they closed."

"To buy us some crisps and such, I'm hoping," Pippa said. She kicked off her shoes and flopped onto the settee. She patted the cushion next to her. "Come here, Duncan."

He crossed the small room and perched next to her. Hat sat down on Pippa's other side and picked up a magazine. *Country Life*. She flipped through the pages idly. I wedged myself onto the settee on Duncan's other side, and he shifted a little to make more room for me.

"Hugh's not gone to the corner shop," her father said, hands on hips. "He had to go all the way to Hethel to the sports shop. He was plenty peeved you'd taken his fishing tackle, Pip."

"I never did!" Pippa protested hotly.

"Well, dear," said Josie. "You do tend to borrow his things without asking…"

Hat looked up from *Country Life*. Duncan shifted uncomfortably next to me.

Ross shrugged. "In any case, *somebody* stole his fishing line, and he needs more if he's to go out on the lake tomorrow before he heads back to university. He thought he saw you rummaging about in his tackle box."

Just then Hugh strode in, his handsome face flushed. "Sorry I'm late."

"We just got here ourselves," Hat assured him. "Come here, give us a kiss, then."

"Give *her* the kiss, but give *us* the food!" said Pippa, holding out her arms for the bag her brother carried. "Crisps and biscuits, an answer to my prayers. Maybe a treacle tart, if there's really a God. We should have something extra nice for our new cousin and Duncan."

Hugh set the plastic tote bag on the coffee table. "Pray to your food goddess all you like, Pip, but whatever we're going to offer our guests is already in the kitchen. I didn't buy food. I was buying replacements for the stuff you stole from me. And this is really getting tiresome! If it's not my music, it's my favorite T-shirt, and if it's not my clothes, it's books—and now the fishing tackle. You don't even like to fish!"

Pippa favored her brother with an equally scornful glance. "Exactly. So why would I want your old fishing gear, you great bloody git?" She shook her head at me and Duncan. "He never puts anything away," she informed us, "and then goes around blaming innocent people when he can't find his stuff. Right, Mum? Doesn't he, Dad? You know it's true. Drives Hat crazy as well."

"I saw you, Pip," Hugh told her. "Two or three days ago. I'd left the box down by the lake, and when I was coming back to get it, I saw you bending over it, messing about. You were wearing my blue sweatshirt, with the hood up! Another thing I'd like back, by the way. Then you sloped off into the woods."

"You're delusional!" yelled Pippa. "I didn't take your old, nasty sweatshirt."

Duncan and I nudged shoulders while brother and sister wrangled. This was getting embarrassing. But Hat just sat back, flipping the magazine pages, a little smile on her lips.

"Get a grip, Pippa," her father said sternly.

Pippa rolled her eyes. "See what I put up with?" she implored us.

Ross frowned at Pippa, then turned to his son. "*Should* your sister take your gear? Of course not. But another question is even more pressing, to my mind. Should you be going fishing, Hugh? I don't *think* so. You know I need you here to help with the hotel accounts."

Hugh's expression darkened. "I've been working nonstop for you this summer. I've hardly had a minute to work on my novel. But tomorrow I'm taking a break to go fishing with some blokes from university, and I need my gear."

"Maybe it was one of the guests," I suggested hastily. "I mean, who took your stuff. You saw the person at a distance, right? Maybe one of those American kids was wearing a sweatshirt with a hood, and decided he wanted to catch his own dinner…"

Hugh shook his head. "It wasn't a little boy. It was Pip."

"Sod off," Pippa said crisply. She favored Duncan with a brilliant smile. "You told me you're an only child," she said. "All I can tell you is: be *glad*. Be *very* glad." She reached for the remote. "Come on, let's start watching something or else Mum's going to say it's too late and that I need to get my rest so I can slave properly tomorrow. I'm telling you, this hotel is like a workhouse."

"Oh…I'm not finding it *so* bad," Duncan spoke up, giving Pippa his slow smile.

Pippa looked at him sharply, then grinned. "Well…maybe not," she conceded. "Not when the off hours come with company like *this*." Her gaze moved over him almost like a caress, and I felt a little kick in the pit of my stomach.

"So let's watch this film," I said abruptly.

Hugh tossed the bag he'd been carrying onto the coffee table, and started flipping through a stack of DVDs. Ross brought us a bowl of salt and vinegar potato *crisps*, wished us a good night, and then he and Josie headed up the steep steps to the upper floor.

But Josie turned back. "Hugh?" she said from the steps.

"Mum?"

"You remember our conversation, dear?"

"Of course, Mum."

Josie laughed. "You'll be a good host and give our guests the royal treatment?"

"Of course, Mum. It's all in good hands."

"What are you two on about?" Pippa demanded.

"I just don't want our guests left sitting there while you and your brother fight," Josie said. "I want you both to be good hosts. Don't stay up too late now. Good night, everyone!"

We all said good night again, and then she and Ross disappeared from view.

Soon there was an adventure flick playing—something set in a jungle with lots of raging rivers, menacing wildlife, and furtive rustlings among the lush tangled undergrowth. It might have been snakes, or aliens, or spies.

Hugh went to the kitchen and brought out sodas. Though the armchair was empty, and seemed the likeliest place for him to sit, Hugh walked over to the settee where the rest of us were sitting in a row. Hat smiled at him invitingly and inched closer to Pippa to make room for Hugh at her end, but he wedged himself in next to me instead. He stretched out his legs and propped his feet on the coffee table, nudging aside the plastic bag from his shopping trip. The bag listed to the side, its contents spilling onto the tabletop.

Duncan laid his hand on my thigh.

I was sitting there, trying to focus on the film, enjoying Duncan's hand on my leg…but Duncan's hand tightened painfully. I put my hand over his to loosen the fingers. His hand turned in mine and his index finger pointed—surreptitiously—at the coffee table. I looked where he was pointing.

The plastic bag full of Hugh's purchases lay on its side, and a few items had slid out onto the table next to Hugh's feet. Fishing gear, that was all. A pack of colorful plastic lures. Another pack of hooks. And a reel of fishing line.

I looked up at Duncan. *So?* What was it he wanted me to see?

On the television screen the jungle foliage was stirring as the enemy crept through it. Duncan's hand pressed my thigh again, and his finger stabbed at the fishing line. I glanced over at Hugh; he appeared to be engrossed in the film. So was Pippa. Hat had her eyes closed; she wasn't watching the film at all. Was that a sheen of tears on her cheeks?

I shifted on the couch and leaned forward, the better to see her—and then I could also see the words on the package of Fishing Line: Nearly Transparent, Extra Strong, Highest Quality "Invisible" Fishing Line.

Invisible?

I felt that same old prickle of unease lift the fine hairs at the nape of my neck. *No way,* I thought, not even sure what it was I was denying.

But the thought wouldn't go away. I stared at the TV screen and tried to watch the film, but instead I saw something else: fishing line stretched across a staircase…

That was just an accident, I told myself firmly. But then I thought: *what if it wasn't?*

Okay, I told myself. *Think straight now.* I had discovered that Mina Fuller was being blackmailed, and had concluded that she had therefore killed Lewis. Now I felt fairly certain she had not, and I could prove her story by checking with the shopkeeper in town to see if she really had told him of her crimes and made restitution by returning everything and paying for it all as well, as she'd claimed she had. So just because Pippa—or someone—had stolen stuff from Hugh's tackle box, that didn't make her—or someone—a killer.

I cuddled against Duncan and tried to make myself focus on the film. But it was hard. My thoughts raced around like sparks from a wildfire, and Hugh kept pressing his leg against mine, making it hard to ignore him.

Had Pippa—or someone—needed the "invisible" fishing line to string across the top of the stairs on the morning that Lewis Paine died?

Think it through carefully, I told myself. Had Pippa tried to trip Lewis? But why would she want to kill him? Because he had come on to her once too often? Would Josie or Ross kill him for that? But why would any of the Foxworths think Lewis would be at the top of the stairs, when they knew perfectly well he slept out in the flat with Duncan? No, Hugh must have seen someone else taking his fishing line, someone else who wanted to get rid of Lewis Paine.

And yet Lewis had not died from a fall down the stairs; he had died from drugs and drowning. So it wouldn't make sense that a trip-line had been meant for Lewis Paine.

So…had the person who'd taken Hugh's nearly invisible fishing line meant to trip someone else? Meant to trip *me*—just as Herr Stifelmeyer suspected?

I had been trying hard all day to believe that nothing here could possibly concern me. But I shivered now despite the soft summer night, despite being seated between two warm-bodied guys. The question pounded in my brain: *Why would anyone want both Lewis and me dead?*

The answer whispered through my head, though I tried to focus on the jungle hero wrestling with the alligator: *Because either of us might inherit Heatherstone Hall someday.*

Without us, the obvious heir to Grandfather's property was Ross Foxworth.

I closed my eyes. Could I really be sitting here in the Foxworths' cottage, with the Foxworths' two kids, who were my cousins—or step cousins, or half cousins, or whatever—and really think their father had already eliminated Lewis and was now out to kill me, too?

And yet Hugh said he'd seen a girl—Pippa—messing with the tackle box. Did that mean Pippa was trying to help her father? She'd already told me how her parents felt threatened by my status as "blood" granddaughter. Or, maybe Hugh was in on it himself. He might have *pretended* to see someone else taking the line, just to cover up his own movements. Because weren't his motives the same as his father's?

Where had Hugh been when the urn crashed down, so nearly crushing me? And where had the rest of the Foxworths been? Pippa and Josie had come running—but weren't they supposed to have been at the dentist? And where was Ross?

I shivered and edged closer to Duncan. When I'd sent those message to my parents this afternoon, I was resolved to put the near-misses out of my mind, to consider it only coincidence that they happened around the same time Lewis had died. But now, while the hero in the action flick fought for his life, I felt my earlier bravado fading.

Now I had to admit that I might be in danger, after all. I had to admit that the beauty of Heatherstone Hall might mask a hidden, murky swamp. There could well be alligators here.

I might have to wrestle.

She has to be got rid of. Soon, soon. First one plan, then another, discarded for being too slow, too difficult. There might well be an automobile accident—if only there were cars for the taking! There could be a nice long drop off a cliff—if only there were cliffs on the estate!

Be serious now.

There might be an offer of swim lessons, private ones. Night-time meetings when both of us are free. Could she be encouraged to learn in secret so as to impress <u>him</u> as a special surprise?

It could work.

Will it be as foolproof as the first plan?

Time will tell.

18

I was desperate to talk to Duncan and assumed he would walk me back across the dark grounds to the house. But when the film ended, Pippa begged him to stay, she *needed* to show him something right now—the book she'd been telling him about.

"Fine," I said tersely. "See you all tomorrow." I headed toward the door.

"Wait, I'll walk with you!" Hugh jumped up.

Hat put her hands on her hips. "Excuse me, but Juliana and I shall walk back together, and you stable-dwellers can just stay put."

"No, I'd *like* to walk Juliana back!" Hugh insisted.

Hat frowned. "You can walk *both* of us back."

I need to talk to you, I telegraphed to Duncan with my eyes. But Pippa was steering him into the kitchen and, infuriatingly, Duncan did not punch her out. In fact, he wasn't resisting at all. But he did wink over his shoulder at me.

"Okay, good-night, then. Have fun." My voice came out sounding tight and resentful. Because, yeah, that's how I was feeling.

"Maybe you should hold Juliana's hand," Pippa suggested to her brother, "so she doesn't trip in the dark."

"What about holding my hand?" demanded Hat. "I feel a trip coming on myself!"

"You *are* a trip, Hat," Hugh said. "Can't a bloke even have a private chat with a long-lost cousin?"

"Depends," replied Hat, "on what that bloke has to say."

Hugh took her hand in one of his and mine in the other. This was ridiculous. I pulled away and strode ahead of them across the grounds. I would walk myself back, thank you very much.

It was after 11:00 and the sun had finally gone down. Summer nights in England were the total opposite of winter nights; it had grown dark by three o'clock in the afternoon when my family had first come to England.

Then Hugh was suddenly at my side, reaching out and taking my hand again, pulling me back to walk with him and Hat. His hand was warm, the fingers strong. And as we walked along the gravel path from the stables to the house, he drew closer and put his arm around my shoulders. "I'm glad you've come to visit," he said, in a low voice, as if to keep Hat from hearing. "I want to get to know you."

"Hmm," I said. I had to steel myself not to pull away from him.

"So how about you come fishing with me tomorrow?"

I was surprised at the invitation, but probably shouldn't have been, the way both Pippa and Josie kept trying to throw us together. "Thanks, but I have to work," I said. "And, besides, you're going with your university friends."

Why *were* they trying to throw us together? I wondered. How did that fit in with a plan to get rid of me? If, indeed, there really were such a plan and I wasn't just being paranoid.

"There are two rowboats. They can have one, and you and I will have one. It'll be fun."

"Um—no thanks, Hugh." I looked up at his handsome, smiling face in the dusk. I imagined us sitting side by side in a rowboat, imagined him rocking the vessel, imagined me toppling overboard into the middle of the lake. Of course, I could swim very well, but an oar bashing down on my head would put a swift stop to that…"Your mum thinks I've had too much time off already," I added faintly.

"I'm coming with you, Hugh." Hat spoke up determinedly.

"That's a great idea," I concurred with a big smile, then said a hasty good-night to them both and let myself in to the quiet manor house before Hugh could say anything more. Hat lingered with him outside.

The kitchen was empty, and the door to Mrs. Grey's suite was closed. As I passed the open doorway to the parlor, I could see one of the honeymooning couples sitting on the couch in a lip lock. I hurried upstairs, hesitating outside Grandfather's door. Then I decided I'd talk to Duncan first before telling Grandfather my worries.

I went into my room and locked the door. Then I flung myself on my bed and checked my text messages:

hey, are you there?

I tapped back to Duncan with relief:

safe and sound. how's your sweetheart?

you're my sweetheart.

yes, that's the right answer.

But what did Pippa want to show you? Her tan lines?

Her new black lace knickers?

your claws are showing.

just a little...

she showed me some earrings she made herself. asked if i thought they looked good on her. asked if i'd have lunch with her at some cafe in the village. flirted outrageously. it's okay, though. but what about you and handsome hugh? He just wanted a little chat?

wants me to go fishing...

don't go.

not to worry. invisible fishing line? very scary.

yeah. so there could have been a trip-line after all.

and he's strong enough to tip an urn over, if he felt like it.

maybe we should tell the police.

I need to tell Grandfather...

and the police!

now you're scaring me.

i'm coming over. now. Okay?

Yes please! I'll let you in the kitchen door.
*no need. Ross gave me a key. So stay in your room and
wait for my knock.*
my hero!!

I could do the text banter as well as anyone, but inside my heart
was soaring with relief that Duncan shared my worries and would help
figure out what to do next. But ten minutes went by, and then twenty,
and no Duncan. I kept opening the door and peering out into the dark
hallway. I listened for his footsteps on the stairs. I checked my phone
for messages, but Duncan wasn't there. **Where are u?** I texted.

No reply.

Puzzled, I slipped out of my room after half an hour, wearing the
old T-shirt I slept in, plus my lightweight sweatpants. I crept down the
stairs. The honeymooners weren't in the parlor anymore and all the
lights were off. I padded along the hallway, through the shadowy
kitchen to the back door, and reached for the knob. Just as I put my
hand on it, it turned. I swallowed a shriek and jumped back, darting
into the adjoining pantry, heart thumping hard. I watched as, slowly,
the back door opened and a stealthy figure stepped inside.

Duncan! I relaxed and stepped out of the pantry, and this time *he*
was the one who stifled a shriek. "Juliana!" he hissed. "You gave me a
fright."

"Well you scared me, too—when you didn't show up! I thought
something happened—"

"Sshh!" He grabbed me in a hug. "Something *did* happen." His
voice was a breath of whisper at my ear. "Let's go to your room and I'll
tell you."

Like cat burglars we tiptoed out of the room, down the hall, and
up the stairs. Inside my room, with the door firmly locked, he kicked
off his shoes, and we sat cross-legged on the bed, speaking in low
voices. He told me how he'd set off from the stable block but had then
seen someone coming out of the house—out the kitchen door—and
heading across the lawn to the maze. He'd ducked behind the screen of

bushes to avoid being seen.

"Who was it?" I asked. "Who would be going into the maze at night?"

"That's what I wanted to know, too. So I followed. I couldn't tell who it was, because he—or she—was wearing a dark sweatshirt with the hood up. It was so creepy, Jule."

"Did you go into the maze?"

"No way—but then I saw something else. Down by the lake. Two people walking."

"Probably the honeymooners. A romantic stroll."

"That's what I thought—at first," Duncan said softly. "But then, while I was watching them, they were gone. Just…gone! I thought they'd somehow fallen into the water, but I didn't hear anything. No splash, no calls for help—nothing. They just sort of…" His voice, already low, trailed off.

"Vanished," I whispered.

He shook his head and scrubbed his fingers through his mop of red hair. "It had to be just shadows I saw, since nothing else makes sense. I was already spooked by whoever went into the maze. Now *that* one was definitely not a shadow!"

I shivered, and Duncan reached for me. "Anyway, I'm here now," he said.

"I wish I knew what was going on," I whispered. "I don't want to be, um, barking up the wrong tree again, like we did with Mina."

"We weren't totally wrong. Not about the blackmail, anyway."

"I have to be careful, Duncan. I want to talk to Grandfather about this, but I can't just accuse his stepson and family of trying to kill me so I can't inherit this place. I don't want to shock him, start him coughing…After all, I don't have any proof of anything."

"Not yet," said Duncan. He sat there looking at me for a long minute, then reached out and traced my cheek with his finger.

Then we were hugging each other, slipping sideways on my bed until we were tangled together, cuddling, making out like honeymooners…and it felt so good, so *normal* after so many things happening around us had been abnormal. So far our relationship hadn't progressed much beyond friendship, kisses, and a caress or two, and we both wanted to take things slowly. But I felt comforted by the bulk of him next to me on the bed, the solid weight of his long legs pressing against mine, his arms holding me tightly. I held him back, kissed him and kissed him, and tried to banish all that was strange and unsettling with all that was…*this.*

Finally we lay quietly, side by side. I smiled into the darkness, feeling safe with Duncan there. The events of the last few days flitted through my head—the flutter of fingers underwater, brushing my thigh; the blackmail note; the scary ride with Mina and her confession; the falling urn; the footsteps in the maze; the theft of Hugh's fishing tackle, and the realization that invisible fishing line could have been strung across the stairs in a deliberate attempt to bring me down. But now I didn't want to talk of murder, or motives, or anything else. I pulled the duvet up over us both, and we dropped off into sleep, fingers linked.

*   *

In the morning I heard the patter of rain against the windows even before I opened my eyes. I cuddled closer to Duncan. Then a brisk knock made us jump, and Pippa's cheerful voice called to me that it was time to get to work. "All right, all right!" I called. "I'll be down as fast as I can." Duncan and I slid out of bed, and I grabbed my black apron from the floor. Pippa knocked again, and Duncan dove under the duvet. I had a wild, hysterical urge to hide him in the wardrobe, like someone in a bad movie. "I said I'm coming!" I called. "You go on. Save me a piece of bacon!"

Duncan's eyes peeked out the top of the coverlet, regarding me with silent mirth.

I headed for the bathroom.

After I had showered and changed, I emerged to find Duncan had made the bed neatly. He was standing by the window, looking out. "Should I slide down the drainpipe, or just try the stairs?"

"I'm thinking bold is better," I said. "You don't need to slink out of here like a shameful secret! You're my body guard. You're my knight in shining armor. We haven't done anything we have to hide, you know."

"Well, we still could," he suggested, cocking one eyebrow suggestively at me. But in the end we just opened the door and walked downstairs together—both of us sweeping our eyes to the corners, checking for trip-lines—and then headed into the kitchen.

"Don't say anything to my grandfather, please," I murmured. "Not yet."

"Eyes open and ears to the ground," he whispered back, with a quick smile, but I knew he wasn't joking. That's exactly what we'd have to do now: watch and listen to everything, and try to figure out what was going on.

It was a bustling scene in the kitchen as some of the staff were eating their own breakfasts and some were preparing food for the guests, and although Pippa's eyebrows shot up when she saw us together, almost immediately John Bainbridge swooped down on Duncan.

"There you are, lad! I went to your flat looking for you. We have fences to build, so let's get started. I've got some men from the village to help us out today."

"But it's raining," I objected. "Doesn't he get the day off when it rains?"

John gave a bark of laughter. Josie shook her head woefully, as if she couldn't believe how stupid I was. "Spoken like a true Californian," she said.

Bee rolled her eyes. "If people stopped working when it rained, no one in Britain would ever be working."

"I thought we were finished with fence posts!" Duncan said before anyone could comment further on my ignorance.

"Finished sinking the posts, yes. But now we need to put in the rails." John raised his bushy eyebrows. "You aren't tired, are you?"

"I'm fine," Duncan said.

It was Grandfather who didn't seem fine. He was trying to eat his eggs, but kept stopping to wheeze and cough. He slurped at his cup of tea, but it did no good, and the next cough sprayed liquid across the table.

"I—I'll be all right," he gasped.

Mrs. Grey hurried to mop him up. "Where is Mina?" she asked. "I thought I heard her come in with you, John."

"She's here," said John Bainbridge. "Somewhere."

"I'll find her," offered Hat, casting a concerned glance at Grandfather.

Grandfather's coughing and wheezing subsided, and he smiled at us. "Don't worry, I'm still hanging in there," he said.

"Of course you are," said Mrs. Grey. "We wouldn't have it any other way."

I glanced quickly at Josie, but couldn't read the expression on her face. Pippa, too, was turned away from me. And there was no sign of Hugh or Ross.

Maggie handed Duncan a plate of eggs and toast, which he gulped down, and then John took Duncan off in a golf cart to join the men from the village. Pippa stomped around clearing the table, refusing to look at me.

Meow!

"Good morning, everyone," said Mina Fuller, coming into the room behind Hat. "I was just chatting with that nice German guest. Now, what is this, Lloyd?" She hurried across the room to him, but gave me a smile, full and friendly, as she passed.

"Just the cough, Mina. Kept me awake last night."

She pulled her stethoscope out of her handbag. "Let's go in the other room, shall we? Let me check you out."

Though I needed to talk to Grandfather—preferably alone—this was clearly not going to be the time or place. Hat and Bee darted in and out between the kitchen and the dining room, serving the last guests to arrive for breakfast and clearing the table of those guests who had breakfasted early. Mrs. Grey set a plate of eggs in front of me, as Josie tried to insist I come with her to the spa straight away.

"It's late," she added in irritation. "Pippa was down an hour ago. Didn't you set your alarm?"

"Let the child eat," objected Mrs. Grey.

I ate as fast as I could, resolving to speak with Grandfather at lunch time. My morning was spent working with Pippa, folding towels, mopping the floor, and adjusting chlorine levels. My cousin worked in silence, snapping the towels into neat rolls, not looking at me. I was surprised that the guests had no qualms about hanging out in the hot tub, now that it had been refilled, but of course every day brought a few new faces. Maybe some didn't even know what had happened. In any case, the hot tub was in use the entire morning, while the rain outside drizzled down the glass-windowed walls. I wasn't planning to get into that hot tub ever again. I shuddered every time I looked at it.

When I stood by the pool and gazed out over the lawn, I could just make out a rowboat on the lake. That would be Hugh, fishing with his university friends—two other guys that Josie told me had driven up to the house in their dilapidated jeep after breakfast. "Fishing in the rain?" I asked, shaking my head. In California rain in the summer months would be about as unusual as snow. I couldn't get used to it.

"Hugh says fish bite even better in the rain," Pippa said, craning her neck. "Look at them. They're gorgeous!"

"The fish?" I teased.

Pippa laughed a little at that. "Both those guys are gorgeous," she said. "But nothing like Duncan."

I looked at her for a long moment. "Duncan's pretty special," I agreed, finally.

"I really like him, Juliana."

"Yeah. Me, too." *And I met him first!* I wanted to add. But I kept quiet.

"They invited me to come with them, those lads," Pippa told me. "But Hugh said no way. Of course Mum would have said no, even if Hugh hadn't, because she was hoping you would go with them."

"I don't like fishing much, either," I said. I imagined myself out there with them, the other boys in one boat, and Hugh and I together. I could almost feel the swell of water slapping against the prow, imagined the boat rocking, rocking, capsizing…my mouth filling with water as Hugh pulled me down…Would the other boys realize what was happening and come to rescue me?

I shook my head to rid myself of such a dark fantasy. Pippa was staring out at the boat, too, but her goofy expression revealed she wasn't thinking of 'accidents.' "I'd have gone if Duncan asked me," she said softly.

"Lovely view, isn't it?" Mrs. Grey asked, coming up behind us with her heavily laden snack trolley and saving me from having to think what to answer.

"Lovely," echoed Pippa. "Those blokes, I mean. But not as lovely as Duncan."

"Do you like to fish, Mrs. Grey?" I asked quickly.

Mrs. Grey stared out at the view with a somber expression. "On the surface the water is all sparkling and inviting, but don't be tempted."

"What do you mean?"

"It's not really a very nice lake," she said, turning to me with beseeching eyes. "It's horribly cold, and very deep. I can't abide water, anyway, but that lake is especially bad. I stay away from it."

Josie walked up with her arms full of wet, rumpled white towels. "Oh, Mrs. Grey," she chided. "Do I hear you railing against that poor lake again? Do you know, Hat told me she even heard you scolding that lake in your sleep! Abusing it viciously!" She gave the housekeeper a teasing look. "Most unkind of you, Mrs. Grey. What has the poor lake ever done to you?"

Mrs. Grey didn't reply, but transferred her damp bundle to my arms. "Poor Hat, it's a wonder she gets any sleep at all, sharing my suite." She shook her head ruefully.

Josie laughed. "Now see here, Juliana, these need to be put through the wash. And don't you listen to a thing Mrs. Grey says! It's a very nice lake, indeed. Look at the lads out there fishing! I wonder if they're catching anything." She fixed me with her cool gaze. "Do you like to fish, Juliana?"

"Not really," I mumbled over the top of the mountain of dirty towels.

"Ah, well, then you've never gone fishing with our Hugh! I wanted him to take you—you could have had the morning off. Perhaps tomorrow. Maybe even this afternoon! It would be lovely, and give you two a chance to know each other better."

Pippa and her mum exchanged a *look*.

"Well, maybe," I said brightly. "And I'm sure Duncan loves fishing. I'll invite him too."

"Then I'll go as well!" Pippa declared.

"Oh no!" said Josie. She frowned. "I can't have both of you taking time off. Now, you have a lot of work to do. Come with me, Pip." And she took Pippa's hand and practically pulled her over to the pool area.

Mrs. Grey met my eyes. "Mrs. Foxworth is an incorrigible matchmaker, I'm afraid. She's got her eye on you, I think, as a match for Hugh, though he's a bit old for you, I'd say. And my Hat has fancied him for years. She adores him, and I think in his heart of hearts he feels the same for her. They'll make a beautiful couple, that's what I've always thought."

"Hat doesn't need to worry," I said. "Hugh isn't my type. Plus he's my cousin!"

"Well, cousins do marry, you know, dear. In fact, Josie once tried to fix me up with a distant cousin of mine—lives over in Hethel, the next village. I hardly knew him, but he was her accountant! A chap half my age!" Her lined cheeks reddened.

So other people were noticing how Josie was steering me toward Hugh. It wasn't just my imagination. I smiled back at Mrs. Grey, shifting my armload of towels. "I'd have thought Grandfather would be a better match for you," was all I said.

"Bless you, child. But Lloyd and I are just good old friends." Her eyes took on a faraway look as she gazed out at the shimmering lake. "No, there was only ever one man for me, there was. Just the one, and then he died."

"When did your husband die?" I asked politely.

Mrs. Grey turned a puzzled look on me. "Oh," she said. "Alf?" Mrs. Grey frowned, considering. "It's been about fifteen years now. He was a good sort of man, was our Alf. Born and raised right in the village. Always had his eye on me, he did. Told everyone there was no lovelier lass than little Edie March! Sweet sort of chap he was, but I liked working here at Heatherstone. Didn't want to leave it to go live in some little cottage over in the village. But he said I could keep working here, if Lady Diana didn't mind my being married. Servants in those days usually didn't marry, did you know that? Stopped working if they did. But she didn't mind, and so it worked out really well. We married and lived in the village, but I came here nearly every day. He was a kind husband and a loving dad…We had just the one son, you know—our Richard. He's Hat's dad. He always was a good lad, and Hat's just like him, but she doesn't see him much. He's in sales. Always on the road for his job."

"Hat said her mum left the family?"

"Oh, she's barmy, that one is. A real loony. Ran off when Hat was a baby, she did, and just as well! I've heard she's remarried half a dozen times, and lives somewhere down London way. Never did make a proper home for Hat. I had moved back to Heatherstone Hall after my Alf died, and I was glad to have wee Hat come stay with me here after her mum left. I raised her right here, and she loves this old place as I do."

"And she'd like to settle down here—with Hugh?"

"Ah, yes. It would be a perfect match. And young Hugh could do worse than our Hat, I'll tell you that much! She's clever and smart, and loyal as the day is long. And I'm not just saying that because she's my granddaughter. I can just imagine the two of them living here at Heatherstone, running the hotel. Ross would like to bring Hugh into the business, you know. And once Hat has done her cookery course, she'll be able to take over running the restaurant. Ahh, it'll be lovely. Almost as if they were the lord and lady, just like years ago."

Mrs. Grey was certainly a gran with a plan, I thought. But it had just become clear to me—and I wondered why I hadn't see it before—why Josie was pushing me at Hugh. If I were to marry him, it wouldn't matter if Grandfather made me his heir instead of Ross. I'd be in the Foxworth family, and could run the place with Hugh someday. Hugh knew very well what Hat was hoping for, but he seemed ready to play along with his parents' plan for him—with me. Was this a warped version of the old expression, 'if you can't beat them, join them?' As in: if you can't kill the heir, marry her?

Out on the lake, the rowboat was nearing shore. Maybe Hugh's ears were burning. Maybe he knew Mrs. Grey was talking about him and I was thinking about him because—though he was still quite far from shore—he raised one arm in a wave. At my side, Mrs. Grey waved back enthusiastically.

I crossed my arms and turned away.

19

Hat and I walked through the dining room after lunch, clearing dishes onto our large trays when the guests were finished. I planned to go looking for Grandfather, but stopped to chat with Herr Stifelmeyer, who sat alone in the guest's dining room with his newspaper.

"Do you have a good aim, Juliana?" he asked. "Are you clever with the bow and arrow, like the American Indians?"

"I've tried archery only once before," I told him. "At school. Why do you ask?"

"Well, now that the rain has stopped, Mr. Foxworth will be setting up the targets. We must try our luck."

Hat stopped at his table. "And are you keen on badminton and croquet?"

"I shall stick to target practice," Herr Stifelmeyer said. "Something I can do from my wheelchair."

"Lawn games are terribly popular with the guests, Juliana," Hat explained as we carried our trays back to the kitchen. "They can get quite competitive."

"And they appreciate it when the staff joins in," Mrs. Grey added. "So I hope you'll both make some time to play with them later today, after we serve Afternoon Tea."

"Sure," I said. "I'd like to."

In the kitchen the rest of the staff sat around the big table, talking in low voices. Duncan, Pippa, and Bee were chatting together at one end; Ross and Josie had their heads together at the other. John Bainbridge was talking to his wife in the doorway; Mina was leaving now to go to her clinic. No one seemed to be talking about Lewis Paine, yet his presence was there. Though his chair at the table stood empty, I kept expecting to hear his sardonic voice ring out among the others as I helped myself to a bowl of Mrs. Grey's fragrant beef and barley soup. I sat down at the table next to Duncan, who was nearly finished with his meal. Hugh came striding into the kitchen with a blue plastic bucket, sloshing water onto the floor. I could see half a dozen fish flopping about.

"Hugh, darling!" Josie looked pleased. "I thought you'd gone back to university with the lads. Look at that catch!"

"Lovely pike, and a few bream. They're practically leaping into the boat. The guys and I are planning to stay for the games. But we'll eat at the flat tonight—have a bloody good fry-up tonight for our supper." He turned his high voltage smile on the housekeeper. "How about it, Mrs. Grey? Half for you and half for me if you'll gut them."

"It's a deal, lad," said Mrs. Grey, taking the bucket from him. "But you should try Hat's fish sometime. Now there's a fine cook for you. In fact, the two of you will make a lovely pair, you running the hotel someday and Hat running a five-star restaurant."

Hugh smiled at the housekeeper. "You've got us betrothed already, eh, Mrs. Grey?"

"Ah, well, a granny can dream, can't she?"

"Gran, you're embarrassing me," said Hat, but she was smiling— smiling right at Hugh.

Hugh winked at her, then turned and winked at me. "Mums have their dreams, too, don't they, Mum?"

"Stop this nonsense, all of you," Josie snapped. "Hugh isn't marrying anybody just now. Now please mop up that water you've spilled, Hugh, and get on back to work with your father."

"I'll do that for you," said Mrs. Grey, taking the towel from Hugh. "Yes, go. Listen to your mum and hurry on to help your father set up the lawn games. Now that the rain has stopped and everything is dry enough, the guests will enjoy a few rounds of croquet or some archery."

"I love badminton!" said Hat.

"How about it, Juliana?" Hugh said, turning to me with his breezy grin. "How about I challenge you to a game of badminton. Or archery if you'd rather. I'm a pretty good shot, I warn you. Belong to the university archery club."

"Hugh has taken me there several times, haven't you, Hugh?" Hat said. "I'm getting better, aren't I?"

"You've come on pretty well," he said without looking at her. "How about it, Juliana? What's your game?"

His words said one thing but seemed to be asking something else. I watched as Hat's expression grew sober. She crossed her arms and leaned against the counter, watching Hugh, watching me.

"Duncan and I will play badminton against you and Hat," I replied. "Doubles. How about that?"

Hat smiled at me.

"And what about me?" demanded Pippa. "I want to play doubles!"

"You can play with Bee," I said firmly.

"Oh," said Josie. "I think Bee should stay out of games until after the baby comes. No, Juliana, you and Hugh will make fine partners, and Pippa and Hat can fight over who partners Duncan. Mix things up a little."

"Ooh," said Pippa, wrapping her arms around Duncan's waist from behind. The girl was shameless. "Let's have a wrestling match to see who gets to play."

I'd wrestle her right down the hill and into the lake.

"I'd have you down on the mat so fast you wouldn't know what hit you," Duncan said with a grin, disengaging himself.

"Ooh!" squealed Pippa in delight. "Let's try it!"

I was getting a splitting headache.

"Bee is perfectly able to play badminton," said Mina Fuller to Josie. "Don't fuss."

Josie laughed lightly. "I'm just trying to get the games going."

"Thanks, Mum, but we can handle things ourselves," said Pippa. She moved away from Duncan—finally—and went over to her brother. She stood on tiptoe to whisper something to him, glancing back me. I couldn't hear what she said next, but Hugh laughed. They moved apart.

Josie was muttering something to Ross. He glanced over at me, too.

What? Had I sprouted blue horns or something?

Mrs. Grey set a small pot of tea and a pitcher of milk on a tray. "I'll just nip up and take this to Lloyd. Dr. Fuller says he ought to stay in bed this afternoon to rest his lungs. But he insists he's getting up for the games. Bee, dear, will you get those fish ready for the fry pan?"

"I won't," declared Bee. "I usually love a good fish-and-chip dinner, but these days I come over all wobbly just thinking about nasty fish. And if I take one more look at those flopping creatures"—she gestured toward the blue pail—"I shall be violently ill."

"It's because of the baby," Hat said soothingly. "Don't worry, Granny. I'll do the fish…and I'll teach Hugh how to do it. A man ought to know these things." She dimpled up at Hugh. "Especially a man who's going to run this hotel with me some day."

Hugh grinned at her, but shook his head.

"Here—" I said in exasperation. "Let me take that tray up to Grandfather, Mrs. Grey." This would be a good time to talk to Grandfather, I figured. "I won't be long," I added, because Josie was looking pointedly at the clock on the wall. She was *such* a slave-driver, as well as a schemer and a plotter.

Was she also a murderer?

"Thank you, dear," Mrs. Grey said to me. "Don't wake him if he's asleep. Just leave the tea by his bedside."

I backed through the swinging door with my load, then climbed the narrow back stairs, careful not to spill a drop, checking for anything that might block my path.

Outside Grandfather's room I balanced the tray carefully and knocked. When there was no answer, I opened the heavy door and stepped into dim quiet.

The room was large and simply furnished with a large carved bed, two small bedside tables, an armchair, and a dresser. The dresser held a small television, but the bedside tables were bare of books or any other personal things. I didn't see any sign of Grandfather—until I looked over to the alcove by the heavily curtained windows. He lay asleep, tucked into a hospital bed under a light brown blanket. His gray head rested on a pile of white pillows. The bed was angled so Grandfather was nearly sitting up, but the rails along the sides of the bed kept him from rolling out. A hospital table on wheels, piled high with magazines and newspapers, stood near the bed, and there were stacks of books on the floor next to it. Another armchair was pulled up near the bed.

I approached quietly. "Grandfather? Here's your tea…" I could hear his wheezing; I could see the struggle of his chest to rise and fall with each labored breath. He didn't stir. I realized then that this grandfather I hardly knew was sicker than he'd led me to believe. Could it really be true that he wouldn't live long?

I felt a stab of loss. I didn't want to be his heir; I wanted *him*.

I hesitated, then balanced the tray on top of his magazines, and positioned the table so he could reach it when he woke. I wasn't sure how long the tea would stay hot, but Mrs. Grey had covered the pot with a quilted tea cozy patterned with daisies. It made a cheerful splash of color in this somber room of whites and browns. Should I stay here and talk to him when he woke up? Should I go ahead and wake him now—and tell him my worries about the Foxworths?

But no, he loved those people. They were the only family he had, besides me. I would need real proof that Ross and Josie wanted me out of the picture.

Out of the picture, in this case, was a pleasant euphemism for *dead.*

"Pssst!" A noise at the door made me turn, and there was Hugh. He beckoned to me. I looked back at Grandfather, who wheezed on steadily. It was so strange that I didn't know how I should feel around this cousin of mine: irritated, or terrified?

I settled for plain *cross.* "What do you want?"

"I came up to get you." He looked over at the alcove. "The old chap looks pretty sad, lying there like that."

"It is sad," I murmured.

"A good reason never to start smoking, eh?" He smiled down at me. "Anyway, I've come to fetch you back downstairs. Mum wants you in the spa—on the double."

I sighed. "I'm on my way." But he caught my shoulders as I started past him out the door.

"Little cousin, you're a beauty, did you know that?" he asked me, his voice husky. "And—er—I love the way you wear your hair."

I pulled out of his grip. "Look, Hugh, give it up. I know perfectly well that your mum and Pippa are trying to push us together, but we don't have to play along! Just go back to—whatever. Novel writing. Bookkeeping. Cleaning fish. Setting up badminton nets!" We heard a cough and a splutter from Grandfather's alcove. "Oh, now you've woken him up."

"Wait just a mo—" Hugh said, and turned to close Grandfather's bedroom door. "We're not through with this conversation…"

"We are totally and completely through," I said and darted out of the room, away from him. Quick as a flash I rounded the corner at the end of the hall. The narrow flight of stairs led down, but as I heard Hugh's footsteps coming around the corner, I jerked open the nearest door and stepped inside, closing it swiftly. I heard him thudding down the uncarpeted steps to the kitchen, calling my name in a soft voice. "Juliana!"

I found myself standing not in a bedroom, but at the foot of another narrow staircase. Fizzing with annoyance at the nerve of my cousins, I sat on the bottom step.

This whole thing was bizarre.

I looked up at the soft daylight filtering down the staircase from a small window at the top. This must lead to the attic where Grandfather stored boxes of my birthmother's belongings alongside the cast-offs from generations of Heatherstone families.

My grandfather was wheezing downstairs in his bed, my mom was in London, my dad in California, but suddenly Barbara-Elizabeth felt nearby. And as I stood at the top of the attic stairs, I almost imagined I could hear my birthmother whisper my name. *Juliana!*

At the top of the stairs, the narrow attic hallway stretched to the left and to the right, four small rooms in each direction, two on each side, with tall windows at the end of the hallway. Far from being the sort of attic I knew from California houses—cramped crawlspaces under the eaves—this one was an entire floor. Once these would have been servants' quarters, I suspected. I discovered that the four small rooms to the left of the staircase were empty, but the four on the right were full of furniture, boxes, and trunks.

I stood listening to the silence. Where would I start to look for my birthmother's things? Perhaps I'd better ask Grandfather before I poked around. But he was asleep…

I decided I would take a look around. A very quick look.

The first little room was crammed with lumpy shapes draped in sheets of white plastic. A peek underneath the plastic revealed dark furniture—antique chairs, bookshelves, tables—enough for a whole shop. As I was heading for the second little room, a soft thud behind me made me turn. Nothing was there. I paused, listening, waiting. There came a soft shuffling sound. Was someone else already up here?

"Hello?" I said cautiously. Was it one of the maids, bringing something up for storage, or perhaps one of the hotel guests, exploring? "Ryan?" I called. "Dylan?" But neither rambunctious boy materialized.

Was there an animal up here? Maybe a squirrel or mouse? Did Heatherstone Hall have *rats?* I hesitated, but when I heard nothing else, I moved on into the second little room. It was similar to the first: full of shrouded furniture. The third attic room contained boxes and trunks. Some of the boxes were labeled with typed tags: **Summer. Winter. Linens.** Others were labeled in brown ink, in a flowing handwriting. I unlatched the trunk closest to me. Its typed label read: **Pantry.** I blew dust off the latches as I lifted the top. The amount of dust alone proved to me that these things had not been disturbed in many years. The trunk held blue and white china layered between sheets of yellowed newspaper. The paper crumbled when I lifted it, but I was able to make out a date: 11 June, 1895. I opened another trunk. In between the layers of newspaper were folded wool blankets.

My little sister would love being up here with me, uncovering the layers of history packed away, I thought. No doubt if Ivy were here now, she'd be feeling all sorts of ancient *vibes.* Far from feeling vibes, though, I was feeling only a desperate tickle in my nose from all the dust.

I sneezed. Sneezed again, harder. Dust mites floated in the air like fairy dust. Closing the lid of the trunk, I made my way around the boxes toward the small casement window. It wasn't easy to open, but after struggling with the handle, I managed to push it out a few inches. The rush of damp summer air was very welcome.

As I was turning away from the window, I spied another trunk, farther back toward the window. I unlatched the catches and lifted the lid, and the reek of camphor assailed my nose, bringing on another sneezing fit despite the open window. *Mothballs,* I thought.

I peeked at dresses and coats, shoes and hats, all in a style I recognized from old movies—cheap, wartime clothes, probably, but in excellent condition. Grandfather—or Mrs. Grey, if they belonged to her—should sell these things to a theater group, I mused. They'd probably get a lot of money for them.

There was a smaller trunk, the size of a large shoe box, pushed back in the far corner, with the initials E.L. painted in flowing gold handwriting. I opened the single latch and looked inside; there were perfume bottles, hair brushes, a nurse's cap. And, at the bottom, a thick home-made envelope fashioned out of blue-checked paper. It was labeled 'Housekeeping Hints' in neat, faded, black print. It looked too old to have been my birthmother's. But maybe it had belonged to *her* mother. I sat down on top of the large trunk and opened the envelope.

Inside were letters, some in envelopes, some just folded sheets of stationary. There were also slips of paper and what looked like pages torn from an account book or ledger, with carefully printed house-keeping expenses. This looked like the sort of miscellany you would find inside anyone's top desk drawer; why had this particular mess been so carefully stored away?

I picked out a couple of scraps and read them:

> *Bed 7. Liquids only.*
> *Bed 9. No dairy.*
> *Bed 14. Poached prunes 2X per day.*
> *Bed 15. Turn patient every two hours to prevent bed-sores.*

These sounded like doctor's or nurse's notes from when Heather-stone Hall was a military hospital. Fascinated, I kept reading, and my guess was validated when the next paper I turned over was a recipe cut from a newspaper. The date at the top was 15 August, 1943, and the recipe was for something called "A Tasty Victory Sponge." This turned out to be a cake made with no eggs or sugar, and the directions exhorted the housewife to make careful use of her weekly rations to provide occasional sweets for her family.

Then I examined the letters that were inside envelopes. I slid off one of the old brown rubber bands, and it broke immediately into three brittle strands. I picked up the first envelope and squinted at the date of the postmark. It was smudged but I could make out 1940-something. I slid the single sheet of paper out of the envelope, feeling a stab of conscience because my parents had drummed into me that reading other people's mail was wrong. But I reminded myself that Grandfather had said I was welcome to look through his old things, so I read it anyway:

> *August 12, 1943*
> *Heatherstone Hall*
> *My dearest, darlingest Dorian—*
> *My sweetest love. I am so relieved you're home, even in this wretched state. I know your injuries pain you, but at least they are the sort that will heal in time. I know you will be a good patient and do as the doctors tell you, and you'll soon be fit as that proverbial fiddle once again. It is a privilege for me to nurse you. Please get strong and well—fast. Those are nurse's orders!*
> *Your E.*

I smoothed the paper with my finger. How old it was...How long it had been packed away...And yet—how the powerful emotion seemed to flow off the page just as it had when it was first written. A love letter! A letter to Dorian, the heir to Heatherstone Hall, from his army nurse. I wanted to sit right here and read through all the letters. I wanted to show Duncan! And I knew Grandfather would want to see them—

Then I heard a sound nearby, a soft shuffle. I sucked in my breath and stuffed the letters back in their blue-checked holder. The sound—the pad of footsteps—was receding. Someone had been up here with me and was now heading downstairs? Who was it?

I carried the blue-checked envelope with me as I edged out of the room. Just as I arrived at the top of the stairwell, the door at the bottom closed with an audible click.

Okay, I told myself, probably those annoying American boys were playing spies.

I wouldn't let myself start thinking it was anybody with more sinister intent. After all, there were no urns to fall on me here. But I'd be in big trouble with Josie if I didn't get down to the spa pretty soon. I hesitated at the top of the stairs, then turned back and hastily investigated the last small attic room.

Here there were six cardboard boxes. These boxes were newer, and they were labeled on their sides in scrawled black marker, in handwriting I recognized from the letter Grandfather had sent inviting me to visit Heatherstone Hall. The labels on four of the boxes read: *Family Photos. Christmas. Tax Records. Train Set.* And then the last two were both labeled the same way: *Misc. Stuff—Barbara-Elizabeth.*

I was aware that I was supposed to be down in the spa, that no one knew I was up here except the little bratty spies, that Josie was probably fuming, but now that I'd found not one, but *two* boxes with my birthmother's name on them, I just had to look inside. Whatever was in these boxes connected me to her.

The first box was heavy. I pulled it over to the doorway and opened the flaps. Notebooks. School papers. Half a dozen hardcover books—adventure and mystery novels by Enid Blyton, who, I knew from my mom, had been a prolific and popular British children's author. There were also some well-thumbed paperback romance novels, the pages dog-eared.

I wanted to read every single one of these books, because Barbara-Elizabeth had once read them.

In the second box I found a pair of white baby shoes, and a folded blue jacket that looked as if it would fit my little sister. I wondered what memory the jacket would evoke for my grandfather, and felt a stab of sadness as I pictured him packing this box, deciding which of his run-away daughter's possessions to save. There were three spiral notebooks of old school notes. I stroked my finger over the ink.

Barbara-Elizabeth's own handwriting, and looking very like my own. I knew I would read every word without caring if they were only Biology notes or vocabulary lists. And there was also a white jewelry box with a picture of a ballerina on top. I opened it to find a tangle of cheap chains, beads, and dangly plastic earrings. At the very bottom of the cardboard carton was a stuffed animal—a faded black-and-white penguin.

As I lifted it out, I felt something wrap around me—a warm, loving feeling. Was this one of the vibes Ivy often felt? Or one of my own memories, however distant, of the first mother I'd ever had? The stuffed penguin smelled faintly of flowers—a flowery perfume? Barbara's scent? I buried my face in the soft fleece.

Then, from far below me I heard my name being called.

I ran along the passage, clattered down the wooden stairs and stepped out of the little closet into the wider hallway. "Pippa, I'm here!" I called.

Agatha Moggs, her penetrating eyes alight with curiosity and cunning, peered at me from around her bedroom door. "Ah, finally down from the attic, are we? Been up there having a look around, eh?" She nodded sagely.

Old busybody, I thought.

"Oh, there you are!" cried Pippa, coming out of Grandfather's room and closing the door. "Where have you been? Mum is *that* furious with you!"

Agatha Moggs, nodding and grinning like a wrinkled Cheshire Cat, retreated into her room and closed the door…but not all the way.

"Um…sorry. I got…sort of sidetracked." I didn't mention I'd been escaping from her brother when I discovered the attic stairs. "I'll come down right now. But look, can you help me? There are some boxes I found—"

"Well, okay…but we'd better be fast." Pippa followed me upstairs. "What were you doing snooping around up here? Mrs. Grey will be spitting nails; she always says no one's to mess about in the attic."

"Well, Grandfather told me some of my birthmother's things were stored up here. He said I could look through them."

I led Pippa to the room with Barbara's boxes. I packed the penguin carefully back with the spiral notebooks. "I want both these boxes," I said. "Will you help me?"

We stacked the lighter box on top of the one with the books inside, and slid them across the floor and down the hall to the staircase. "Wait just a sec—" I hurried back down the hall. I slipped back into the third room and picked up the blue-checked envelope. "There's this, too," I told Pippa. "Some really old letters that Grandfather will want to see." I balanced the 'Housekeeping Hints' envelope on top of Barbara's boxes, and we lugged everything down the attic stairs, nearly crashing into Hat, who was passing in the hallway just outside the attic door as we kicked it open.

She carried a wicker basket full of clean linens, and nearly dropped it. "Bloody hell!"

"Sorry, Hat!" Pippa and I exclaimed together, skirting around her with our boxes.

"To my bedroom," I directed Pippa, and we headed down the hall. We had to set the boxes on the floor while I unlocked my door.

Hat walked over to us. She scooped two rolled towels from her basket and handed them to me. "Clean towels for your bathroom."

"Oh, thanks." I opened my door and nudged my birthmother's boxes inside the room.

"What's that lot?" she asked, nodding at them.

"Just some of my birthmother's old books and school stuff," I said. "From the attic. Grandfather said I can have them."

"And some old letters." said Pippa. "Maybe they're love letters that your mum got from her boyfriends!"

"No, they're older than that," I said. "War-time letters."

"Really!" Hat looked intrigued.

"I know Grandfather will want to see them," I said. Then just as we were about to leave the room, Duncan came along the hallway. "Hey!" I felt my smile stretching across my face and my cheeks growing warm.

"Hullo, my Yankee Beauty," he said, stopping at my open doorway.

Hat snorted.

"What are we, chopped liver?" Pippa asked Hat.

"And ecstatic greetings to all English beauties, too, of course." Duncan's smile was friendly, but his eyes were on me.

"You two go ahead," I said to the other girls. "We'll be down in a minute."

"Oooh!" hooted Hat. "Time for a quickie!"

"Mum's going to kill you," Pippa sighed, glancing longingly back over her shoulder at Duncan.

"Come on, Pip," said Hat teasingly. "Let's leave them to it."

When we were alone, Duncan stepped into the room and wrapped his arms around me. "How are you doing? I've been worrying about you all day."

"No attempts on my life so far." I kept my tone light. "But Josie's going to strangle me if I don't get down to the spa." I struggled against him because the blue-checked envelope was crushed between us.

"That's a woman with no romance in her soul." He stepped back and smoothed the envelope. "Sorry. I got carried away."

"No problem," I said. "It's a bunch of old wartime hospital notes, and some letters. Love letters, maybe. I'm bringing it all down to show my grandfather."

Duncan took the envelope in one hand and reached for my braid with the other. "I'd rather get on with *modern* romance than read about old-timey ones," he said, winding my long braid around his hand.

"Me too," I said, "if I can wrench you away from Pippa's clutches." I stowed the homemade blue-checked envelope in the deep pocket of my apron.

"Ah, she's all right," he said. "But I'd rather hang out with you." His eyes were bright and his lips warm as we kissed again. "Want to be my partner for badminton doubles?"

"I want to be your partner—period," I murmured. Then we ran downstairs together and went our separate ways: he to finish hauling compost for the flower garden before setting up the badminton and croquet games, and I to slave for Josie at the spa.

20

When I entered the atrium, Josie shot me a *look*, but didn't say anything. I knew she wanted to chew me out, but she was ushering a guest into the massage alcove, and it would hardly be professional if she started scolding me over the lilting notes of the peaceful, meditative music playing. I turned away and opened the dryer. I pulled out the freshly cleaned towels and started folding them as I'd been taught: in half, then again, turn and roll up…The compactly rolled towels fit neatly into the wicker baskets placed in strategic spots around the pool and hot tub.

"Juliana, do you have a minute?" Grandfather called to me. He was sitting at a table in the snack bar with Hugh and Herr Stifelmeyer.

"Yes, please would you join us for a minute?" Herr Stifelmeyer indicated an empty chair at their table.

In the alcove behind me, Josie sighed audibly.

"I'll just be a second," I muttered in Josie's direction, and abandoned the towels.

She stepped out of the alcove to glare at me, hands on hips. "I'm sure I don't know what your grandfather is paying you for. You've had more time off than you've had on the job."

I bit back whatever comment I might say in reply; it was sure to be unpleasant.

I walked over to the men, smiled at Herr Stifelmeyer and Grandfather, and avoided looking at Hugh. Talk about awkward.

"Hugh told me you were looking for me after lunch," Grandfather said to me. "Found me snoring in my bed."

"I was bringing up your tea," I said. "And I wanted to ask if I could look up in the attic. You were sleeping, so I went up there anyway. I hope that was okay."

Hugh winked at me.

Jerk!

"Of course," Grandfather said heartily. "Though there's not much up there but my junk, and Mrs. Grey's stuff, and some old Heatherstone family bits and bobs. Did you find anything of Barb's?"

"Yes, I did!" I grinned at him. "A couple boxes with books and school notes in them, and a stuffed penguin. I hope you don't mind."

"Of course I don't. And if you'd like to have anything of hers, it's yours. Take the lot. She was your mum, after all."

"Old Heatherstone family bits and bobs, you say?" Herr Stifelmeyer's sharp blue eyes lit with interest. "What does this mean, *bits and bobs?*"

"Assorted junk nobody needs anymore," translated Hugh.

"Well, there might be something interesting," I replied. "I saw a couple of old trunks. And inside I found old papers and stuff. I think they were written during the war."

"Papers?" Grandfather looked intrigued.

"The war?" Herr Stifelmeyer frowned.

"Notes about patients, maybe written by a doctor or nurse," I said. "And, best of all, love letters! At least I think they are. From that guy—Dorian Heatherstone? And his girlfriend who was a nurse."

"Could be quite a story there," said Hugh. I kept forgetting he was a writer, or wanted to be. Of course he'd be on the lookout for material for the novels he planned to write.

Grandfather's eyes brightened. "Excellent. Capital! I'd very much like to see these papers. You, too, Otto?"

Herr Stifelmeyer nodded. "Ach, yes, I would enjoy that. Voices from the past."

I had my hand in my apron pocket, about to bring out the blue-checked envelope to show them, when Mrs. Grey came up behind me, pushing the snack trolley. Hat was at her side, arms laden with the empty coffee urn.

"What's all this about voices?" the housekeeper inquired sharply. "Are you telling your silly ghost stories again, Lloyd?"

"Not at all, Edith," he replied, his eyes twinkling. "I know you don't approve of such nonsense. No, indeed. It's just that Juliana was up in the attic—"

"The attic!" The housekeeper's brow furrowed. "Oh dear, it's probably very dusty up there. I haven't gone up for ages."

"You're the most organized person I know, Gran," replied Hat. "I'm sure Juliana can survive a little dust."

"I have survived," I told Mrs. Grey, smiling. "It was fine."

"Oh, well, that's all right, then," said Mrs. Grey, smiling back at me.

"Juliana found some letters from Dorian Heatherstone and his nurse," said Grandfather. "The lass who died of a broken heart."

Hat made a strange sort of snort. Maybe she didn't believe in broken hearts. "It's all just old news," she said dismissively. "Nothing worth looking at, if you ask me."

Not that I'd been asking her.

"Such a long time ago," said Grandfather. "Wasn't it, Edith?"

"Indeed it was. " Mrs. Grey smiled distractedly. "So long ago as to be of no interest now whatsoever. What is of interest is whether you two old soldiers are going to have a swim! I'm sure Hugh will help you in and out of the pool."

"Of course," said Hugh with his charming grin and a dramatically low bow to both men. "That's what I'm here for."

"I wasn't planning anything so strenuous as a real swim," Grandfather said with a rueful laugh. "Just a nice time in the hot tub for a few minutes. We've got to carry on as usual, eh? And the hot water is wonderful for getting the blood moving."

Mrs. Grey shuddered. "I have never liked the water," she said.

"And I like it less now."

"Ah, but you used to like swimming very much," trilled Miss Agatha Moggs, walking into the atrium with her sister, Sue-Sue, in tow. "I recall you were the nurse who offered swimming lessons to those soldiers who did not know how." Miss Moggs turned to her sister. "It was quite brazen of her, really. But, then, we all looked quite fetching in our swimming costumes back in those days."

Sue-Sue tittered behind her hand.

"You've got me mixed up with someone else, Agatha," said Mrs. Grey with a shudder. "I've never liked the water, but I do remember *you* were quite an exhibition diver."

"I did love a good high dive," Miss Moggs said complacently. "I was quite amazing, or so people said. Not," she added quickly, "that I ever had much time for swimming. Worked to the bone, I was. Day in and day out…"

She and Sue-Sue found chairs by the pool and settled into them. "I've always liked to watch young lovers," Agatha remarked loudly, nodding at a pair of honeymooners smooching at the side of the pool. "Never get tired of it! It's all right for some, isn't it? But as for me, I never got much chance at romance, worked to the bone as I was…"

We all tuned her out.

"So how about it, Herr Stifelmeyer?" asked Hugh. "Are you going in the hot tub?"

"*Jawohl,*" the old German replied. "I enjoy the heat on my legs. But I am quite able to climb in and out myself, thank you."

He demonstrated this by heaving himself out of the wheelchair just as Josie came out of the massage alcove and stalked over to the snack bar, with Pippa at her heels. "Juliana, have you finished with your chat? If so, the towels are waiting your attentions. Pippa has done more than her share."

"When you have finished your towels, lass, come back and show us those letters," said Grandfather.

"What letters are these?" asked Josie sharply.

"Old ones she found up in the attic," said Grandfather.

"Snooping around," murmured Josie under her breath, but I heard her just fine. She frowned at me and I glared back. She made her voice falsely bright and said, "All right, Pippa, Hat, Juliana—you girls all get back to your work, please." As Pippa and Hat followed Mrs. Grey off to do whatever else needed doing, Josie added to me in a low voice, "You are not a pampered guest on holiday here. And don't you forget it! "

Fuming, I carried a basket of towels over to the hot tub as Herr Stifelmeyer and Grandfather eased themselves down into the bubbles with sighs of contentment. I averted my eyes from that foaming water but still felt again the nudge of Lew's body underwater, bumping against my legs.

I shivered despite the steamy air around me. Even among all these people, I felt very alone. Across the spa I saw Josie laugh at something Pippa had said and put an arm around her daughter's shoulders. It was unusual to see Josie being affectionate.

Suddenly, very badly, I wanted my mom. Not Barbara-Elizabeth, but my own mom who was far away in London being a trendy artist and getting written up in the newspapers. I wanted her to throw down her paintbrush and loop her arm around my shoulders, and keep me safe.

Across the room, Josie glowered at me with narrowed eyes.

*   *

The afternoon passed slowly. Back at the snack bar there was talk of ghosts. The American mother listened agog to one of the honeymooning couples, who had been walking by the lake that very morning…

"And we both saw them, didn't we, Ron?" The young woman in her sleek black bathing suit sat at the small table, wrapped only in a towel after her fifty laps. She and her husband were waiting for Mrs.

Grey to serve their coffee.

Her husband, Ron, chuckled. "Well, we saw some people walking, just as we were walking, darling," he said, his tone slightly guarded. "But we don't know they were ghosts."

I was wiping off the empty tables and could hear everything they said. Probably he knew this and didn't want anyone thinking *he* believed in ghosts. But the woman had no such qualms.

"We both saw them vanish. You know we did." She nodded vigorously, and the American woman leaned toward her. "What could they be if not ghosts?"

"What did they look like?" the American asked eagerly.

"Ever so focused on each other, they were. He was leaning on her arm and carried a walking stick in the other. Limped quite a bit. But they were gazing at each other—the way you used to gaze at me, Ron!"

Both women looked over at Ron and giggled.

Ron saw me watching this exchange and shrugged. "It was strange," he acknowledged. "They were there, walking just ahead of us. Then it started to drizzle, and Judi and I turned to go in. When we looked back, they were gone. Just—gone."

"Maybe they went into the boat house to get out of the rain," I suggested.

I remembered what Duncan had seen. This sounded like the same couple.

"It was locked," the woman said. "I checked when we first came down from the house because Ron was going to take me out in one of the rowboats."

"Oooh," said the American enviously. "I'd love to see a ghost."

"I've seen a couple sort of like that," I volunteered. "A few times, actually. Walking just as you said, down by the lake. And then the mist came down and I couldn't see them anymore. Duncan has seen them, too."

Judi and Ron turned eager, wondering eyes to me.

But Mrs. Grey's voice was brisk as she arrived at the table with their coffee. "There are no ghosts here," asserted Mrs. Grey. "Absolutely not. It's crazy to think so."

"I think it's romantic," sighed Judi. "They looked so in love!"

"Star-crossed lovers from some ancient time," suggested the American.

"Not very ancient," said Ron. "They were wearing ordinary clothes. Well, not exactly ordinary, but not ancient. It was a little strange, actually. I think the man was in a bathrobe!"

"Probably both were stark naked under their robes, and they just jumped into the lake," cackled Agatha Moggs from her chair by the pool some distance from the snack bar. She was sitting there with her sister, Sue-Sue, still ogling the swimmers. But she seemed to have excellent hearing for a woman her age. "Probably just lovebirds out for a morning swim."

Sue Sue tittered behind her hand. "Oh, Sister! Stark naked!"

"Well, they aren't guests at this hotel," Judi said firmly. "Not that I've seen, anyway. And there was no sign of anyone in the water…"

"Complete and utter nonsense," muttered Mrs. Grey, moving to the next table with the coffee pot. But her face looked pale, and I wondered if maybe she *did* believe in ghosts, after all.

* *

At four o'clock tea and scones were served in the conservatory, but Josie pointed out that I had missed considerable work time while snooping (*her* word, of course) in the attic, and so I was to skip the tea and scones and remain in the spa until dinner was ready to be served.

"What about archery out on the lawn?" I asked. "Mrs. Grey wanted me out there to play games with the guests."

"I think you've forfeited your time for games today, don't you?" replied Josie.

You're just like mean old Mrs. Brooks, keeping me in from recess in third grade for giggling with my friends, I thought. But I smiled tightly. "No problem, Josie."

I swept the floor and checked the chlorine levels, and sat at a little table in the snack bar eating a package of potato crisps. I watched idly while one of the honeymooning men swam lap after lap, his body slicing through the water, somersaulting under to kick off, and then slicing through again in the opposite direction. I wondered why he was already wanting time alone; presumably his new wife was sipping tea and chomping Mrs. Grey's delicious scones and would soon be battling someone in badminton or croquet. As if he'd heard my thoughts and felt a stab or two of jealousy, the guy jumped out, grabbed a towel, and left the atrium.

Now I was alone. I could see people jumping around outside on the lawn, presumably hitting the birdy. I could see others lining up with croquet mallets in hand, striving to hit colored wooden balls through the course of hoops. Further away, near the tall green wall of the maze, two archery targets had been set up.

I pulled out my cell phone and phoned my mom in London. She answered on the first ring, her voice sounding clipped and professional, and much more British than it used to. It seemed the longer we lived in England, the more she reverted to her previous, pre-American, self. "Hedda Martin," she said. She'd dropped Dad's name—Drake—from our family last name of Martin-Drake practically as soon as we'd moved to England.

"Hi Mom."

"Jule! Darling, how are you doing?" I could hear the smile in her voice. "I thought you were the gallery owner ringing me back. We're having a little problem with the lighting…"

"I wanted to hear your voice."

Mom's voice lost its professional veneer. "What's going on? Are you all right?"

"Yes…" My voice trailed off. I wasn't sure why I'd called, but I was clutching my phone pretty tightly.

"Are you upset about that cousin's death? Silly question—of course you are. But I mean, are you *very* upset? Shall I come collect you? It's what I said in my email; you don't have to stay there with strangers, you know. You must come to me here in London! I'm staying in a lovely little flat, but there's plenty of room for you as well. It'll be heaps of fun."

I half wanted to leave, to join her in London in her little flat. It would be interesting visiting all the museums and galleries, to help her set up her special exhibition, to see her in her professional persona. Hedda Martin, *emerging artist extraordinaire,* as last month's review in the *London Times* had said. *A bright new star ascending. Someone to watch.*

"They're not strangers," I found myself saying instead.

"Well, practically strangers!"

"They're my birth family, Mom. Except for the guests, of course. And staff." Why in the world was I claiming Ross and Josie, Pippa and Hugh as my own?

Mom was silent. Then she sighed. "Well, if you don't want to come here, would you like me to come there? I can stay a few days, if you want me. Is that why you rang, Jule?"

Why *had* I called? I pressed the phone to my ear but couldn't think what to answer. I had needed her, needed to hear her voice, needed the safety she'd always provided. I still needed all that. But if I left Heatherstone now, how would Grandfather feel?

I was surprised that how he felt mattered, but it did.

"I'm fine, Mom. I just wanted to say hi." I couldn't tell her about the invisible fishing line or the falling urn, or she'd drive up to get me no matter what I said about wanting to stay. Her voice softened. "Love you, Jule. Text me! Or call anytime."

We said good-bye, and I sat there staring at the still blue water of the pool. Then I looked up to see Duncan outside the spa windows, waving at me. I waved back, and he beckoned me over to him.

I opened the window. "Hey, Handsome."

"All is forgiven," Duncan said. "Or, rather, your grandfather sent me to bring you out no matter what Josie says because Herr Stifelmeyer is asking for you. Seems he's challenging you to hit the bullseye. Talking about cowboys and Indians. Odd sort, really."

"Oh, he's all right." I pocketed my cell phone, eager to get outside. "I just have to lock up here. Hold on a sec." I secured the glass windows and doors of the atrium behind me and together we set off across the lawn.

It was a friendly, fine-spirited group engaged in traditional English summertime garden games. The honeymooning guests, including Ron and Judi, the couple I'd met in the snack bar, played a round of croquet along with Bee, Pippa, and the two handsome university students who had come to fish. Josie and Grandfather stood together, watching Ross and Hugh battling hard at badminton. Father and son both wore frowns of concentration that mirrored the other's. They played in near-silence, grunting occasionally as they strove after a particularly difficult return. I was pretty sure their battle was over more than who could hit the birdy. Did Grandfather and Josie understand that as well?

Then it was time for Duncan and me to play Pippa and Hat. Hat and I should have been a team instead—because at least we were each intent on winning. It seemed to me that Duncan and Pippa were just playing to each other, lobbing easy shots back and forth, smiling and laughing the whole time. Pippa kept making suggestive remarks about the shuttlecock, which is what they call the birdy in England, and Duncan bantered right along with her, until I'd had enough.

I put my hands on my hips. "Some game," I said in disgust. "If you two could stop flirting for ten seconds, maybe we could actually get a volley going!"

"And if you would stop stomping around like some sort of…baboon," Pippa shot back, "maybe you'd be able to hit the shuttlecock someplace other than into the net!"

"Girls, girls," said Duncan in an infuriatingly patronizing voice. "It's only a game."

Hat tossed back her cloud of dark hair, threw down her racket, and wandered off.

I followed suit. So much for *that* game. And *that* partner.

Flirt with Pippa, see if I care. I stormed off after Hat, but she had already disappeared. The American father and mother were trying to interest their boys in the croquet game, which Agatha and Sue-Sue Moggs were winning impressively, but the two boys kept veering toward the archery contest.

Herr Stifelmeyer waved to me. "*Ach*, here comes a worthy opponent!" he called to me jovially. "And Duncan! And Pippa!"

I turned in surprise, and there was Duncan striding along, with Pippa tagging right behind him. "Sorry," he mouthed to me.

"Come here, my young friends!" called Herr Stifelmeyer. "*Jetzt*, let me see you try to hit the—the how do you call it? The cow's eyeball?"

Duncan snorted, and I had to laugh, too. "The *bull's eye*," I corrected. I accepted a lightweight fiberglass bow from the German, and picked up an arrow from the leather holder. "All right—now, stand back and watch this!"

"No, me! Me next, me next!" cried Ryan, the American boy. His mother grabbed him by the shoulders protectively and steered him away from the line of fire.

I let my arrow fly and missed the center by about six inches.

"*Nicht schlecht,*" said the old man, his eyes twinkling. "Not bad at all. But I do not see any tribal talent in you, my dear. Now, Duncan, what about you? Any native Scotsman talent? And then, yes, young Ryan, you shall also have a turn. Perhaps *you* can harness some American Indian talent!"

Duncan's arrow missed by a mere inch. Ryan's went up wildly off course and landed amidst the croquet game. "Oops!" he called.

"In my day, children were kept out of sight and out of trouble," Agatha Moggs informed everyone within hearing distance.

"Oh dear," his mother fretted. "Be careful, boys!"

"Madam, you are next," said Herr Stifelmeyer.

"Oh dear!" The American woman took the next shot, and managed to hit the bale of hay that the target rested upon.

Then it was Herr Stifelmeyer's turn. He lined up his shot carefully, pulled his arm back, and sighted along the arrow. He let the arrow fly…Bull's eye!

Everyone watching applauded. "You always were a good shot, Otto," Grandfather said, and Duncan teased the elderly guest about Ancient Germanic Barbarian Hordes.

We took turns, with more guests coming by to try their hand at it. Hugh managed a bulls-eye, too. Grandfather handed me his cane while he took his turn. His arrow landed in the hay. The hotel guests applauded politely, anyway.

Then John Bainbridge drove up in the tractor, pulling a wagon full of five more bales of hay. Ross and Hugh hurried to unload these, and rolled them into a line. Then John set up five more targets, and all the guests thronged around to try their hand at hitting the 'cow's eyeball.'

"Everyone may try with three arrows," said Ross. "Then it's the next person's turn!"

Dylan, the younger American boy, shot an arrow up into the air and was sternly reprimanded by his father. "You could have hit someone!" he shouted.

The tips of the arrows were sharp, but only pointed wood. *Good thing*, I thought, because now, with all the guests laughing and trying for the bulls-eyes, arrows were flying all around.

Then it was my turn again. I had three chances to make a bulls-eye. The first arrow was off by only three inches. The second lodged in the hay. I sighted carefully along the third. Duncan came up behind me and helped me line up the shot. I leaned back against him and his arms tightened around me.

"Sorry," he whispered again. "She's just such a flirt. It's nothing serious."

Before I could answer that I *guessed* I would forgive him, Herr Stifelmeyer approached us, walking shakily with Mrs. Grey at his side. Duncan moved away.

"Position your arm back a bit," the old German instructed. "Aim carefully. I know you can hit this one! *Ja, gut*—that's right…"

Mrs. Grey had to hold onto his arm as he swayed. "Let's get you back into your wheelchair, Mr. Stifelmeyer," she said solicitously.

"In a minute," he replied. "I want to see Juliana make a bulls-eye."

I lined up my shot while Herr Stifelmeyer and Mrs. Grey watched attentively.

"*Yay!*" shouted Dylan, who must have finally hit a hay bale.

"*Oooh!*" shrieked Pippa.

"*Damn,*" moaned one of the honeymooners, whose arrow had gone astray.

"Good shot, Bee! Pregnant mums rule!"

Arrows whizzed toward the hay bale targets on both sides of me.

The voices of the others receded as I concentrated. I took aim, pulled back my bow…but a whistling sound made me turn my head— a whooshing sound coming from behind me. And that's when I felt the searing burn against my cheek—and heard Herr Stifelmeyer's shout of alarm as I stumbled against him. The two of us fell onto the grass in a tangle.

For just a second, time hung suspended, frozen. I put my hand to my cheek and brought it down, sticky with blood. As I stared at it, incredulous, people surged around us, pulling us up, brushing us off, exclaiming and demanding to know what had happened. In the next instant Duncan's arms were around me.

What happened? I couldn't think, couldn't make sense of it. I stared up at Duncan, then over at Herr Stifelmeyer's ashen face, as

Mrs. Grey and Ross helped him into his wheelchair. The old German raised his arm and pointed with a shaking hand at the target I'd been aiming for. There south of the bulls-eye, was an arrow. He let loose a torrent of harsh, angry words—all in German. I couldn't seem to open my mouth to say anything at all.

Who had shot it? Who had stood behind us and aimed even as I was aiming, with Herr Stifelmeyer's help, at the target? Who had let the arrow fly right at us—so close that had I not turned my face at the last second, the last *split* second, the arrow would have plunged into my neck? Instead, it had whizzed down past me so close it grazed my face, taking off a couple layers of skin.

Stop shooting!" shouted Ross, waving his arms above his head. "Bows and arrows *DOWN*, everybody!"

There was a roaring now in my ears, as I stared around at the scene. The American mom was gathering her sons to her, shrieking at them: "Did you shoot that arrow, Ryan? Did you? *Did* you? *Dylan!* Come here! Didn't I tell you to be careful?"

The honeymooning husbands bent protectively over their brides, leading them away from the games area.

Mina Fuller walked across the lawn from the drive. "What's all the commotion?" she called. "I just arrived and heard screaming!"

Hat hurried across the lawn, clutching her apron. "Is something wrong out here?" Her eyes were wide.

Maggie called from the conservatory door: "Is someone hurt?"

"It's all right, it's all right," Grandfather called to the crowd. "Juliana's just got a scrape. Mr. Stifelmeyer is not hurt. It was just an accident! Too many people letting fly at once. We must all be very careful with the arrows, and wait our turn to shoot."

The American mother gathered her sons close to her, as if fearing they were being accused—and maybe they were. Hugh pushed Herr Stifelmeyer's wheelchair across the lawn to the house. I stayed in the circle of Duncan's arm, and nodded my assurances to Grandfather that I was, indeed, not badly hurt. Mina came over and looked closely at my cheek. "Goodness, that was a close call," she said quietly. "Now let's just get you up to the house for a wash and a plaster," she said.

"Plaster?" I asked, confused. "It's my face—not a broken arm…"

"For your poor cheek," murmured Duncan, coming up to me and nuzzling my ungrazed one. And then I remembered that in England a *plaster* is a bandaid.

Something else tickled at the back of my mind, another memory…something I'd noticed? Something I'd seen? Something I'd realized without realizing that I'd realized it? In a daze I walked with Duncan and Mina back to Heatherstone Hall to wash my face, the two of them marveling over my latest narrow escape.

21

Mrs. Grey hurried after me. "Come to the kitchen and I'll make you a nice cuppa, luv. That's the best thing for jangled nerves, I always find." Her voice was twittery, her offer kindly meant. But I shook my head.

"I'm going up to my room." My head was pounding, and my hands were clenching and unclenching at my sides as I tried to keep my rising panic in check.

"Oh, do you think you should? Is it wise to be alone when you've had such a scare?" She put her hand on my arm and peered earnestly into my face. "What do you think, Dr. Fuller?"

Mina gave me a searching look. "I think she'll be fine. It's a shock, but you're not badly hurt, are you, Juliana?"

I shook my head.

"Well then. I'll leave you in the care of our resident nurse. She'll coddle you a bit. I have to get back to the clinic."

Mrs. Grey fluttered around me. "You're not badly hurt, but you might have been. What kind of holiday has this been for you, poor girl? Just one trouble after another! I hate to think of you alone in your room, brooding."

"She won't be alone," said Duncan tersely, "because I'm going up with her."

"Oh, my goodness—" Mrs. Grey looked alarmed at the impropriety of his announcement.

"What about your work?" asked Josie, coming into the kitchen.

"What about *her* work?"

"It'll get done." Duncan reached for my hand. "Come on, Jule." He looked at the women. "We'll be down in time for dinner."

I didn't appreciate the little smile Hat gave me as we passed her on the stairs, as if she knew what we'd *really* be up to in my bedroom. But I said nothing, just hung onto Duncan.

We climbed up the main staircase in silence, then walked down the hallway to my bedroom. I pulled my key out of my pocket, inserted it in the lock—

But—wait. The door was already unlocked. The doorknob twisted easily in my hand. "That's weird," I said to Duncan. "I know I locked it before I went to the spa…"

Alarm bells in my head rang faintly and then more loudly as he pushed the door open. I gasped at what was revealed through the open doorway.

Complete chaos.

My room was a shambles. Bedding had been hauled off the bed and the mattress pushed off the frame. The wardrobe door hung open and the clothes spilled across the floor. Likewise, the drawers of the dresser had been pulled out and my underwear and T shirts and everything dumped. I hadn't brought much with me, but whatever I had was now strewn across the floor. Even my suitcase and backpack had been opened and searched—for what?—and tossed aside, and the contents of the boxes I'd carried down from the attic earlier that day had been dumped in a pile by the dresser. I snatched up the penguin and clutched it against my chest.

"Bloody hell," said Duncan tersely. "What about your wallet—your money?" Then he saw I was about to bawl and he put his arms around me—penguin and all.

"Who would *do* this? What do they want?" My voice rose.

"Where's your wallet?" he asked again.

We searched the room and finally found my purse upside down in the corner by the windows, with my wallet and hairbrush and all the messy contents scattered around it. Loose change, crumpled tissues, a chocolate bar, a couple of embarrassing tampons…Hastily I gathered everything and stuffed it all back into the purse. I opened my wallet, held my breath—

The money—what little I had to begin with—was still there.

"Nothing taken," I said softly. I stood up again and stepped back, then abruptly sat down as I tripped over the mattress.

"Nothing at all?" Duncan strode back and forth, his agitation making his already pink cheeks flame red. "What about jewelry?"

I laughed, and heard the high, hysterical note in my voice. "You mean my diamonds and pearls?" I made myself take a deep breath. Freaking out wasn't going to help. "I don't wear jewelry anyway— well, just earrings."

"Are *they* missing?"

I went into the bathroom. The cupboard doors were open and the towels had all been tossed around, but my make-up bag, shampoo, and toothbrush were just where I'd left them. The little velvet box that held about ten pairs of earrings lay on the floor. I picked it up and opened it. All the cheap, funky pairs I'd received from friends or family for birthdays, plus the new ones of red beveled glass that Ivy had made in an after-school stained-glass workshop and given me for my sixteenth birthday, all were right there.

I slid those red glass earrings into my ears now, feeling comforted by the thought of my little sister, of my family.

"Nothing is missing." I walked out of the bathroom and surveyed my bedroom. "Will you help me get the mattress back on the bed?" I felt heavy and tired, as if my body wanted to sleep.

Together Duncan and I lifted the mattress and maneuvered it back into place. Now there was room for me to gather my scattered belongings. Wearily, I started shoving everything into the suitcase.

"Hey, hold on." Duncan put his arms around me. "Deep breath, Jule." He pushed me gently toward the bed and I flopped across the bare mattress. My raw cheek burned under the bandaging. My eyes—

stinging with unshed tears—finally spilled over.

"What could someone have been looking for?" I sobbed. I felt violated, and furious. "Why did someone do this to me?"

"Shhh," Duncan said, smoothing my hair. "I'm thinking another question to ask is why *now*? What do you have in your room that you didn't have before?"

"My birthmother's boxes?" I considered what he was asking. "Yeah, but they're *here.*"

"But what about those letters?" he persisted, intent on this line of thought. "What about the blue envelope?"

"The letters haven't been stolen. I've got the envelope right here." I reached deep into my apron pocket and pulled out the blue-checked envelope.

"Right," he said, standing up and pacing around my room like some sort of red-headed panther. "You took them with you. But they're *new*. They came into this room only today. Only a couple hours ago. Along with that penguin, and the rest of your mum's old stuff. You took them down with you to show your grandfather—and did you? Did you show him? I'm betting you didn't!"

"I didn't, because he was going into the hot tub. It wasn't a good time to bring out old letters. I thought I'd wait till after dinner." I sat up, staring at him. "What are you thinking?

He scrubbed his hands through his red thatch of hair until it stood on end. "That envelope," he said slowly, "is the only thing I can think of that might have been here, but wasn't here."

We stared at each other, and my cloudy brain seemed to clear. "You mean," I said slowly, "someone came looking for it. Someone wanted the old letters. Someone wanted to read them."

"Or didn't want you to."

His words sent a prickle up my shoulder blades. The arrow wound on my cheek throbbed painfully. I put my hand to the bandages.

"Who knows you had them?" demanded Duncan, lowering his

voice to an urgent growl. "Think!"

Think back before the arrow attack? It was as if the pain and shock of that mishap had wiped out my memory. What *had* I been doing? My mind was a blank.

"You were going down to the spa, remember?" Duncan prompted me. "And Pippa said Josie was pissed off…"

"Yes, that's right. Well, yes. I went down. And of course before that we were up here, and so Pippa knew about the letters because she helped me bring the boxes down from the attic. We saw Agatha Moggs skulking in the hallway, and Hat knew because we were talking about them. And…oh, then in the spa practically everyone heard about them because I told Grandfather I'd found my birthmother's box and the packet of letters. Herr Stifelmeyer was interested, and so was Mrs. Grey. And Josie was there, and Hugh, and…" I tried to remember. "That awful Agatha Moggs again, and her weird sister."

Duncan nodded. "Okay, and did you show any of them the letters? Did they know you had them with you in your apron?"

I shook my head. "I don't think so."

"So, let's say we're right, and one of those people wants the letters," Duncan said slowly. "They think the letters are up in your room. So they sneak in while you're out playing games—"

"They had to have a key!" My stomach twisted.

Duncan pressed on with the scenario. "Somebody has a key or knows where to get a master key. He or she comes in here and tears the place apart, searching. But they don't find the letters. So, what do they do next?"

"Shoot an arrow at me?" I asked, my tone ironic. "Really? Like that was going to help find the letters? Or are you thinking they're just pissed off now?"

"Seems a bit extreme," he admitted. "When you put it like that. And all the other stuff—the falling urn, and the trip-line, if there was one, and your cousin's death—none of that has anything to do with the letters either because you only just found them today." He slumped back onto my bed.

So what was he saying? That my life was just full of random, bizarre moments? It was a depressing thought. But then I remembered something my dad always told us kids when we were stuck on homework or couldn't solve some problem with our friends: "Look for the pattern," he'd urge us. "See how things connect." It was 'builderspeak,' coming from an architect. And even though he was many thousands of miles away in California right now, the advice hovered in my room as if my dad had walked in and spoken the words.

Look for the pattern.

"Do we call the police now?" he asked.

"Not yet," I said decisively, pulling the blue-checked envelope out of my apron. "Right now we sit down and read these letters."

22

I opened the packet and fanned out the contents. There were letters in envelopes, and letters without envelopes. There were slips of paper torn from a ledger. There were a few faded newspaper clippings. One fluttered from my hand, landing face-up on the bed. `Winning Ways with Carrots`, read the bold-faced headline. Then in smaller print: *Carrot Jam for Frugal Families.*

"Yuck," I said.

"It was wartime," Duncan replied simply. "I remember my grandmother telling me about the odd things she ate, just trying to get by."

I held the fanned out papers toward him. "Pick a card, any card."

Duncan plucked an envelope from my hand and opened it. The letter was handwritten on a single sheet of thin paper, folded neatly and inserted into an envelope with a stamp bearing a man's regal face in profile. King George—father of the present queen. The postmark cancelling the stamp read 1943, and sent a prickle of anticipation along my shoulders. These were Dorian Heatherstone's letters, sent to him during the war. He had saved them, brought them home when he was wounded. Someone had packed them away in the attic after his death, along with his uniforms, his books.

They were love letters, and little love notes, nothing too spicy, but sweet, many along the lines of 'I miss you and love you and want you home safely…' We shuffled the letters as we read them, trying to put them into order. Some had dates, others did not. I squinted at the faded postmarks inked across the stamps. I read the letters aloud to Duncan, trying to figure out why someone would search my room to get hold of these. Nothing jumped out at me. The letters told a story of a couple in love, that was all. The miscellaneous clippings and scraps of notes were the seasoning, garnishing their story. I wondered if Dorian's young nurse had been studying up on how to be a good housewife. Certainly the intruder who searched my rooms had not been looking for *Tips for the Wise Wartime Housewife:*

1. *Shop early.*
2. *Carry your own parcels and take your own wrapping.*
3. *Save fuel, light, and time.*
4. *Use vegetable water for nourishing soups.*
5. *Use Family Rations carefully.*

Duncan and I read everything, drawn into the long-ago story.

Heatherstone Hall
14 February, 1943
Dear Dorian,
 Leaving your unit behind in France whilst I and the other nurses were sent home to serve was one of the hardest moments of my life. But you will laugh to know where I have landed. You told me your family home had been turned into a hospital for the war effort, but I could not picture how grand a place it was. And whoever would guess I would end up serving in this very place?! It is a delightful house, my love—even this dreadful war, robbing it of gaiety and family life, cannot hide the centuries-old splendor of the place. Though the great rooms are now hospital wards, filled with the sick, the maimed and the dying, Heatherstone Hall shall be made joyful and elegant again after we beat back the Nazis, as surely we must.
 I am honored to be here, nursing our fallen soldiers. I think of you on this St. Valentine's Day with longing, and

I pray to God for your safety.
Love from
Your E.L.

The next letter was folded into an envelope:

Heatherstone Hall,
10 April, 1943
My beloved Dorian,
I think of the words to that old children's song about the Owl who loved the Pussycat—another match as unlikely as our own, and considered by many just as unsuitable—"O let us be married / too long we have tarried." I can't wait until this war is over and you are home again. We have tarried too long, my Owl. And yet, shall I really become mistress of Heatherstone Hall? I can scarcely believe it as I walk the ward daily, administering to the poor lads who have been wounded. So many boys, Dorian, who wrench my soul—and I cannot picture this place as it must have looked before. I try to picture it as the grand home it must have been before the war, the home it surely must become again when you—the heir!—are back where you belong. I want to be a worthy mistress of it, my love. Of it—and of you.
Stay safe, my soldier boy.
Your E.L.

A loose sheet of paper without an envelope seemed to be a draft of a note Dorian himself was trying to write from his hospital bed, after he'd returned to Heatherstone as a wounded officer.

Oh my darling girl,
No hand on my brow feels so soothing as yours·
No other smile offers such comfort! I can almost wish never to recover, because getting well means

having to return to my unit· I do not want to be away from you· As soon as I am on my feet, these shaky legs shall walk with you down by the lake· I shall take your hand—the hand that soothes so many fevered brows—and help you into a rowboat and we shall have a picnic on the island· I shall teach you to swim, my darling, for of course you can learn, no matter how late! Remember you taught me to ride a bicycle in France and we thought it funny that I, growing up with horses to ride, had somehow never mastered a simple bike! Yes, my darling, we shall one day ride through the woods and swim in the lake and wander the maze hand in hand· And in one of those places I will sink to one knee—if only my knee will bend properly again—and ask you to be my wife·

Oh, I know every man here wants to ask you this! I do not doubt that every soldier here is in love with you· Of course you tend to each one devotedly, because in your profession as Head Nurse there is no one more dedicated· But it is my great fortune that you favor only me with your love· As soon as I am well, as soon as I am released from this awful pain, we must marry!

D·H·

"So romantic," I murmured. "If you weren't so busy playing badminton with Pippa, you could write me letters like this."

"But you already know how to swim," Duncan countered with a grin.

"Dorian never did get well." My voice had a catch in it. "They never did get married."

On the top of the next page there were some little doodles, and initials entwined: EL and DH. The letter read:

Heatherstone Hall
Tuesday morning.
My brave soldier boy—
You are sweet to want to teach me to swim, but I warn you I always sink like the proverbial stone. Many have tried before you and failed utterly, well, not really many! I don't want you to think I've had many suitors, all gazing upon me in my bathing costume! No, no, it was only my brothers and my father who tried so hard and failed so miserably. But for you I will try once more. I have every trust in you. Not just around water, but in every aspect of life. I feel safe in the world because you are there with me.
Your EL

"Why don't you say such romantic things to me?" Duncan teased.

"I could, actually," I murmured, and scooted closer to him. "I do feel safe around you."

Now that Dorian and his nurse were in the same place, the letters turned into little notes, which they must have passed back and forth, like teenagers between classes. The snippets of paper offered a glimpse into a happy relationship between two people with a lot of respect for each other, who also liked to play. I was beginning to feel I knew these two, and that they weren't so different from Duncan and me, though our relationships were separated by more than half a century. I thought about all our text messages vanishing into cyberspace. Some saved, but there was nothing to tie up with a ribbon to read again when we were old.

O Beautiful Nursie! O Nursie of Mine! What a beautiful Nursie you are, you are! What a beautiful

Nursie you are!

Unfortunately I'm not up to giving the swim lessons myself—yet. But I shall give them to you by proxy. You know how well Nurse March can swim. Let us ask her to give you lessons while I watch! Oh, how I shall enjoy watching you in your trim swimming costume...

D.H.

No, my darling, let's not trouble Nurse March. She has enough to do as it is. And having you watching me would only serve to make me nervous, and nervous nurses never float! So I shall wait for you to teach me yourself. You will soon be well enough. Now what is this about a ball your sister wants to give for the soldiers who are recovered enough to dance? It is a noble idea, though I don't know how many of my patients will actually be able to get up and dance. We nurses can each take a partner and spin his wheelchair, however!

Ever your devoted mermaid, EL

My lovely mermaid! What a fantasy you're painting: You—clinging to me in your bathing costume while I teach you to swim? And you—spinning me around? Ah, the thoughts of such delight make me dizzy. You, Nurse Lambeth, are a tease. And teasing girls must be severely dealt with! I order you to appear at my bedside this evening, 9:00 sharp.

D.H.

Esteemed Soldier Boy,

If I am a tease, then you are a bad lad in need of a bedtime kiss. I shall indeed be at your side tonight, as I am every night, not because you order it to be so—but because I wish to be there!

—shaking in my (army) boots, I remain,
Your EL

At the back of that message, in the same neat handwriting, was a more practical note:

Summer Drinks for Pennies. Delicious—Nourishing.
—Mint Tea
—Blackberry Leaf Tea
—Barley Water
—Lemonade with Honey

My darling,

Now I can walk—with your arm to lean upon on one side, and a stout stick on the other—we will take that moonlight stroll· It's been our fantasy for a long time now· But I want fresh air, and I want it with you· See you tonight! Instead of the bedpan or the pain pills, let's just have a walk down by the lake...
D·H·

Darling!

Your fantasy is also my own fantasy—we are well matched! Except for a few of the details. We mustn't go at night; the night air is not healthy for my patient. (And you are still my patient!) The bedpan we can dispense with, if you're sure you won't miss it, but the pain pills will help you rest peacefully. The walk itself can take place before your afternoon rest time. I'll be there with my walking shoes on and my strongest arm to offer you.

Much love from your obedient—

EL

You call that obedience, young wench? Well· I see I have no choice: I am in your power, and you are still the Head Nurse· But I did think a night-time walk would shield us from prying eyes...

D·H·

There was just one last letter, and we read it silently, our heads bent together over the page.

My dear Dorian,

Yes, yes, a thousand times yes! I want to shout our betrothal to the treetops. I want the sound of my voice to ring out across the lake. I want everyone to know! But I am so glad you agree to keep our betrothal a secret until you are strong and well again. I thought you might fuss and fume—you know you're very good at doing both!—but, as you said yourself, you won't be prepared to battle with your parents over your choice of bride until you are 100% in top form. I worry that any stress will set you back. You are so strong, my love, but you were badly injured and several times the doctors despaired of saving your life. Now that you are on the mend, I can wait. I can wait for you as long as it takes, my precious one. And then, like the owl and the pussycat, we shall dance by the light of the moon, the moon!

Your eternal EL (soon to be EH!!)

"So that's all there is," I said, and folded the last letter. "It's so romantic, and so sad because you know he died before they could get married."

"Yes, it is sad," Duncan agreed. "But I still can't see why someone would tear your room apart, searching for these letters! There's something we're missing."

I looked inside the blue-checked envelope and withdrew a pile of scraps. "Well, there are these," I said. "But they aren't letters." Some were brittle newspaper clippings, some were handwritten notes.

The first one I unfolded had been cut from a newspaper. It offered more advice for thrifty housewives:

```
           If you want to win the war—
           Save and Salvage more and more.

       A soldier' s blood is on your head.
       If you waste a scrap of bread.
```

The second was a handwritten message—not in Dorian's handwriting, nor that of his nurse:

> *I shall be happy to teach you. It's what he'd want, and what a nice tribute to him if you learn!*
> *He would be so proud of you. Let's meet tonight at 8:00 by the boat-house. I'm sure you'll learn fast.*

"I wonder who wrote this one," I said. I unfolded the others and saw they were all written in the same hand, though some seemed scrawled hastily and were harder to read. Before I could decipher them, there came a light tap on my door. I quickly handed the pile of scraps, unread, back to Duncan.

"Lass?"

Duncan stuffed the notes back into the envelope, and then slipped the blue-checked packet under my pillow.

"Hello, Grandfather," I called. I rolled off the bed and was about to open the door and show him my ransacked room, when I hesitated. No need to shock his heart. "I've been resting."

"It's almost time for dinner," he said, "But I've told Josie you need to stay quiet. You must have the night off again, and I'll come up and sit with you after I eat. Is your young man in there with you?"

"Yes, Sir," Duncan called. "We've been talking."

There was a silence from the other side of the door, and I thought Grandfather might rap harder and demand that I open the door and that Duncan come downstairs. Then he would see the wreckage of my pretty bedroom, and I'd have to explain what had happened. But an idea had come to me, and I wanted to put it into action before anyone knew my room had been ransacked. Anyone but the one who had done it, of course.

"I'll be down to help serve," I said through the door. "I just need to get cleaned up, and then I'll be down."

Duncan looked at me like I was crazy. And Grandfather cleared his throat. "I think working tonight might be too much for you," he said through the closed door.

"No, I'll be fine," I said firmly. "I want to do my job."

"Brave lass," he said, and I heard the pride in his voice. "Your mum was like that. Couldn't keep Barbara down for long. Seems you inherited her pluck. It's a good family trait."

"Thanks," I said.

I listened to his wheezing as he continued down the hall to his bedroom. Then I started picking up my scattered clothes.

"Okay," Duncan said. "I don't get it. Why didn't you open the door and show your grandfather what happened here? Aren't you going to show him the letters?"

"I will—but later. Now I want to go down and pretend nothing has happened, and watch which one of them is freaked out. Somebody knows what I found in here when I opened my door, and that person is expecting me to be crying and raging and telling Grandfather and everyone. Somebody wanted me to be very upset. It would have been possible for whoever it was to search quietly, and neatly, but they made the biggest mess possible. *On purpose.*"

I jumped up and folded clothes and put them back in my drawers. I hung my two sundresses neatly in the wardrobe.

"I get it, I think," Duncan said, and knelt to repack the books. He set the stuffed penguin on my dresser.

"We'll watch everyone at dinner," he suggested. "See who does what, says what. Somebody is very surprised right now that you haven't screamed about what happened to your room, or rung your mum and demanded to be taken away from here. Maybe your silence will make them edgy and they'll give themself away somehow. We'll both be watching with every bite we take."

"I don't feel much like eating," I said. "This is way beyond creepy."

"It is. Your grandfather is right. You do have pluck. If it were me, I'd probably be running for home right now."

"No you wouldn't. You'd be angry."

"I am bloody angry. But I think you're amazing." He dropped a kiss on the top of my head. "Bring the letters down in your apron, all right? Keep them with you—or better yet, give them to me. I'll keep them for you."

I took the packet out from under the pillow and watched him shove it into the waistband of his jeans. Then he pulled his shirt down over the bulge.

"Um—you look nearly as pregnant as Bee," I said.

"All right, I'll take it to my flat," he said. "I'll go now. Wait for me here, okay? We'll go down to dinner together. I want to see you make your grand entrance."

He slipped out the door and I locked it behind him. Then I went into the bathroom and stared at my wounded face in the mirror. The bandage high on my cheekbone made me look lopsided, and my face throbbed, but now that the shock had faded, I felt much stronger.

I washed my hands, re-braided my hair, and then went out and tidied up the rest of my room. I made myself keep cleaning so I would not have time to feel nervous about going downstairs and facing everyone.

When the tap came on my door, I jumped a mile. Then I said, "What's the password?"

I heard Duncan's laugh on the other side. "Let me in so I can kiss you."

"Correct. You may enter." I opened the door and he stepped inside. He was carrying an arrow.

"Okay," he murmured. "I've stashed the letters under my pillow. They should be safe enough now. But, listen, there's something else." He took my hand and led me over to the bed and sat down beside me. "Look at this. I pulled this out of the hay."

I took the arrow and rolled it across my palm. "I don't think I really want it as a souvenir," I said.

"No, look at it. See the tip? It's a steel tip. But all the other arrows were just wood."

"So…this is a different arrow. Someone shot a different arrow…" My words came out slowly as I considered what this might mean.

"And it went into the hay at a very different angle from all the other arrows. Much lower down. As if it were shot from…" his voice trailed off.

"Much higher up," I whispered. "From above. From the roof of the portico."

"That's what I'm thinking." His voice was terse.

I could see it all happening. All the people out there milling around, lining up to try their luck with the bows and arrows, aiming for the targets pinned to the bales of hay. Except for one person who had gone inside, climbed the stairs, opened the window, and stepped out onto the roof of the portico. Walked over to the edge, perhaps crouching to hide behind one of the large stone urns while taking aim with a bow and a steel-tipped arrow. Taking aim at me.

"Whoa," I said shakily.

Duncan hugged me. "So now I'm thinking you should tell the police. And of course your grandfather, too."

"About my room, too?"

"About everything. See what he advises you to do."

"And if he thinks I should leave?"

Duncan led the way downstairs. "Then at least you'll be alive to look for another summer job."

Swimming lessons are out. I offered, but He has already offered to teach her! Sweet of him to be so kind. It's a good ruse.

My clever lad.

Something else will be better, more efficient.

Something will be more secret.

What is the daily routine?

Where might an accident naturally occur?

The possibilities are quite fascinating.

People fall down stairs sometimes. Slip in the bath. Eat something that doesn't agree with them.

The possibilities are endless.

23

"How are you feeling now, lass?" asked Grandfather, coming upon me in the hallway as I reached the bottom of the long staircase.

He reached out a hand and touched my uninjured cheek.

"Oh, I'm all right," I said quickly. *For someone who was nearly murdered.* But I liked the feeling of his hand on my face. "I was lucky."

"I don't want you overtaxing yourself—" He broke off, coughing hard.

"I'll be fine," I said, and forced a smile. "Grandfather, I need to talk to you."

"Right now?" He had to double over before the coughing spasm subsided. "Or do you have time to watch me win a battle before our meal begins?" He grinned, then gasped a bit.

"A battle?"

He nodded toward the billiard room. Herr Stifelmeyer emerged from the room and stood in the doorway.

"No thanks," I said distractedly. "I've already been in battle today. That's more than enough for me."

The old German saluted me, but his eyes searched mine, and there was no teasing in his voice. "How are you feeling?"

"Ready for dinner," I said.

Dinner was ham and fresh green beans, potatoes and gravy, salad, and fruit and bread. I carried trays of food to the dining room and chatted to the guests, who exclaimed over my poor, bandaged cheek and my lucky narrow escape. I cleared tables and wiped them, and wondered why Herr Stifelmeyer had not come to sit at his usual table. Perhaps the billiard battle had gone into overtime.

When I joined the staff in the kitchen for our meal, I discovered Herr Stifelmeyer sitting at the far end of the long table next to Grandfather. Grandfather saw my look of surprise and winked.

"I've asked Otto to join us," Grandfather announced. "I've beaten him soundly at snooker. No reason to add insult to injury by making the old chap eat alone as well, eh?" He laughed his deep raspy chuckle.

Herr Stifelmeyer laughed, too. "I admit defeat like a gentleman," he said. "And it's lovely to be asked to join you all for the meal."

Mrs. Grey pursed her lips, and Josie frowned. But everyone else smiled and welcomed him. They all seemed in fine spirits, ready to put my mishap behind them as just another one of those things. But I was aware with every single bite that one of them could be the person who had searched my room. Was that the same person who had shot the arrow? And was that the same person mixed up in Lewis Paine's death? As platters of ham and boiled potatoes were passed up and down the table, I watched to see who might be watching me, who might be planning another 'accident.'

Everyone looked so *normal*. But someone was definitely not normal. Wasn't there some sign that would tip me off? Why wasn't real life like those old Nancy Drew mysteries, where the villain was always the sullen swarthy man who spoke broken English or the tall woman with evil, shifty eyes and large, masculine hands?

Hugh wasn't there. He had gone out to eat with some of his university friends, Ross told us, adding dourly, "If the lad spent as much time learning the hotel business as he does larking about with his mates, he'd be running this place and still have time to write his blasted novel!"

"Ross, dear," remonstrated Josie.

Mina Fuller, John Bainbridge, and Bee weren't eating with us either. They had all gone home early. "Bee wasn't feeling in top form,"

Mrs. Grey said to me, "after your accident in the garden, so John and Mina thought she should have a nice lie down, put her feet up."

"It's Juliana who got shot with the arrow," Hat observed. "But *she's* not having a nice lie down with her feet up!"

"Juliana's not preggers, either," said Mrs. Grey reprovingly.

"Sorry, Granny." But Hat winked at me.

They conjectured about Bee and her baby, and how would the fledgling marriage fare once Henry Harrison came home from Iraq. They talked about the fences Duncan and John had built, and wondered whether the workers hired from the village might be hired for the rest of the summer. They discussed the game of snooker and how it differed from billiards, which was different again from the game I knew in America as 'pool'—and questioned whether the rules for scoring were different in Germany. They talked about everything under the sun, it seemed, except to wonder who had trashed my bedroom, and who might have been behind my run-in with a steel-tipped arrow.

When we had finished eating, Maggie and Pippa cleared the table. I started loading up the two huge dishwashers. But Grandfather put his hand on my shoulder. "You've done more than your share," he said. "Now come and talk to an old man."

"All right," I said. This would be my chance to tell him everything.

Pippa cornered Duncan and begged him to watch a film with her. "It's the sequel to the one we saw last night. Juliana's going to be busy with Grandfather."

"I am, too," Duncan said. "If that's all right." His eyes met mine.

"Yes, please," I said.

Pippa flipped back her blonde hair and pouted. "Hat? Do *you* want to watch it?"

"Sorry, Pip-squeak, I've got other plans." Hat untied her apron and hung it on the hook by the back door. Then she checked her face in the small mirror by the pantry, fluffed her thick dark hair, and left the house. We could hear her feet crunching on the gravel as she crossed the courtyard.

Pippa flounced out of the house after her.

Duncan and I found Grandfather and Herr Stifelmeyer sitting in leather armchairs flanking the fireplace. The wheelchair was parked in the corner by the long windows.

I had not wanted the German guest to be there, too. I needed to talk to Grandfather alone. There was no need to alarm any of the guests with my news of the arrow shooter and the room search. And Herr Stifelmeyer was already anxious about me.

"There you are, lass," Grandfather said. "And Duncan. Please join us. Mrs. Grey will be bringing us some tea shortly." He gestured to the couch. "Sit down, sit down, both of you. Get yourselves comfortable. Otto and I are both eager to have you read those letters—"

"*Ja, ja,*" agreed Herr Stifelmeyer. "A little trip into the past."

"Oh, sorry," I said. "I didn't bring them down."

"I can go get them," offered Duncan. He and I exchanged a look, then he left the room.

"Have you read them yet?" asked Herr Stifelmeyer.

"Yes," I replied. "And they were interesting. Sad, really. You feel you get to know Dorian Heatherstone and his fiancée, but you know their story doesn't have a happy ending. The letters are happy, though."

"They bring young Dorian to life again, eh?" Grandfather asked. "He and that sweet nurse, what was her name again, Otto? Eve, wasn't it? Or Eva?"

"Yes, Eva—that's it," said Herr Stifelmeyer. "I remember now."

"She was a dear lass, very professional, but a spot of sunshine to all of us wounded men who lay in the wards. And can you believe," Grandfather asked me, "that this very room where we're sitting now was a ward? Beds lined up on both sides of the room, wounded lads in every bed, and Mrs. Grey and this Eva lass tending to us."

"I wasn't in this room," said Herr Stifelmeyer. "The prisoners of war slept in the back parlor. Because the room could be locked, I suppose."

I kept forgetting that Herr Stifelmeyer hadn't been here as a regular soldier but as a prisoner of war. It was hard to look at that old gentleman and imagine him wounded and frightened, in enemy hands.

"You were a prisoner, true, but I didn't notice you trying very hard to escape!" Grandfather chuckled, then broke off with a cough.

"No," Herr Stifelmeyer agreed. "It didn't feel like a prison, except for the locked doors. I was treated decently. And when Nurse Eva tended me, I forgot I was in enemy hands."

"I think we all forgot ourselves completely when she was around!" Grandfather said. "The wards didn't seem so depressing at all when she came along with her smiles—and those vials of painkillers." His laugh again turned into an alarming wheeze.

I jumped up to pound him on the back if necessary, but the wheezing settled into a cough, then subsided. As we waited for Duncan, I looked around the room and tried to imagine it as a ward, as the old men described. Strange to think that the man who had written those ardent, teasing love notes had lain in a bed right here.

"He was getting better," I said. "The nurse—Eva?—was planning to take him for a walk by the lake. How did he die? Did his wounds get infected again?"

Grandfather looked uncomfortable. "No, there was no infection, my dear. No one knows exactly what happened, but he died of an overdose."

"What!? You mean he committed suicide?"

"Not at all, no, no dear. You've got it wrong. It was an accident."

"He took too much medicine by mistake?"

"Well, not exactly." Grandfather and Herr Stifelmeyer exchanged a glance. "As I recall, he was inadvertently *given* an overdose. Of morphine. In error."

"Tragic," muttered Herr Stifelmeyer. "So impossible for her to bear."

I sucked in my breath, suddenly understanding. "You mean, *Eva* gave him the overdose? By mistake?"

"I'm afraid so," Grandfather said.

"Poor Eva! She must have felt terrible. What happened to her? Did she lose her job?" I looked at their lined faces and another thought came to me. "Or—oh no, she wasn't put in prison was she? For a mistake?"

Grandfather and Herr Stifelmeyer shared a glance again. *"Nein,"* said Herr Stifelmeyer. "Not prison."

"Then what happened?"

Grandfather reached out and patted my hand. "Now, now, don't fret. It was a very long time ago. A terrible mistake. She must have measured out the wrong amount. The poor nurse was in shock afterward; she couldn't believe it. She said she had simply done her rounds as always, giving each patient the correct dosage of morphine as prescribed. And yet when an autopsy was done, Dorian Heatherstone was found to have many times the amount of the drug in his body as he should have had. Of course it killed him. And then the poor young Eva—Eva... " He broke off, coughing.

The door opened just then, and I turned to welcome Duncan, but it wasn't Duncan. Mrs. Grey bustled in with a tea tray. "Have a cup of tea," she urged Grandfather. "I've got a good fresh pot here. It will help clear your lungs. I could hear you clear out in the kitchen."

"I'm never one to turn down a hot cup of tea," Grandfather said, clearing his throat. He tried for a smile. "But as for clearing my lungs—ah, Edith, the damage was done years back. As a nurse you know that perfectly well." He fixed a stern eye on me. "Never start smoking, lass. It's a death sentence. Your mum, that is, my Barbara—now, she took it up when she was younger than you. I know I didn't set a good example, but I did tell her not to start. She smoked—and probably other substances than tobacco as well, at least that's my guess. And look what happened to her! I'm telling you, you put anything in your lungs, and it's a death sentence. You remember that, Juliana."

"I will," I said, uncomfortable with all this sad talk of sickness and death. I glanced at the door. Where was Duncan? How long could it take to bring the letters from his flat?

"Do you remember that nurse's last name?" Herr Stifelmeyer asked, neatly changing the subject. "We can't recall it. Eva somebody. The one who—you know."

Mrs. Grey pressed her lips together. "Nurse Lambeth, wasn't it? Eva Lambeth." She shook her head mournfully. "Really Lloyd. I don't think this is a very nice topic of discussion for Juliana after the sort of day she's had! It's all in the past now."

"What happened to Nurse Lambeth?" I asked. "Wasn't there an investigation?"

"It's all in the past now," Mrs. Grey repeated severely. "And it's just upsetting. It's not good for the story to get around—the guests won't like it. They'll see this as a place of tragedy. Not a place to spend their holidays."

She left the room and closed the door firmly, as if it, like the sad subject, was not to be opened again.

I turned back to grandfather. "The guests won't like *what*?" I demanded. "What happened to Eva Lambeth?"

Grandfather and Herr Stifelmeyer looked at each other. "There's no reason she shouldn't know, is there, Otto?"

"*Nein,*" he said. "I see no reason."

"She told everyone she *hadn't* given him too much morphine...but the facts were staring her in the face. Her loved one was dead, of a huge overdose. She couldn't live with her own terrible guilt," Grandfather said. "So she walked into the lake one night...and drowned herself."

I stared at him, shocked. "So it was a double death." That really *was* a tragedy. How much sadness had this house known over its long history? I wondered. It put what had been happening here over the past week into a new perspective.

The parlor door opened then and Duncan was back. But his face was nearly as red as his hair, and his expression was tight with fury. "What is it?" I cried.

"Juliana, they did it to my flat, too. Totally ransacked!"

"You mean—?"

"Searched. Everything torn up. And this time they *did* find the letters."

"They're gone?"

Grandfather pulled himself to his feet. "Are you saying your flat has been burgled?"

"My room was, too, earlier today," I said. "I was going to tell you—"

"And you say the packet of old letters has been taken?"

"Yes," Duncan said, plopping down on the couch. "I'd hidden them, but obviously not well enough. Sorry, Jule. You should have just brought them down with you to dinner. Then you'd have them safe."

"But what was in them that anyone could want?" Grandfather asked, perplexed. "This is preposterous! There must be an intruder on the property! Or one of the guests is a thief!"

Herr Stifelmeyer gripped the arms of his chair. "Bring in the police, Lloyd!"

"Not so fast," replied Grandfather sharply, and I looked at him in surprise. "They're just some old letters."

"But they must be valuable, or nobody would steal them," protested Herr Stifelmeyer.

"Perhaps. But the letters were up in the attic of Heatherstone Hall, which is my property. Those letters belong to me, and unless I press charges, there is no case for the police."

Herr Stifelmeyer sat back in his chair and glared at Grandfather. Duncan and I met each other's eyes. Did Grandfather think he knew, after all, who might have searched our rooms and stolen the letters?

Was he protecting someone?

"Was anything else of yours stolen?" he asked Duncan.

"No, sir. Not that I can tell."

"And anything ruined? Broken in the search?"

"No. It's all just a mess. Stuff pulled out everywhere."

Grandfather sighed. "I'll ask Pippa and Hat to help you clean it up in the morning. But for now, please do not bring in the police. I need to think about this." His raspy voice was weary.

He *knew* something, or thought he did.

And the shiver across my shoulder blades as I stared at him told me that maybe I knew something, too. Something I had seen, or heard...Or something I had read? There was something in those letters that made them worth stealing—if only I could figure out what it was.

Duncan opened his mouth to speak, then closed it again. Herr Stifelmeyer sat rigid, his face like a thundercloud. Grandfather fell into a coughing fit that left him gasping, and Mrs. Grey popped back into the room so quickly she must have been hovering out in the hallway. "Let me call Mina," she fussed.

"I'll just get myself up to bed," he wheezed. "That's all I need. A good sleep." His eyes caught mine, and I saw that he did not want me to mention the ransacked rooms or missing letters.

"I'll help you upstairs," Duncan offered quietly, interpreting Grandfather's look.

"I shall head to my bed as well," said Herr Stifelmeyer, struggling out of his armchair.

"I'll get your wheelchair." I jumped up.

"No. Just leave it there for the night. My old legs need the exercise." He paused. "Or maybe I should keep it with me for safe-keeping. Who knows if it will be stolen in the night?"

Mrs. Grey looked at him curiously. "What a thing to say, Herr Stifelmeyer. I'm sure our guests can be quite sure that their personal possessions are safe here at Heatherstone Hall." She stacked our teacups on her tray. "Will you be wanting anything else then?"

"Nothing for me, Edith. Thank you," said Grandfather, frowning at his German friend.

"Your hot chocolate, Mr. Stifelmeyer?" inquired Mrs. Grey.

"Not tonight, thank you."

"Well, then, I'm off to watch the telly," she told us. "But you just ring me if you need anything." Halfway out the door she turned back. "And you young people don't stay down here talking about the past. What happened years ago is over and done with. There's no sense sitting around feeling bad about it. You weren't here then, and you weren't part of it, and there's nothing you can do to make things right." She hesitated. "It's over and done with, and the past can't be changed, as much as any of us wish it could be."

Grandfather rubbed his chin. "No nonsense, eh, Edith? No ghosts—and no nonsense."

She nodded, though her eyes were troubled. "Exactly." Her voice became brisk again. "Ghosts *are* nonsense."

"We make our own ghosts," Herr Stifelmeyer said quietly.

24

No use sitting around feeling bad about what was long past, Mrs. Grey had said, and of course she was right. And no sense sitting around feeling angry and frightened by intruders that quite likely had found what they wanted and would not bother us again. But such occurrences left echoes—*vibes*, as Ivy might say.

Dorian Heatherstone and Eva Lambeth hadn't made it into their future, but I wanted to make it into mine—with Duncan beside me. I didn't want anything awful to happen to break us apart as those long-ago lovers had been. War, illness, injury, accident, tragedy—so many things could happen to people. My birth parents had not planned on dying young, either.

So now Duncan helped Grandfather out into the hall and I took Herr Stifelmeyer's arm. He leaned on me to steady himself, and we followed.

Duncan and I climbed the long stairway with the elderly men. We saw them into their bedrooms. Then we left the house by the kitchen door and hurried over to Duncan's flat. There was no need for Grandfather to send Hat and Pippa to clean it up in the morning. We would do it together—now.

As we stood in the lounge, surveying the mess, I wrapped my arms around Duncan tightly, as if to close the space between us because—you never knew—into that space *anything* might come creeping. *War, injuries, accidents. Blackmailers, intruders, thieves.*

And ghosts? I felt uneasy, as if the shades of Dorian Heatherstone and Lewis Paine lingered with us in that ransacked room.

Duncan wrapped me snuggly in his arms, but still my mind was racing. Someone had come with a key to unlock this door while we were at dinner. I cast my mind back over the evening. Who had been where?

Who *hadn't* been where?

Josie and Ross had been in the kitchen during dinner, but what about afterward, while I was in the parlor? Were they home with Pippa, watching the film? Bee had gone home early with her parents. Maggie and Hat had served dinner, but I hadn't seen them again after we'd washed up. Hugh's parents told us that Hugh was eating with university friends...but who really knew if anybody was where they'd said they were? Any one of them could easily have taken the master keys from the kitchen and headed over to Duncan's flat while he and I were with Grandfather.

And what about the guests?

Somehow I couldn't imagine the American family or any of the Japanese businessmen or honeymooning couples sneaking into my room or Duncan's flat to look for the box. None of the other guests even knew about the letters—except Herr Stifelmeyer.

My memory sharpened. Herr Stifelmeyer *and* Miss Agatha Moggs knew about the letters. And both of them had been at Heatherstone Hall years ago during the war. I did not think Herr Stifelmeyer was nimble enough to have raced to Duncan's flat and stolen the blue-checked envelope—but what about spry Miss Moggs or her side-kick, sister Sue-Sue?

Duncan bent his head to kiss me, then we, reluctantly, parted. We set to work, stowing books in shelves, returning cushions to the couch, clothes to the wardrobes. We remade the beds; Lew's bed had been stripped as well as Duncan's.

"Your grandfather has a suspect in mind," Duncan's tone was terse. He replaced the pillow on his bed.

"I know." I smoothed the bedspread.

"There's something about those letters. Something we're missing."

"I know."

Despite everything that had happened, there suddenly wasn't a whole lot more to say. We finished clearing up in near silence.

"Want to stay tonight?" he asked me.

And I did want to stay, but I shook my head. "Not tonight," I said. Not with so many shadows hanging over us. So he walked me back to the house, our feet squelching across the wet grass.

Upstairs, he waited while I unlocked my bedroom door. We peeked inside together—and saw that the room appeared to be just the way we'd left it.

"All right?" he asked me.

"Yeah."

"Want me to come in?"

Yeah. "No, that's okay." My cheek was aching, and I was exhausted.

"Sure?"

I kissed him again. "I'll see you in the morning, then. Bright and early."

I locked the door behind him and then crossed to my bed. I hugged Barbara-Elizabeth's stuffed penguin, inhaling the faint, flowery scent. Then I picked up the first of her spiral notebooks and flipped through the lined pages. Equations, computations, formulas, all scrawled in messy pencil. Trigonometry, I thought it was. There were check marks in red pen in the margins—a teacher's assessment that these problems were all correct. It looked like Barbara-Elizabeth had been no dummy at math.

Wishing I had inherited her skill, I opened the second notebook. Lists of French vocabulary words covered the first few pages, but after that there were few notes. Instead, doodles filled the notebook. Spirals, swirls, hearts, suns, and stars. And then a little sketch of a motorcycle, with two stick figures bent together over the handlebars. Instead of the French dialogue she was probably supposed to be writing, my birthmother had written:

> Je suis bored out of my mind.
> Je suis counting the days.
> Je absolutely can't wait to hit the road with my best bloke. Vvvrrooom!

I smiled and opened the third notebook. This one contained lab notes from science experiments for the first few pages, then turned into more doodles. Barbara-Elizabeth had not been a very attentive schoolgirl. The last pages of the notebook seemed to be a dialogue between my birthmother and a friend. Perhaps they'd sat in their chemistry lab, passing the book back and forth between them across a lab table, pretending to record results of an experiment while really carrying on a conversation wholly unrelated.

> I can't wait to get out of here. Soon!
> **Where will you go?**
> Anywhere! No—it's got to be someplace warm. I want sun, sand, surf…

It was almost like texting, except they didn't do that back then. Reading my birthmother's words made the link between us feel stronger, tighter. She had been real. She had been, briefly, mine.

> **Maybe I'll come with you. South of Spain? Florida?**
> Hey, yeah! Or California. New bloke I met is going there. Wants to visit a cousin or something. Says I can come with him…
> **WHAT NEW BLOKE? You never said!**
> Dead dishy, he is. And smart, with a fab motorbike. Named Clark.
> **A motorbike named Clark. I like that.**

Don't be daft.

My parents won't let me ride motorbikes. Think I'll be killed.

Yeah, well, be glad they care. My dad wouldn't care if I did get killed.

Now who's being daft?

Damn right he doesn't care. Spends all his time in his bloody hotel. He might as well live there fulltime, much as I ever see him.

Don't look now, but Miss P. has her evil eye on us...!

The notes reverted to Chemistry formulas. I closed the notebook and sat there, running my fingers along the spiral wire, lost in the sense of my birthmother. She had been a girl my age, gone to school, confided her unhappiness in a friend. And who was the dishy Clark with the motorbike? Had she gone off to California with him?

A new thought stabbed me: Could Clark have been my birthfather?

I knew next to nothing about him, only that he'd died in a road accident when I was a baby. My birthmother had struggled on, sinking into the world of drink and drugs, until one day she was found dead. I was only five years old, and had few memories of my life with her before my adoption. But sitting here now, holding these links to her, I felt that our connection still existed—stretching beyond time and death.

Links in a chain, as my mom might have said.

I rubbed my wounded cheek gently on the stuffed penguin's soft head, and reflected that Barbara-Elizabeth had been very wrong about at least one thing: her dad had cared about her. He'd cared very much.

Then I heard a noise out in the hall. Footsteps. Had my thinking about Grandfather somehow brought him out of bed?

Immediately I was off my bed and opening my door. And there was Mrs. Grey, not Grandfather, carrying a small tray with a green thermos on it, and wearing a frown on her face. She looked startled at the sight of me. "Gracious, girl! I thought everyone was asleep." She shook her head, looking just as exhausted as I felt. "Hat and I were just heading to bed, when our German guest decided he needed his midnight snack after all." She shrugged her shoulders. "Well, what can you do? It's all part of running a hotel."

"Here," I said. "Why don't I take it to him?"

"You're a thoughtful girl," said Mrs. Grey, handing me the tray with a grateful smile. "He's in room twelve. Hat made his cocoa just the way he likes it, with real cream and a dash of cinnamon." She headed back down the main staircase.

I walked along the silent hallway to Herr Stifelmeyer's door. I balanced the tray in one hand, nearly tipping the thermos onto the rug as I knocked.

"Juliana!" exclaimed Herr Stifelmeyer, opening his door. "They have you working late tonight."

"It's okay," I told him, entering the room as he stood aside. "I offered to bring you your hot chocolate."

"It is my special treat. Mrs. Grey has been very obliging in sending someone to bring it to me when I ask. But I did not request it tonight."

I set the tray down on his dresser, opened the flask, and poured the hot creamy drink into the china cup. "Smells good, though."

"This is a fine surprise. And will you join me? I had wanted to talk to you further."

"About the letters?" I guessed.

"Yes. It is wrong that your grandfather does not go to the police."

I looked around his room, which was tidy, except for the rumpled bed. The covers were bunched and tangled as if he had been tossing and turning. I wondered if he had nightmares about the war, or just found it hard to get comfortable. Or maybe he was lonely. There were a couple German books lying next to a pair of reading glasses on his bedside table.

"Here," he said to me. "Please sit down and have a cup with me. There's more than enough for two."

"Well, all right. For a minute." I took the offered cup. "Thank you."

"I've been sitting here thinking," he said. "I am baffled."

Baffled, that was the right word for what I was feeling, too. "I'm baffled, too."

Herr Stifelmeyer lowered himself into the armchair and reached for his cup of cocoa. He stirred it but did not drink. "The stolen letters, of course. That is very baffling. But more important: the arrow today. It could have killed you."

"Yes, I know," I said, drinking deeply. "Believe me, I know." The cocoa was very sweet and hot, and slid down my throat like a warm river.

"*Ja*," continued Herr Stifelmeyer. "It could have killed you—just as the falling urn could have killed you. Just as the string across the stairs could have killed you. This worries me."

I gulped down another hot mouthful. "Me, too. And Duncan pointed out that the arrow wasn't even one of the hotel's regular arrows. It's a different kind, with a metal tip! We think it was shot down from the roof of the portico."

"That is terrible, but I am not surprised. Things are very wrong here. And I am wondering why this is all happening *now*, Juliana. I am wondering what is different at this hotel now than at other times." He nodded at me. "I think you know."

"You mean—me?" I asked in a low voice. "You mean, that I'm here? That I've come to visit my grandfather?"

"*Jawohl*," he said, nodding. "That is what I'm thinking is different."

"You think my being here has set something in motion."

He nodded. "I do believe this. I believe someone feels threatened."

So many accidents—well, I believed it, too. But why should my presence threaten anybody? I knew I should be sitting on edge, letting anger and fear fuel my next actions, but instead I felt my worries ebbing away as the warm drink calmed me.

I curled up in the armchair, sipping the drink I held cupped in both hands. "Duncan and I already figured that the 'accidents' might not be accidents at all. But it's hard to see why anybody would want to hurt me."

"There's something strange going on," he said. "Something to do with those letters." He peered at me over the rim of his mug. "Do you not agree?"

"Yes. Somebody stole them…" My voice trailed off sleepily. I took another sweet sip.

"Tell me about the letters," the German said. "Someone searched your room?"

"Yes," I said. My eyes felt heavy, sitting here. I was *so* tired. It was an effort to make my lips shape the words. "And…the same person—at least I'm thinking it was the same person—also tore up Duncan's flat. We were just over there cleaning up. There was no sign of the…envelope."

"Which envelope is this?" Herr Stifelmeyer's gaze sharpened.

"The big blue and white envelope. Labeled 'Housekeeping…Hints.' My tongue somehow felt too big for my mouth, and as if it were made of rubber. I was speaking slowly, slurring my words a little. "The letters…are inside it."

"Ah?" he said. He paused, then opened his mouth to say something else, when the room around me seemed to waver. What was wrong with me? Was I going to throw up? I stood up and held onto the bedpost.

I lurched toward the bathroom. "Excuse me…just a minute," I gasped. I closed the door and reached for the sink to steady myself.

I stood holding the cool porcelain sides for a long minute, then splashed water onto my face. It made me feel better. I bent down to drink deeply of the cold water, right from the tap. I stared into the mirror at my pale complexion.

I do look sick.

Then I stared deeper into the mirror, past my face. I stared at the toilet behind me—at the blue checked envelope resting on the shelf above the toilet.

Oh, this latest one is a lovely, perfect plan, a gem of a plan. The best plan yet. And this one can so very easily become real, yes as it can, as it must!—with just the right amount of cleverness and the right amount of daring (two traits he once said he admires in me), mixed with the special stash, saved up for weeks now...

> *Ah, my lovely special stash!*
> *Ah, my cunning, foolproof plan!*
> *My perfect recipe—*
> *For doing what must be done.*

25

I wheeled around—and the room seemed to spin with me. My stomach rolled and my brain screamed DANGER. I needed to leave here. *Now*.

"Juliana? Juliana, are you all right?" Herr Stifelmeyer's deep voice with its heavy accent (*Yooliana? Yooliana*) came to me through the door.

I grabbed the envelope. It was empty.

Dropping it, I pulled the door open. "I'm fine. But need to go—" I made a mighty effort to walk past him without staggering. Like a wobbly sailor I headed for the bedroom door. "Thanks for the hot chocolate," I said. "G good bye—"

"My dear girl, you don't look well."

"Oh, I'm fine, just fine," I slurred.

"But we must talk about those letters. Come sit down…"

I left his room, pulled the door closed behind me, staggered around the corner to my own room. I sagged against my door. I let out a shriek when it opened and I fell inward—into Duncan's arms.

"There you are!" His voice was low, tight. "I've been so worried, Jule. You weren't answering my texts, so I had to come over. And I was getting frantic, thinking about what 'accident' might have happened to you *this* time." As I sagged against him, he broke off and his arms tightened around me. "What's *wrong*? What's happened? You look—"

"Drugs," I whispered.

Duncan half carried me, half steered me over to the bathroom sink. He turned on the tap and filled my plastic cup with water. "Drink this."

I slurped at the water. It ran out of my mouth. I could barely swallow. I just wanted to sleep. "Stifel…meyer," I managed to get out. "Gave me…cocoa…"

"You've got to throw up," Duncan said urgently. "You've got to throw up everything you drank. Here—quick! You do it." He grabbed my hand. "Stick your finger down your throat. Go on," he pressed when I pulled my hand away. "Do it! Or I'll do it for you. You've got to get that cocoa out of your system—*fast*."

I was too weak and too dizzy to fight him off. But the desperation in his voice got through to me, and I slid my hand into my mouth, jabbed my finger at the back of my throat, and retched into the sink. Up came my dinner in a hot rush of fluid. Up came all the hot chocolate.

Heaving, moaning, I gripped the sides of the sink until it was all out of me. I sagged against Duncan.

"Good girl," he whispered, and the relief I heard in his voice touched me. I reached for the glass; I wanted to wash out my mouth and brush my teeth, but he stopped me. "Wait—" he said, and scooped a trace of the vomit into the glass.

"Ew," I whispered.

"Evidence," he said grimly, handing me my toothbrush. "All right, then. Go ahead now."

I brushed, spit, drank from the tap. I splashed cold water over my face, rubbed it with a towel, then let him lead me out of the bathroom. We sank onto the bed.

"How do you feel now?"

I lay back and stared at the ceiling. "Weak. Sort of fuzzy. But better, I think." Actually I still felt shaky. I could taste the bile in the back of my throat. My skin was clammy.

"You need a doctor."

"No, I think I'll be okay." I could feel the veil of sleepiness settling like a fog over the lake. "I just want to sleep."

"No—you need to stay awake and tell me what happened!"

And, groggily, I told him how I'd taken the hot chocolate to Herr Stifelmeyer, how he'd offered me some and I'd grown woozy and weak…How I'd seen the blue-checked envelope on the shelf in his bathroom.

"The drink was definitely drugged," I murmured. "So *he* must be the one who took the letters! And he must be behind all the incidents. And that means—oh, Duncan, he's got to be the one who killed Lewis…" I curled on my side, holding my stomach, closing my eyes.

"Same method," agreed Duncan grimly. "Drugs in a hot drink. But *why* would he be after Lewis? And why *you*?"

I didn't know. I couldn't think, but tears pressed behind my eyelids at the betrayal. I liked the old German so much. I had thought Grandfather's old friend was becoming a friend of mine. And all the time he had been plotting…

In my mind I saw again the blue-checked envelope on the shelf in his bathroom, just perched there as casually as if he'd just happened to find it and set it there.

"He was always there," I said, fuzzily. "He was there at the top of the stairs with me when I nearly tripped. And he was right there with us when the stone urn crashed off the portico. And out in the garden—he was right behind me when the arrow nearly skewered me! He's always been *right there*—!"

Duncan stroked my hair as I shuddered. "But wait," he said. "He didn't make his own cocoa, did he?"

Then I sat up, clutching my dizzy head as it dawned on me. "Ohmigosh—I'm an idiot." I stared at him, my head clearing. "Duncan, Herr Stifelmeyer's been with me every time. So he *couldn't* have pushed the urn, since he was with us. He couldn't have shot the arrow since he was standing with me." I searched Duncan's face. "Why didn't I see it before? Of course he didn't make the hot chocolate. Each and every accident has been as much a near miss for *him* as it was for me."

"So *he* could have been the target all along?" Duncan's voice was hard.

I shivered and tried to stand up. "Oh, Duncan, we have to go to him. That was *his* cocoa. And if he drank the rest of it. . ."

Wobbling, I staggered into the hallway. Duncan tore ahead of me to room twelve. The door was slightly ajar. He tried to push it open, but it wouldn't budge. I joined him and shoved—but it was stuck—no, it was blocked. It was blocked by a body lying on the floor just inside the room.

Herr Stifelmeyer's body.

26

I was just thin enough to push myself through the opening in the doorway. "Herr Stiefelmeyer, Herr Stiefelmeyer!" I knelt by his side and tried to shove him out of the way so that Duncan could open the door wider. The old man was heavier than I expected. *A dead weight*, I thought—but no, his heavy breathing proved he wasn't dead. Not yet.

I rolled him onto his side, and Duncan was able to enter the bedroom. He knelt at my side. "He's alive," I said.

The old German groaned. "*Ich bin…unheimlich…schwindlich.*"

"He's incredibly dizzy," I translated, my high school German coming in useful. "That's just how I felt. How I still feel."

"It must be some kind of tranquilizer," Duncan said grimly. He tried to pull Herr Stifelmeyer to a sitting position. "Herr Stifelmeyer, can you hear me? We want to help you."

The old man's eyes fluttered.

"We'll get it out of him," I said. "Same way you did with me." I looked around the room, then wobbled into the bathroom. Grabbing two towels and Herr Stifelmeyer's toothbrush, I returned to Duncan. Whatever drug had been in that drink, I was still feeling the effects of it. I felt like I was moving underwater.

Duncan had the old man sitting up now, leaning forward. Herr Stifelmeyer moaned a bit as Duncan held his shoulders steady. "You have to do it, Jule," he told me. "I can't hold him and stick the toothbrush down his throat at the same time!"

"We need a doctor. Or a nurse! Should we get Mrs. Grey? And call for an ambulance?"

"We will as soon as he throws up."

It was horrible, but I did it. Stuck the toothbrush back far enough to make the old man retch. He fought against me, but we held him tightly until it all came up. Then he sagged in our arms again and closed his eyes.

"Bingo," said Duncan softly. "But now what?"

"Now we get Grandfather," I said firmly, wiping the old man's mouth with a towel. I smoothed his gray hair back from his forehead. "And Mrs. Grey. *And* we call the police."

"Right," Duncan said, struggling out from under Herr Stifelmeyer's weight.

"The police have to be told that Lew was murdered. It *wasn't* an accidental overdose and drowning. He was probably drugged just the same way Herr Stifelmeyer and I were. A drug in his drink."

It was terrible, horrible—but I couldn't help but feel relief at the thought that I had not been the intended victim of the various *accidents* after all.

At the sound of his name, the old man groaned. His mouth moved. He wanted to speak, or was he going to throw up more of the hot chocolate? "*Wasser…*" he whispered. Then he closed his eyes.

"He wants water," I translated, and Duncan leaped up to bring Herr Stifelmeyer a cup from the bathroom. I leaned over the old man and helped him sip it. "Hold on, we're going to get you a doctor now. Just stay quiet. You'll be all right soon. I'm already feeling better."

Duncan helped the old man lie back on the pillow. "Now if only we could figure out how the two men are connected. Lewis Paine and Herr Stifelmeyer. There must be a connection."

"There has to be," I agreed. "Because someone wanted them both dead."

Herr Stifelmeyer's eyelids fluttered. "March," he mumbled. "March, march!" He tossed his head from side to side. "*Wasser...schwimmen...*"

"He's talking about marching, I think. Remembering being a soldier, maybe? Or something that happened in March? And he said 'water,' and 'swimming.'" I told Duncan. "I'll go tell Grandfather what's happening. Can you call the police and the paramedics?"

Herr Stifelmeyer stirred agitatedly. "*Sie kann doch sehr gut schwimmen...*" he said clearly, though his eyes remained closed.

Duncan reached down and patted the old man's shoulder. "Can you say it in English?"

"He said, '*She can swim very well,*'" I translated, frowning. "Or '*very well indeed.*' But who? *Who* can swim very well, Herr Stifelmeyer?"

I felt I was on the edge of understanding something vitally important. There had been something in those letters about swimming, no—about *not* being able to swim! Dorian Heatherstone had wanted Nurse Eva to learn to swim...But what could that have to do with anything now?

Duncan took out his phone. "I'll call for help and stay here with Herr Stifelmeyer while you get your grandfather."

"Right," I said, and rose to my feet, still feeling light-headed but better than before. I reached out for the window sill to steady myself, and as I looked out, I saw a white figure stagger across the lawn. "Wait—who is that?" I stared out at the darkness.

Duncan opened the window, and a gust of cool wind puffed past him into the room. He leaned out. "Hey—it's your grandfather! In his bathrobe!"

I leaned out of the window, too, and cupped my hands to my mouth. "Grandfather!" He did not turn, but hurried on toward the lake. I turned around. "What in the world is he doing out there in the dark?"

"I'll go after him." Duncan went to the door.

"No, I'll go. You stay here and call the paramedics."

I stepped out into the hallway, only to bump right into Hat, who was standing there with a tray. She was wearing a dark blue bathrobe, belted at the waist. "Oops, sorry!" I cried, my exclamation merging with her own small shriek.

Duncan leaped forward to steady the teapot and cup that had nearly overturned.

"You nearly scared the life out of me!" Hat exclaimed nervously. "I'm just on my way to take tea to some of those awful honeymooners. They never sleep! It's positively indecent! Anyway, you know how it is in this hotel—no rest for the wicked, as Gran always says. That old Agatha Moggs is right—worked to the bone, we are!"

"Hat!" My voice cut through her babble. "*Listen*. Herr Stifelmeyer needs a doctor. Someone has drugged him!"

"Pardon? *Drugs*?" cried Hat. "Did he take an overdose like Lewis? He suffers from pain in his legs, didn't he say? Poor fellow! Here—you stay here with him; I'll call the ambulance for you!" She hurried down the hall, the tea things rattling on the tray.

"I've got to get Grandfather." I headed out into the hall.

"That's odd," Duncan said. Something in his voice made me turn. "What's odd?"

"I have a feeling those honeymooners won't be getting their tea,"

"But Hat said—" I peered out the long window in the hallway, one of those that looked out across the portico roof, down at the silvery, moonlit lawn. No sign of Grandfather.

"Hat said," Duncan parroted, "but that teapot was empty."

"What?" I looked back at him. "I caught the teapot so it wouldn't fall—and it was empty. Bone dry."

"Weird," I said, frowning. Why would Hat say she was taking them tea, if she wasn't? But there was no time to ponder this behavior, because out of the corner of my eye I caught sight of a flash of white on the lawn, heading for the lake. "There he is!" I turned and hurried for the stairs. "You'll watch for the paramedics? They should be here any minute if they're just coming from the village."

"I'll call them myself, and I'll stay with him till they come."

I took the stairs two at a time, and raced along the corridor to the kitchen. The back door was ajar. "Grandfather!" I shouted, leaving the house. I careened around the side of the manor to cross the gravel drive. Heading across the lawn, I stood for a moment in the summer dark, looking down to the lake. Where had Grandfather gone? I couldn't see him now.

My legs felt wobbly, rubbery—the residue of the drug, I supposed. Herr Stifelmeyer had drunk more than I had, as he was clearly more strongly affected. And whatever drug it had been in the cocoa, he'd taken it on top of whatever pain medication he'd already taken. I listened for the sound of sirens. Where was that ambulance?

My eyes were heavy, and my legs seemed like the bendy, elastic limbs on Ivy's and Edmund's puppets as I set off after Grandfather. Like the couple who had disappeared into the mist, the figure in white seemed to have vanished. Then the moonlight and shadows separated as clouds scudded overhead, and—*there!*

"Grandfather!" I bellowed, but the night wind whipped the word away. My throat felt dry. What I really needed to wake me up and keep me alert was some tea—no, not even tea would pull me out of this fuzzy cloud. I needed a strong, hot cup of coffee, the kind Mrs. Grey served.

I stopped walking. *Coffee?*

I was remembering my first morning in the spa, when Herr Stifelmeyer sat at the cafe table and Mrs. Grey served coffee. I was remembering how Lew swaggered over to the table and boorishly snatched the cup poured for Herr Stifelmeyer, dumping it into his own mug.

Lew had taken Herr Stifelmeyer's coffee.

Not long afterward I had seen Lew staggering across the lawn. I'd thought he was drunk—or in pain from his back.

But he could already have been drugged.

He might well have headed for a soak in the hot tub, thinking the hot water would make him feel better…But the drug made him lose consciousness, and he'd sunk beneath the bubbling water, his swimsuit catching on the underwater light cover. There he had stuck fast until Duncan and I discovered him.

Lew had taken Herr Stifelmeyer's coffee.

That meant—that might mean it had never been about Lew at all. If Herr Stifelmeyer had always been the intended victim, then Lew had ended up dead in the hot tub by mistake.

Nothing was making sense, but an urgency was filling me, a feeling that I must gather all the strands of this strange tapestry together—and *quickly*. I must weave them smoothly, because the fabric was coming unraveled, and danger gathered in the shadows.

Why is this happening now? Herr Stifelmeyer had asked me, and I told him how I'd figured that *I* must have been the catalyst. But if Lewis had died because he'd taken someone else's coffee, I might have become yet another person killed by mistake, just by being in the wrong place at the wrong time.

My mind whirled as I tried to reason it out. I stopped stumbling through the darkness and stood staring up at the manor house. Why would someone want Herr Stifelmeyer to die?"

"No one could be afraid that he'll inherit Heatherstone one day," I whispered to myself…and my mind started leaping all over the place, trying to pull the threads of the events of the last few days together into some tapestry that made a whole picture. The German was in no way related to this family and would have no claim on the hotel. He was just someone Grandfather had met many years ago, during the war, when both were wounded soldiers and Heatherstone was an army hospital.

Why is this happening now?

If the answer had nothing to do with Lewis, and nothing to do with *me*, after all, then it must lie with Herr Stifelmeyer, and with something that had happened here at Heatherstone Hall during the war, something that still mattered now—like ripples still moving outward from a stone flung long ago into the lake. It was nothing to do with Lewis Paine's nasty blackmail, nor was it to do with the Foxworth family wanting to inherit Heatherstone Hall someday. It was happening now *not* because I had come to visit my grandfather, but because Herr Stifelmeyer had come back to the hotel where he had once been a wounded prisoner of war.

Who was here during the war? Grandfather was a patient, of course, and Mrs. Grey was a nurse. Agatha Moggs was an overworked maid—

Something was niggling at the back of my mind.

March, march, march, the old soldier had muttered.

Dorian Heatherstone had wanted his beloved Eva to learn to swim. He had suggested a teacher, but she wanted to wait until he was well and could teach her himself. One of the little notes in the blue-checked envelope, a note not in Dorian's or Eva's handwriting, seemed to be an invitation to a swimming lesson. But who had written it?

She can swim very well!

I sucked in my breath. The cool night air blew mist across my face. "Oh no," I whispered as understanding dawned. I ran like the wind.

"Grandfather!"

He came out of the boat house. "She's not there," he called to me, waving his cane in a gesture that might have meant I should hurry and join him or might have meant I should go back to the house.

I joined him. He was wearing his white bathrobe and his bedroom slippers. "Grandfather! What are you doing out here?"

"I must find her," he rasped, his voice quavering. He wheezed heavily, could hardly get the words out. "Must stop her!"

So he already knew! I took deep breaths to calm myself, and held on to his arm, steadying myself as much as steadying him. "Don't worry—Duncan has called the police," I said. "They'll stop her!"

Grandfather bent over, leaning on me heavily, coughing mightily. I tried to pound him on the back, but he pulled away.

"What's that?" he said, cocking his head. "Police? We don't need police. We need—wait, hear that? Listen! She's in the maze!"

And he stumbled away from me, heading toward the entrance. He startled a family of ducks huddled by the bushes.

I lurched after him. The lawn was bathed in misty moonlight. Grandfather bent nearly double, coughing, but he kept striding along with his walking stick. As he disappeared into the maze, I hesitated, looking back up toward the house, hoping to see Duncan and a whole fleet of police cars. But there was no sign of anyone.

"Please listen to me, Grandfather." I tried to keep my voice calm. "Lewis didn't die by accident. He was murdered. And tonight Herr Stifelmeyer was nearly murdered, too. And so was I!"

"You're talking nonsense," he snapped, rounding a corner, then another as I stumbled along behind him. "You don't understand." Left, right, right, right again, left.

"No, you're the one who doesn't understand!" He had vanished again, but I could hear him coughing up ahead. It was astonishing how fast this old man could go, striding through the maze he knew by heart, darkness no obstacle. He made each turn—left, left, right, left, right, right, left—with assurance, waving his cane ahead of him to break the cobwebs from our path. *March, march, march.*

I had lost all sense of direction. But the cool night air blowing behind us seemed to push us toward the center. "Grandfather—listen!"

Then as we stepped into the circle I gasped in horror, for there she was, seated on the stone bench: a plump spider in the center of her web.

Now for the final step.
Quick, painless oblivion.
Comforting after a long day. Creamy, warm. And quite tasty, too!
What more can one ask for in a death?
And then—and then she'll be out of the way.
Out of our way.

> *And we'll be together as we are meant to be.*
> *Finally and*
> *forevermore*
> *with my beloved.*

27

M rs. Grey dropped her knitting into her lap as Grandfather and I stepped into the center of the maze. "Oh my," she said mildly.

"Out for a midnight stroll? I often come here when I can't sleep. It's very peaceful. And the moon—so bright tonight."

I stepped in front of Grandfather. "It was *you*," I said. "Nurse Edith March."

"Ah," she said, and sat looking down at the ball of yarn. "So you've found me."

"Yes, we've found you, Edith," said Grandfather in a hearty voice, "and we're going to get you back up to the house. I don't know what in the world is going on, but it will help to talk it out. I've been your friend for many years, and I'm not going to desert you now."

"My old friend," Mrs. Grey said softly, "you have been very good to me." She smiled at him, then reached over and picked up the thermos. She unscrewed the cap and poured out a cup of milky tea. "That's why I left the note on your pillow. It's true: I am thinking of leaving Heatherstone."

"Leaving? That means you're thinking of running away," I challenged her, "because you're afraid to get caught for what you've done."

Grandfather turned to me, surprise in his eyes, but Mrs. Grey just smiled. "Oh dear," she said. "You've not only found me, you've found me out. Haven't you, child?" Her voice was calm.

"I found out that Lewis Paine didn't die by an accidental over-dose," I said clearly. I wanted to sound calm and normal, too, though this meeting was anything but normal. But my voice quavered. "You killed him—and that was the accident. Because you meant to kill Herr Stifelmeyer! You've been trying and trying to kill him!"

"Juliana!" Grandfather's voice was harsh. "How dare you say such a thing?"

"No, Lloyd. Let her speak. My dear girl, why do you make this accusation?"

"Because it's something to do with Dorian Heatherstone and that nurse, Eva. It's something to do with swimming."

"I don't swim," Mrs. Grey said. "I've told you before. I hate the lake. But I do love this maze. Do you know how many times I've sat right here, right here in the center?" She met my eyes, and held my gaze as she raised her cup and took a sip of tea. "Ahh, yes. That's lovely." She winked at me. "Chases the chill away. Such a cold summer. Typical English weather!"

"Maybe you don't swim now," I said, refusing to let her change the subject. My pulse pounded in my temples so hard I could practically hear the beat. "But you used to swim. You swam very well. Dorian Heatherstone asked you to teach Eva to swim!"

"Ah," she said, "Dorian," and there was a catch in her voice. "So you read the letters and figured it out? Well done, you!"

"What's going on here?" asked Grandfather. "What are you talking about?"

"Confession is good for the soul, isn't that what they say? And my soul, believe me, Lloyd, needs all the help it can get." Her voice grew dreamy. "I came here to be alone, but now that you're here, I shall tell you my story."

I had not come here to listen to a story. I had come to get Grand-father, to take him back to the house, where I hoped the paramedics were tending to Herr Stifelmeyer. Where I hoped the police had been summoned to arrest this woman. But Edith Grey's words wafted around us like gossamer strands of sticky web. They pulled me in, and held me captive. I licked my lips and they felt dry, swollen. My head pounded.

I crouched at the entrance to the circle, leaning against the hedge for balance. And listened.

"I remember when I first knew I was in love with Dorian Heatherstone," Edith Grey began. "I was just a young girl, a young girl in service as a maid. It was one summer afternoon, balmy and warm, not drizzly and cold like *this* summer. Lady Heatherstone had a caller—the vicar's wife, I think it was. I had just brought in the trolley of cakes and was going to pour the tea, when Dorian burst in all in a bother because his little dog couldn't be found, not anywhere, and his sister would not help in the search! He was a couple years older than me, and the loveliest lad I'd ever seen. His mum gave him a scolding for interrupting, and sent him out. She ordered me to fetch his governess, and as I hurried from the room, I wanted so much to call back to him, 'Don't worry! I'll help you find your dog!' but of course I didn't. It wasn't my place to speak to the young master. But later on I searched all the rooms in the servants' quarters—and in fact I *did* find the little dog! It had got locked in the laundry room somehow, poor thing. I carried it right up and knocked on Master Dorian's schoolroom door. I wanted to speak to Dorian myself, of course, but twitchy little Miss Diana snatched the dog and closed the door without even a thank you. I never did like that girl much. Even as a grown woman she was…twitchy."

Her voice trailed off. I waited, tense, shifting my weight from leg to leg. How could any of this story relate to Herr Stifelmeyer? The night air blew through the maze, and I shivered.

"The first time I actually spoke to Dorian was a few years after that. He was about seventeen, and home from boarding school," continued Mrs. Grey. "He was sitting in his room reading, and I came in to build up the fire—the manor was still heated room by room in those days. I couldn't bear to leave him without saying *something*. So I screwed up my nerve. 'The fire is laid, sir,' I said, which was of course a ridiculous thing to say because he could see that for himself, and one of the chief rules for maid servants was that we were not to speak to the family. But he looked up from the book he was reading—a fat red leather book about King Arthur, it was—and he smiled at me." Her voice softened. She was staring off into space as if seeing Dorian there in the circle with us. "And he answered me: 'I thank thee, sweet maiden.'"

Her voice grew even softer, and the thermos cup trembled in her hands. "I'm sure I blushed, and I backed out of the room, and didn't dare to speak to him again for a very long time. I spent my days imagining how we would next speak again, what he would say and what I would answer. How he would look at me, his sweet maiden, and how I would look back at him. Oh, I grew to love him, and I loved his home *because* it was his home, and despite all the hard work, the beautiful manor house was a joy. As I worked, I day-dreamed I would one day become the mistress of Heatherstone, married to Master Dorian. It was all I ever wanted." She gazed at me with a penetrating stare. "I believe there has never been a happier servant girl, Juliana."

She unscrewed the thermos and poured out another cup of tea. "I wanted to marry Dorian Heatherstone—and I believed he shared my passion! Oh, I could feel it like an electric current between us, even when he was away at school and later at university, and even when he became an officer in the army and was sent to France."

Was that a siren in the distance? How long could it take the police to arrive? Why was it taking so long for them to come and find us here? I knew from TV crime shows that it was good to keep the murderer talking. Mrs. Grey was doing a fine job talking. I could see where this terrible tale was going, I thought. But I kept quiet and hoped she'd keep telling her story till the police found us. But if they didn't come soon—well, she was old and fat and I was sure Grandfather and I could overpower her.

"Then one day I had a dream that my Dorian was wounded in

battle," Mrs. Grey was saying, "and so I decided I must train to become an army nurse."

"Ah, yes, the army," said Grandfather. He bent over and coughed rackingly.

The coughing nearly toppled him. The sound was terrible. Alarmed, I reached for the thermos. "Here—give him some of that tea!" I said, but Mrs. Grey held it tightly and did not share.

"Heatherstone Hall was requisitioned as a military hospital," Mrs. Grey continued her tale, even as Grandfather coughed harder. "I was posted here to nurse the wounded and dying. Sister Edith March—how well that sounded! I worked hard—you remember how hard I worked, Lloyd! I loved serving the wounded men because each and every one of them could have been my Dorian. And then—it proves that dreams can really foretell the future—one day one of the wounded men *was* my Dorian!"

Grandfather shuddered, but his coughing stopped.

"You told me and Hat that dreams don't mean anything," I interrupted coldly. "You said they were nonsense."

"I've said a lot of things," Mrs. Grey acknowledged slowly. "To cover my tracks." She drained her tea. Overhead the clouds scudded past the moon. We fell into darkness, then we could see again. Then darkness, then moonlight.

"My poor Dorian was in a coma for weeks," she continued softly. "Everyone thought he would die, but I couldn't let that happen. And when he finally came round, he was in dreadful pain. I sat by his bedside to give him his medicines or change his dressings, and we were able to talk. Really talk! Not as master and servant, but as equals. He told me about the dreadful bombing in France, where he had been wounded. He told me about the other men, about the battles. He told me he was ready to stay home now and marry. And I saw my future—the future I'd always imagined—opening up right in front of me!"

"Goodness, Edith," said Grandfather, taking her arm. "You're talking nonsense tonight. First you're going on about murder—and

now, did you really think Dorian would marry you? His family's servant?"

"I was his nurse," spat out Mrs. Grey.

"So was Eva," I said boldly. "So tell us what happened to *her*."

"Eva Lambeth!" Mrs. Grey pulled her arm out of Grandfather's
grasp in a sudden burst of animation. "Can you imagine my fury when
I found the packet of letters in his bedside table? Letters from that
woman. Of course, I went straight to Eva's room and checked *her* bedside table. In the drawer were more letters—his letters to her! It made
me sick. I meant to throw everything away, but they were in his handwriting...his own, dear handwriting...She'd saved his letters, and
other things. I saw a note I'd written myself! And all sorts of com-
ments on the various patients' progress. I didn't have time to sort
through everything in her drawer, and I didn't want to be caught in
her room. So I just gathered everything up and stuffed it under my
sweater. In my room I hid it somewhere no one would think to look."

"'Housekeeping Hints,'" I said. "The blue and white envelope."

Mrs. Grey looked at me and her tone sharpened. "So you found
it, did you? I'd made the envelope for all the useful clippings I found in
the newspaper, and for all the little notes I wrote to myself. I shoved all
Eva's letters and papers in with my own, for safe-keeping."

Her voice chilled me. She tipped the thermos again, but there was
no more tea. Then she put her head in her hands and was the picture
of woeful remorse. "Of course there was no excuse for what I did
next."

I knew it. "What did you do?" I asked carefully.

Grandfather patted Mrs. Grey's back. A long moment passed as
Mrs. Grey's shoulders heaved. She seemed now not a predatory spider
but a sad old woman—a woman who had done something terrible,
but was sorry, so sorry. But then I saw her spread her fingers and peek
out at me from behind her hands. Checking out how we were taking
her tale?

I crossed my arms and stood up. "Your thermos is empty," I said brusquely. "Let's go back to the house." The police must be there by now. They would know what to do with this woman.

"No thank you, Juliana. I've had as much as I need." She lifted her head slowly. Her voice, ragged now, continued the story. "I stole that packet of letters from Dorian's bedside," she confessed. "I took them to my room and read them all. That wretched nurse, that Eva—she had met him in France. So what? I had known him since childhood! This woman—how dare she reach out and take his hand? How dare she push his wheelchair through the maze, or down to the lake!" She started to tremble. "Who deserved to be his bride, mistress of Heatherstone Hall? Such rage I felt, you wouldn't believe. I followed them and hid in the boathouse so I could watch what they did. I listened as they made their plans. I heard him promise he would teach her to swim. I heard him promise he would teach her to ride. I heard him promise to marry her as soon as he could walk again…"

Her lined face was paper white in the moonlight. The eyes were shadowed and distant.

"You were jealous," I said softly. "So you made a plan…"

"Oh yes indeed." Her smile looked more like a grimace of pain. "I made a plan."

She swayed on the bench and Grandfather steadied her shoulders. "Enough is enough, Edith," he said. "You're looking terribly pale all of a sudden. I don't know where you're going with this story, but you can tell it to us just as well at home. Come on, now."

"I'll be all right," Mrs. Grey whispered. "I'll be fine. The story is almost over. You must sit and listen while I still have time."

"We're listening," he said. "But what do you mean, while there's still time?"

No doubt she knew the police would be looking for her soon.

"Drugs," murmured Mrs. Grey. "I saved up the strong drugs that we gave to the men in small doses, and when I had enough, I slipped the medicine into Nurse Lambeth's evening hot cocoa. Oh, yes, loaded it right up…enough to stop her heart. I intercepted Eva at the end of her shift, when she usually made herself the hot drink, and I handed her the mug. "

Her voice slurred slightly as she told us these details. She must be very tired now, but was driven to finish her confession. "But how was I to know she wouldn't just drink it down right then, the way she usually did?" Mrs. Grey asked, her eyes widening. "How could I know she would take the mug with her and go to his bedside? How could I know she would offer *him* the hot cocoa as a special treat? It was against doctor's orders—'No sugar for the patients!' he was always telling the nurses—but she gave him his regular dose of medicine and then offered him her cocoa."

"Edith, surely this isn't true," groaned Grandfather, wheezing at her side.

"Oh, it's true!" laughed Mrs. Grey. "My darling died, and the world crashed around me. I was sick, I could not work. Everything was ruined."

"And so you killed Nurse Lambeth, too," I could feel my heart hammering under my T-shirt as I made this accusation, but I knew it must be true. Some of the puzzle pieces of the last week were beginning to fit into place. "You offered Eva a swimming lesson—and drowned her!"

Grandfather gasped for breath. "Juliana—what a thing to say!"

"Hush, Lloyd. I'm afraid your clever granddaughter is right. At first I thought I wouldn't have to kill Eva; I thought she'd be dragged off to prison for giving Dorian the overdose. Hanging would have been too good for her, as far as I was concerned. But the military authorities decided the overdose had been accidentally given. And so it was left to me to make sure she paid for what she had done."

Grandfather leaned away from Mrs. Grey. He looked dazed. She was looking pretty dazed herself. "I-I can't believe what I'm hearing, Edith!"

Mrs. Grey's shoulders slumped. "I am terribly ashamed," she

murmured. "*Now*. Believe me, I am a haunted woman. Even at night, there's no escape from thoughts about what I did so long ago. I dream about it, and babble about it in my sleep. Hat was getting suspicious because she heard me saying things about Dorian and Eva. Finally I had to tell her, and she promised to keep my terrible secret, though I know it was a burden on her, poor girl. But back *then,* at the time, I was not remorseful. No, back then, I needed revenge! And I saw my chance one night when Eva came to me. She came to me! That's the beauty of it! She said she couldn't sleep, night after night, thinking of Dorian. She said she thought of all the things they'd meant to do together—and now would never do. Oh, I could relate, I tell you! She said he had wanted her to learn to swim, had even suggested she have lessons from *me*, but she'd told him no, said she'd wait for him to teach her. Foolish girl! Now that would never happen. So I offered to teach her. I said if she learned to swim he would be watching from heaven. He would be so thrilled, I told her."

Mrs. Grey's chuckle chilled me. "At first she said no, but I kept after her. I wrote notes to her, telling her how proud Dorian would be if she learned to swim. How his spirit would rest more peacefully if he knew she was a safe swimmer. I finally convinced her, and one day we set a time to meet after work."

"Eight o'clock," I murmured. "At the boat-house."

Grandfather looked at me in surprise, but Mrs. Grey nodded. "So you know that, too, eh? Clever, meddlesome girl."

Again, that low chuckle. "We met at eight, and changed into our bathing costumes. Easy as pie, I towed her into deep water, told her to hold her breath and dive down, down, down as deep as she could. She trusted me, the fool. And I just swam away. "

"No, Edith! You didn't!" Grandfather gasped. "I'm sure you would never—"

"You think I wouldn't kill her? Well, technically I didn't kill her at all! I didn't hold her under; I just left her there, and she deserved it."

Now she was holding her hand out to Grandfather as if for

understanding, for sympathy. He moved forward and sat next to her on the bench.

"I can't believe this," he said. "Tell me it isn't true."

"Oh it's true, every word," she whispered, and leaned her head on his shoulder for a second.

The woman was mad. How could I get Grandfather away from her? How could I get us both safely back to the house?

Now Mrs. Grey raised her head and glared at me. "But all this recent trouble—that's the fault of your German friend. He was always nothing but *trouble*. That night when I left the lake, I passed a pair of soldiers on the lawn. What were they doing out at that time of night? They shouldn't have been there! One of them was the German prisoner. He wasn't easy to forget with his carrot-red hair. The German prisoner should not have been out at night! But there he was, leaning on two crutches. His guard was helping him get in some extra practice walking, that's all. What I'd been doing was none of their business, but as I passed, the red-haired lad raised his head and looked in my direction. I was terrified he had recognized me."

Mrs. Grey seemed desperate to get it all out, every last word, though now she seemed to be so tired she could barely shape the words. "When Eva's body was found," she whispered, "everyone thought poor Nurse Lambeth had drowned herself out of grief—or guilt—for having caused Dorian's death. I worried myself sick, waiting for the German soldier to say something about seeing me. But he didn't, and then when he could walk, he was sent elsewhere, and I finally relaxed. The war ended...and I carried on."

I just stared at her. Grandfather's wheezing was the only sound in the maze.

"I see them sometimes," the housekeeper whispered, slumping against him with a sigh. "Arm in arm by the lake. Always together. Can they really be ghosts, Lloyd?" She turned her gaze to me. "What do you think, Juliana?"

I did not reply. But here in the heart of the maze, with the high, dark hedgerows towering around us, anything seemed possible.

"And so that's what you've been afraid of since Herr Stifelmeyer came back to Heatherstone Hall," I stated, keeping my voice as calm as I could. "You thought he'd recognize you, so you tried to kill him."

"Edith, you sicken me," Grandfather said heavily. He pushed her away from him. Mrs. Grey swayed on the bench. For a moment I thought she was going to fall, but she recovered herself. "Yes, yes," she whispered. "That's right. I thought he'd recognize me. So I tried to kill him. The urn, the arrow—that was me! That's what I was trying to do!"

Her voice grew fierce. "And I did everything. I did it alone! All…by myself. Tonight—the final attempt. Poison in the hot chocolate, eh? That would do the trick."

Wait. What? I stared at this spider in the moonlight. The hot chocolate. The urn. The arrow? Her memory seemed perfectly detailed when she was recalling her long-ago crimes, so why was she saying she'd shot the arrow at me when she must know perfectly well that she'd been standing right next to me, helping to steady Herr Stifelmeyer while he helped me line up my shot?

Then came the soft sound of running footsteps on the path, and Hat's voice calling desperately, *"Gran? Granny?"*—and I finally understood.

"You liar," I hissed to Mrs. Grey. "You horrible, pitiful *liar.*"

28

You're covering up for *her*!" I cried. "It *wasn't* you after all! It was—"

"*Hat...*" murmured Mrs. Grey in a distant voice. "My lovely Hat will become mistress of Heatherstone now instead of me. She must! She loves the place as much as I ever did. She'll marry Hugh...Tell her...I've taken care of everything."

The footsteps rounded the corner. "Granny!" Hat cried. "What are you doing out here? What did you tell them? Don't say anything!"

Mrs. Grey collapsed sideways, then slid off the bench onto the ground. The empty thermos fell with a thud and landed next to her. With a howl, Hat was at her side. "Granny! Granny!"

"She must have put something in the tea," I told Grandfather urgently. "Some drug. Tranquilizers like the ones she put in Herr Stifelmeyer's hot chocolate—or something stronger, I don't know!"

Grandfather reached down and shook her shoulder. "Edith!"

"You stupid old man," shouted Hat. "Why did you let her drink it?"

"I didn't know," said Grandfather brokenly. "I didn't know."

I hadn't known either, but now it seemed I should have guessed.

"I did it...for you, Hat..." whispered Mrs. Grey. "Now...hush."

"*You* hush, Granny!" hissed Hat. "Just shut up now."

"We have to make her vomit," I said. "Help me, Grandfather!"

The housekeeper's eyes rolled back in her head. Her breath gurgled in her throat. She tossed from side to side in Grandfather's arms. I gripped her chin, pried open her mouth and thrust my fingers against the back of her throat to trigger the gag reflex that might still save her. Throwing up the drug had saved me tonight, and I hoped it had saved Herr Stifelmeyer.

But now Hat was on me in a fury. "Get off my granny!"

"I'm trying to save her life, you idiot," I panted.

Mrs. Grey was a dead weight now, slumped on the ground in the middle of the maze. Again and again, while Grandfather tried to keep Hat off me, I forced my fingers into the housekeeper's mouth, but nothing came up.

"You drove her to this!" screeched Hat.

"We need the paramedics—fast. Hat, you stay here with her and we'll get help."

"If she's dead, then you killed her!" shrieked Hat. "You could have stopped her from drinking that tea!"

"I didn't know…" I said.

The hatred in Hat's look chilled me. I released Mrs. Grey and backed away slowly. My head ached. I felt tangled in the strands of this spider web, trapped with Mrs. Grey, who had killed two people long ago, and with Hat, who had known this and was trying to protect her grandmother by killing Herr Stifelmeyer. It made a sort of terrible sense, but it also meant Grandfather and I were in this maze with a killer *now*. And this killer was not elderly, was not drugged, was not dead.

I reached out and took my grandfather's hand. We needed to get away from there quickly—now. We needed to get out, get help—and get away from Hat.

She was bent over the body of her granny, sobbing. She was taking off her dark blue bathrobe and tucking it around Mrs. Grey. Hat's white nightgown with its long ruffled sleeves gleamed in the moonlight. Was that a glint of metal—something silver—in her hand?

I sucked in my breath, then let it out as I hissed at Grandfather:

"Run!"

I pulled him by the hand and we set off, trying to put as much distance as possible between the two of us and Hat.

I could go faster, but I needed Grandfather to take the lead or we would never find the exit. Paths branched left and right. *Left? Or right?* Wheezing badly, Grandfather moved ahead of me. We heard rustling, then the padding of footsteps on the other side of the hedge. We stopped. Listened to the silence.

Grandfather pointed to the right. Away from the entrance, down a path Hat wouldn't expect us to take? It was the best way.

More rustling, and then I screamed as Hat's arm stabbed suddenly through the hedge, the knife held out like a sword—narrowly missing my shoulder. Grandfather bellowed in terror, and I pulled him back, and the arm in the white ruffled sleeve pushed through again and again, the fabric tearing on the boxwood branches, the blade of the knife gleaming bright.

"I know you're there," Hat said calmly from the other side of the hedge. "And I'm coming to get you."

I turned and ran, though I knew I would just as likely run into Hat as escape from her. And what about Grandfather? He knew the maze like the back of his hand, but couldn't go fast enough.

"Juliana—go faster," Grandfather wheezed at my side. "Leave me. Save yourself."

I wouldn't leave him. Couldn't, either, because I didn't know which way to go. We moved together, down one path and up another, trying to be silent but hindered by Grandfather's uneven gait and harsh gasping. "Not far now," he wheezed close to my ear. "We're almost out."

But at the last turn before the exit, there was Hat. Her face in the moonlight was a pale mask of fury. Her arm was pulled back, the knife poised to slash. "You won't get by me," she hissed. "You won't get by me alive."

Gallant Grandfather stepped bravely in front of me, shielding me.

He put one arm behind his back and pressed his cane into my hand. "*Why*, Harriet? Have you gone mad?"

"It's because she knows I've figured it all out," I said slowly. "She knows I know that she was the one who killed Lewis Paine, *and* that she was trying to kill Herr Stifelmeyer. Killing must run in the genes, eh, Hat? But not smarts—because your granny at least, got away with no one knowing for decades! But how do you think you'll get away with it if our bodies are found stabbed in the maze? That won't look like another *accident*, Hat!"

Hat's shriek of rage merged with my own as I shoved Grandfather out of the way just as Hat lunged at us with her knife. I wielded the cane as a sword to fend her off, blocking her knife thrusts and finally knocking it out of her hand. Grandfather kicked it out of the way. She whirled around to try to get past me, but I raised the cane threateningly. I would smash her if she so much as stepped in my direction, so help me.

Then she turned back toward Grandfather—"Out of my way, old man!"—and leaped at him, knocking him to the ground. In a flash I jumped onto her back, clutching her around the neck, hitting out left and right wildly with the cane. In my mind I heard my mom's voice: "*You never know what you can handle until you're wrestling in the dirt.*"

This was it. This was the dirt.

A fierce, primal loyalty flooded me, giving me strength. Hat was *not* going to hurt my grandfather. She was not going to kill me, either! I would stop her or die trying.

Hat was strong and wiry, but the cane gave me an advantage, and Grandfather struggled to his feet to help. The two of us were able to hold her down at last. Grandfather's coughing filled the night, but he did not release his grip on Hat's arms until I'd pulled the sash from Grandfather's robe and trussed her hand and foot.

"Hogtied," gasped Grandfather with satisfaction, looking down at her. "Harriet, I am thoroughly ashamed of you."

I wanted so badly to give her a good hard kick, but I didn't. In the distance I could hear the most welcome sound—Duncan calling our names.

"Juliana? Mr. Ellis? Juliana?"

"We're here! In the maze!" I howled. "Duncan, we're in the maze!" I followed Grandfather out to meet Duncan and the police.

We left Hat, cursing viciously, there on the ground.

29

What happened next was like something in one of those classic Agatha Christie movies that turns up on late-night television.

My mom thinks they're corny, but my dad loves how all the suspects are brought together for a debriefing by the clever detective, who explains why it has turned out that one of the least-likely suspects is, in fact, the murderer.

Except in our case, I already had figured out most of it. And it was scary, and tragic, and the farthest thing from corny I could imagine.

Nothing was corny about how the police raced past us into the maze, either. I recognized Detective Inspector Richards and Constable Henderson, the two officers who had come to the hall after Lewis died. Nothing was corny about the third man, tall and lean and wearing a suit instead of a uniform, who strode across the lawn after Duncan. The man strolled casually, as though apprehending criminals in the dead of night was all in a day's work for him. And maybe it was. The sight of Duncan made me feel shaky as I realized how much had happened since he'd gone his way and I'd gone down to the lake after Grandfather—not so very long ago, but also a lifetime ago.

Mrs. Grey's lifetime ago.

The man introduced himself as Detective Chief Superintendent Pape. We stammered out our names. He shook hands, first with Grandfather, then with me, his grip hard as iron. "First question," he said. "Are you hurt, either of you?"

"Just shaken," Grandfather said, leaning heavily on his cane with both hands. "But Edith Grey is dead. And her granddaughter, Harriet, attacked us. Poor Juliana took the brunt of it, I'm afraid."

"I'm okay." My voice came out shaky. Duncan wrapped his arms around me and I leaned into him in relief, but I still couldn't stop trembling. "Duncan, Duncan, you won't believe this. Hat tried to kill us! Hat! She had a knife…Oh, Duncan, we've tied her up with Grandfather's bathrobe sash—I hope it holds—" I was babbling now, and tears were streaming down my face. "I thought Mrs. Grey was the one who did everything, but it was Hat who killed Lewis and almost killed me! She was trying to kill Herr Stifelmeyer the whole time—"

"Shh," murmured Duncan, holding me tighter. "Shhh. The paramedics have already taken care of Herr Stifelmeyer. They say he'll be fine."

"I waited and waited for the sirens!" I wailed.

"They came without sirens so they wouldn't tip off the murderer."

"Hat—in the hallway—with the tea cart," I babbled. "It was just a cover! She was coming to Herr Stifelmeyer's room to finish him off! Hat…Hat's totally crazy —" I was gasping and sobbing now.

"Tried to stab us—" interjected Grandfather, then stopped as Detective Chief Superintendent Pape raised his hand.

"We need to get you two back to the house," he said. "You need something hot to drink, and we'll need statements from you all."

"Mrs. Grey will make tea—" I began, and then stopped as I realized Mrs. Grey would never make tea again.

"Edith," said Grandfather dully.

"This person called Hat—is this the young woman my men are bringing out now?" The detective chief superintendent nodded toward the entrance to the maze.

We all looked, and there were the two officers, with Hat in her white nightgown stumbling between them, her hands in handcuffs behind her back, their hands gripping her upper arms. She was fighting them every step of the way, shaking her head wildly and kicking out at their legs.

"Yes, that's Hat." A shiver slid down my spine at the memory of my close call, her breath hot on my cheek. "Harriet Grey."

Then another voice rang out in the darkness. "Lloyd, what in the world? What are you all doing out here in the middle of the night?" Ross's shadowy figure was followed by one—no, two, no, three others—all running across the lawn. Pippa and Hugh clustered with Ross around us. Josie came behind. "Bloody hell—will someone tell me what's going on here?" Ross demanded of the detective chief superintendent.

Hat, writhing between the two officers who held her, threw her head back and howled. "Hugh! Hugh, you've got to help me!"

"Hat?" Hugh's voice sounded anguished, incredulous. "Hat, what's *happened*?" He ran to her, but Detective Chief Superintendent Pape followed and put a stern hand on Hugh's shoulder.

"We'll handle this, thank you," he said.

"But what *is* this?" demanded Hugh. "What's going on out here?"

Hat sagged suddenly in the officers' arms. She stared at us dully. "That bloody German. It's all *his* fault! He's like a bloody cat with nine lives. No matter what I tried, *he wouldn't die!*"

"Who?" shouted Hugh, much agitated. Josie and Ross and Pippa gathered close. It seemed none of them could quite believe that it was their own Hat—friendly, feisty Hat—who was handcuffed here in the darkness, wild-eyed and dirt-streaked. Only I could believe it, could still see the flash of her blade through the hedge.

"She means Herr Stifelmeyer," I murmured to Hugh. "It wasn't Mrs. Grey who was trying to kill him. It was Hat the whole time! She tried to kill him so many different ways. I started thinking that some-one was trying to kill *me*, because I was with him on the stairs, and when the urn fell, and shooting arrows. Hat was trying to protect her gran because of something that had happened back during the war—"

I broke off and stared at Hat. Then I turned to the officers who had come when Lew had died. "Lewis Paine's death wasn't suicide, and it wasn't an accident!" I clutched Duncan. "Hat killed him. It wasn't Mrs. Grey, though she did kill Dorian Heatherstone and Eva Lambeth."

At his incredulous expression, I nodded vigorously.

"That was a mistake," Hat spat out. "But Lew was a bloody idiot. He deserved what he got. He thought he was God's precious gift to all females. I'm not sorry he died! And it was his own bloody fault for pinching other people's drinks!" She drooped between the officers, and her voice grew truculent. "Do you think it was easy for me to collect all those painkillers? Only to have them all wasted on the wrong bloke?"

"Save it for your statement, young lady," said Constable Henderson tersely. "We'll want the whole story."

"I want my granny!" Hat shrieked at him. "I want my gran!"

Ross tried to go to her, but the detective superintendent put a restraining hand on his arm. We watched as the officers bundled her into the police van waiting on the gravel drive in front of the house.

"Where *is* Mrs. Grey?" demanded Josie. "Where's Edith? What's going on here?"

She wasn't my favorite person, but I put my arm around Josie. "She's in the maze," I said gently.

That's when things took the Agatha Christie turn. Detective Chief Superintendent Pape ushered us all up to the house and asked us to wait in the library. Josie said we preferred the kitchen, and he agreed. Then he left the house again, this time with Ross, whom he asked to lead him to the center of the maze. I offered to go with them, but Ross, putting a suddenly fatherly arm around my shoulders, said, "No, Juliana. You're the hero of the hour, but you need to sit down. And your cheek is bleeding again. Let the police handle this."

Hero of the Hour? Was that like Heir to the Kingdom? I put my hand to my arrow wound. My fingers came away streaked red.

Josie took my hand. "Come with me," she said, and led me to the little bathroom off the kitchen. She washed my cheek very gently and bandaged me up again, and even gave me a little pat on the head. "There," she said. "All better now." She squeezed my shoulder. Tears came to my eyes as I thanked her because it felt so good to know she *wasn't* trying to kill me and never had been.

Pippa and her father made the tea. Herr Stifelmeyer came in from the hallway, pushed in his wheelchair by a paramedic. "May I join you?" the old man asked politely. "I seem to be the only guest awake, and it's rather lonely in the library."

"Of course, come in and have something hot to drink. Or perhaps brandy?" Josie fluttered around him worriedly. "Herr Stifelmeyer, are you quite sure you won't go to the hospital just to be on the safe side?" she asked. "We all feel so dreadful that you've been treated so abominably while you're here as our guest."

"Thank you, Mrs. Foxworth, but I shall be fine. Thanks to Juliana and Duncan, the drugs Hat gave me did not have much time to do their work."

"The ones Mrs. Grey took in her tea must have been much more potent," I murmured.

"Well," said Duncan. "She was a nurse, after all. She'd know exactly what to concoct to do the job. Hat was just guessing at dosages."

"Amazing that the danger was Hat all along," Herr Stifelmeyer said, and rubbed his veined hand over his face wearily. "I never suspected I was the target. I was convinced that Juliana was in danger. But how lucky I am that Duncan stayed in my room until the doctors came because I think Hat had come to...how do you say it? Finish me off?"

Duncan nodded. "I think so, too. That teapot and story about the honeymooners wanting a midnight drink was a lie."

"*Everything* was Hat?" Hugh asked heavily. "The falling urn? The arrow attack?"

"The steel-tipped arrow didn't come from Heatherstone,"

Duncan told him. "We'd already figured that much out."

"The university archery club," he muttered. "She must have stolen an arrow when she practiced there with me."

"Shhh." Josie closed the kitchen doors and urged us to speak in soft voices. "The last thing we need is for the other guests to wake up and join us. There's going to be enough bad media coverage once the police reports are filed."

"Maybe not," Hugh said, his voice ironic. "Try to look on the bright side. Scandal and tragedy always bring out the crowds."

I listened, sipping my hot tea. I breathed in the aroma, as if by filling my nose with the fragrance of tea, I could wipe out the other smells of this awful night: sweat, fear, tears.

It seemed ages before Grandfather, Ross, and Detective Chief Superintendent Pape were back, but at last they came through the kitchen door. Ross and the officer supported Grandfather, who was breathing heavily. Hugh jumped to his feet when he saw how ill Grandfather looked. Otto Stifelmeyer rolled his chair over to Grandfather. I stood up and walked to his side, too.

"Edith is dead, just as we feared." Grandfather's voice was hollow. "Dead in the middle of the maze." Tears ran down his face as he pointed out the window at the dark. "I thought there was still a chance she was only unconscious." He pulled a chair out roughly and sank into it. His hands shook. "They've taken her body, and there will be an autopsy. The coroner says we'll know then what drugs she put into her tea."

Ross took out his phone. "I'm going to call Mina," he said. "You look a right horror."

Herr Stifelmeyer put his hand on Grandfather's shoulder. "You tried your best, Lloyd. And you were a good friend to her all these years. But no one could save her from herself."

"I could have saved her," Grandfather whispered despairingly. "We were *right there*! But I didn't see what was happening."

"I didn't either." I took his hand. "She would have hated to be arrested and taken off to prison, though. Like—like Hat. Mrs. Grey didn't want that."

He squeezed my fingers. I saw there were tears in his eyes for his old friend. But my eyes were dry. Edith Grey was responsible for the deaths of two people—one by accident, one on purpose. And her granddaughter repeated the pattern decades later, killing Lewis Paine in error while intending to kill Herr Stifelmeyer. I had only narrowly missed becoming another of her 'accidents.' So many lives ruined—including Mrs. Grey's and now Hat's—and for what? Hat was the villain tonight, but Mrs. Grey, despite having grown into a sweet old lady, had set all the scary events of the past week in motion decades ago with her obsessions and jealous nature. Perhaps the residue of Nurse March's rage and the tragedies it had led to was what my sister Ivy had sensed here—that little bit of evil from the past.

"What I'm still confused about," said Duncan, "is whether Mrs. Grey and Hat were in on everything together."

"I don't think they were," I replied. "Not until the very end. You see, I remember Hat telling Mrs. Grey that it was hard sleeping in the same room with a granny who talked so much in her sleep. She must have heard enough to figure out that Mrs. Grey had a terrible secret to keep. She figured that Herr Stifelmeyer was the danger—if being back at Heatherstone Hall triggered his memory and he told the police what he remembered about the night Eva Lambeth died, Mrs. Grey would be arrested. Hat thought it would be simple to arrange an accident that would kill him. I don't think Mrs. Grey realized at first what Hat was doing. But then, when all the accidents started happening, she must have guessed what Hat was up to. She knew that sooner or later Hat would kill him—or someone else, like me, for instance—and get caught. She decided that if *she* were dead, then there would be no one for Herr Stifelmeyer to turn in to the police. And so Hat would be safe."

"So she'd kill herself to protect Hat?" Ross sounded skeptical.

"I think she would," I said. "I think that's what she did tonight."

"She loved Hat," Josie reminded him. "Hat was her pride and joy. Hat was everything to her devoted Gran."

"But what did you mean about the night Eva Lambeth died?" Pippa asked. "Who is Eva Lambeth?"

They hadn't heard Mrs. Grey's terrible story. They didn't know! "Listen," I said. "What happened tonight started a long time ago…" And I filled them in, told them everything.

"I might never have suspected there was more than one killer," I said finally, "except that after Mrs. Grey took the drugged tea, she said a few things that didn't quite fit. She said she had been the one behind everything, behind the falling urn and the arrow, too—but that made me realize, finally, she had not tried to kill Herr Stifelmeyer. She had been right with me when I got hit by the arrow! So she was lying, but *why*? If she hadn't been behind the attacks, then who had? I remembered that Hat knew I'd found old wartime letters from Dorian—"

"So she's the one who searched our rooms, desperate to find them," said Duncan.

"Yes. When she heard I'd found old letters, she must have worried there'd be something to link her granny to Dorian's and Eva's deaths. And there was—but not so much a letter as the note in Mrs. Grey's own handwriting, setting a time for a swim lesson."

"I'm not sure there was really enough evidence to convict Mrs. Grey of murder," Duncan said musingly. "Without her confession, I don't think we could have proved a thing."

I'd thought of that, too. "Yes, if Hat hadn't panicked and thought she needed to protect her granny—as well as protect her own plan for running Heatherstone Hall with Hugh someday—none of the rest of it would have happened. And Lewis would still be alive."

Grandfather sat at the table with his head in his hands. He was listening, I thought, but he had nothing to say. His heart was too heavy.

"Hat was a very unstable person," Duncan said grimly, "but nobody saw it."

"Until tonight," Pippa spoke up, "when Hat came into the maze looking for Juliana, and found her granny dying. That's when she snapped."

I rubbed my bruised shins, my aching shoulders. "In a big way," I said.

30

Josie phoned Mina Fuller to come check on Grandfather, and Mina soon arrived with John Bainbridge and Bee. Agatha Moggs and her sister Sue-Sue woke up and came downstairs, demanding to know what was going on. Things like this never happened back in *her* day, Agatha Moggs let everyone know. Heatherstone Hall was certainly going downhill.

"I got here as fast as I could," Mina said, rushing to Grandfather's side. "Do you need to be in hospital, Lloyd?"

"No, Mina," rasped Grandfather. But he didn't look well, wheezing hard and slumping in the chair.

"It's ever so awful," declared Bee. Her eyes were dark in her pinched white face. "I couldn't believe when Josie told us the news. To think that Hat—oh, I can't believe it."

"Believe it," I said. "Hat fooled us all. I didn't suspect her until the last minute."

"Now that the family and staff are all assembled," announced Detective Chief Superintendent Pape, "I'd like Juliana and Duncan and Mr. Ellis to go over what happened tonight. I'll need statements from the rest of you as well about what has been going on here at Heatherstone Hall."

I was sitting next to Duncan at the table. He reached over and took my hand. I held on hard. Pippa, watching us, sighed.

And so we spoke, and we listened, and I looked around at the faces of everyone I had suspected of *something*. Mina Fuller smiled wryly at me. Josie frowned. Hugh raked his hands through his hair, looking dazed. Herr Stifelmeyer reached over and patted my arm.

"I still don't understand something," I told him. "Why do you have the 'Housekeeping Hints' envelope in your bathroom?"

He raised his bushy brows. "It was lying on the floor in the front hallway when your grandfather and I finished our snooker game. It was empty—so I just picked it up and carried it up to my room with me when I was getting washed up for dinner. I was surprised when you mentioned it, as I had not guessed it was something to do with…all this."

"It's the envelope the letters were in," I told him. "Hat must have dropped it when she raced back from stealing the letters from Duncan's flat. She probably stashed everything from the envelope in her pocket or something, and dropped the envelope in the front hallway without noticing. When I saw it in your bathroom, I practically fainted. I thought—" I shook my head.

"What you've been through tonight is enough to make anyone faint," Ross said kindly. "This has been one bloody awful night."

"We have searched Harriet Grey's room," the detective chief superintendent said, "and we discovered this pile of letters and papers and scraps under her mattress." He handed me the pile. "Do you recognize these? Are they what was stolen?"

Yes, there they were—all the letters, the newspaper clippings, the scraps we hadn't had time to read. I unfolded one and read it swiftly to myself.

> *I know he is meant to be mine. Only mine.*
>
> *Knew it from the first time I saw him.*
>
> *Sat with my darling today, took his poor hand in mine. His hot brow under my fingers …oh how I wish I could heal him with my touch. Talked of his time in France. Talked of childhood, the village, his family…He seemed cheered by the talk of times gone by. I've known forever that we're destined to be together, but I didn't speak of that. Know in my heart he feels the same way.*

These, then, must be the notes Mrs. Grey—Edith March—
mentioned in the maze, the notes she had written to herself long ago. I
felt chilled as I read the next one, and the next. The scraps formed a
sort of diary of her longing for Dorian Heatherstone, and her plan to
secure him. Her recipe for murder.

> *It is a perfect plan. And afterward, freedom. Hand in hand we*
> *can leave the house, no need to skulk, no need to wait for dark. We*
> *will show everyone.*
> *We will not have to hide.*
> *We will not have to slip into the quiet of the boathouse, nor will*
> *we seek privacy in the heart of the maze. We will stand right out in full*
> *sunlight, ready to start the rest of our lives together.*
> *It is time now.*
> *Ready...steady...*
> *Go.*

Herr Stifelmeyer cleared his throat now and shifted in his wheelchair. "It was a most puzzling case," he said in his gravelly voice. "I felt
a mood here from the first night I arrived—how do you say it? An
atmosphere. I sensed undercurrents. But I misunderstood them. I did
not for a moment suspect that I was in danger! I feared for Juliana,
because she was the newly found granddaughter." He glanced at Josie
and Ross. "I feared someone was feeling threatened by her, someone
was worrying that she would inherit Heatherstone Hall someday."

"The very idea," declared Josie in a tone of outrage.

She and Ross were looking fairly complacent, probably pleased
with themselves that no hint of scandal was attached to them in this
case. But I knew that, though they wouldn't ever admit it, they were
probably not very sorry that Lewis Paine had died. They hadn't liked
him coming on to Pippa, and besides, Lewis dead was one fewer

person standing in line to inherit Heatherstone Hall. Yet it was a huge relief for me to know they had not set up the trip-line, nor levered off the stone urn, nor shot an arrow at my neck. Josie was guilty only of throwing her son in my way, hoping that somehow love would blossom between cousins, and that Hugh and I would decide to marry and run Heatherstone Hall together, whichever of us inherited the place. Maybe she figured I'd make a better daughter-in-law than Hat.

But blood kinship wasn't always an easy relationship, I'd learned. I almost hoped Grandfather would just leave me out of the inheritance loop altogether.

Almost.

"It was the letters that jolted my memory," Herr Stifelmeyer continued. "The old letters from the attic. When you told us about them after dinner, I started to think more clearly about the time I had spent here during the war. I remembered the lovely Nurse Lambeth and her devotion to Dorian Heatherstone. I remembered, too, another nurse who was devoted to him. A nurse I'd seen talking to him often. Nurse March. I remembered how he'd been polite to her, but his eyes lit up only for Nurse Lambeth. I'd been a wounded soldier, you must remember, numbed with pain medication, so I recalled only hazily that I had seen Nurse Lambeth out in the middle of the lake with that other nurse—with Nurse March. And I'd seen Nurse March walking back from the lake alone that night. Why would they be having a swim lesson at night, I wondered."

"I told you Edith Grey was a swimmer," Agatha Moggs reminded us in her prim voice. "But would anyone listen to me?"

"You didn't suspect murder, though?" I asked Herr Stifelmeyer.

"No," he said regretfully. "Because I didn't quite remember. Not then. But because Mrs. Grey felt so worried I would remember—so worried that she babbled about it in her sleep—an innocent man was killed."

"That wasn't your fault!" I told him.

"Perhaps not." But he didn't sound convinced.

"What will happen to Hat now?" asked Pippa.

We all looked to Grandfather as if, somehow, he as head of the family and owner of the hotel would be the one to decide. But Grandfather looked to the police.

"Harriet Grey is in police custody," Detective Chief Superintendent Pape said. "That's where she'll stay until she has a hearing to determine whether she's mentally fit to stand trial. If she's not, she may end up in a psychiatric hospital for treatment. Otherwise she'll be tried for the murder of Lewis Paine, and for the attempted murder of Otto Stifelmeyer."

We sat in silence, letting his words sink in.

"I do wish I had recognized Edith March earlier," Herr Stifelmeyer said finally, his expression anguished. "As it is, I feel my memory lapse was one of several events that led to Lewis Paine's death."

"Now Otto, don't stew over this." Grandfather leaned across the table toward his old friend. "I might say the same thing about myself. Why didn't I figure out the truth—after all these years of living under the same roof as Edith Grey?"

"Why didn't I see the madness in Hat?" mumbled Hugh. "You'd think I would have noticed something! Maybe more than once of us is responsible for Lew's death."

"Links in the chain," I murmured.

Duncan pulled me close.

The detective chief superintendent shut his notebook.

"Well put, young lady," he said. "We often turn out to be links in chains we don't even know we are part of. And it's the truth of every case I've worked on."

His words made me shiver.

Then he left us there, linked forevermore—but without Lewis, without Mrs. Grey, and without Hat.

*   *

The next morning, early, I called my mom in London to tell her about everything. I wanted to give her all the details before she heard some version of it in the news. Mom's reaction was what I expected: she drove straight up from London, determined to take me back with her.

I called my dad in California, and his reaction was also what I expected. He wanted reassurance that I was safe now, and he wanted to speak to Grandfather, and he asked if I would like to fly home and spend the rest of the summer with him and Ivy and Edmund. When I assured him I was fine, and wanted to stay, that was it. But Mom arrived full of fury, even when I just plain told her I was staying the full month as planned.

"Oh, my dear Lord, the danger you've been through!" she cried, outraged, stumbling out of her car, parked haphazardly on the gravel drive in front of the hall. "I knew it was a bad idea to let you work in this terrible place."

"It's not a terrible place, and the danger is over now," I protested. "So now is not the time to make me leave!"

I convinced her to come inside, to have lunch in the dining room as an honored guest, to spend the night—she shared my room with me and wouldn't let me out of her sight—and I tried to show her all the good things about Heatherstone Hall.

Josie gave Mom a free massage and an herbal wrap at the spa. Ross and Hugh walked her around the gardens, down to the lake. Duncan and I took her out in a rowboat. We all played croquet, and Grandfather won despite stopping several times to cough and cough.

The next day Mom and I drove into the village and had a snack at the Dirty Duck. Then Mina Fuller invited us to her house for tea. I hoped Mom would see that my time at Heatherstone had not been completely terror-filled. And Grandfather told her how helpful I'd been, and what a delight to have around. "A little bit of Barbara," he said. "Same sparkle. Same daring. You should have seen her tackle Harriet on that terrible night. But still," he hastened to add, "Juliana's quite different from Barbara. Strong. Won't be pushed around—or led astray, I'm willing to bet. And that part must come from your side of the family."

It was definitely the right thing to say to my mom. She agreed to stay another day, then another, and seemed to enjoy herself. "I've needed a break," she told me. "The London art world makes me dizzy sometimes." She watched me at work, and I folded towels and served meals with a great big smile plastered on my face to show her how great it was to be here.

Thing is, it's how I really felt about Heatherstone Hall now.

At breakfast, the morning of the day she planned to return to London, Mom asked to wander the maze. That was just about the last place in the whole of England that I wanted to see again—and my face must have shown my reluctance. "Oh, sorry!" Mom shook her head. "Of course you don't want to go in there. I don't blame you at all, after such a nightmare."

"I'll take you," Pippa offered, smiling at me. "Juliana can hang out in the garden. Duncan's working there, and he'll keep her company."

I smiled at my cousin, accepting her olive branch. "Thanks," I said. "You're the better guide, anyway, because you can get to the center and out again in this same century." But then I took a deep breath. "If you lead, I'll come, too."

"Brave girl," said Mom approvingly.

The maze was shady and damp, but the grim shadows I'd felt there before seemed to be gone. I entered the center cautiously, standing aside while Mom and Pippa sat on the stone bench together. Mom moved over to make for me, but I shook my head. I couldn't bring myself to sit where Mrs. Grey had sat while confessing to murder, drinking her poisoned tea. Brave, yes, but not that brave. Not yet, anyway.

"It really is a lovely estate, Jule," Mom conceded as she was getting ready to drive back to London. "And how lucky you are to have it in your family." Then she set off, waving out the window, calling back that I should ring her if I needed anything before the end of the month.

She let me stay. And Duncan stayed, too. But Hugh went back to university; he'd been hanging around a few extra days, he told us, because he wanted to see if he could figure out who was taking his stuff. "It wasn't just my fishing line that went missing; there were other things. Scary things." His cricket bat. The fireplace poker. Hugh had searched Mrs. Grey's suite of rooms and found his things hidden under Hat's bed.

I felt sick when he told me. These were all things Hat had taken to use if her other plans to kill Herr Stifelmeyer failed. Now that Hat was gone, so was the danger, but just thinking about her could make me start sweating.

Herr Stifelmeyer's holiday lasted another week. On his final morning with us, he toasted our health at the breakfast table, and insisted that Grandfather must visit him the following spring.

"If my doctor allows me to travel," Grandfather wheezed, "I'll be there."

"Perhaps you will bring him, Juliana," the old German said, turning to me. "Come to Bonn with your grandfather, and I shall introduce you to my grandchildren. You will be able to practice your German."

"I'd love to come sometime. Vielen Dank!"

We all saw him out to the gravel drive, where a taxi waited to take him to the train station. "And you must promise to take care of yourself," he said to me, shaking my hand vigorously. "No more close calls or narrow escapes. No more accidents."

I promised. "Same with you," I said.

The American family left a few days later, to be replaced with another American family, this time from Chicago, with two little girls who took to following me everywhere. The honeymooners all went home, to be replaced by a convention of birdwatchers. Agatha Moggs and her sister Sue-Sue stayed on. There seemed to be no budging them. In fact, Agatha Moggs announced she intended to apply for the housekeeper position, now that Mrs. Grey was no longer with us. I was worried for a second until I saw Grandfather and Ross crossing their eyes and making faces behind her back.

Duncan and I explored the maze every evening before dinner, and astonished ourselves by eventually learning not one, not two, but three routes that got us to the center and back out again. Entering the center grew easier, and I was surprised that it remained a peaceful, pleasant place. Eventually I even sat with Duncan on the stone bench. "I'm crazy about you," he told me, gathering me into his arms, where I fitted so perfectly. "Do you know that? All the near misses this month have made me realize how much I need you in my life, healthy and whole and unhurt." His mouth came down on mine, hard, and tender, and my arms pulled him down onto the soft grass.

No ghost of Mrs. Grey lingered there in the center of the maze.

But speaking of ghosts, it was on our very last day that we saw them.

Duncan and I took a picnic, packed for us by Maggie, who was acting as housekeeper until someone new could be hired, and rowed out to the middle of the lake. We toasted each other with glasses of fresh lemonade and shared kisses between courses. We ate cold chicken pies and salted crisps, and threw the crumbs to the pair of swans swimming majestically past.

When the interminable drizzle began again, we picked up our oars and started rowing for shore. Suddenly, there they were.

It was the couple we'd seen before, walking arm in arm, toward the boathouse. They might have been hotel guests from the bird watching society, but I could see from this distance that the man was slightly stooped, leaning on a cane. The woman, her arm linked through his, was wearing a nurse's cap. They looked across the lake, through the rain, right at us—and then somehow simply weren't there anymore.

Duncan gulped. "Did we just see that?"

"We did." I squeezed his arm. "And now we don't."

We rowed in silence until we reached the shore. We pulled our boat out of the water and turned it over. Then, linking our arms in the same manner as the misty figures, we walked up the lawn. We reached the manor house, still silent, still arm in arm, but then stepped away from each other and raced each other up the wide stone steps.

It was time to go home.

I would be taking my birthmother's stuffed penguin, and her boxes of *misc stuff* and the doodled sketch of the motorbike zooming off into the unknown. I would take new friendships with my cousins, Pippa and Hugh. I would take the knowledge that I had a special place as blood kin in Grandfather's heart. But it was to my own family that I was so eager to return: to Mom and the Goops and, intermittently, Dad. Links in my chain.

Another thing I was bringing away from Heatherstone Hall was Duncan.

We were leaving on the train after dinner.

"But there's still time before we eat," Grandfather said. "So what about a last stroll around the lake?"

Pippa grabbed Duncan's arm and beamed at him. "Count me in!"

Duncan smiled over at me. "Coming?" And held out his hand.

But Pippa clung to his other hand. "I bet Juliana still has tons of packing to do," she said, and her eyes met mine. I could see the longing in them, and how much she hated that Duncan was going back to Blackthorn, how much she hated that he was going back with me.

"You two go," I said. "I have things to do here."

Pippa brightened. Duncan looked back over his shoulder, and dropped a wink as they left together. I laughed a little as I ran up the stairs and spun down the long hallway to my room.

That wink connected us, as so many things had connected us this harrowing month. And Duncan would be with me, not Pippa, on that nine o'clock train. I could be generous, feeling the strength of our future stretching out before me.

Forevermore links in each other's chains?

I could live with that.

The End

Acknowledgments

Shortly after the publication of Blackthorn Winter: A Murder Mystery (Harcourt, 2006), my fans started writing to me asking what happened to Juliana and Duncan next. And since some of my very favorite books growing up were mystery series, I decided there should be at least one more Juliana book, if not more. Heatherstone Hall and the village of Heatherstone, like the village of Blackthorn, are places I made up. But they are based on places I've visited and places I've lived. England is a vibrant country to which my British husband and I, along with our seven children, return as often as we can. My love for this country includes its tiny villages, ancient churches and friendly pubs, its stately homes and crumbling castles, its drizzly gray weather and verdant green fields, and (maybe especially) its daily teatime ritual. But most dearly I love the people there—our relatives and many friends— and I am grateful for their continued hospitality over the years. These include Doreen and Gail Ellis, and David Henderson, Dave and Mon Pape, Maggie and Mike Durkee, Elaine and Henry Mitchell, along with Thomas and Lily, Chris Richards, Phil and Dianne Martin Sommers, Louise and Andrew Shekell, Christine and Graeme Coulthard, and our own daughter, Angie Strychacz, who was an amazing London tour guide. Thank you all for putting us up—and putting up with us—so I can soak up the *vibes* of England at regular intervals! Thanks especially to my long-time editor at Harcourt, Karen Grove, who helped shape many drafts of this novel and others, and to my agent, Ginger Knowlton of Curtis Brown, Ltd., for getting me the rights back after Harcourt merged with Houghton Mifflin. For careful proofreading, I offer up eternal thanks to Tom Strychacz, Dorothy Molnar, and Donnell Rubay. And a heartfelt thank you to the hardworking and talented Daniel Strychacz, Bonnie Britt, and Kelly Eismann for shepherding this novel into print and e-book form and calming my fears along the way.

About the Author

Kathryn Reiss is the author of many mysteries for children and teens, including *Time Windows,* an ALA Best Books for Young Adults, and Edgar Award nominees, *Pale Phoenix* and *PaperQuake*. She lives with her family in northern California and is a Professor of English at Mills College.

Other Novels of Suspense
by Kathryn Reiss

Time Windows (Harcourt)

The Glass House People (Harcourt)

Pale Phoenix (Harcourt)

Dreadful Sorry (Harcourt)

PaperQuake: A Puzzle (Harcourt)

Riddle of the Prairie Bride (American Girl)

Paint by Magic (Harcourt)

The Strange Case of Baby H (American Girl)

Sweet Miss Honeywell's Revenge: A Ghost Story (Harcourt)

Blackthorn Winter: A Murder Mystery (Harcourt)

The Tangled Web: A Julie Mystery (American Girl)

Puzzle of the Paper Daughter: A Julie Mystery (American Girl)

A Bundle Of Trouble: A Rebecca Mystery (American Girl)

The Silver Guitar: A Julie Mystery (American Girl)

Intruders at Rivermead Manor: A Kit Mystery (American Girl)